10/15/10

Preemptive
Strike

By D. L. Wanna

MAJOR CHARACTERS

FICTIONAL:

Dominic Benvenuto: Counter Intelligence Chief, FBI New York

Agent Sonya: Lead Soviet Operative for "Wet Operations" in the Americas

"Oryol" (Eagle): Principal Russian Spy inside the American Rocketry program

Lieutenant Colonel Igor Tolstoy: America's Senior Spy inside the MGB-KGB

Catherine Bowers: Assistant Producer, NBC's Today Show

Vladimir Bodkin: Veteran Sniper and Principal MGB-KGB Hit Man in New York

General Iuri Strelnikov: Head of MGB-KGB Operations, New York Consulate

Prudence: Dominic's Personal Assistant, FBI, New York

Francois Duborg: Prudence's Lover

HISTORICAL:

AMERICAN:
President Dwight David Eisenhower

J. Edgar Hoover, FBI Director

Allen Dulles, CIA Director

John Foster Dulles, U.S. Secretary of State

George Kennan, U.S. Ambassador to Moscow

RUSSIAN:
Premier Joseph Stalin

Nikita Khrushchev, Future Secretary General of the Soviet Union

General Sergei Kruglov, Director of the MGB-KGB, Moscow

Colonel Iuri Andropov, MGB-KGB Moscow, Future General Secretary of the Soviet Union

TABLE OF CONTENTS

FOREWORD

Some historical facts for your consideration:

- On October 4, 1957, the Soviet Union successfully launched the first space vehicle, Sputnik 1, from its secret launching site in Tyuratam, Kazakhstan on a large K-7 rocket. The satellite was encased in highly polished aluminum. It burned up on reentry on October 6.

- Only one month later on November 3, 1957 the Soviet Union launched the much larger Sputnik 2, weighing 1,118 pounds. The dog "Laika" was sent aloft in this vehicle and perished in about a week. This satellite also burned up on reentry 162 days later.

- Sputnik 3 and 4 also burned up during reentry. It was not until almost 3 years later that a Soviet space vehicle successfully reentered the Earth's atmosphere. Launched on August 19, 1960, Sputnik 5 contained two dogs, Belka and Strelka, who were recovered in good condition. The Soviets had finally solved the reentry problem with a material that would protect the returning cargo, be it a dog or a nuclear warhead.

- This success led to the launch of the first man, Colonel Iuri Gagarin, into space by the Soviets in 1961.

- Meanwhile, no American space equipment launched in this period ever experienced reentry destruction.

- Following the Gagarin achievement, it was widely accepted that the Soviet Union had a meaningful lead on the U.S. in deploying large, nuclear tipped Intercontinental Ballistic Missiles (ICBM's), making conceivable a preemptive nuclear assault by the soviets.

- The "missile gap" played a significant role in the 1960 presidential campaign.

- Several sources have reported that in this period, Chairman Mao of China suggested to the Russians that they launch a preemptive first strike on the United States.

- In late 1960, after it was clear the Russians had solved whatever reentry problem they had earlier experienced, the Corning Glass Company went public with an advertising campaign featuring NBC news anchorman Chet Huntley leaning on a missile nose cone. He stated that the same "space age" materials invented by the company and used in the cone were in the company's consumer line of Corning Ware kitchen products, demonstrating their strength and ability to withstand substantial fluctuations in temperature.

- Lastly in 1961, when Soviet Premier Khrushchev visited the United States, he brought one of the six puppies born to the space travelling Strelka, and gave it as a gift to Caroline Kennedy. The symbolism was quite clear.

All of these developments were set in motion by certain events in the early 1950's, when the nuclear balance of power in the cold war between the Americans and the Soviets hung very much in the balance. Those events are the subject of this journey.

Chet Huntley – 1960 Corning Glass Commercial

CHAPTER 1

BIRTH OF PROJECT DEATH STAR

World War III started right on time.

It was cataclysmic for the United States. The first Russian nuclear warhead to detonate, just as planned, was the R-7 Semyorka, an airburst at 3,000 feet just over the Capital building in Washington D.C. Seconds later, Major General Taborsky, head of Soviet rocket forces, received an effectiveness report.

"Sir, given the altitude, the precision success of the strike, and the last telemetry messages from the missile, we estimate complete annihilation of the city's center, including the capitol building, the White House and the Pentagon. We know the American President and vice President were at a White House state luncheon and therefore are certainly dead, as are most of congress and the military leadership. We have caught them totally unawares."

"Excellent," the general responded, breaking a controlled smile.

Eight seconds later he received the confirmation of a double warhead R-7 blowing at 1500 feet above the Empire State Building. "Sir, our theory of using the double warhead is proving correct. The force of the dual pulse is causing many of the Manhattan skyscrapers to fall into each other. All of the 2.5 million people in Manhattan and most of the outer boroughs are now being incinerated. Few will survive."

And those who do survive will wish they hadn't Taborsky thought.

With amazing exactitude in the next 57 seconds, Chicago, Philadelphia, Los Angeles, San Francisco and 13 other American cities suffered comparable blows, all from Semyorkas launched in the last hour from the Soviet Union and timed to detonate within two minutes of the initial blasts in Washington and New York. The telemetry data from the missiles and the satellite images were clear.

Eight minutes into the attack, the commander received a more extensive report. "Sir, a complete success. The attack is estimated to have destroyed 30 % of American economic productive capacity, eliminated the federal government and military apparatus, and resulted in the immediate death of 17 million Americans. Radiation will kill an equal number in the next 48 hours. Nuclear storms and fires are raging in all these cities according to our satellite images."

"*Excellent. And when do you expect the strikes on the American Strategic Air Command bases around the world? Will we wipe them out before they can get their 400 bombers airborne and headed toward us?*"

"*Absolutely. The first has just hit the center in Omaha. Twenty six others should be hitting their airbase targets in the next three minutes. The 400 fueled and nuclear armed U.S. bombers on the runways will be destroyed on the ground. We are not monitoring any communication out of Omaha or Washington to their worldwide air bases.*"

"*Taborsky asked. "What's the current radar and satellite read on the number of American bombers airborne at the inception of our preemptive strike?"*"

"*We count 23, sir, with the closet to Soviet soil being three planes off our eastern coast of Siberia.*"

"*Good, a manageable number. Our interceptors are already moving toward them?*"

"*Yes Sir. 1609 MIG fighter interceptors, all we've got, were airborne at the moment of first strike, and all have been assigned to the 23 incoming American bombers.*"

"*Report to me every two minutes,*" the General ordered.

Twenty-eight minutes after initiation, the operational commander reported. "Sir we have shot down 21 of the 23 incoming bombers. One aircraft was badly damaged but has successfully dropped below our radar. We believe it is approaching south central Asia, probably Irkusk and our ICBM launch facility west of there. We can't find the last one, a B-47 from the 348th Bomb Squadron, part of the 99th Bomb Wing out of Westover, Massachusetts."

Four minutes later the damaged plane was reported to have crashed 300 miles west of Irkusk. The one unaccounted- for bomber 17 minutes later dropped a nuclear payload over the secondary city of Omsk in Siberia. It was the only American weapon to find its intended mark – a remarkable defense of the Russian homeland by the Soviet fighter aircraft armada. And a small price to pay for the effective destruction of the United States.

One hour into the attack Taborsky's operational deputy reported, "Sir, American response activity has ceased. Their defense communication system is silent, their airbases destroyed, no planes left in the air. Satellite images show massive destruction and fire in the 17 attacked cities. There is nothing left standing in New York or Washington. It's over."

Taborsky responded with a broad smile enveloping his face, "We have crushed them. As I knew we would."

Two hours later the soviets received a call from the Montana ranch of Senator Mike Mansfield, the Speaker of the U.S. House of Representatives and the new U.S. President following the confirmed death of both the President and Vice President. He offered complete surrender of all United States forces and an immediate stand down, accompanied by acceptance of any reasonable demands of the Soviet Union. He pleaded for an end to this "holocaust."

The commander gave the order, "It's over. Stand down. All offensive operations to cease!"

The control room of the command center broke into a spontaneous cheer. The war game had ended. Two years in the planning and hundreds of millions of rubles later, it had been an extraordinary success. The total elimination of the major enemy of world communism had been accomplished in a mere four hours.

It was a full-blown simulation of a surprise missile onslaught against the United States at a future date. At a time when the Russians would have ICBM capability and the Americans would not yet be operational. Their rockets against the U.S. bombers – an unfair fight launched in total surprise.

Taborsky stood up to cheers all around the command base. Phoned accolades came in from all the regional commanders who had led the war game. The Mig fighters were recalled to their bases. The exercise had demonstrated that the soviet command and control system could manage multiple simultaneous ICBM launches; have the entire soviet fighter interceptor fleet in place to destroy surviving American bombers; and easily withstand the few hits that would occur on their soil.

Of course, all this was completely dependent on the key premise of the war game – no retaliatory American missile force in place.

The Soviet Union did not yet have these ICBM missiles in 1950 either. But it had underway a massive program to get them, all a deep secret from western intelligence. Meanwhile the unsuspecting U.S. was pursuing its own rocketry plans at a rather lackluster and desultory pace.

That evening General Taborsky got a call from the Defense Minister of the Soviet Union. "Congratulations, comrade. You have an appointment with Premier Stalin in three weeks. And you better be ready. He is very enthused."

May 31, 1950 – Three Weeks Later
Premier Stalin's Private Kremlin Office, Moscow, USSR

The three men entered the Premier's office with trepidation.

Colonel General Kruglov, head of the entire MGB Soviet security and secret police apparatus, entered in military step with Major General Taborsky, the young rocketry "genius" who had designed the missile battle attack plan.

They both followed behind politburo member Nikita Khrushchev, an up and coming leader who had become famous as the political commissar of Stalingrad during its stirring victory over the Nazis in 1942-1943.

Kruglov was somewhat scared. He was always scared in front of Stalin. He had seen men go into this office and never come out. The three stood at attention, Stalin saying nothing and continuing to write, pointedly ignoring them, a subtle means of intimidation he frequently employed.

The office was spectacular, awe inspiring. It was the most elaborate in the Kremlin. The office had been the Moscow headquarters for the last Czar, Nicholas II, when affairs of state had brought him from St. Petersburg. It dripped in gold façade and imperial splendor and bore the gravitas of momentous moments in history and portentous decisions.

Kruglov's eyes sought out Stalin, the leader of the world communist empire. With the recent addition of China, the new "religion" of one third of the world's population. And this Stalin was the very man who had broken Hitler's back and thrown the mighty Nazi's empire into the junk pile of history. Smashed Hitler and his "1000 year Reich."

Stalin took his sweet time, finishing the paragraph he was writing and puffing on his pipe. Finally, he looked at each, and then said softly, "You may be seated."

He ignored Khrushchev and Kruglov, addressing only the junior ranking Taborsky, who had just been promoted head of the new Soviet Rocketry Command. "Yah prochital vash doklad, tovarich. Eta ochen interyesna" *(I have just read your report, comrade. It is very interesting)*. "And you think you can do this? In seven years, by 1957, have a fleet of these intercontinental ballistic missiles outfitted with nuclear warheads? Enough to destroy America's leading cities and its nuclear bomber fleet on the ground? A weapon that would reach American soil from here in less than an hour and be impossible to knock out of the skies? Is this all correct?"

"Yes, sir!" the general said. I just proved it in our simulated strategic war game he thought – of course I can. And the boss knows it.

"When do you expect the Americans to have this weapon?" Stalin responded.

"Sir, our best intelligence indicates that America is at least five years behind us. Their early work is around rockets that are hopelessly small. They don't even have drawings for such a high payload, high thrust rocket. We also believe they are behind on the fundamental physics involved and the complex guidance systems needed to accurately hit a target."

"Five years," Stalin uttered softly. He rose, went to the window and looked out, lost in thought, slowly inhaling on his ever-present pipe.

Taborsky thought, he has to let me lead it. I designed the whole battle plan. I can do this. Or is the boss getting timid, worried about Russian civilian casualties?

So nervously Taborsky added, "Sir, of course, it would also be possible to just threaten America. Have missiles land perhaps 50 miles east of both Washington and New York, detonating in the ocean. Let them know there are dozens more behind these that would target their cities, if they didn't immediately disarm NATO, permanently cede all of Europe to us and abandon northern Asia. Or whatever other demands you would deem appropriate."

Stalin raised his eyebrows. He puffed slowly, deep in concentration. "No general that would put the American Strategic Air Command, their bomber fleet, on guard. Let's stick with the total surprise attack, smashing their largest cities and bomber air bases with one thunderous nuclear blow. Just like your very successful war game that we spent so many rubles on. Having destroyed their ability to retaliate, we could then concentrate every fighter plane we have on their already airborne and incoming bombers, just like your plan. It would be all our interceptors against maybe several dozen of the American B-47's or those new B-52's now in design."

Taborsky's mind raced. Shit, the boss isn't troubled at all by the frying of 30 million Americans? He is tough, ruthless. Better give him what he wants to hear.

"Yes sir, we could do that. That is what we just proved. We would have all our fighters, over 1,600, airborne at the moment of simultaneous missile detonation in the U.S., and direct them by radar to intercept the incoming airborne American bombers. It would be a turkey shoot. Maybe one or two bombers would get through, if any. And their command and control system would be shattered, like a chicken's last flailing steps after its head has been chopped off."

Stalin smiled slightly; he appreciated analogies to Russian peasant life. "Yes, that's our objective here. General, I appreciate your briefing, and I applaud your ambition. I want you to go forward with all possible speed. You'll have any resources you need. Anything for this program – our little nuclear death stars. And this must be a secret known only to those intimately involved in the process. No lose lipped political blowhards. And I want a report from you in person each month. Do you understand all this?"

"Sir my mission is abundantly clear, and I will carry out your instructions explicitly."

Stalin shook Taborsky's hand, an unusual gesture. "General, you're dismissed. You are to be congratulated on your work to date. You two remain," he said to Nikita Khrushchev and Sergei Kruglov.

Taborsky exited. He thought, with a few words the boss has just authorized a first strike that could kill and maim 30 million or more Americans. Jesus, like you would order chai. And I will have the honor to plan, manage, and command it. With the unlimited resources of the Soviet Union behind me. Without political interference. It's mine – I own it!

He levitated down the Kremlin's magnificent steps. Every illuminated bulb in the massive overhead chandeliers seemed to be shining only on him. Maybe some day he might run this colossus, the Soviet Union, the future undisputed ruler of the world.

Back in the office Stalin leaned toward the two remaining men, staring at them with his wolfish eyes in laser focus.

"The key in this whole thing is the five-year lead. That gives us the time to bring the American bastards to their knees, before they can also arm with these weapons and neutralize our advantage. It's a crucial window we will never have again. If we get there first with these ICBM's, America is finished. FINISHED," he emphasized loudly.

"Koba, as always in these great strategic matters, you have come to the right decision," the always sycophantic Khrushchev responded.

After a quiet pause for effect Stalin leaned forward and now in a hushed, almost reverential tone asked, "I assume this intelligence has been influenced by input from our delicate little bird in America, Comrade Oryol *(Eagle)*?"

"That's correct, sir," Kruglov replied. He was actually in charge of running Oryol, their most important agent in the world. Only two others and the three men in this room knew his true identity.

"So, I can feel extremely confident of its accuracy?"

"Completely" Kruglov responded. "Oryol is deeply immersed in the American rocketry program, and has given us extensive data. He knows everything. Oryol reports that they are still designing small rockets that can't launch more than 30 – 40 pounds. They are way behind. And most important, the Americans have no idea Oryol passes on to us everything they're doing."

Stalin smiled and replied, "Take superb care of Oryol, Sergei. That agent is the key. With his vital input we will know where the Americans are on this and can time our preemptive strike exactly. Then annihilate them. Maybe we spare them ruthless slaughter by giving them 24 hours to surrender to soviet occupation… or else. We will achieve the final victory of world communism, years ahead of schedule. And…I will live to lead it! Today you have made me a very happy man."

Then Stalin dropped the slight smile and added menacingly, "But don't fail me." He looked deep into their eyes. Enough said. An involuntary quiver ran down Khrushchev's back. Stalin dismissed the two men. They rose, saluted and departed.

Now alone, he contemplated the victory celebration. I will stand erect on the viewing platform of the Lenin Mausoleum on Red Square, receiving the accolades of the greatest victory parade in the history of man. People will come from around the world to express their homage and fealty to the new Soviet super state - the acknowledged center of the world. And I will eclipse all men who have gone before, at last recognized as the greatest man in all history.

He took a prolonged full puff on his pipe and exhaled. He gazed at the rising smoke, catching the symbolism – the mushroom clouds that would envelope New York, Washington and the other American cities he would incinerate if the Americans did not submit.

It had been a very good day.

CHAPTER 2

THE PROBLEM

Two years later
Saturday, July 26, 1952
10:00 a.m. – Kazakhstan, Soviet Union

The simulated missile velocity and nose cone temperature increased. Conditions approximated the extreme heat that would be encountered as an R-7 rocket reentered the atmosphere at 24,000 feet per second.

Everyone in the room knew this was it. Millions of rubles and the best Soviet scientists had produced this new polished aluminum nosecone solution. Would it work? They knew they could launch a 1,000 pound payload as soon as 1957. That would be enough to deliver a multi-kiloton nuclear warhead to any spot on the earth in less than one hour. There would be no defense against the death star. It would hit its target at a high terminal velocity. The Americans would lie vanquished, and the rest of the Western world would bow to their new Soviet masters.

But was this material strong enough to protect the nose cone from the heat and pressure of reentry? In the last two years there have been nothing but laboratory failures in the attempts to solve the problem.

The lead engineer watched the group standing in the laboratory, built in great secrecy in Tyuratam, Kazakhstan, part of a new rocket launch site complex still under construction. Security was extreme. The laboratory was buried 200 feet below the surface and built to withstand a direct hit from all but a nuclear weapon. It was reachable only by a steel reinforced elevator. Fewer than 30 Soviet scientists even knew of its existence.

The core of the test facility was a super wind tunnel, reinforced by five feet of concrete. It could be heated to the intense levels that would be faced by an incoming warhead and also accurately replicate the pressures of reentry.

In attendance was Major General Taborsky, the commander of the astoundingly successful war game two years earlier and now the head of the Soviet Rocketry Command. Stalin's fair-haired boy. The boss of the top secret program that contemplated the potential nuclear annihilation of America. He would be reporting the results immediately to the minister of defense, who would then report to Stalin.

The tension was palpable.

With a siren's blaring, the test began. The nose cone had to withstand enormous heat for four minutes, simulating the maximum temperature that would be reached around a reentry altitude of 60,000 kilometers. Two minutes into the test, the cone glowed yellow, then red. Things seemed to be going well until…

In the third minute and fortieth second the protective shield split and 1/1000 of a second later exploded off the simulated payload, leading to its destruction. A burning, charred mess. The combustion actually destroyed part of the test chamber.

The lead scientist turned catatonic. Amidst the silence, the general blasted out of the viewing area and ran over to his control station. "Fuck your mother," he shouted at him. "You and your wonderful engineering breakthroughs. Now I get to report this to the minister of defense, you academic idiot. And then he calls Stalin himself. Place this incompetent under arrest," he called to a guard.

No one in the room ever saw that man again. In fact, he was shot that evening on direct orders from Stalin.

Later that day
Kremlin Private Living Quarters, Moscow

The news of the test failure was a brutal disappointment to Comrade Stalin. His plan to achieve Soviet world dominance would now be materially delayed. And he wasn't getting any younger. He reviewed these events with his number two, Lavrenti Beria.

"The test failed. I already ordered the death of the lead scientist and internment of three others. I have to act strongly in such failures. The people correctly think of me as a military and scientific genius, and nothing can be allowed to tarnish that reputation. I am Stalin, literally the Man of Steel."

Beria nodded, "absolutely, Koba." But he knew in reality that Stalin was no longer the man of steel, the man who had lead the destruction of the Nazi empire and then outfoxed Roosevelt and Churchill at Yalta. He was a desperate, sick man and a raving insomniac.

It was 3 a.m. Beria watched him move to his window overlooking Red square, gazing toward St. Basil's Cathedral, built by another man of steel – Ivan the Terrible.

"I can't let anyone on the Politburo perceive my health problems as a weakness," he said in hushed tones to Beria. "Any of my key people may be plotting my elimination. My old ally Malenkov is always kissing my ass, but who knows if he's loyal? I don't trust Khrushchev at all. As the political Commissar at the battle of Stalingrad, he strutted like a peacock, but it was my genius alone that won back MY city. Mikoyan is a modernist who wants to liberalize. And these doctors – they had better keep their miserable mouths shut about my troubles. Maybe it is time I send some of these insiders to join the others who have doubted me – Trotsky, Yagoda, Kirov, Zinoviev – all now filling the cellars of the dead."

Beria just nodded. He had become Stalin's father confessor. He was also Stalin's chosen successor, so he had to be supportive yet careful and clever. The old bastard could strike like a cobra at any time, have anyone shot or hauled off to the gulag. Beria had seen him do that thousands of times.

Stalin added, "People have always plotted against me. I know this. I will be strong, as my countrymen expect me to be."

But standing there in his underwear, Beria knew he was not the man of steel, the Stalin of old who had kicked Hitler's ass. He's a pathetic figure now, a depressed, paranoid old man, taking ten pills a day. No woman in his life, his favorite son killed in 1943 in a German prison camp, only his daughter, pesky Svetlana, still around, and she too flighty, untrustworthy. And the blood of 20 million innocent Russian civilians on his hands.

Beria spoke up, "Koba, you are right. These obsequious advisors have to be watched. They don't respect your great legacy. They are just ass kissers."

But Beria thought to himself – you prick, you killed millions of your own people with a mere nod. The details of that slaughter won't long remain a secret. You have a right to be paranoid, you psychopathic madman.

Who would betray Stalin, Beria thought – Malenkov, Bulganin, Khrushchev? I don't know. But then I will take charge, mourning over the body and declaring my fidelity to the glorious history of our fallen leader. I will ascend to my rightful position – his chosen successor.

Stalin resumed, "Lavrenti, I have concluded that I must activate agent Oryol in America. I have no choice. He can get us the details on their new American solution we have just learned of to this miserable nosecone problem. With it we can still accomplish operation Preemptive Strike years before the Americans can catch up. We are way ahead on all the other parts of the puzzle."

He had reached a decision. Stalin picked up his phone, reaching his aide who worked the midnight to 8 a.m. shift, a busy one for the depressed insomniac. "Tell MGB director Kruglov to be in my office tomorrow at noon, alone. It's a matter of great urgency."

He turned back to Beria. "Oryol is the answer. Our brilliant little bird, right in the middle of all the American secrets. He will get their answers to this reentry puzzle. Then we will change the world."

"How will you activate Oryol? Who will be his handler?"

Stalin smiled for the first time that day. "Our cunning and vicious, young American, agent Sonya, of course. She is our greatest asset there, totally unknown to their FBI and the rest of the American idiots. She has already done incalculable damage to them on the atomic secrets, and they still have no idea she even exists. Remarkable."

He puffed on his pipe. "She can do anything – a born and raised 100% American, beyond suspicion."

"Yet the most deadly, professional and committed agent we have ever run abroad," concurred Beria.

Stalin rose and left for his bed chamber. As he lay in bed, he recalled Sonya's history, remarkable for a 32 year old woman. The pleasure of those thoughts finally allowed sleep to come.

CHAPTER 3

MURDER ON THE *OWL*

Four Months Later
Tuesday, November 11, 1952
6:00 p.m. New York City

FBI head of New York counterintelligence, Dominic Benvenuto's eyes circled the room. Can I trust everyone here, he thought. All these university types, academicians, mushy do-gooders. The same kind that had populated the Manhattan Project designing the first atomic bombs in Los Alamos – whom we now know leaked them to others who worked directly for the Soviets.

We and the CIA have checked them out head to toe but who knows? Scares the crap out of me. These guys can change the world, and if one of them isn't clean, and I don't find him or her…

He began his opening presentation to the Rocketry Commission, a brain trust secretly appointed directly by the Department of Defense and President Harry S. Truman. It's dual-mission was to lead the top secret effort to develop strategic rockets capable of both delivering nuclear tipped missiles anywhere on earth and put Americans in space.

"Ladies and gentlemen, before you begin your meeting let me stress again the absolute need for total security. Nothing reviewed here can be shared with anyone outside this room – not your academic or military colleagues, your families or friends. I also remind you to keep in place all the security precautions we have put in place in your homes, offices and when traveling to and from these meetings. Is this all clearly understood?"

He watched the heads all nod. A bit too casual for me, Dominic thought. I hope these eggheads know they might have the ultimate fate of the United States in their hands.

Nearby

The voice on the untraceable pay phone spoke slowly and clearly.

"The meeting of the Rocketry Commission won't break until after dinner. So, he's leaving on the late train, just as you hoped. He'll probably get to the terminal between 9:30 p.m.-10:00 p.m. There will be a treasure trove in his briefcase. Are you ready?"

"Of course, Oryol," the woman on a clean payphone on the other end responded. "My man is already in place. Now I will join him. The material will be in Moscow day after tomorrow."

"Good." The caller hung up.

The woman, who had planned every aspect of this pick, dialed the number of the freight yard phone where the operative on the scene was standing by. "It seems we will be taking a little trip tonight on train number 15, the *Owl*. Just as we hoped and planned for. See you shortly."

"I'm ready," a gruff male voice responded in Russian and then immediately hung up.

Same Day
Four Hours Later
10:00 p.m. Hoboken, New Jersey

As Professor John Dickinson exited the drab government sedan and entered the Hoboken terminal to board his westbound train, he looked in admiration, as always, at the beautiful structure that housed the eastern terminus of the Delaware, Lackawanna and Western Railroad. Completed in 1907 in the peak period of railroad prosperity, it was a blend of classic French Renaissance architecture and practical utility, sharing common grandeur with its contemporaries, Grand Central Terminal and the Pennsylvania Station but on a much more human scale. Every time he passed through, he noticed a new detail – the glass ceiling, the small floor tiles, the iron staircase rail, and the exterior copper, now graced with a remarkable green patina. At this hour of night the terminal was peaceful, the commuter crush long over, ambient sounds slowly being absorbed by silent osmosis into the 50 feet high glass ceiling, personally designed by Tiffany himself in 1907.

But this was no night for architectural ruminations. The Princeton physicist had been told in no uncertain terms to go directly to his sleeping compartment, lock the door, conceal his papers, and not come out until he reached Corning, New York, his destination. Dominic Benvenuto, the head of the FBI task force providing security, had offered an armed bodyguard, but Dickinson had declined with a chuckle. These FBI guys see spooks around every corner, he thought.

There were two Lackawanna options in the evening hours to get from Hoboken to Corning – the 7:30 p.m. departure of train No. 7, the *Westerner*, or the 1:05 a.m. departure of No. 15, the *Owl*. Dickinson preferred the later *Owl*, because you got a good night's sleep in a comfortable Pullman bed and arrived at Corning at 9:28 a.m. This allowed time to dress and enjoy a Lackawanna breakfast in the diner lounge car in the morning.

To Dickinson the *Owl* was a subtly mysterious, even romantic carriage of the night, moving gracefully through the darkness. This luxury capsule sailed alone through the quietude of New Jersey and eastern Pennsylvania at high speed before the sun came up, passing thousands of homes, somnolent factories and mines, shops and schools. Many along the mainline knew it only as the "night train" and were comforted by its patterned rumble, almost always right on time on the punctilious Lackawanna.

He boarded the lightweight sleeper car, *Kittatiny*. It had 10 roomettes for single occupancy and six double bedrooms. It had been delivered to the railroad in 1950, practically brand new in railroad product cycles. He was in bedroom F, the most desirable room in the car. It was in the center where it would be smooth and quiet, farthest from the clickety-clack of the wheels on the rail joints. Although unknown to all, tonight would hardly be smooth or quiet.

Dickinson bought the closing stock market edition of the *New York World Telegram* newspaper for a nickel and boarded the train at 10:26 p.m. Although the train did not depart until 1:05 a.m., first class passengers were free to board after 9:30 p.m., go to their assigned space and go right to sleep if wished. He was led by an affable porter to his bedroom F in the *Kittatiny*. It had two chairs facing each other, which had been collapsed prone to support a lower bed which dropped from the wall, and a small enclosed private bathroom. The crisp white sheets and light brown Pullman blanket were already turned down, inviting entry into this welcoming cocoon of promised restfulness.

"Yessuh, your bed is all set, both pillows out and extra towels. Will you be needin' anything else, suh?" the veteran porter inquired.

"No thanks, just a wakeup buzz around 8 a.m. See you in the morning." He gave the porter a dollar tip.

Dickinson changed into his bed clothes, climbed in between the crisp, clean linen sheets and read the newspaper. It was an enjoyable moment – safely packaged in this secure nest. The paper trumpeted depressing news from the Korean War, but there were several upbeat stories on the president-elect, Dwight D. Eisenhower and his proposed cabinet appointments. It seemed surreal to Dickinson that a Republican had actually won, first time since 1928.

The sports section featured a story on the football Giants' new rookie star, Frank Gifford from USC. And there was speculation as to who would win the 1952 Heisman Trophy, succeeding the 1951 winner, Princeton's own Dick Kazmeier.

The *Owl* boarding at Hoboken

Well before the train departed, Dickinson was sound asleep. But there were others on board who were not sleeping. They had very different agendas – far more sinister.

Just as Dickinson was nodding off in his warm bed, Vladimir Bodkin came out of the cold night shadows 800 feet east and slipped behind a Railway Express car.

Bodkin had done his homework. This long distance car had been fully loaded hours earlier in the terminal's yard before the train had been formed. It had been sealed closed, ready to begin its 3000 mile sojourn to San Francisco. The other head end cars were still being filled with packages going to less distant locations. Around midnight, one hour before departure, he would move quickly from behind the express car into the coach passenger car. No one would see him in the terminal or on the long platform.

Just like none of his 58 confirmed German kills had ever seen this wirey sniper in his six months in the bowels of Stalingrad.

At the same time Kenny Weinstein was at the other end of Hoboken terminal, finishing his sirloin steak dinner in the restaurant and getting ready to board the *Owl* for his return home to Syracuse. He noticed the shapely woman and her long flowing red hair as soon as she came in, and his eyes followed her to the seat she took at the bar.

He had been thinking about the women's apparel he had just purchased for his clothing store in Syracuse. The "shmata" boys know what I want by now –the latest fashion but at reasonable prices for middle age women getting fat and older in suburbia. But not realizing they are starting to look like shit. My stuff makes them feel better, particularly when I lay on the compliments, as they exit the changing room. It also helps that sometimes I even go into the room with them to help them change. Hell, I'll do anything for a sale. My new portfolio for the cold months is a winner. I'm satisfied with my work this trip.

But he was profoundly dissatisfied with something else – he had not had his usual explosive sex with the tall lithe blond model at Cedric Rosenberg's woven goods firm. He usually spent his last evening with her in the city. She had been fired for some trivia and was nowhere to be found. He knew Cedy from army days and Cedy was close to Kenny's wife, so he could not him ask about his lover's whereabouts. So, he thought, just another date tonight with my hand on the train. Oye vey.

Kenny was one of those men that needed satisfaction almost every night, a real horn toad. Many nights he would awaken his wife from a sound sleep just so he could get off. Sometimes she would even fall back asleep before he finished. It didn't matter. He would have gotten what he wanted and slept all the better (fifty years later in 2003, living in a nursing home, he would be caught attempting sex with another octogenarian which resulted in his being ejected from the facility).

So when the redhead with the gloriously ample figure entered the bar, his eyes locked right onto her. She looked about 30, quite stunning but with a sad demeanor, like she was upset about something. He paid his check, got up and sat two bar seats down from her.

"Excuse me miss, but do you happen to know when we can board the night train?" He knew it was already free to board.

She turned and looked at the source of the inquiry. "I believe it's open now," she said. "What time is it?" She seemed quietly melancholy and a bit disoriented. "I'm sorry if I seem a little scattered. I've had a bad day."

Kenny slid over one bar stool so as to be next to her. "Gee, I'm sorry, are you comfortable telling me what happened? I had a miserable disappointment also." Not getting laid was always a disappointment for this Jewish Fountain of Tivoli.

"It's just a very sad time for me."

"Maybe you can tell me a little about it, might make you feel better. I'm actually a doctor." As he said this he started to feel a slight stir in his pants. "By the way, I'm Ralph. What's your name?"

"Martha." She also didn't give a second name. A good sign.

His eyes turned downward to his feet. "My Manhattan girlfriend of six months just dumped me. Said I was boring, a hick from upstate and just not exciting enough for her. Man, just because I tried to treat her with some class and dignity. I bought her roses, took her to Broadway shows, bought her a beautiful necklace…she said she didn't like my cologne. I thought it smelled nice." He slowly looked up into her eyes to see if she was buying. He thought he saw a hint of a connection, a tweak of compassion.

It soon appeared to Kenny that he was making progress. After a few more minutes she started to really open up with tears welling up in her eyes.

"My husband has long had a lover in the city. He lived with her on his business trips, away from our home in Buffalo. I found out about it, and for six months we tried to reconcile, but it had finally just come apart."

As she finished she broke down in tears. He put his arm around her.

"I have an idea. We should order some champagne. As a beautiful young woman you actually should be celebrating. This happened soon enough for you to still reconstruct your life. Forget this idiot."

They spoke with growing animation as the champagne started to work. Soon Martha was actually smiling. They left the bar together at 11 p.m. with the remnants of the bottle under Kenny's arm, both laughing. She had a coach seat, Kenny had a deluxe drawing room in the *Syracuse* sleeping car, the largest room on the train, so he suggested they finish their libation in his accommodation.

They wound up making love for two hours until the train departed at 1:05 a.m. Drunk and covered with the juices of salubrious sex, Kenny passed out shortly after she had given him the last drink left in the bottle. As he crashed into sleep, groaning with satisfaction, he thought about how much he loved deluxe train travel on the staid *Lackawanna*, the "Friendly Service Route." It certainly had been friendly tonight.

Same Morning, 1:30 a.m.

"Martha" was negotiating the car hallways with the train at full speed, as she left the sleeper headed for the coach. She had transferred much of the champagne from her cup to the increasingly woozy Ralph or whatever lover boy's real name was. Then to really put him out, she had slipped the sleeping barbiturate into his last drink. He was soon snoring loudly as she exited the deluxe drawing room compartment.

She was very comfortable with her performance. He would remember a tall, busty redhead, whom he graciously transformed from a grieving divorcee to a wildly hot, multiple orgasmic, reborn woman. Her orgasms, all fake, had been very skillfully orchestrated. Next life maybe I'll take up acting, she thought.

Before leaving the drawing room, she removed the red wig, replaced it with a graying hairpiece in a bun, took off the elevator shoes and changed into a doughty outfit. She also marked her face with artificial aging lines and the slight hint of an old woman's mustache. No one could reconcile this look with the redhead. She was fully transformed from the bombshell who boarded the train to a graying and fading mediocrity.

She reached into a pocket to retrieve the note she had written three hours ago as Dickinson boarded the *Owl*. She reached the last row in the dark coach car and sat next to a man sequestered in the corner, furtively slipping him the note.

Vladimir Bodkin, the sniper rat from Stalingrad, never even looked at her. He opened the note. "J. Dickinson, Car 150 – *Kittatiny* – bedroom F." Two minutes later Bodkin was on the move. Just as they had rehearsed it.

1:48 a.m.

Bodkin was an accomplished thief as well as a deadly assassin. As he rode in the rear of the coach car, he had thought about how as an 18 year old he had found himself in 1942 in the 42nd Guards in the dregs of Stalingrad with the famous Yaakov Pavlov and his sewer rats.

Then he was promoted to sniping. No Russian spider was better –a lot of dead Germans could vouch for that. It always helped him to think about Stalingrad – particularly when he was about to undertake an assignment like this one, so easy by comparison. He couldn't believe how stupidly naïve these Americans were. A weak, unarmed, unguarded American professor up against him, a man who had broken German necks with his hands in the sewers.

He had boarded the *Owl* with an unreserved coach ticket bought in a general ticket sales office in Manhattan. There would be no record of his travel. He took the rear most seat, wore thick but clear glasses, shoes that elevated his otherwise 5'6" stature by three inches, and a well traveled hat that hid most of his face. He'd ridden the *Owl* several times in different disguises. He knew precisely when and how he would strike.

————————————

At 1:45 a.m., the train had entered the high speed cutoff, a raceway of 28 miles of straight track in Northwest New Jersey with a speed limit of 79 miles per hour. No one will be out for a stroll at this hour, and the high noise level in the car is covering every sound. Exactly why I had hoped that Dickinson would take the late train.

He entered the *Kittatiny* sleeper. Just as the train crossed above the tunnel for the railroad's Sussex Branch at Andover, he slowly opened the door of bedroom F with the master key he had stolen on his practice run on the *Owl* last week.

He entered the room slowly. He knew the double bedroom by heart. Dickinson seemed asleep, his watch and wallet in the small bag above the bed. Bodkin grabbed both as planned to make it look like a robbery. Then he found the briefcase, opened it.

Empty. Damn! Dickinson had hidden the papers somewhere else. There was nothing in the small closet, the waste baskets, even the shoe box for the porter. Finally Bodkin found the papers under the bed, and stood up.

————————————

As he did, suddenly and out of nowhere a metal ice water thermos smashed into the back of his head. He staggered back in intense pain. He heard a yell, "Porter!" from his adversary, whom he turned to face. The metal thermos was again coming at his head, with the cry, "You god damned thief."

He ducked and slammed a fist into Dickinson's gut. That stopped the yelling. A blow at the larynx ensured silence. But Dickinson, a former collegiate boxer, didn't go down. He jammed an upper cut with surprising power into Bodkin's jaw, the blow knocking the Russian onto the floor.

Bodkin saw the thermos coming at his face again. He dodged it. "Mother fucker," Bodkin growled in Russian. The two, tightly interwoven, struggled in silence until Bodkin pushed Dickinson away, giving him the room to kick Dickinson hard in the balls. But Dickinson fought on.

Then Bodkin lost it. Enraged, he grabbed his military knife, sharp enough to split hairs, and drove it below Dickinson's sternum and punctured his heart. "This show is over, asshole professor," he spat in Russian into Dickinson's face. He pulled the knife up and out, tearing Dickinson's chest apart. "Die you miserable asshole," he said through the splitting pain of his head wound.

Bodkin stood panting, still reeling from Dickinson's blows. What a disaster he thought, picking up the papers. I hope this bastard's yelling didn't wake anyone up. The covering noise of the speed and the rain against the windows helps.

He moved quickly back down the sleeping car aisle and entered his coach unseen, returning to his rear-most seat. He took off his bloodied jacket and replaced it with another from his suitcase.

He looked at the graying woman across from him and nodded. He transferred Dickinson's documents, wallet and watch into a locked suitcase, breathed deeply and tried to regain his composure. Was any blood still apparent?

When the *Owl* reached the next stop, Stroudsburg, Pennsylvania, at 2:52 a.m., he departed the train as did the aging lady a minute after him. He exited forward and she left toward the rear of the coach.

3:03 a.m.

He was the first to reach the waiting escape car, set in place by others, two blocks from the Stroudsburg station. He unlocked it and took the passenger's seat. The gray lady came 30 seconds later and got behind the wheel. One look at Bodkin told her there had been complications. He carried the smell of fear and the scent of anxiety. Since his English was poor, they spoke in Russian. She was totally fluent.

"I had to kill the son of a bitch," he whispered. "He jumped me in the bedroom while I was looking for the material. Almost knocked me out with a thermos, started to yell and kept coming at me. My head's killing me. The room looks like a stinking meat plant, blood everywhere. At least I got his notes. They better be as important as we were told. They look good – very technical and extensive."

"Were you seen?" she asked.

"I don't think so. With luck he won't be found for five hours when the porter tries to wake him in Elmira. By then I'll be safely in the New York consulate. Just drive." He started restoring his hair color and removed the elevator shoes.

She glanced at him. "When we get to Manhattan make sure you go into the consulate through the back passage next door."

"I always do," he responded.

"Good. We don't need you on any FBI film."

7:30 a.m., Soviet Consulate, 136 East 67th Street

The MGB (intelligence) station chief in New York was an old and seasoned Bolshevik, General Iuri Strelnikov. He was 59, bald and overweight; vodka frequented his breath. He had served his party and later the Soviet Union since 1916, when he joined the Czarist army two years into World War I, when any recruit was accepted without any background check by the Czarist authorities. If they had investigated, they would have found his arrest record in 1912, when he was accused of complicity in the murder in Kiev of Czar Nicholas II's prime minister and reformist, Pyotr Stolypin. Because nothing could be proven and perhaps because he was only 19 years old, he was released.

What they couldn't have expected to easily discover was that he had been out of the country from 1912-1916, mostly in England, where he worked as security muscle for a group of radical Marxists, becoming quite proficient in English. He snuck back into Russia through Finland in 1916 and joined the army with the clear orders to infiltrate the rank and file and help turn them against the collapsing old order.

Somehow in the next 36 years he had survived Stalin's purges and World War II, where he had distinguished himself on the northern front, helping break the 1000 day encirclement of Leningrad. More importantly for his career, earlier in July 1941, immediately after the German invasion, at Stalin's behest he had destroyed all written record of numerous agents' warnings of the coming German "Operation Barbarossa" invasion of Russia. Stalin had ignored them all, never believing Hitler would try such a bold strike. Strelnikov shot the keepers of those records, recalled the providers of that information to Moscow and also had them shot. As of 1952 none of that information had ever surfaced. Stalin trusted Strelnikov as he did few others and, in fact, that trust was well placed.

Bodkin gave Strelnikov the full detailed account of the evening and handed over all the professor's notes. The latter were immediately sent for photographic copying and placement in the diplomatic pouch bound for Moscow that night. When he was finished, Strelnikov addressed his chief muscle man in New York.

"Obviously, comrade, this was not one of your shining moments. There will be much concern at the Center about your sloppiness. How could you be surprised by a middle aged academic, a miserable amateur? This will now lead to a massive counter espionage effort, probably overseen by that closet faggot, J. Edgar Hoover himself. The reaction to the murder of a prominent American scientist, who happens to be a leading expert in rocket reentry physics, will be nasty. Given that he had just come from their special task force meeting, we can expect a strong response. You better hope that what you got was worth all this."

He glared at Bodkin. "That's all, I'm disgusted with you. A supposed professional. You performed like a rookie in training. You're dismissed –get out of my sight."

After he left, Strelnikov thought of other implications, known only to him. I oversee the Soviet Union's most important American agent. Right in the middle of the Americans' most secret rocketry program. The night's events clearly put that agent, Oryol, at risk. Bodkin may be losing it from too many years of killing.

Strelnikov reached for his vodka.

8:00 a.m., a Manhattan Apartment

The woman had slept for a few hours, then awoke and had some coffee, staring out the window. She hated America in general and New York in particular.

She smiled as she found a strand of red hair from the "Martha" wig she had worn last night. It's always so easy getting some guy to hit on me and then use him for my needs.

She reviewed the events of the previous night and early morning and their potential ramifications. She prided herself in conducting such complicated and brutal matters with a cold, analytical detachment, truly remarkable for a 33 year old operative, particularly one born and raised in America. But then, everything about her was highly unusual.

Last night's complications didn't bother me at all, she thought. Sometimes extreme action done intelligently is necessary to achieve one's objectives. In fact, I find it stimulating to be involved again in wet operations. Frankly, I don't get enough of it. Reminds me of my training in Russia in the Urals in 1943. I love every aspect of the work – the cunning implementation after meticulous planning, and then the occasional stunning brutality. All of this for the cause – the movement that will liberate the world and, with some good luck, eventually place me with the top of the new ruling elite. We'll destroy all these capitalist bastards.

She lifted her cup of coffee, and pointed to the east, "Na zdoroveya, o moya dorogaya novaya Rodina (to your health, oh my sweet new motherland). I will do whatever asked of me to destroy our greatest enemy – America – and advance the final victory of glorious communism. With me at the center of it all – pulling the strings of power with the leadership, disposing of anyone who tries to get in my way."

Sonya took a shower, got dressed for work and departed with a joy in her step, fully satisfied with her night's work. She could still taste the subtle vestige of adrenaline lingering in her body – the joy of a successful kill.

CHAPTER 4

THE INVESTIGATION BEGINS

Same Morning – Wednesday, November 12
8:00 a.m. Aboard the "Owl" Train En Route

As requested, the porter of the sleeper *Kittatiny*, 26 year veteran Thurgood Randolph, knocked on the door of bedroom F to awaken his guest. Dickinson had been clear that he wanted to be awakened 30 minutes outside of Elmira, giving him time to have a full breakfast in the diner lounge before disembarking at Corning at 9:28 a.m.

Sleeping car porters had been doing this ritual since before the civil war. In fact, Randolph's' father had been a Pullman porter for 38 years, and his brother in Los Angeles was one now. He worked the Santa Fe *Super Chief*, the elite train for the stars as they played their bi-coastal ballet.

That weeknight over 50,000 people were still sleeping in beds as the guest of America's railroads in first class overnight rail accommodations. Dickinson had been one of them – but clearly the only one whose chest had been punctured and guts eviscerated.

Randolph's first knock met with no response. This was not at all unusual, as the passenger could be using the facilities. However, when there was no response to a second longer knocking ten minutes later, Randolph got concerned. Several years ago he had a passenger die in his sleep of a heart attack, and he didn't want to go through that again. He went to get the master key and then opened the door.

"Oh, sweet Jesus!" Dickinson lay on the floor in a pool of blood that spread over four feet of the carpet. There was a gaping hole in his chest. His head was partially detached from his body. Thurgood ran to get the lead conductor, the man in charge of the train. "Lawd have mercy," he cried.

When the conductor saw the carnage, he almost passed out. Then he grabbed his radio and told the engineer, "Call the station agent in Elmira and ask for state and local police in force to help secure the train when we stop. A first class passenger has been brutally murdered. His head is detached from his body. He's been robbed by some maniac. The killer might still be aboard. We gotta get this thing shut down…tight."

Dominic Benvenuto, the newly appointed 42 year old head of the New York counterintelligence office, sat bored and somewhat exasperated at the meeting table. A senior FBI agent from San Francisco was lecturing his group on Harry Bridges and his renegade left leaning West Coast Longshoremen's Union. He thought the guy was somewhat paranoid, and in any case what he had to say had no relevance to the East Coast union which was run by the mob, not some left-wing gigatz (idiot). Crooks but patriotic crooks. And Dominic knew everything about them. He had to – the port was the New York entry point for all to gain access to the U.S. from abroad, except for the few super rich who could afford $1,000 airplane tickets and had nothing to hide from passport security.

The visiting agent was preaching, "So this guy Bridges is a pinko, left leaning creep. He may not answer to Moscow, but he does a lot to help their cause. He's had the balls to call two wildcat strikes, right in the middle of all the war material flowing to our boys in Korea from the port of San Francisco."

"But what has that got to do with New York?" Dominic interrupted, growing tired of this waste of time. He had real work to do. "I guarantee you if some red showed up on these docks he would disappear real fast, with no forwarding address. The mob boys and their union members would see to that. You can say what you want about these hoods and their union, but they are loyal Americans. This is the last of my worries in counter intelligence. Go see the guys in the crime task force – that is their territory."

At that moment Ed Booth, Dominic's agent in charge of everyday security for the new top secret rocketry task force, burst into the room. "Boss, I need to talk to you. Now. Could you please step out?"

"Why not Ed, I could use the break and maybe get some real work done," he said, looking with disdain right into the visitor's eyes.

They moved to a deserted corridor, "Dr. Stookey at the Corning plant just called. Professor Dickinson is uncharacteristically late for his 2 p.m. meeting to review the Rocketry Commission's work yesterday here in New York."

With anxiety suddenly dancing in his eyes, Dominic asked, "Your guy put him on the train last night, right?"

"You bet. The professor hates security, but Miller followed him from a distance until he boarded the train."

"It may be nothing then. Maybe he's got the trots. Tell our guy at the plant to call us back in half an hour if he doesn't show up."

"Okay, boss."

25

Dominic hesitated to go back into the meeting. What the hell, just in case, might as well check the teletype that receives all messages from Northeastern law enforcement. He strolled over to the clattering machine.

The usual crap, he thought, scanning the rolls of paper, not unlike the stock market news ticker you'd find at Merrill Lynch. A dozen missing person reports, 95% of which would be resolved in 24-hours as the drunk slept it off or lover boy returned to his wife.

Then his eyes caught it – a report from the Elmira, New York police department and New York State police asking for help in identifying a murder-robbery victim on the Lackawanna's *Owl* night train. Dom raced through the report to the last sentences. "The Pullman conductor aboard the train identified the victim as one 'J. Dickinson'. No confirmation has been established as his being a resident of the immediate area or employee of an area business, school or hospital."

"Jesus Christ," Dominic moaned, "Ed, get over here, now." He showed him the item. "Get on the phone with Corning. I'm calling the railroad. Prudence," he yelled as he ran toward his assistant's desk. "Get me the General Traffic Agent of the Lackawanna railroad, Mr. Farmer at their 140 Cedar Street Manhattan office."

Within minutes he had reached Farmer. "Yes, we had a brutal murder on train #15, The *Owl*, last night" Farmer said. "Looks like a robbery, wallet and watch gone and briefcase emptied out. We have both local and state law enforcement on the scene."

Each of his words seemed to further liquefy the very floor Dominic was standing on, opening a chasm he was cascading into. The physical evidence and the empty briefcase sealed the issue. Dickinson was dead and the papers, secrets that could change the world, were gone. God almighty!

He raced back to his office. Phones started to light up throughout the Northeast, including the FBI emergency command post in Washington, the Officer in charge (OIC) desk at the Pentagon and the duty officer at 1600 Pennsylvania Avenue, where a note was slipped to outgoing President Truman.

Thirty Minutes Later
Elmira, New York

Agent Jesse Morgan and two associates were the first FBI personnel to reach the train at the Elmira Station. They had raced there from the Corning plant half an hour away, where they oversaw security of the highly classified work being done there on missile reentry nose cones.

He pushed people away, flashing his badge, until he reached a Captain Donald Schultz of the New York State Police, homicide division. "I'm FBI

26

senior agent Jesse Morgan. This crime scene is of Federal concern, and I am now declaring it under the control of the FBI. There will soon be dozens of agents here. We expect and know we will get your full cooperation and support. Your own commanding officer from Albany is also on his way by plane."

Jesus, Schultz thought, what is falling on my head? "Agent Morgan, can you give us any background on this John Dickinson and what the issues are here?"

"No, I cannot. Please have your men announce that no one who has worked on this crime scene can leave, nor can anyone who was or is on the train."

"Yes sir," he replied.

"Now please tell me concisely what you know at this point"

There followed a short briefing that reflected the kind of police work expected at the site of a murder where robbery seemed the motive. Photographs of the body had been taken, and then the body was rushed to the county coroner, a prime goal being the establishment of the time of death. Finger prints were taken, passengers and employees were being interviewed and nobody was going anywhere, including the train.

Ten minutes into it, Dominic reached Morgan on his car radio and got a quick debrief. "I'm on my way," Dom told him. "I'm getting on a Bureau plane to Elmira and expect to be on site in less than two hours. Don't let the locals screw it up anymore than they probably already have."

He hung up the phone and jumped into a car for the waiting Bureau two engine Cessna aircraft at LaGuardia airport.

The drone of the engines and the interlude of the flight allowed Dom to put his thoughts in some order. He tried to put this crisis that had ambushed him out of nowhere into the context of his life to date. So far he'd lived a charmed existence, a remarkable series of achievements and successes for a young, second generation American.

Dominic had been appointed New York Chief of Counter Intelligence for the FBI two months ago at the impressively young age of 42. He stood six feet tall, had a tight body of 195 pounds with a 32 inch waist. His chiseled jaw with a Clark Gable dimple complemented the jet black hair and deeply expressive brown eyes. He resembled an Italian count in a Hollywood movie. The eyes of women constantly danced after him as he moved through a room. You could feel his energy with your back turned.

Truesdale Colliery 1910 – World's Largest Anthracite Mine

He was a graduate of the United States Military Academy, class of 1942, where he had been a halfback on the football team. He was a decorated war hero, having served two years in Europe. He loved his country with a passion, and his commitment to his beloved FBI was sacred.

Dominic's father, Alfredo, had arrived from Calabria, Italy in 1908. He got off the steerage section of the boat and looked for the Lackawanna Railroad agent, as he had been instructed to by his uncle, who was a foreman at the Truesdale Colliery in northeastern Pennsylvania, the world's largest anthracite coal mine. Within hours he was departing from the brand new Hoboken Terminal for the anthracite country around Scranton, Pennsylvania, one of a group of over 150 able bodied men who had been recruited in Europe by agents of the coal mining companies who operated in northeastern Pennsylvania.

The economy there was booming. There were two driving forces – high quality anthracite coal, the "black diamonds," found only in this region, and the rapid growth of the steel production. Both were essential to the new American economy, the fastest growing in the world. One of the largest steel plants in the world was Bethlehem Steel's plant in its namesake city, right in the heart of hard coal country. From this 1300 acre complex would later come the steel that built the Golden Gate Bridge, the Empire State Building and the Holland and Lincoln tunnels.

Dominic thought about his father's work to feed his family – the hard, dangerous and filthy life of a coal miner. Helped by a strong back and an innate sense of mechanical engineering concepts, he had risen rapidly from apprentice to master miner to shift boss to foreman over the 1000 men in the day shift. The men and the bosses respected him. The Serbs, Poles, Czechs, Hungarians, his fellow Italians, even the Irish bosses seemed to like this highly effective man. Simply stated he was a man of integrity who did what he promised. Everyone sought out his sage advice on all kinds of matters.

He had met a young Italian-American beauty, Giovanna Carreri, six months after arrival, was blasted by the "thunderbolt" and married her in 1909. They had Dominic in 1920, the third child after two older sisters.

Giovanna, or "Gianna" as his mother was affectionately called, was an extraordinary woman. One Sunday a group of men from the "Black Hand" had knocked on the door, basically asking for a share of the sweet, flowing nectar of union dues. Alfredo invited them in and offered a glass of wine and homemade Italian desserts. They chatted and danced around the issues. Finally, Alfredo said no. As the lead thug rose to approach him, a shot, fired by Gianna from the kitchen grazed his ear.

"My next shot will be right between your eyes. Now do you want that or should we all sit down nicely and finish our desserts?" The lead hood, visibly shaken, voted for the latter. They were never seen again at the Benvenuto home.

Alfredo left the mine in 1928 to open a fuel oil distribution company, ironically the commodity which, with natural gas, would ultimately kill anthracite. He never said it, but everyone knew the father worshipped his son, such a glowing success in one generation. West Point, an officer and war hero and now an FBI rising star. Dominic's mother and sisters shared the father's deification of the son.

Dominic married the former Laurie Wolski, a striking blond and a former Miss New Jersey. They had two boys and a daughter, lived in the fancy suburb of Chatham, New Jersey, owned their own home and were basically living the American dream. And Dom would often say, "not bad for the son of a paisan who fell off the boat right into a 300 foot deep coal mine."

He had only one issue in his life – his weakness for beautiful women. He blamed it on his Italian gene pool. He was working on this problem, but it clearly was still a work in progress. And the women liked him.

All of this life experience had forged Dominic into a man of unlimited confidence tempered by the proper humility. Deep within he viewed himself as up to any task, any challenge. Failure was unknown to him – as a student leader, a star athlete, a decorated warrior, a husband and father and a fast rising FBI wunderkind. He had joined the Bureau for all the right reasons – to give back by serving his country that had been so abundantly generous to him and his family. And his record of accomplishment so far was exemplary – the poster boy for the "new" FBI.

As the Bureau plane bumped to its landing in Elmira, he was brought back to the present. While it taxied, he spoke to Ed Booth, one of this accompanying agents.

"I let a naïve academic talk me out of proper security safeguards, and the result's a disaster. He gets murdered and the killer takes papers vital to the national interest. Now I have to get on top of this fast and set it straight. Don't expect much sleep the next few nights, Ed."

They bounded out of the plane and ran to the waiting car to take him to the scene – Dominic, a man possessed.

5:10 p.m.
Elmira, New York

Dominic's first interview on site was with the Pullman porter of the car Dickinson had occupied.

"Randolph, did you notice anything unusual about Mr. J. Dickinson?"

"No sir," Thurgood answered. "I welcomed him in Hoboken. He boarded early, and I took him to his bedroom. I believe he had traveled with me before, he looked familiar. In any case he needed no explanation of the room's

30

features. He said it had been a long day and that he would turn in early. He asked to be awakened 30 minutes out of Elmira and slipped me a dollar. A very nice gentleman."

"Was he carrying anything out of the ordinary?"

"No, a small suitcase and a heavy briefcase, like a lot of my businessmen. They's the ones who keep us going on the *Owl*, you know."

"Did he seem nervous, agitated, troubled or anxious?" Schultz asked.

"No sir. He looked to me like a man who was very happy to be in a comfortable place and looking forward to some sleep after a long day."

"Did you see anyone enter his room or the sleeping car itself that did not belong?"

"No. We were about three quarters full in my car last night, 16 people. Busy. I greeted them all and remembered the faces. No strangers came in the car that I saw. But ya do know, sir, that we leave Hoboken late, and few people ever get on the *Owl* until Binghamton, New York. And I have to get up very early for folks disembarking at Scranton, Binghamton and Elmira. So I always tries to get some rest between Hoboken and Scranton. It's the only rest I get."

"Where did you sleep or…rest last night?"

"In roomette 1, which was vacant and closest to the next sleeping car. By the way, that's also furthest from the coaches. I wouldn't of seen anyone comin' in from the coaches."

"Describe the scene when you opened the bedroom door just outside of Elmira."

"Never seen the likes of it. Mr. Dickinson on the floor, blood everywhere. I rolled him over and saw the hole in his chest and the slashed throat - a nightmare. In all my days, I…" He stopped and put his head in his hands. He had told Dom all he knew. This interview was over.

Dominic asked for a summary from Captain Schultz, the New York State Police homicide captain. "We interviewed everyone in the sleeper. Only two gentlemen, each in roomettes, had gotten off before Elmira, both in Binghamton. Our state police are trying to locate them. Everyone else in the car checked out, subject to further investigation. The two other sleeping cars also seemed devoid of suspects."

Dom moved to the coach. There had been only ten people still on board in that car. The conductor's collected tickets, showed that nine coach passengers had bought tickets to detrain before Elmira at station stops Scranton and Binghamton. No one had bought a ticket to get off at Stroudsburg, although one remaining coach passenger thought he saw someone walking by on the outside on the dark side of the train away from the station. And of course, all the unreserved coach passengers who did get off before Elmira were nameless and not immediately traceable – a major problem. Coach tickets were anonymous – exactly what a perp would do.

Dominic interviewed the conductor in charge, followed by Dickinson's fellow passengers in the sleeper. Afterword Dominic turned to Agent Morgan, "There's no way the killer or killers stayed on this train. The county coroner confirmed death between 2-4 a.m., so our perpetrator got off somewhere shortly thereafter. His options really were only Stroudsburg, even though no one had a ticket to there, or Scranton. Why stay on to Elmira?

"Boss, what about the sleeper that got cut out in Binghamton to join the Syracuse branch line train waiting there? Could any of the guys on that separated sleeper be our man?"

"No way. Why stick around in broad daylight and ride to Syracuse? If this killer is a professional foreign operative, he got off with his precious cargo as quickly as possible and is probably back where he came from – New York City or Northern New Jersey. I have 25 men each scouring Stroudsburg and Scranton right now and a new command post being set up in the Hotel Casey in Scranton. I'll go there now but that's just to oversee the local investigation. I'm sure our boy is long gone – probably had someone or a parked car waiting for him. You keep turning over stones here. I'm off to Scranton and Stroudsburg."

8:00 p.m. Same Day
FBI Command Post, Hotel Casey, Scranton, Pennsylvania

Dominic waited for the call from his boss' boss, J. Edgar Hoover himself, the Director of the FBI. He had organized his notes for the call and was as ready as he could be. Most of the night's events had been documented. He would now lay it all out to Hoover.

Meanwhile, he had the sinking feeling that his life, this marvel of one success after another until now, was about to be immolated in a firestorm of disaster. But he couldn't let fear get in the way of his now focused sense of mission. This is the biggest challenge of my life, he thought, and I will attack it with a passion, destroying anything in my way. I will remain professional and laser focused in pursuit of those who have disgraced me, killing a key guy I was responsible for. I'll find these bastards. And destroy them.

"Mr. Benvenuto, pick up line one. It's Director Hoover's office," screamed the secretary there in the Hotel Casey temporary office.

"Bureau Chief Benvenuto, this is the Director. Please report your progress in the Dickinson case."

Hoover was consistently concise and always formal. But his voice had a strange sort of rallying effect on Dom, an in-your-face challenge that got Dominic even more energized, if that was possible.

Dom began with a reflexive, almost paramilitary law enforcement demeanor, spitting facts. "Mr. Director, we have 160 agents working on the case. They are coordinating with state and local law enforcement personnel in New Jersey, New York and Pennsylvania."

"What makes you think that's enough?" Hoover interrupted.

"I don't know if it is, sir," Dominic responded. He wasn't going to bullshit the Director.

"But let me tell you what we learned in the last three hours. As you know, sir, the train was stopped at Elmira when the body was found, and no one was allowed to leave before being interviewed by state and local law enforcement. They recorded names and addresses, deemed no one a logical suspect and allowed a fair number to leave. We're following up with all of these passengers now and so far, although it's early, share the view of the state and local people. We'll continue to investigate with interviews of employers and friends, detailed reviews of phone records and personal histories. There is one coach passenger who describes himself as an active socialist, on whom we will conduct active surveillance and further checks. So far he seems an unlikely, however."

"What about the passengers who got off before Elmira or were on the sleeper to Syracuse which was switched off in Binghamton?" Hoover asked.

The Director was well briefed. "Sir, the train had stopped at Stroudsburg, Pennsylvania; Scranton, Pennsylvania and Binghamton, New York before the body was discovered and the train searched in Elmira. The perpetrator or perpetrators could have exited the train at any of these spots. The conductor's manifest showed no coach or first class passengers scheduled to detrain at Stroudsburg, but of course, that makes me believe they probably did get off there, the first stop after the murder. There were two coach tickets to Scranton, and two first class fares and seven coach fares to Binghamton. We interviewed the two first class passengers, businessmen well known in that community, but we're trailing them for a while anyway."

"What about the rest?"

"The coach passengers who left the train at Scranton and Binghamton are unknown. No one, including the conductor, saw anyone leave at Stroudsburg, although one drowsy coach passenger thought he saw a man with a suitcase walking on the dark side of the train away from the lights of the station. Descriptions of those who left in Scranton and Binghamton are marginal. Regarding the Syracuse sleeper, we do have the names of the fourteen passengers on that sleeper and have located and are interviewing all of them, but I'm not optimistic that any of them were our killer. Why would he stay on any part of that train?"

"Bureau Chief Benvenuto, what ARE you optimistic about?"

Dominic hesitated. Then he felt his Calabrian ire rising rapidly. Mr. big shot director, sitting in his huge office barking at me.

"Sir, no one regrets the events of the last 24-hours more than I do. I know that I failed – failed in a matter of the gravest national import. But the victim was a very difficult academic who wanted no part of bodyguards or anything like it, similar to most of these Rocketry Commission guys."

Then it just blurted out. "You know the type sir. Just like that crowd you had to deal with at Los Alamos and the Manhattan project."

As soon as it was out of his mouth, Dom couldn't believe he had said it. Everyone around the Bureau knew of the catastrophic security breaches within the Manhattan A-bomb project and the Los Alamos, New Mexico facility where the first bombs had been built. Grave atomic secrets had leaked from both to communist sympathizers, accelerating Soviet atomic bomb development by years. It was Hoover's and the army's biggest security failure. Dominic had just counterpunched right to Hoover's glass jaw. Basically pissed in the boss's face.

The director said nothing for 10 seconds. My career is hanging on a thread. The first five words from Hoover would tell the story. He could be finished–the wonder boy from the hard coal region, crashed and burned. A failure. The silence seemed endless.

Finally Hoover just said gruffly, "Give me your thoughts on where the killer exited the train." Jesus, I made it, thought Dom, resuming his breathing. The Chief doesn't want to talk about the Manhattan Project or Los Alamos. He's backed off, it worked!

"Sir, that's the key question," Dominic said, trying to flatter the Director while avoiding being obsequious. "The autopsy done immediately in Elmira put the time of death between 1:00 and 5:00 a.m. This means the killer potentially exited the train at Stroudsburg or Scranton. My personal theory is Stroudsburg at 2:52 a.m. Stroudsburg was the first stop after the time that the coroner established as the time of death. It would be a great place to disappear into the darkness. As is true most nights for this train, no one was scheduled to get on or off there. Only mail was loaded and unloaded and a crew change.

We interviewed all the homes around the station," Dominic continued. "There's one very interesting lead. A retired railroad engineer, who lives two blocks from the station, and has a direct view of it, was awakened by the arrival of the *Owl*. He is apparently a light sleeper, and actually enjoys seeing #15 come in and leave, as he used to run that train himself. A few minutes after the train's arrival, he saw a man silently enter a car two houses up his street on the passenger side of the car. Then he saw what looked on the surface to be an older lady about 60, who moved like a much younger woman, dash in behind the wheel. He identified the car as most likely a 1949 or 1950 fastback Pontiac with New York plates, but couldn't make out the numbers. He couldn't tell the car's color, other than it was dark. The activity struck him as strange, but he went back to sleep. We are following up on this aggressively."

"Agent Benvenuto," responded the Director, "You've been briefed on the extreme importance of this case. You know of our suspicions that this was the work of foreign agents, who somehow knew what professor Dickinson was involved in and his travel plans on Tuesday night. Your progress is not satisfactory. It sounds like all you have is a theory on Stroudsburg as the point of exit and a possible link to a vehicle. Some very important classified information may be about to leave the country. I want it stopped. Do you understand me?"

"Sir, we are leaving no stone unturned, but I must say that this all looks very professional. I'm already ninety percent sure the killer bought an anonymous coach ticket for Scranton, but actually snuck off at Stroudsburg. He is untraceable. He had scouted his escape and had that car waiting for him. He knew the train, its process, its rhythm and how to disappear off of it. A deadly pro."

"But why would a professional have to kill Dickinson to get his material. Why not a simple theft?"

"The forensic study of bedroom F indicates some kind of struggle. We're reviewing the prints picked up and hair follicles found but expect only confusion, given the number of occupants of a Pullman bedroom and those who service it every week. We're also attempting to understand how the responsible parties knew what Dickinson was doing and his last minute travel plans, made as the task force meeting ended. These issues raise some very disturbing questions."

"Disturbing indeed. We're very aware of those issues. I expect more progress, and soon." Hoover hung up.

Dominic exhaled. For the moment he had survived. He kicked his desk, threw his clenched fist up into the air, got up and exited his office for a little sleep before a 6:00 a.m. drive to Stroudsburg.

Next Day, Thursday November 13; 9:00 a.m.
Stroudsburg, Pennsylvania

Stroudsburg was, as advertised, a small town. It had the marginally subtle feel of an area that was not depressed but was not as prosperous as it once had been. Production of anthracite was declining. The other big area employer, the railroads, were declining both as a result of decreasing anthracite output and the major productivity gains the diesel engine brought versus its steam engine predecessor. There actually were seven so called anthracite railroads that crisscrossed northeastern Pennsylvania, and all of them were meaningfully reducing their payrolls.

By the time Dom arrived at 9:00 a.m., the FBI had scoured the town. Their conviction that the suspect(s) had detrained there grew by the hour. By now they had interviewed almost everyone who had ridden in any accommodation on the *Owl* the night of the murder. It was the kind of thing the Bureau was very good at, Dom knew, particularly with major resources employed. The strongly held view now was that the perpetrators had indeed snuck off at Stroudsburg.

This was old news to Dom. He sighed in frustration.

"Tell me again about the first class passengers in the sleeping cars, particularly this guy Weinstein."

"Boss, we've accounted now for all of them. This Kenny Weinstein, a married guy, who had been in the Syracuse sleeper, admitted, after much reassurance of discretion from us, that he had met in the terminal restaurant and invited onto the train a rather stunning, red headed woman around 30 with a very attractive full figure.

"What do you mean, full figure? Fat?"

"No, big tits" agent Morgan replied.

"Did this bombshell have a name?"

"Martha, no last name given. She had a coach ticket but joined lover boy in his private drawing room. They had vigorous sex for several hours. He said he had fallen asleep, and she was gone when he awakened just outside of Syracuse at 9:30 a.m., strangely late for him to arise he says. My bet he was drugged. The room has been dusted for fingerprints – so far none match anything on file. Problem is that the railroad estimates 25 passengers and 40 railroad employees would have had access to this deluxe drawing room in just the last month. We also are looking for a woman of that description in her supposed hometown of Buffalo, recently divorced, per Weinstein's description of their conversation. No luck yet and frankly we don't expect any. My strong bet is that the woman, heavily disguised, was part of the hit, maybe its leader."

"Did she have an accent?" Dom asked.

"None according to Weinstein. Straight up American."

"Has any passenger acknowledged seeing either this "Martha" or the old lady that the retired railroad guy, Pochick, talked about?"

"No, Sir."

"I bet we never see either of these women again. This Martha shacks up with Weinstein to have the privacy of the sleeper. Then she probably drugs him, which explains why he slept so late. She disguises herself as an old lady and moves to the coach where she meets her male accomplice who will do the pick. It gets messy as Dickinson resists. They leave the train separately in Stroudsburg, get in the car, pre-positioned near the retired engineer's house, and leave in a hurry."

So far he was sure he was right. But who was the mysterious woman? No accent? And the barbaric killer?

Dominic studied the geometry of the tracks and its relationship to the station. As previously reported, there was nothing on the north side of the tracks, and it presented an easy route for people to slip off into the darkness of the streets. They then followed the two block route to the home of George Pochick, the retired DL&W engineer, who had seen the man and woman who entered the car up his street. He lived alone in a small home, following the death of his wife of 51 years the previous winter.

"Mr. Pochick," Dominic opened, "We greatly appreciate all your assistance in this difficult case. You've been most helpful. I'm from New York City and in charge of this investigation. I have read all your previous comments to our agents. Is there anything you think particularly significant that you would like to emphasize directly to me?"

"Well sir, it was very strange for me to see people moving on this street at 3:00 a.m. I know that was the time because I like to get up to see the *Owl*, #15, and it was right on time that night. You know, I really miss my old job running the trains. A man spends his whole life working up the ladder – freight conductor, then fireman, then freight engineer, then passenger engineer on the minor runs and finally the big time luxury trains. Then one day it all stops. Two, four, six, eight…and then zero. That's life, I guess. Then you think you'll enjoy takin' it easy, but after three weeks you're bored out of your mind.

Then the missus ups and dies on me, leaving me alone in this old house with many beautiful memories of yesterdays but no todays. My two kids live in Dallas and San Francisco." He paused, with moisture welling up in his eyes. Dominic did not hurry him.

"But you don't want to hear an old man's life story. Back to that early morning. As many nights as I have been awakened by that train, I'm a light sleeper, ya know, I never remember seein' anyone on this street at that hour. Until that night. And I know all my neighbors. Hell, they all go to bed around 9:30 – 10 o'clock just like me," he smiled.

"So here I am starin' out my window at the depot and switch tower, when I see this figure in a dark coat approach a parked '49 or '50 Pontiac, you know, the kind with the sloped fastback. He opens the door and gets in. About one minute later some lady gets in on the driver's side. I barely saw her she moved so fast and quietly. Don't know where she came from. Like she came out of the shadows – a ghost.

Then they drive off. Car had New York plates, you know, with that empire state stuff on it. My eyes are still good. So that was it. Thought it was odd, but I went back to bed."

"You didn't get a look at either face?"

"It was too dark. First was a man though. The second I only caught for a split second. Only reason I say she was a lady was I got a quick look at her balled up hair, you know like an older gal would wear it."

"Was her hair red?"

"Don't think so, but it was real hard to see 'cause the car was parked away from any street light. Then…wait a minute. I just realized something - they didn't have their car lights on. When they turned right up the street a ways, I should of seen the beams. There were none. Funny, I never thought of that until now."

"So you're sure the car was moving without lights?"

"I guess I am."

Dominic looked at the other agents. After a few more questions, they thanked Pochick and left. They got in a car and began the ride to Scranton.

"I think that's the icing on the cake, " Dominic offered, "People who belong here aren't walking around at 3 a.m. in this town, dashing silently into a car, well away from any street light and skulking off slowly in the dark with their lights off. Now we have to figure out where that dark Pontiac was heading. Probably around Hoboken, where they had to get on the train, or New York City.

I'm betting the lady is the earlier young redhead, undoubtedly in some kind of disguise both on the train and later as she walked to the car. And an American with no accent. Very troubling.

We have to find that car. Put out an APB through the locals for the Pontiac. See if any have turned up somewhere, any stolen, the usual drill."

Returning to New York on the Lackawanna's premier train, the *Phoebe Snow,* Dominic organized his thoughts in the luxury and quietude of its finest car, the tavern lounge on the end of the streamliner.

When he first boarded the train in Scranton for the three hour return to New York he found himself reflecting on the joys and accomplishments of his life. But now all this accomplishment – the star student, the football player, the war hero, the young FBI dynamo – the whole thing was falling into a chasm of crap. Whatever had been in Dickinson's bag, vital secrets in the new cold war, were probably now on a long trip east. And…there is almost certainly an enemy operative inside our rocketry group or even in my organization, and we don't have a clue who it is. How did they know Dickinson's last minute plans?

At least I survived the first sparring contest with Hoover. But that was just round one. These secrets may turn the course of the cold war. And history may treat me and my FBI as the incompetent idiots who let the Russians grab it.

This whole notion was beyond debilitating for Dominic - the boy wonder, the A student, the football hero, the FBI star. He felt subtle tugs at the base of his enormous self confidence and optimism, the core of his foundation. How could he have been so unbelievably careless?

He mentally laid out a timeline of the events on the night of the murder and listed every human being, who could have seen or come into contact with John Dickinson. All members of the task force, the commission's staff, my 18 agents, my office and their people - a total of at least 87 men and women. Then there were about 30 people in the train terminal, but only one man who had contact with Dickinson, the newsstand employee. Agent Bugliari, who had surreptitiously followed Dickinson until he saw him board the train, reported no other contacts and nothing suspicious. Finally there were the 16 train employees and 48 first class passengers in the sleepers. Only the Pullman porter in Dickinson's car and the ticket-taking conductor reported any contact with him.

The coach passengers did produce one new lead – a German-American guy who lives in the Yorktown section of Manhattan. The Bureau had actually noted him during the war and had records of some social contacts he had with the German-American Bund in Sussex County New Jersey. But why would an ex-Nazi sympathizer want to help the Soviets?

My money's on the hot American "redhead," who did Weinstein in the sleeper.

Dom got out the teletyped memo from the statistical cone heads in the bureau's Washington case management group and reread it:

> To: Bureau Chief Dominic Benvenuto
>
> From: Ralph Kubiack, Manager, Statistical Case Management
>
> Cc: Clyde Tolson, Assistant to the Director
> _____
>
> We have reviewed the data submitted by all sources on the Dickinson case. We have quantified the input and have run the values through our Mean Expected Value program in our new Univac computer. The results appear below:

1. Probability that the actual murderer was a lone man: 53.7%. One standard deviation: 6.8%
2. Probability of an accomplice: 72.7%. Standard deviation: 21.3%
3. Probability that one of the interviewed passengers or railroad employees committed the murder: 7.1%. One standard deviation: 2.2%
4. Probability of the murderer and possible accomplice(s) being one or more of the six non-interviewed coach passengers: 91.2%. One standard deviation: 4.8%
5. Probability of the murderer(s) detraining secretly at Stroudsburg: 84.6%. One standard deviation: 7.8%

Let us know if we can serve you further in this most grave matter.

He scanned the lounge car, focusing on the group of attractive female college students sharing drinks with some Cornell guys, all coming home for Thanksgiving vacation. How simple their 21-year old lives seemed. His eyes returned to one particularly attractive blond in a red dress with a bullet-type bra. Great body. No harm in looking at attractive snatch. He looked a lot but rarely touched. He tried to keep that side of him under control. Sometimes he failed.

———

Unknown to Dominic, at that very moment a teletype report from the Bayonne, New Jersey police department reached the FBI counter intelligence office in Manhattan:

"In response to your inquiry we advise the recent disappearance of a 1949 dark green fastback style, Pontiac sedan on October 16, 1952 from the driveway of the owner, a Miss Mary Coleman, a veteran teacher in the Bayonne public school system. There has been no report of the car's whereabouts since its disappearance."

The next morning at 11:28 a.m. Dominic received an update from the Bureau's statistical evaluation group, having been given the new data point of the stolen car matching the description of the escape car in Stroudsburg.

They had raised the probability of an accomplice(s) from 72.7% to 96.8% and an escape at Stroudsburg from 84.6% to 99.3%. Issue closed.

The Tavern Lounge Car at the rear of the *Phoebe Snow*

Dominic called in his five top agents. With the strong tone of calculated certainty he said, "Gentlemen, let's quit dickin' around here. We know we've got an elegantly planned and orchestrated robbery of national secrets from an academic, who wouldn't let us protect him. He was killed resisting the theft. In my opinion this was led by a female sleeper agent using clever disguises. A full blooded American, helped by a muscle guy."

Then he stood up, pounded the table and let loose his frustration. "I failed in an assignment for the first time in my life. We all screwed up. And it's at least 50/50 that some son of a bitch somewhere among us on the inside is helping the redhead. I've missed him or her – right under my nose." Then he totally lost it, kicking over his chair, moving smartly to his office and slamming the door. He didn't come out for two hours, and his assistant, Prudence Owens, had the good sense not to go in or let any calls through.

Inside he seethed. He thought, it's now me versus this female American traitor. I'm on a mission – that's all I'll be or do 'til I find her. Dead or alive.

And hope this bitch doesn't find me first.

CHAPTER 5

REACTION IN MOSCOW

Wednesday, November 19, 1952
9:00 a.m. - MGB Security Headquarters, Dzerzhinsky Square, Moscow

As Lieutenant Colonel Igor Tolstoy glanced out his window onto the square, he was struck, as was often the case, by the apparent normalcy of the surrounding scene, ironically right across the street from the nerve center of the entire gulag complex that had imprisoned and killed millions of the traitors who had plotted against the motherland.

He looked right onto the city's biggest toy store, Detsky Mir. In the streets there were women in their babushkas carrying bread home, children going to school and workers walking to their jobs. To add to the irony, this building, built in pre-revolutionary times, once housed a capitalist life insurance company.

Now the Lubyanka prison in the basement was a scene out of hell – a center of incarceration, torture and death. The floors were even constructed with a slant to assist washing down the frequent flood of blood after a normal work shift.

Igor was rising rapidly in the regard of all his superiors in the MGB, the agency responsible for intelligence activities outside the Soviet Union. He also was part of the group implementing a far more subtle plan – the growing disinformation program directed at leading American agencies to wrongly label prominent citizens as communist agents, allies or sympathizers. They'd recently gained major traction with the very helpful effort of one Senator Joseph McCarthy and his House Un-American Affairs Committee.

McCarthy, the junior senator from Wisconsin, had begun in 1950 to build his political base as a "commie hunter." Igor knew there were no Soviet agents in the State Department, but the MGB began to water this fertile ground. Through sympathetic true believers, they leaked a story to Roy Cohn, McCarthy's lead counsel, that the democratic candidate, Adlai Stevenson, had known Alger Hiss, the convicted Russian agent. On October 27, days before the

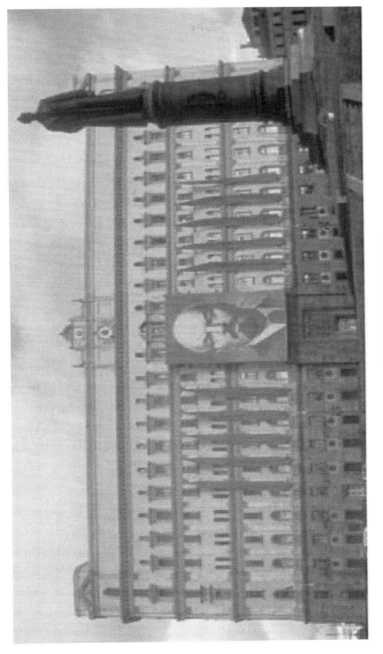

MGB HEADQUARTERS
Dzerzhinsky Square, Moscow

Presidential election, McCarthy began a stemwinder political speech with an attack on "Alger (loud laughter) I mean Adlai Stevenson."

Later the MGB duped a McCarthy staff member with the information, later publicly repeated by the senator, that the American Civil Liberties Union was "listed as a communist front." (It clearly was not). It even encouraged the "Daily Worker," the public face of the communist party of America, to attack McCarthy. What better way to build the anti communist credentials of this demagogue than to have "the party organ" call him the greatest threat to the cause?

Igor's immediate boss, Colonel Iuri Andropov, was convinced that eventually this McCarthyism/red baiting of the wrongly accused would create a strong counter reaction by an attack on McCarthy and his followers. In the process this could lead to a lessening of anti-Soviet vigilance and counter intelligence zeal. Then the real KGB's operatives could go about their work of undermining the United States from within with less attention. The old Bolsheviks had not liked the plan initially, but even they had to be impressed by the department's success in manipulating the U.S. Senate from 6,000 miles away. Amazing!

As a key player in the effort to gain intelligence from the new American task force on rockets and space weaponry, Igor prepared to assist his boss, Colonel Andropov, in his presentation to the presidium board of the entire MGB security apparatus. We're in the spotlight, and we'd better perform, he thought. Andropov had in fact ordered the theft of Professor Dickinson's papers but was upset by the excesses of that evening. That meant trouble for him. The entire team had by now reviewed the material seized by Bodkin, and were about to present their findings.

At 9:00 a.m. sharp Tolstoy and Andropov entered the board room where the boss of the entire MGB, Colonel General and MGB Chairman Sergei Kruglov, was already waiting. The boardroom was spectacular - ornate moldings, high vaulted ceiling and beautiful large chandelier. Another irony, Igor thought briefly – capitalist excess encasing the core of Soviet espionage, murder, foreign mayhem and death to the enemies of the new order.

His boss came to attention and saluted Chairman Kruglov. "Sir, Colonel Andropov reporting as ordered."

"At ease," responded Kruglov. "This joint presidium of the MVD – MGB is now in session. We are most interested in your presentation today. We are concerned about the events in America last week and have great hopes that the material obtained was worth the risks taken. As you know, the highest level of our government is vitally concerned with this matter. Please begin your report colonel."

"Comrades," Andropov began, "since the arrival of the Dickinson notes and calculations, we've been working without rest to evaluate their meaning and significance. Dickinson's mathematics prove the feasibility of an intercontinental ballistic missile, an ICBM. Similar to our own conclusions, a large rocket with adequate thrust can be put in orbit and returned anywhere on the earth in less than an hour, an unstoppable and deadly weapon that will be able to deliver a nuclear warhead anywhere. The rocket's superstructure and engines can clearly withstand the g-forces and stress. The Americans' version is different in apogee and trajectory from ours, but is essentially similar. However, and this is most important, we are well ahead in rocket size, throw weight capacity and guidance sophistication. But we have one very troubling problem – the right nose cone material to protect the nuclear payload from the extreme heat on reentry. And the Americans apparently have it." He paused briefly for effect.

"Our physicists, Cerenkov and Maksimov agree with Dickinson's computations. Generally, they feel these Princeton applied physicists, working with Albert Einstein and his colleagues at the Institute of Advanced Studies at Princeton, are the most accomplished experts in the United States on these matters. While, of course, not the equal of our own soviet scientists, they are distinguished practitioners."

He was interrupted by one of Stalin's men on the board. "Speak in plain Russian, Andropov. Does this nosecone crap mean we won't be able to deliver our ICBM's to Comrade Stalin on time?"

Andropov thought what a bunch of stupid peasants most of these old Bolsheviks were. Then he answered, "Yes sir, it means we could be late on our promises."

"Could the Americans have this weapon before us?"

"Absolutely – we can't deliver an atomic weapon if it melts on reentry."

Stalin's man didn't know anything about nose cones and H-bombs, but he knew the potential heat of his boss. This whole miserable group could be on a rail car heading East – way East.

After a pause, Andropov resumed, "I will now distribute to you our written report. I must demand that none of this leaves this building, and insist you return all this material to Lieutenant Colonel Tolstoy as you exit." Andropov circulated an 87-page report plus exhibits.

"The second focus of our work was the review of Dickinson's notes and reports on the American effort to develop an effective nose cone or missile shield. Since this was not Dickinson's area of expertise, what he was carrying were his personal notes on the presentations of others, experts in material science, metallurgy, exotic plastics and, most important, high technology glass-ceramic composites. His work had, in effect, informed these researchers of the temperatures and stresses that the materials would need to survive and they, in turn, have been working to find a solution. And I am afraid that they have found it."

The boss, Kruglov, looked around the room, as Andropov paused for effect. Some eyes rolled and others looked down at their hands. Kruglov felt the beginning of an urge to puke. We have 95% of the puzzle. They have the other 5% but little else. They got it, we need it. This could get real ugly for me. The boss could order me to get Oryol out, a really dangerous operation with everything at stake.

"They appear to be convinced that a glass-ceramic solution will work," Andropov resumed. "This work is being done at the Corning Glass Company by a group Dickinson's notes refer to as 'Stookey's people'. Apparently a Donald Stookey recently had a fluky accident while heating a piece of pre-exposed fotoform glass. The oven controls went out of control and took the glass to 300° C above the desired maximum of 600° C, yet the glass not only didn't break, it withstood an accidental drop to the floor. They are now convinced that they have figured out how to chemically reformulate these ceramic materials to create a shield that can withstand both extraordinary heat and severe pressure. We've never considered this as a possible solution to the re-entry problem, but these Corning people have apparently achieved it, at least in the laboratory. We will continue to study Dickinson's notes but don't expect much further clarification."

At this point the crusty old Bolshevik interrupted again, "Then tell us, my young genius, how do you expect us to get more details on this latest American breakthrough? Strelnikov's man in New York has already roiled the waters with his thugs. Cutting this guy's heart out onto the floor. Like a damn butcher. Now our people report the FBI is heavily involved. There'll be no more of the usual careless American surveillance. I bet no one on that Rocketry commission can take a shit now without security watching and then wiping their ass."

Kruglov rolled his eyes – this guy's got the mouth of a true peasant.

"General we will look for openings," Andropov responded, "but you're correct, security is now extremely high. I think we will have to rely on our best American asset, agent Oryol, to produce either the scientific papers for the material or tell us in general how it is done. He'll be directed and managed by our chief MGB operative in North America, agent Sonya. Yet, as our most important asset in America, we absolutely cannot put Oryol at unnecessary risk. Oryol is in a position to be of enormous help to us in all these rocket weaponry issues.

Oryol can change the world."

Later in the week

At the center of the Kremlin in a secure outdoor area, where electronic eavesdropping was impossible, Nikita Khrushchev, the senior member of the ruling politburo, came up to Kruglov.

"Our dear friend, Koba (the boss), is very upset with you on the American matter," Khrushchev said. "Malenkov and I calmed Stalin down and diverted his attention, but he was ready to send you away. Of course, he has conveniently forgotten that it was he who rushed the rocketry work, and this nose cone problem is fallout from his own haste. This is the final lunacy for a number of us – we can't have this sick bungler leading us any longer, particularly at such an opportune time when we have just won China and are holding the U.N. forces in a stalemate in Korea.

And Stalin's health is going south fast. The boss is really out of his mind now, up all night, screaming at his doctors, taking a basket of medications every day. He apparently has also had some minor strokes. I don't expect him to last long."

"It's that bad now?" Kruglov asked.

"Absolutely. Our wonderful 'great hero and military genius', this psychopath who has killed over 20 million of our own people, may go at any time."

Then Khrushchev stopped, touched Kruglov's arm and looked right into his eyes. "Of course, sometimes a man taking so much medication can get confused on the dosage. Or…the doctors accidently order medicines that don't mix well. Tee panamyush? (You understand?)"

Kruglov stared back. Then he nodded twice. He didn't have to say anything; they were now allies in a treacherous and highly dangerous effort to do nothing less than eliminate the leader of the new communist empire.

That evening when Kruglov returned to MGB headquarters, he called Igor into his office. The light colonel was the general's kind of man, the type he had wished his own sons had become, instead of one dead coward and one bum chasing skirts. He felt real attachment to him–Igor Tolstoy had never failed him.

He stared at him for a few seconds, tension in his eyes. "Do you ever have doubts, my dedicated young friend? Do you ever question the wisdom of decisions made by those senior to you?

"Comrade General, if you are referring to yourself and my immediate superiors here, absolutely not. The agency is, in my opinion, more effective now than at any time in our history."

"No I don't mean us. I mean our bosses, the guys who can shake our world with a few words. Make us disappear."

Igor squirmed, the tension palpable. "Sir… I really don't ever give that any thought."

Kruglov locked onto Igor's eyes. "I know you well enough to be sure there are some policy decisions that have pissed you off. You're too smart not to have noticed some of the recent idiotic moves–quarreling with Mao, potentially alienating one billion new communists. And how about making a non–person of our great hero, Marshal Zhukov, the man who broke the back of the Nazi siege of Moscow in December 1941, when those bastards were 20 miles from where we now sit.

Stalin is sick in more ways than one. Let me tell you, there will soon be major change–at the top. You need to tell me RIGHT NOW that your balls are on the line with me and the rest of us who support change."

He awaited Igor's reply, monitoring every tick in his face or any other involuntary body movement. He prided himself on his ability to read a man – it had kept him alive all these years. If I have any doubt after this meeting about Tolstoy, I will order him shot. No question or hesitation. He would be just another corpse in the basement, where many others have died for the wrong answer to a superior's question in this building.

The young man fidgeted briefly, then met the General's stare. "Sir, you know I'm with you now and forever. You've been my mentor and my inspiration. I'm ready to follow you anywhere, any time."

The general released his breath. He smiled. "Good. Then stay close for the next few months. I may need you at any time for a show of force. You're greatly respected around here. You can be a big help. And tell no one of this discussion. NO ONE!"

"Yes sir. You know you only have to ask for any help and I will be there. We sink or triumph together." Igor extended his hand, a gesture emblematic of deep respect. The general gripped it firmly and drew him into a warm embrace. He kissed him on each cheek in the Russian style of dearest friends, comrades in arms.

They were committed now to go forward with a plot to eliminate the leader of the most powerful police state in the history of the world.

Igor left the building spinning. They're going to throw out the old man, the man of steel, the exalted leader – or at least try. Dangerous moments lay ahead.

I will back my boss – I've tied my fate to him. I just hope to hell that he succeeds. That bastard Stalin – I hate him with a passion. And apparently he is now out of his mind and will go sooner or later anyhow. I just hope the general and his allies have thought this all out. And also how they would deal with the Stalin loyalists like that pervert number two, Lavrenti Beria.

When he reached his apartment, he mentioned nothing to his wife. He feigned extreme tiredness and retreated to that beloved Russian institution - a hot bath. Before entering the tub, he looked hard at himself in the mirror. He thought of his meeting with the Americans in Germany in 1945 and a young American major by the name of Dominic Benvenuto, who had befriended him after the fall of Berlin.

And…what that bastard Beria had done to his beloved sister in 1948.

CHAPTER 6

TOLSTOY REMINISCES

Igor Tolstoy had only been in the West once, in 1945, in Germany, and he had fought his way there. He was part of the First Byelorussian Army that liberated Minsk, Warsaw and then finally merged with the forces that took Berlin in May 1945. At that point he had been assigned to a field intelligence unit that ultimately reported to Marshall Zhukov, the supreme commander of all Soviet forces. He had rushed into the burned out Berlin Reichstag two hours after it had been cleared by the Russian infantry and began gathering intelligence in a large basement storage room. As he was glancing at a file in Russian apparently about Russian Ukrainian officers who had defected to the Nazis, automatic weapon fire opened up on him and his men, instantly killing a squad leader and a young private.

"Down. Fire at will!" he screamed at his men. "Three Germans – two o'clock." A fusillade of lead laced the moving Germans. They fell. One was still alive as Tolstoy turned him over.

"What's in this room, you bastard? What's so important about it?" he screamed in passable German into the man's face.

The Nazi officer replied in perfect Russian, "You piss face Communist. Now you miserable bastards will keep my beloved Ukraine imprisoned."

"So is this room filled with the history of traitors like you who would fight against the Motherland?" Igor yelled. The Ukrainian Nazi slipped into death before he could answer.

Igor's unit had been the first to stumble upon the Nazi records of Russians who had been turned – men who in the post war confusion would try to return to their villages, communicate with each other and work against Mother Russia, the Rodina. He received a citation for this from Marshall Zhukov himself, who was quite taken by this fine physical specimen and model communist soldier.

Tolstoy, then a captain, wound up being invited to a celebratory dinner in Frankfurt, where both Zhukov and Eisenhower spoke to an audience of the military leadership and distinguished young officers of both armies. There was excellent food and an abundance of Russian vodka and western liquor; mutual praise and genuine warmth and toasts flowed between the representatives of the two allies. All the junior officers were pretty much drunk at the end.

He was seated at a table of his Russian peer group and three young officers in the U.S. Army, one of whom, a Major Dominic Benvenuto, was on General Patton's G-2 intelligence staff. Benvenuto had grown up with Russians in the coal fields and had taken it for four years while at West Point. He spoke respectable Russian, and Igor had studied English for eight years. They became friends immediately, discussing military life and the future of Europe and U.S.-U.S.S.R. relations. Afterward the two of them, already three sheets to the wind had gone out to a late night bar.

As he soaked in the soothing, near scolding tub, Tolstoy recalled that night and all that it would set in motion in the years following.

May 28, 1945
Berlin

The two warriors left the dinner drunk and with their arms around each other. They entered the first late night hofbrau they found, a dump filled with sour drunks and scummy hookers. Germans in post-war Berlin were having trouble feeding themselves. German scum, Tolstoy thought, let them die of hunger.

Tolstoy got Major Benvenuto talking first. He asked him about life in the West – how they lived, what they ate, did he own an apartment (he owned a whole house!), where his kids went to school, did they have to join a political party to get ahead. Dominic answered everything candidly including political and religious questions. And no, there was not a political officer connected to each U.S. army unit.

Benvenuto was honest. He was critical of a lot of American society. "My father had many tough years in the coal fields. Management and the union hated each other. A good friend of my father had been a labor organizer, helping form the Master, Mates and Pilots Maritime Union and helped the New York Police Department get an eight hour day. He had been thrown in jail once, after picketing the Lehigh Valley Railroad docks. I'm a strong Roosevelt democrat. I despise how some working men are abused by their companies, businesses that have politicians in their pocket.

Truth is America is a great, imperfect experiment in democracy, trying to balance liberty with justice, sometimes succeeding and sometimes not. I love my country, but it's a work in progress."

Igor had never heard such a frank and unfettered view of one's country, certainly not in the Soviet Union. You could disappear real fast talking like that. Like his father and uncle had.

Then Dominic went on the offensive. "So tell me about you and your family, Igor. Are you married, kids, what's the story? Also, what attracted you to the army?" His smile was benign, warm and guard lowering.

Igor replied, in English, "I'm married to a wonderful girl I met at University. We have two young kids, a boy and a girl, and I love them very much. Marriage has filled an enormous void in my life created by the passing of my parents and their generation – all my three uncles and two of my aunts."

"Were they all killed in the war?"

Igor was silent for a second. "Not exactly," he responded. Then he became silent again. Dom caught the slight quiver in his upper lip. They were on their fifth drink.

He resumed, "In case you've been wondering where my famous name Tolstoy came from, Leo Tolstoy was, in fact, my great grandfather. He sort of became an intellectual communist at the end of his life, taking on an anti-war and anti-noble class bias. As such, the Communists claimed him as one of their own.

Helped by this Tolstoy pedigree, my father became a Bolshevik General in the war against the whites right after the revolution of 1917. He commanded the forces that finally destroyed Admiral Kolchak's counter-revolutionary white army in Siberia in 1919 and scattered them for good. Zinoviev gave him the highest combat medal of the time, and Lenin himself pinned it on my father's chest. This success and the Tolstoy name, allowed my father to advance rapidly. His career prospered until early 1939.

In February of that year my father sought out Marshall Voroshilov, Stalin's leading military flunky. He was then the minister of Defense and supreme commander of the Soviet armed forces. My father complained bitterly about the slaughter of top leadership that had resulted from the military purges begun in 1938. It had wiped out almost half of our general officer leadership corps.

Three days later my father disappeared. I never saw him again. His brother, Vladimir, my uncle, who I was very close to, was a party official. He searched for my father in the camps for eight months and then word came that Vladimir had been arrested. We got two letters in six months and then nothing. His wife, my aunt, was arrested while looking for him and only released after the war broke out in June, 1941. My family's home was in Smolensk, taken by the Germans on September 10, 1941, after a two month battle, and my mother and last uncle were killed.

All this unnecessary tragedy infuriated me. Stalin had so decimated our officer corps that in the early days of the war we fought without real leadership. We were led mostly by political sycophants. Millions died or were taken as

POW's, most never to be seen again. What a disaster – all because of Stalin's purges."

Dominic, an intelligence officer was amazed at Tolstoy's frankness. Obviously he was drunk...but still. "So how did you get beyond all this and so distinguish yourself in the war?"

"When the motherland was attacked you had to forget everything in the past and turn all attention to the German bastards who were slaughtering our people. Personal grievances had to be forgotten."

"And now that the war is over, how do you feel?"

Tolstoy stared into his drink, "I don't know. I'm still an ardent Communist and love my country, but I can't forgive what the leadership did to my family. I also have an idealistic streak that makes me want to achieve a national leadership position where I can help achieve Lenin's idealistic vision of true Communism – from each according to his ability, to each according to his need.

Dominic, I've spoken too freely and I've drunk too much, but I've been deeply troubled since 1939, very confused. There is no one in my country I could dare to talk to like this. I've said more than I should have. So now I've opened up to a new friend, as you did to me, and must ask that you never mention a word of this to anyone."

Dominic smiled. "Of course, Igor. But we must stay in touch. You know, Marshall Zhukov has invited General Eisenhower to visit Russia in August, and Ike has accepted. I just learned that I'll be part of the entourage. Should I try to get you invited on part of the tour? Or could you get your new friend, Marshall Zhukov, to include you?"

"I don't know, but I'd be honored to be part of the group to show our country to General Eisenhower – and to see you again."

August, 1945 Moscow

Eisenhower and his touring entourage of 50, including Major Dominic Benvenuto, were warmly welcomed during their tour of Russia. As is often the case, military men share a certain common heritage, discipline and work ethic, particularly when they are allies, and indeed allies who had just eliminated one of the great scourges of world history. Captain Igor Tolstoy, to the mild surprise of his peers, had been invited to participate in Marshall Zhukov's hosting party. Dominic and the young captain had been able to spend time together. Igor's wife was introduced to Dominic at a dinner at the Metropole Hotel, where the Americans were lodged.

On the final night of Eisenhower's trip, there was a large gala in the vaulted halls of the Kremlin with toasts and praises on all sides. On that evening, everyone was a friend. Igor and Dominic found themselves bidding each other a very warm farewell.

"Igor," Dominic said in Russian, "I hope I'll see you again, but that may never happen. I'll always remember you and the warmth you have shown to me personally here in Moscow. I know things have troubled you in the past, and if you should ever want to be in contact with an American, about anything, let me just mention something to you."

Igor froze. Dominic grabbed him in an embrace, so he could whisper in his ear.

"There is a store in Moscow, Reeba Magazin numeer vosem-adin (Fish Store Number 8-1) on Gorkova Ulitza (Gorky Street). Ask for Nicolai, the manager. Inquire if they have sturgeon. He will say no. By the way, they never do. Then just leave. In time someone will contact you very, very discreetly. You should have no fear, as it will be totally untraceable. That's all you need do."

Dominic released the embrace and laughed heartily, as though he had just told a joke in Igor's ear. After a second or two, Igor joined him in laughter. The ruse completed. The night ended with embraces all around.

However, no one in that room ever saw their counterparts again. Not General Eisenhower and Marshall Zhukov nor Major Dominic Benvenuto and Captain Igor Tolstoy. Yet the latter two would become inextricably involved in the course of events in 1952-1953 that would change the world.

October 4, 1948
Three Years Later, Moscow

Igor had always been close to his younger sister Ludmilla. She was six years his junior and worshipped her god-like older brother. She grew up to be a tall, Slavic beauty – high cheek bones, blond hair, deep blue eyes and a perfectly proportioned body that caught every male's eye – an absolutely stunning figure, very atypical for even young soviet women of that era.

When their father and uncles had disappeared in 1939, brother and sister found solace in each other. After the war they had contact once or twice a week, the two families joining for dinner on most Saturday nights. Both were married now, Ludmilla to an architect who was involved in post-war reconstruction in several major Russian cities. Igor loved her intensely. He would die for her.

In university a male student had gotten physical with her after she had denied him. Igor sought out the student and beat him with his hands to within an inch of his life. The kid was unconscious for three days and required 74 stitches. Igor told him he would kill him with his hands if he ever went near his sister again.

Now 24 years old, Ludmilla was a highly skilled technical stenographer typist, who worked on government projects at a very high level. Typical was her assignment in September, 1948 to type and assemble political/military assessments of the Russian blockade of Berlin and the subsequent U.S. air response to resupply the city.

In the course of her work she came in contact with Lavrenti Beria, former head of the old NKVD security complex and Stalin's likely heir. Beria had seen her at a meeting where she took stenographic notes of intelligence estimates of American airlift capacity to continue to assist Berlin.

The next day she received a message from an aide. "Comrade Beria wants to review this material directly with you, and your presence is required at his office in the Kremlin at 7 p.m. Be prepared to work late." The aide hung up not allowing any response.

Beria was well known as the biggest womanizer in Stalin's inner circle. He had probably had sex of one description of another with 10,000 females, age 11 to 75. Trains would stop so he could get a blowjob.

Stalin just laughed about it. I trust him – that's all that matters. Keep him happy, was Koba's view.

Aware of Beria's reputation with women and concerned with the late time of the appointment, Ludmilla entered his office with some trepidation. At first he was charming, praising the transcription she had already done and had her record further dictated notes on the subject. Then half an hour into the meeting, he went to his bureau and poured two glasses of chilled vodka, presenting one to Ludmilla without even asking her if she wanted it. He drank, and they finished the dictation.

Then he calmly rose and without saying a word began to fondle her perfect breasts as though inspecting them for construction quality. He manipulated her nipples like a carpenter might set a nail, with his silence daring her to utter even a sound.

Ludmilla just stood still, passively trembling, unable to resist the second most powerful man in the Soviet Union. He pulled down his pants and sequentially forced his manhood into every orifice of her body. Finally, he reached satisfaction. Then he made her clean him up.

This led to her throwing up on his rug. He screamed, "Get out you pig." He picked her up threw her out on the hallway floor, and then closed his door. After a minute he returned to his work like he had just had a satisfying break for chai.

Ludmilla ran down the hall, out of the building and into Red Square, where she took the subway to Igor's apartment. She fell in a heap at her brother's feet, crying in powerful waves. Igor's children were gathered by his wife, Natalia, to the back bedroom, so the brother and sister could have privacy. She finally was able to describe the experience between the tears and screams. She didn't spare one detail. Igor had never heard his blessed, genteel sister speak so graphically.

Igor simmered in silent, building rage. With internalized fiery hatred he was unable to move or speak. Finally he embraced her, but still in silence.

Eventually, he brought Ludmilla back to her own apartment. When they arrived, Igor explained to Dmitri, her husband, what happened. Dmitri was a gentle man of culture and art, who adored his wife. He began to weep and then rushed back to his wife's side, where they clung to each other, both realizing that they lived in a barbaric society where logic, order and love could be atomized in a moment by certain superior beings, and there could be no recourse. They expressed these horrific thoughts to each other and then to Igor. But Igor did not hear their utterances; he already was well along in a chain of thought and fury that was now coursing through his body.

When he left their apartment he began a long walk in the dark around Moscow. He thought, whatever the merits of Lenin's moral and idealistic case for "final communism," true equality and justice for all, he now knew it would never be realized in a Soviet Union led by the likes of Stalin and Beria. It was all a monstrous fraud. It would stall at the stage of the "dictatorship of the proletariat," Lenin's supposed middle step between revolution and the final realization of the perfect communist state. In a country where power was won by leaders who liberally used fear and incarceration of their own people, as well as each other, communism had become and would remain a convenient label to justify the captivity and subservience of the people by these monsters. A vile serpent that needs to be destroyed.

He did not go to work the next two days, calling in sick. He considered all his options, including getting close enough to Beria to kill him. In the end he rejected that. What would it really accomplish? The evil communist hydra would just produce another venomous head to take the position of Stalin's number two.

There is a far better way that I can be highly effective and dangerous to all that I now hate, he realized. I will continue to ardently strive to advance in the intelligence community and be the model of the "new communist man," with a public persona devoted to my heroes, Marx and Lenin. No one will question my loyalty, and I will reach ever higher into the nerve center of world communism. Then I will strike at the heart of the beast when it really matters.

The next day he visited fish store #8-1 on Gorky Street, asking Nicolai if sturgeon was obtainable. It wasn't, but his life's new mission was set in motion. He was given the code name Levin, after the lover of Anna Karenina in his great grandfather Leo Tolstoy's classic novel. He had directly caused her suicide and destruction. He liked the American sense of literature and symbolism.

"I will crush these bastards and their evil system," he said to himself.

At the end of that first day of the rest of his life, he thought of Major Dominic Benvenuto and their meetings in 1945 that had set all this in motion. He lifted a glass and offered a silent toast.

Wherever you are Dominic, I bless you for looking deep into my core, helping me see the truth and giving me this option. You will probably never know what you started, but it might change the world.

You're probably sitting in your beautiful suburban American home now, long out of the military and enjoying some nice comfortable job like banking, something safe and civilian. You come home each night to your family and enjoy your American way of life. Well God bless you, enjoy it. You deserve your world of peace and quietude.

We are now on courses that will never again intersect, but I have not forgotten you. And now I am a man on fire, laser focused on bringing down this evil charade that has captured my country.

Moscow. 1952

Igor rose out of the tub, his reminiscing complete. He knew what he would do. The next evening he left a coded typed message in the water closet above a toilet in the bar in the National Hotel. It read simply, "Uncle Joe is in serious trouble; expect an attempt to eliminate him."

As he left, he asked one of the regular waiters, "How's your daughter doing? Has she recovered from that nasty fever?"

"Yes she has comrade colonel. Thank you for asking."

The waiter had no daughter. She had perished in the gulag years ago following a brutal beating. As the signal called for, at the end of his shift the non- descript waiter entered the bathroom and retrieved the note from the back of a toilet, the method Igor had been using to communicate with the Americans since 1948.

The next morning the waiter went into that same fish store, number 8-1, on Gorky Street. He too asked Nicholai for sturgeon. The manager, whose brothers had been executed by Stalin in 1936, said, "What? Are you crazy? We never have sturgeon, you old fool. I only have herring and it's a few days old." The customer shrugged and bought the woeful herring. He handed the manager a five ruble bill, the Tolstoy coded note well folded within it. Ironically, a bold visage of Lenin on the obverse of the bill covered the covert message – the very same Lenin who had allowed the madman Stalin to succeed him.

By 11:15 a.m. the note had successfully reached its intended address on Mokhovaya Place. Outside the entrance sign in both Russian and English read in large letters "Embassy of the United States of America." At 11:22 the new and already distinguished U.S. ambassador, George F. Kennan, met with his head CIA officer, and both read the brief message.

Kennan instructed the CIA man, "Encode this message from agent Levin immediately. Make sure you use the new Univac computer machine and transmit it to Washington in cipher, the one we know is beyond the computer ability of the Russians to decode. Snooping bastards. Our agent Levin is proving to be a real gem."

"Well Mr. Ambassador, he's doing a lot better than his namesake, Constantine Levin, the seducer of Tolstoy's *Anna Karenina*." He smiled, pleased with the irony of their chosen code name for Leo Tolstoy's great grandson.

Kennan replied, "Yes, but even more devastatingly disruptive than Tolstoy's Levin. This man is an extraordinary asset!"

The next day the message was read by incoming CIA Director Allen Dulles. He let out a quiet whistle, picked up the phone, and requested meetings both with outgoing President Harry Truman and President – elect Dwight Eisenhower, both of which were summarily granted.

Then Allen Dulles picked up the highest security phone and called his brother John Foster Dulles, the incoming Secretary of State. "Some news from a very reliable source – Uncle Joe may be on his way out. His enemies are gathering to strike."

The aristocratic older brother whistled a low response.

"Also, on another subject the Russians are not satisfied with the rocketry information they got from the Dickinson murder. Stay tuned for chapter two, brother John. There's something they desperately need. We've got to find Oryol, this Russian Eagle in our midst, before he passes on these secrets that apparently could be devastating. I'll also have to now bring Hoover into the loop on our agent Levin in Moscow."

"Hoover's such a pompous windbag," John Foster said. "But I guess we have no choice in something as grave as this. Are you going to tell him that his man Dominic Benvenuto originally recruited this guy Levin in 1945?"

"No. No reason to. Screw him. That's too big a secret."

The incoming Secretary of State raised his eyebrow. The Brahmin Dulles family rarely used even mild expletives.

CHAPTER 7

CATHERINE BOWERS AND THE *TODAY* SHOW

Friday, November 14, 1952
10:00 a.m. - NBC Studios, New York City

Friday mornings were a delight for the *Today* show productions staff. The show signed off at 9 a.m., the week was done and the on-camera hosts high-tailed it for home. Once the feature production segments were done for Monday, they could then leave for the weekend. Catherine Bowers, the 31 year old lead feature writer, was beginning to feel the usual end of week euphoria.

"God, I need the weekend. This getting up at 4:30 a.m. really gets old by Friday," she said to her aide Kelly. "But we're on a roll. Forget all those nasty January reviews from the press snobs. Our ratings are taking off."

"Who else does what we do – we got the formula now. Hard news, current stories from around the world with a mix of the lighter stuff – fashion, entertainment, sports. And let's be honest we couldn't do it without our boss, Dave Garroway. He's the perfect host, smooth, funny and charming. A closet intellectual who makes us all laugh and relax."

Catherine was stunningly attractive. Fair skinned, blue eyed, tall and lanky with a model's body. Slim and taut, with a very modest bust and 24 inch waist. She looked and moved like an athlete, which in fact she was. Her naturally light brown-blond short hair capped this visual treat for the eyes.

Her job was to produce segments on serious hard news stories. She was tenacious in looking for the undiscovered and unreported facts that others may have missed. Right now she was intrigued by both the unsolved murder in Manhattan of a South Korean who spoke in favor of the war, and charges of labor racketeering reported in the longshoreman's union. As she liked to say, "I have no aversion to swimming in dangerous waters."

"I can't wait to get out of here," she said to her research assistant. "This has been a tough week on all fronts, particularly the union story. How's your research going?"

"I'm still checking the possible interconnections between the leadership of the construction trades and the ILA. They always seem to take the same political position, they socialize together and even eat at the same joints. Is it all mob run?"

"I'm working that angle," Catherine replied. "There's a new lead. I have an interview later today with the key FBI guy in New York counterintelligence. Met him at a news conference on the murdered South Korean a month ago. I'll see what he can tell me about the waterfront. Ever hear of Dominic Benvenuto?"

"Never have."

Same Day 11:00 a.m.
Downtown New York

Catherine took the elevator in the downtown federal building to the FBI offices that housed Bureau Chief Benvenuto, carefully planning her approach. I'll start with the praise of his work on the Korean case, she thought, warm him up with a sales pitch about the *Today* show and then see what he can tell me about the waterfront.

She was struck by how ordinary the offices looked and sounded. She thought, this place could be an insurance company – phones ringing, people conferring, cheap linoleum curling up on the edges and doggy furniture. Except for their size and physical condition, they look like a bunch of bureaucrats, having their late morning coffee. Yet this is the place where our guys track their spooks, protect American assets and looked for the traitors.

She was shown to Benvenuto's office. Dom said, "Hello, Miss Bowers, good to see you again. Thanks for coming."

"The pleasure is mine, chief." She viewed the partial title as the most appropriate, until she could work her magic and get closer to the guy. "Thanks for seeing me."

"So what's a nice Midwestern girl like you doing working on these tough stories?"

"Hey, how'd you know I'm originally from the Midwest? You've been checking up on me?" she said with a lightly suggestive smile.

"Not at all. Part of our training includes recognition of regional accents. There's actually a guy in this office who can guess within 50 miles where you grew up. I'm not that good, but with you I would guess Wisconsin."

"Damn, you're good. I grew up in Iowa but went to the University of Wisconsin. I'm impressed – I thought I had lost that little twang." He just smiled back at her. This guy is sharp, she thought. And a real hunk – six feet, great Italian features, dark hair, chiseled chin with dimple – have to keep my mind on work.

"I saw your *Today* show today. First time. Got to say it was better than I expected. A little light but some good stuff. Do you ever get in front of the camera?"

"Only once so far."

Too bad he thought to himself. With her looks and body she would probably help the ratings. And why is that top button of her tight blouse open. But forget that Dominic, concentrate on this media bloodhound and see what she wants.

She was well prepared. "We've been undertaking some background research on the ILS union that runs the New York waterfront. It's no secret that the control of the union rests in some strange hands. Things seemed real smooth in the War – the ports handled record volumes, and there were no issues. They stepped up and met the challenge.

Now there's noise that the union bosses are really getting greedy. Shakedowns are going on, violence, people disappearing. We're doing some work on this. Also, I assume you guys have noticed what Harry Bridges and the West Coast boys are doing. Their wildcat strikes are slowing the flow of war material out to Korea. Aren't you afraid the guys here might follow?"

"Miss Bowers," Dominic responded, "I really can't comment on that. As you know, I run counterintelligence here, not the organized crime detail. We do watch closely for any external threat to the port. That's part of our mission but not domestic criminal activity. I'm busy enough without that noise."

He quickly thought about the boys who ran the port. In fact, he knew a ton about them. He had an unspoken understanding with them – don't do anything outrageous, keep us informed and we won't bother you. As long as you let us know about anything that looks suspicious – strange cargo, strange people, strange meetings. In fact we're all over the port. No one and no strange goods are getting in or out of this country though New York by boat without my knowing about it.

And Hoover doesn't need to know any of this. An undocumented accommodation among Italians who quietly respect and understand each other. Just so long as they're not pigs. Dominic had learned from his parents on these matters.

A 15-minute further discussion followed of how they might work together. There was friction – Dominic thought this is just another news hound trying to get some pearls from me for this flashy new show of hers. Catherine's mind kept returning to her core premise – how can this master spy catcher not know about the crooked guys at the top of the port? Why's he messin' with me, won't open up?

Finally Dominic said, "I've got an important meeting. Don't worry about the port. You've got better fish to fry. Good luck with your new show. But let's stay in touch, maybe I can help you with something. And who knows, maybe you can help me sometime."

They agreed to reconnect at some later date. She rose, shook his hand warmly with both of hers and gave him a broad smile.

"And better luck getting a cab going back to your office," he said.

"What?

"You're dry, but your expensive shoes show a water stain. Your umbrella protected your head and body, but the shoes got wet as you splashed through the surface water on the streets, trying to hail a cab." He stopped and smiled.

She grinned back, a smile with the texture of feminine interest in her eyes. The guy is good. And one handsome SOB.

For a few seconds both seemed to drop their guard, and a little direct current electricity jumped between their eyes. She turned and departed, Dominic watching her sculpted ass until she rounded the corner.

He thought, I can't help it. I'm Italian and no *Paisan* is perfect, particularly when an ass like that moves right in front of my face.

Lunch, Monday, November 17

This was a special day for Catherine – Dave Garroway, the host of the *Today* show, had asked that she join him at lunch for a progress review of her work for the show and her year end compensation package.

They entered the elegant Edwardian room at the Plaza Hotel, which looked onto Central Park South. They were escorted to a window table. On their way Dave nodded to Vice President elect Richard Nixon, who was seated in a central table with secret service personnel around him. Garroway had gently interviewed him some months ago in connection with the so called Checkers dog scandal.

After a few social amenities and typical Garroway subtle humor, he formally went right into the laudatory task at hand. "Catherine, I want to commend you on your work, both your original stories and your editing role. You have demonstrated a real knack for developing original news material and editing the work of others. You're a significant factor in our first year's success, and let me say personally how appreciative I am of all you are doing."

"Well thanks boss," she said cheerily. "I've got to tell you that I just love this job. I should pay to work here – we're working out the kinks, developing the morning format that fits this exciting thing called television. What a hoot!"

Garroway then reviewed her salary structure and offered a whopping 25% raise in pay and benefits. "Catherine, I just hope this expresses how we all feel about you and that includes my bosses at the network. You are becoming one of the early movers and shakers behind the scene in television."

Before ordering desert, Dave asked, "So tell me what you're working on now that will light us up?"

"Dave, I'm fascinated by the port here. Everybody knows the mob runs it, yet nobody seems to do squat about it. What gives? On Friday I went downtown to the FBI office in the Federal building and connected with a guy named Dominic Benvenuto, a bureau chief. Smart, well spoken, presentable guy, but I got zippo out of him about the port."

"Catherine, you're working a tough story," Garroway responded. "Nobody talks about certain things in this city- the port, the vending business, construction trades. People who do seem to wind up missing. What got you going on this?"

"The 180 degree difference with the West Coast longshoremen's union. Those guys led by Harry Bridges are left-leaning liberals who go out on strike at the drop of a hat, and they're doing this while the Korean War is red hot. Here the guys are red blooded Americans with the flag all over their equipment."

"Don't know, but I'm afraid it would be dangerous to try to find out. In our business you've got to pick your spots. We want our share of hard news, but you've got to allocate your time to stories you can close on."

She didn't give up easily. "Dave, do you have any contacts that could help me on this before I do give up? You know everybody," she said with a flattering smile.

"Well, I did meet a Jewish lawyer at a cocktail party recently who has those kind of connections. You could try him but be careful. And make sure you really think you can come up with a story we can go with without blowing too much time. Hey, the *Today* show has the whole world as it's feet- why mess with the mob?"

Catherine smiled and raised both hands in a what-can-I-say gesture. "Boss, I just like the action. I guess you could call me a shit disturber, to use a little of my college French. I like to go where others fear to tread."

"Well just be careful. We want you around."

CHAPTER 8

DINNER IN THE DINER

Friday, December 7, 1952
Downtown Manhattan

Agent Sonya, secluded safely in a shadow, waited for the banker to emerge from the lobby of 30 Pine Street, the home of Goldman Sachs, a smallish but highly profitable investment bank. It was predominantly Jewish, but its growing success was beginning to shake up the bluebloods at Morgan Stanley, Merrill Lynch and Dillon Reed.

She thought, I despise everything about these Wall Street bloodsuckers. They're at the heart of the American system of allocating capital, paying for much of the vital defense work aimed at my beloved Russia. We'll cut the balls off this serpent.

She earlier had told her boss, General Strelnikov, of her weekend plans. "I've got a line on the guy who raises money for Corning Glass. This Friday he is off for a social weekend with the executives of that company. I'm goin' to try to hook up with him."

"Hasn't Moscow concluded that this Corning company makes the American missile shield material?"

"Yes, and I think this Wall Street money creep can give me some real intelligence."

"Good, sounds like a nice way to get what we need through a secondary source who won't have FBI men all over him. Very shrewd."

"Exactly. And let me add something. I know the stakes here. And I'm proud to be in charge" Then she bent toward him, staring into his old, cold and empty eyes. "And, I WILL NOT FAIL. Nothing will stop me, and I will stop at nothing."

The woman's eyes caught the banker as soon as he emerged from the building, stopping on the curb to bid goodbye to another blue suit, blue tie, white shirt guy. She moved closer to hear their conversation.

"Henry, I hope you share my view that this was a very productive day. Ford Motor Company needs this public capital to finance this new generation of cars you are planning – the stunning new Fords, Mercurys and Lincolns. And that Thunderbird sports car, what a winner. Save me one of those for my garage," he said with a smile.

She recognized the other pig as the young Henry Ford II, the grandson of the founder of America's largest private company. She hated the formal, stilted structure of their conversation – so elitist and aristocratic. Who else talks like this but these high level leeches from all the right colleges and families.

"Bill you made a very persuasive argument today. I have no doubt you're right. Now the hard part starts – convincing my board that we should give up our private status and join this new world of publicly traded companies. Slumming it with the likes of General Motors and Chrysler," he said with a grin.

Sonya felt like puking. These capitalists repulsed her.

"Well Henry, travel back safely and call me when convenient. Are you flying back to Detroit?"

"Yes, American to Willow Run. I like that American Airlines service, all first class DC6B which gets me home in three hours after a dinner of fois gras, beef Wellington and a fine Bordeaux at an altitude of 23,000 feet. Then I land at Detroit's Willow Run airport, built by my grandfather for the Tri Motor Ford plane produced by the company in the 1930's. Right next to the Ford automobile plant there."

She thought, you boastful jackass. All of it made possible by your exploitation of the workers for generations.

"Well, enjoy the flight. Think of me still on the train as you get back to that beautiful home of yours, Henry."

"Say hello to the Houghton family at Corning for me, will you. I played golf with them last year. They run a gem of a company – Corning Glass is a powerhouse."

"Absolutely," the banker responded, as they parted company. "See you soon my friend."

She thought, how incestuous – this whole little covey of top capitalists cavorting like some new band of inbred royalty. We'll burn them just like we did the Romanoffs, but we'll scatter the ashes of this crowd in the sewers of Red Square. She spit at a manhole to emphasize her sentiment.

She walked over to where Bodkin waited in another stolen car, repainted and with new plates, and said as she got in, "Follow the older guy, our banker. He's going to Hoboken to get on a train. And so am I."

Both she and the banker exited their cars at the Christopher Street ferry terminal where they got on the *Elmira* boat to Hoboken. They boarded Lackawanna Train #5, the *Twilight*, the deluxe afternoon streamliner that would get them to Corning just after 11 p.m.

She checked her first class parlor car ticket, purchased in a false name. This would put her close to the Goldman banker. In case he had spotted her, she now wore a brunette wig. The staid blazer was replaced by a rather tight sweater over her 36C breasts. She followed him onto the train one minute behind and noticed a vacant seat across from him.

She turned to the Pullman porter, "Would it be possible for me to switch my seat and take that one. I really do enjoy the view to the south." With that she tactfully handed the porter a dollar. "Yes ma'am, absolutely. That seat is vacant tonight" and with that he dusted off seat 7A and stored her bag above.

The train left Hoboken at 4:50 p.m., packed as usual on a Friday afternoon with businessmen returning home for the weekend to Pennsylvania and New York state, as well as personal travelers getting an early start on a weekend in the Poconos. Also, there was a sizeable contingent on the through sleeping car to Detroit, which arrived in the motor city at the comfortable hour of 8 a.m. the next morning for those who wanted luxury but, unlike Henry Ford II, could not pay the threefold higher price of first class air.

She caught the banker deftly removing his wedding ring. These slimy capitalists, she thought – they're all the same. Figure they can get in any girl's pants with all their money and power. They should be physically castrated, just like what I did to that German sniper during my training in the Urals. I learned how to make any man talk.

Sonya recalled it clearly and with pride, as the train pulled out of Hoboken and onto the main line.

It was 1943, and I was completing my intelligence training in central Russia, well behind the front lines. Our interrogation classes had gone well, but now there was a final challenge for our elite group of dedicated communists from around the world, being honed to be super agents in their native country. Each of us had to break an actual German prisoner who had successfully resisted to this point. By any means possible.

The *Twilight* gate at Hoboken

When I got to him the German had nearly been drowned and his face was a red pulp, but he had revealed nothing to our people. A real tough German prick who loved killing important Russians. A nice challenge.

My case was a Waffen SS captain of strict Prussian military descent, the son of a baron. Typical university guy – a fencer with the scars to prove it and a good proficiency in English. He had been in charge of an elite group of snipers, all fluent in Russian, who had infiltrated behind our lines. They were having some success in killing Russian senior military officers in numerous sectors. One of their victims was one of Marshall Konev's chief adjutants.

In decent German I began, "Helmut, you haven't been cooperating, have you. Now I regret to inform you that you will now experience the worst pain and indignity imaginable. You don't have to suffer this; before we begin would you like to talk and then have a cigarette and some food? You will talk eventually; why not save yourself this horror? We are reasonable people."

He didn't move or speak. He just stared back at me defiantly from the pulpy red mess that once was his face before three days of torture. I sighed and took out some extremely sharp surgical instruments and donned some filthy gloves.

"I will now begin your castration, Captain, with a surgical incision into the upper left of your scrotum. Then I will cut your cremasteric and dartos muscles which hold your left testicle." The Prussian quivered involuntarily.

I crudely sliced the skin's connection to his body and cut those muscles – a procedure that without anesthetic had been described by our interrogation doctors as perhaps as painful a procedure imaginable. Tweaking those nerves as the muscles were removed was like a man being constantly hit in the balls.

"Now I've removed the left testicle, largely intact," I told him. He screamed in excruciating pain and blood flowed rapidly from the gaping hole onto the table. He passed out.

I revived him with smelling salts. He yelled in agony as he returned to consciousness. "Now I will show you your testicle. Quite healthy actually, a shame you had to lose it." The sight and the pain made him throw up. "Now I will dice it into neat sections and force it into your mouth and nose."

He screamed, "Just kill me, you bitch."

"Oh no, that would be your reward for good behavior. Do you now have things you would like to tell me?"

He said nothing, just more moans of agony.

"Well Captain, you leave me no alternative than to take out the second one, only more slowly so you remain conscious and suffer greater pain."

This went on for eight more minutes until he found himself yelling, almost as an uncontrolled delirious response, the names and location of six Waffen SS snipers and the Russians they were targeting.

I looked at my commander, who smiled at me and said, "Excellent job – a very creative approach. You are developing into one of our best. He's done, dispose of him," and he left the room.

Then for practice I sliced his jugular vein, which would produce a slow death, threw his second testicle in his face and left the room. This success was later described to me as the key contributor to the decision by my superiors to name me the outstanding graduate in my class.

Her mind returned to the present, breaking the reverie of her past triumph. The banker was smiling at her as they pulled out of Newark. He had a fresh drink in his hand. She quickly thought how much she would enjoy the recreational castration of this capitalist blood sucker.

"Where you off to?" he opened with a smile.

"Corning actually. Off to see an old college roommate from Wellesley, her husband and two young kids. And you?

"Oh, a little fun with some business friends. Golf, weather permitting, a dinner party, the usual."

Oh how sweet, you asshole, she thought. But she replied, "Corning is a great little town, kind of place I might settle down in some day."

"What do you do if you don't mind my asking?" he probed.

"I work for ASCAP. The American Society of Composers, Authors and Publishers. Great job, get to meet almost everyone who ever put a successful musical note on paper and all the stars who sing them, from Irving Berlin to Marilyn Monroe."

"Hey, that's got to be exciting. I can see why you don't want to settle down. By the way, my name is Brian Suitor."

You lying moron, she thought. This one thinks he's going to get lucky this weekend and doesn't want me to have his real name. Of course, I'll do the same.

"I'm Suzannah. Suzannah Johnstone. Pleasure to meet you."

A second drink followed for each, but she quietly spilled most of her second on the carpet unnoticed. Then they walked to the dining car, resplendent in its starched napery, silver plated utensils and flowers on each table. The smells of roasting meat, fresh vegetables and just baked desserts were yummy. After dessert and a French burgundy (almost none of which she actually drank), Sonya had skillfully directed the conversation to Corning Glass by drawing out of him his role as a financial advisor to the company.

"You know my girl friend tells me Corning is really a great company. Her husband sells them laboratory equipment, a lot of high tech stuff."

"You don't know the half of it," he responded, starting to slur his words. "These guys have more new inventions than Carter Wallace has liver pills. All kinds of stuff, including things they're doing for the government that I don't know much about."

"Yeah, I've heard some of that also. My friend's husband says there's some guy there named Dr. Stookey who is spooky smart."

"Wow, your friend does know the company. Stookey's working on something now that they won't even tell us, their bankers. Really top secret I guess. All I know is he's been taken off the consumer area, where he was working on some kitchen products that I'm very excited about and part of the reason we financed them. He's now tied up for some time in this other classified work. Whatever it is, I do know they expect big volume by early 1954. It better be there or they won't be able to pay our loans off," he laughed.

She thought carefully. Even though this asshole is close to plowed, I have to be cautious now. When he tries to find me in New York next week and can't, I don't want him thinking that he might have said something to me he shouldn't have. Also, I'm pretty sure he doesn't really know any more. He doesn't realize he already has given me a gem.

She cleverly turned the conversation to other areas. They were the last to leave the diner, laughing and flirting. As he held the door open for her, his hand lightly brushed her ass. Her only response was a smile. She gave him permission to call him next week in New York at ASCAP.

He did so on the following Tuesday, a reasonable compromise between sounding too anxious and too casual. He was very surprised and confused to learn from the secretary to the president, Sylvia Metzler, that ASCAP apparently had no employee named Suzannah Johnstone and never had. He started to review their conversation and concluded nothing troubling had been said to her, whoever the hell she was. Nothing ventured, nothing gained. The little unappreciative bitch.

At that moment he was interrupted by his secretary announcing that Mr. Ford was on the line from Detroit. The news was promising; a relationship was being forged.

Dinner in the Diner

He never thought of Miss Johnstone again. Why should he – there were a million of these type ladies in New York for him to play with, eager to be graced by such a financial luminary as he. There always was pussy for masters of the financial universe. We control the bucks that everyone wants, and the women always follow that intoxicating aroma of power.

She spent her weekend scouting Corning and preparing the way for the new agent she would soon drop into the world of Corning Glass. She also hung out in a local bar Saturday night where she got a load of plant gossip and some interesting names.

She wound up screwing and faking orgasms for six straight hours with an accountant named Herman Mook, who worked in the classified area of the plant. He pleaded for her address and phone. Sonya made one up and then claimed that she worked in the plant's personnel department. As she left the idiot told her he thought he had fallen in love.

On Sunday a coded message was sent from the New York consulate to Moscow by General Strelnikov:

Major General Sergei Kruglov, Director, MGB

Dzerzhinsky Square, Moscow

Agent Sonya has confirmed from two credible sources that the Corning Glass Company intends to ship meaningful volumes of Dr. Stookey's new missile nose cone protectant material in 1954. They are highly confident in the material's performance, even though not fully proven yet. This information comes from a financier who has seen internal revenue and profit projections for the company in support of certain company loans and is corroborated by a local accountant in the plant.

Agent Sonya has also set in motion the plan to introduce agent Traveler into the Corning complex. It is clear that penetration into the Corning facility and access to the specifications of this material is crucial. We now have agent Sonya devoting full attention to this matter exclusively. She also is the only one in contact with Oryol. We will update you on our progress.

Respectfully submitted,

Major General Iuri Strelnikov
New York Station, Commanding

It was a concerning piece of news for the boys at Dzerzhinsky Square, but they shook their heads in awe that their star agent had produced once again. And the Americans had no idea who she was.

General Kruglov called Lieutenant Colonel Igor Tolstoy into his office. "Igor, this woman is a piece of work. Smart, cunning, vicious and wonderfully ambitious – and 100% American – an unbelievable resource."

"General, how did we recruit her?"

"Ah, my model communist officer, even you can't be told any specifics about agent Sonya. Only Stalin, Khrushchev, Beria in Moscow and Strelnikov in New York know her full details. Even I have only part of the picture. Not that I don't trust you like a son, Igor, but the five of us are sworn to absolute secrecy on every detail of her life. She's more valuable than 100 generals – and a lot less trouble!" he said with a laugh.

Igor smiled back, but internally he felt a wave of nausea. Two days ago he had received a coded instruction from the Americans running his case that his primary and most urgent task going forward was to identify this agent Sonya. Using any means possible, extreme as they might be. Strange he thought, these Americans with all their principles – except when it really mattered.

But how the hell can I find this information. The only people who know who she is are the five highest ranking people in the Soviet Union. And those guys never talk to anyone except their inner circle. I'm in real trouble.

CHAPTER 9

THE ROCKETRY COMMISSION MEETS

10:00 a.m., Wednesday, December 12, 1952
111 John Street, Lower Manhattan

The Rocketry Task Force met for the first time in its entirety since the death of Professor Dickinson. Dominic was charged with security for the group and had secured a separate office and meeting site just for the committee members and the support staff at 111 John Street in the downtown insurance district near Wall Street. It was a busy building where people would not be noticed coming and going. The eleventh floor, where they were located, had only one other tenant, the Standard Claims Adjustment Company. This small business, led by a Harold O'Brien, settled claims for out of town insurance companies related to accidents occurring in the Northeast. Dominic was convinced these guys were no threat and in fact perfect neighbors and cover.

Dominic looked out at the group – the best of the best. There were 34 formal members of the task force. They included a rocket propulsion scientist from Thiokol Chemical Company; IBM computer engineers; aeronautical engineers from Lockheed, Douglas and Hughes Aircraft; metallurgists from Alcoa; and academicians from MIT, Cal Tech, Stanford, Georgia Tech, the University of Illinois - and formerly one physicist from Princeton. They were all men except for a youngish and attractive woman from Stanford's engineering school, a Dr. Sharon Hallman, who was an expert in material science, particularly exotic metals – titanium, beryllium, etcetera.

The task force was chaired by the distinguished Werner Von Braun, a father of the German V-1 and V-2 rockets, who had by now become fully Americanized. The vice chair was Dr. Peter Harsanyi, a native of Hungary, who was a very senior engineering professor at MIT and possessed Noble Prize type brilliance. He had barely escaped the Nazi crackdown in his country in 1944-1945 at the end of the war. Most of his wife's Jewish family had been wiped out in that final orgy of slaughter when the German's took control and thousands of Jews were rushed to Auschwitz. In the last days of that house of horrors, the Germans had actually set "production" records gassing and burning Hungarian Jews.

The mission of the task force was to be the coordinating leadership for the new and somewhat scattered American rocketry program. Under the control and financing of the defense department, work was going on around the country.

President Truman had reportedly responded to the first mention of a weaponized missile that, "it doesn't take a rocket scientist to understand the implications of such a nuclear delivery system." As was his custom, Truman made a fast decision and quickly allocated funds from defense department contingency reserves to support the commission's work. And then as always, he slept his usual solid eight that night.

The meeting was brought to order by Dr. Von Braun precisely at 10 a.m. The first order of business was an update by Dominic on the Dickinson case and related security issues. He spoke in his best FBI formality.

"Gentlemen," Dominic began, "the investigation of the tragic death of Dr. Dickinson is proceeding with vigor and urgency. I will now give you a brief overview of our progress with the hope that perhaps some of you may recall helpful information and also so that you are all fully forewarned of the potential dangers. I can not overstress, as always, the absolute top secret nature of what I will tell you. Particularly since we now realize the desperate lengths our enemies will go to.

The murder on the *Owl* train, although excessively brutal, was professionally planned from inception to implementation to clever escape. Early on we strongly suspected that the perpetrators were agents, directly, or indirectly of the Soviet Union. This has now been confirmed by certain sources. We strongly believe the killers, probably one man and one woman, exited the train at Stroudsburg, Pennsylvania around 3 a.m. and walked a short distance to a waiting car. We know the car used was a dark 1949 Pontiac and have traced it to a vehicle stolen several weeks before in northern New Jersey. There has been no trace of that vehicle since the murder. Do any of you recall seeing such a vehicle?"

At this point Dominic held up a generic photo of a 1949 Pontiac. There was no response. Dominic thought, these eggheads probably don't know the difference between a Pontiac and beer truck.

"Please be alert to any vehicle that might be following you or consistently parked anywhere around your daily routine. And any sighting, no matter how seemingly innocuous, of a 1949 Pontiac. We will check out each report.

We have by now interviewed all of you regarding what materials Dr. Dickinson might have had with him, all of which was taken. He definitely would have had his own presentation at the last committee meeting of his calculations of missile flight path options, trajectories, altitude, time to target, etc. We suspect he also would have taken copious notes on the discussion of both the new designs for a nose cone and material options, particularly the review of the Corning alternative, as he had spent a great deal of time with those people. Indeed, as you know, he was traveling to Corning the night he was murdered. Let me now ask if any of you have more to add on that subject."

Dr. Harsanyi, the vice chair, offered, "It's hard to say what else John might have had with him that night. He was extremely well informed on almost everything we are doing. He may have taken notes on anything the committee reviewed that day, including our favorable testing of the ceramic nose cone composite at my MIT laboratory."

Van Braun chimed in, "John was a compulsive note taker, a true academic. He also was brilliant and understood more pieces of this puzzle than all but a few of us. We have to assume a lot of data was lost."

Dominic groaned internally.

The lone female member, Dr. Sharon Hallman then asked, "But what did John really know about the Corning material? Sure he heard explanations but he couldn't reproduce the chemical formulas on his own. And I still have doubts this stuff will work in a real test outside a laboratory."

Dominic thought, what's her story? I know she's a metallurgist and has been pushing exotic metals, not Corning glass, for the nose cone. But since the ceramic worked in Harsanyi's test, why doesn't she yield on this. Pain in the ass.

Von Braun responded, "It will work. We're there. And my fear is that if the Russians just know such a protectant is possible, they will get there. Just like the atomic bomb.

Remember what Heisenberg and the other Nazi physicists did right after the Hiroshima bomb went off? They were under house arrest in that British estate, and English Intelligence MI-6 bugged everything right to the toilets. In two weeks they figured out how the Americans did it, just knowing it had been done. This was after they had been stumped throughout the war years."

Dominic thought, that's true – just like our crime cases. Once it happened, we put together the "how" real fast. We've got to find these bad guys – now.

After a painful silence Dominic continued, "We will now be implementing a much higher level of security around the task force. All of you will travel to these meetings, as you did today, with an armed escort. We discourage you to bring with you or take away any materials that are not essential to the day's discussion. We will use the internal FBI mail delivery system to distribute your work and use our secure storage for your research.

Now I must introduce a sensitive concern of ours," continued Dominic. "We know that Dr. Dickinson's exact travel plans were not finalized until late on November 11th. He was considering an option of staying over in New York and leaving the next day for Corning. He had a backup reservation on that afternoon's train. He apparently made his decision late, right after your working dinner. That begs the obvious set of questions. How did the perpetrator and his conspirators know he was going to Corning? Was it from previous post-meeting surveillance by them? Or did someone somewhere on the inside inform them? If the latter, how did he or she know that the doctor at the last minute decided to take the night train?"

He stared for awhile around the room to see if anyone blinked. Silence – no response. The thought flashed through his head – I may be looking at the traitor right now. Right here under my Roman nose. And notes on this meeting may be sitting in the soviet consulate tomorrow. Jesus, we may be feeding the devil as we speak. His body shivered involuntarily.

After an extensive review of the science and the schedule going forward, Von Braun adjourned the meeting at 7 p.m. As Dominic returned to his office, he thought about a possible traitor in their midst. Acting like he or she knows nothing, a calculating traitor blending right in with these academic dreamers.

7:45 p.m.

Later that evening the phone rang at the usual midtown garage. "This is Mrs. Brown," said Sonya. "You know the car I have been storing there for my vacation to the mountains?"

"Yes," was the laconic reply.

"I don't think I will be using it after all. You can sell it to the highest bidder."

This was the agreed upon code for the immediate but careful dissection, chopping and disposal of the 1949 Pontiac, the getaway car from Stroudsburg.

After a pause, the garage voice responded, "Of course, Madame. I will see to it myself."

Two nights later the parts, encased in a heavy container, were loaded on a truck and delivered to a fishing trawler, which then sailed into the Atlantic and, using its on board crane, dumped the heavy remnants of one 1949 fastback dark green Pontiac into the deep waters just off the continental shelf. It came to rest at a dark depth of 1100 feet, where it would now spend eternity.

Sunday, December 16, 1952

It took some time for further instructions to arrive from the intelligence center in Moscow. New York MGB station chief Strelnikov hoped the Dickinson's papers had done the trick, requiring no more such dangerous expeditions. When the new instructions arrived, he realized they had not.

He always worried about coded messages, even when hand delivered in the diplomatic pouch. Every officer in the KGB knew the full history of the British breaking of the "Enigma" code of the German high command and the American decryption of the Japanese codes in World War II. Why should we feel secure in our codes, Strelnikov thought? We know the Americans are far ahead in the new field of electronic computers, and that these computers have the ability to identify patterns in seemingly random bits of data. That's exactly why I have three active agents employed now inside IBM in Poughkeepsie full time.

The decoded message read as follows:

From: I.S. Andropov, Colonel, MGB

To: I.N. Strelnikov, Major General, MGB

Comrade General,

I report to you on the status of the missile and rocketry intelligence project. These conclusions are for your eyes only.

Your recent package was quite helpful, although in other respects disturbing. Our major concern now is the American research into potential missile nose cone protective material and a new design structure for the nose cone. The area of greatest interest is work apparently being done at the Corning Glass works in Corning, New York. In conjunction with your field agents you are to attempt to infiltrate and get the research on a new glass composite material that they apparently have developed that can withstand the heat and pressure of high altitude reentry.

That is all you need to know on the science and physics of our request. We will activate a sleeper agent, code name "Traveler" in the United States, who will know our full needs. He is aware of the reporting chain. He contacts agent Sonya, who will get it to you.

We are, however, not confident that Traveler can get the job done. We may eventually have no choice but to resort to direct utilization of Oryol, as risky as that may be to our most valuable asset in America. Time will dictate our decision.

Upon reading, destroy this message immediately.

By order of the MGB Central Committee

I. S. Andropov, Colonel
[SEAL OF THE MGB]

CHAPTER 10

RECALLED TO LIFE

Same Sunday Evening
East 9th Street, Manhattan

Prudence Owens, Dominic's assistant, had worked all yesterday (Saturday) at her boss's request. The work load on the Dickinson case and the Rocketry Commission was reaching unmanageable levels. In addition to her boss's normal responsibility and work load, he now had control of 200 extra FBI agents throughout the Northeast temporarily assigned to him. Plus calls from Hoover and his staff to deal with.

She stumbled out the office door Saturday evening at 7 p.m. The only thing keeping her going was the joyous thought that she would spend tonight and all Sunday with her new French boyfriend.

They had met through a chance encounter at a packed Horn and Hardart's restaurant on 42nd street, each grabbing a quick snack at the inexpensive eatery. He was a part time actor with a day job translating legal documents for the Credit Lyonnais Bank office in midtown.

As she walked toward her apartment, her step quickened at the thought of what she would soon be doing. God, do I deserve to be this happy at 40 years of age? I've been divorced from my ex for two years, two terrible years. He just up and tells me one day he is leaving me out of terminal boredom and that he never should have married me in college just because our daughter got conceived. What a bastard.

Then I meet the love of my life – this young, artistic French intellectual, a graduate of the Sorbonne. And what a lover – Francois takes me to levels of physical intimacy I'd never even fantasized about.

She opened the door, and Francois stood at the kitchen counter, with nothing on but an apron, cutting vegetables into a sauté pan and sipping a nice Bordeaux. She started her usual tempestuous swim into that sea of passion.

"Hi honey. Do you like my apron? I thought it might improve my cooking." Then he lifted the front, ostensibly to dry his hands, creating a full frontal nude shot. He gave that goofy smile. Then he lifted her off her feet, kissing her with passion.

Five minutes after they had completed dinner, he carried her to the bedroom. His lips moved all over her body. Are there any Americans who can make love like this? She began the familiar convulsive lead up to her first climax. This time he keeps taking me to the edge without allowing me to go over. What an artist.

Nine minutes later she exploded with profound ecstasy and almost lost consciousness for a few minutes. As she began to move again, he started pleasing her anew but in another way. This went on until 2 a.m., when she basically dissolved in a delicious flood of emotions mixed with physical joy. He was unreal! The best lover in the world. And it just kept getting better.

The next morning they awoke and left for work. After these weekend marathons, everyone in the office, including Dominic, noticed a profound difference in the normal Miss Efficiency. Frequently she would be asked if she was feeling all right. With each inquiry she smiled, but finally lost it in laughter when the senior female administrator asked her what had gotten into her. Not what, she thought, but who. And thank you, God.

CHAPTER 11

THE DON

Monday, January 7, 1953
New York City

Catherine had followed up on Garroway's suggestion to contact the lawyer who had certain "clients" that might be helpful in providing an introduction to the longshoremen's union leadership. She had set up call with one Bruno Sabatini, a vice president of the ILW.

After opening pleasantries she said, "Mr. Sabatini, I appreciate your taking my call. I work on the *Today* show and also help provide stories to NBC News. We've covered the story of the west coast strikes on their waterfront and are intrigued by the labor peace here in New York. Seems to be a real contrast in union leadership. Can you help me out on this?"

There followed several minutes of repartee, jousting, an exploration of each other's bona fides. She began to progressively engage him and finally got him pitching the union.

"Well, Miss Bowers," in a heavy New York/Italian accent, "You have to realize we are very different. Those West Coast guys are weirdos. Our boys are real Americans. They work their tail off, do their job, and we make sure they're taken care of. We have nothin' to do with Harry Bridges and those gigatsos, excuse me, squash heads in California."

Colorful, she thought. "Yes, I can see the obvious differences. Would it be possible for me to visit you to discuss this in more detail? We might run a little story comparing the two unions. You guys would probably come out looking pretty good."

Sabatini was silent for a second. Then for the benefit of the other man in the room, he said out loud, "We have to think about that, Miss Bowers. Maybe we could help you in a story showing how different we are from those unpatriotic idiots in San Francisco." He glanced at the man for his reaction, who made the gesture of a maybe sign with his hand. "Let me get back to you on this. We appreciate your interest."

After they hung up, Bruno asked the other man, "What do you think boss?"

Dante Bonsignore, aka "the Sausage," controlled the longshoreman's union. He was also the Don of New York's strongest family, the head of the council of the five New York crime families. The don of dons.

He took a puff on his Cuban cigar. In Sicilian he replied, "You know, Brunes, maybe we have to come into this twentieth century. This new TV thing is big. The right PR might help us. We could kiss their ass like we do with the boys at the papers. Maybe an envelope or two with some cash could help them clarify their understanding," he smiled.

"I agree, boss. And this lady sounds like she's working a good angle—how patriotic our boys are. This could work."

Don Bonsignore took another puff on his cigar and slowly exhaled. Bruno could feel the wheels turning. He thought, the boss has great instincts – he'll figure it out. After all he didn't get to the top being an idiot.

"Call her up and invite her in for a tour of the docks. If it's going well, invite her into my office to meet me," the Don answered. "I think we want to work this."

"You got it, boss," Sabatini replied and then left.

The Don got up and walked out to his receptionist. He winked and motioned for her to follow. He closed and locked the door.

He thought, I love my midday intermezzo with Miss Abadanzo. It always clears my mind. It's an essential part of my life. Espresso in the morning, Abadanzo's blowjob at noon, dinner in a private room at the Blue Grotto with some of the boys and Mass on Sunday. Perfecto mundo.

And killing any son of a bitch who even mildly threatens to disturb my position on this gleaming, lustrous waterfront of gold.

The report of the call from Bowers to the Don reached Dominic's ears the next morning. Not bad he thought for a guy who, as he had told Bowers, has no knowledge of the Port. In fact Dominic had a man high in the union and two guys on the FBI cash payroll actually working inside there 40 hours a week. Nothing important happened on the docks that Dominic Benvenuto didn't know about. And he planned to keep it that way.

It will be interesting to see if this pushy broad gets a story from the boys, he thought.

CHAPTER 12

THE TRAVELER AND AN EXECUTION

Saturday, January 10
Corning, New York

They met in his rented house. Today she was a brunette with hints of gray capping a middle aged countenance. Sonya had called this first face-to-face meeting with the Traveler on this frigid weekend in upstate New York.

His name was Hermann Mannesmann. The guy had quite a personal history. Unbeknownst to the American security people, he had actually joined the communist party in Germany in 1928. A promising young aerospace engineer, he was kind of a quiet intellectual communist until Hitler came in, and his brown shirts took his homosexual lover off to Dachau. Then Mannesmann went underground on both the communism and his sexual preference – either of which could have landed him in the same camp.

What he didn't know was that Moscow ordered the death of his lover on his third day in Dachau and then the murder of the arresting Berlin cop, so neither could expose Mannesmann. He survived as a hidden Russian agent working deep within the German rocketry program for 13 years, until the Americans grabbed him out of Germany at the end of the war.

"So now that you've settled in, tell me what you make of the situation," Sonya opened.

Mannesmann followed with an unemotional and methodical twenty minute dissection of the potential and challenges of his assignment to infiltrate Corning Glass and obtain, however possible, the secrets of the nose cone breakthrough.

"It will be a daunting task," he concluded, "but doable if I am careful."

Sonya stared at him without comment for ten seconds. Then she said, "You know how vital this is to us Mannesmann. In a few short years we will be able to launch multiple nuclear warheads to any spot in the U.S., maybe five years ahead of the Americans. We will have the thrust, payload capacity and guidance systems to do this, if we can just get the last piece of this puzzle - the nose cone material to protect the payload on reentry. The damn answer is right here. Five miles from where we now sit. We can smell it – it's right under our nose. You work in the plant that houses the secret. With this we can change the world…overnight."

She then raised her voice several decibels and pointed her right index finger at his face. "And you, Traveler, will get this secret for us. If you fail, we will save the Americans the trouble of dealing with you. Do I make myself clear?"

Traveler was speechless with new found fear. He had never had a controller like this. His handlers had all been understated, calm, encouraging – kind of like him. This woman was different, terrifying – a coiled serpent, whom he had no doubt would destroy him if disappointed or disobeyed.

But sensing his palpable fear, she then smiled and said, "But of course, you will not fail us, and you will continue to serve our great cause in complete anonymity."

After she had left, he stumbled into his bathroom and threw up- his reflexive response to this new master of his life. As risky as it might be, he had to succeed.

One Week Later
Moscow

Lieutenant Colonel Igor Tolstoy read the latest report from agent Sonya in his door-closed office. The super spy was clearly making progress. She had facilitated agent Traveler's successful insertion into the Corning plant engineering design team.

His work gets him close to the nose cone secret. They have him drawing a revised design for its physical shape. It seemed two American aeronautical engineers have just demonstrated, quite counter intuitively, that an inverted conical shape is most effective in defeating heat on reentry, making the nose cone protectant's job less challenging. This was big news. Traveler already has part of the answer, but just a small part.

But getting the composition of the nose cone would be more challenging. Traveler says that work is being done by a separate and tightly isolated group elsewhere in the building, with heavy FBI security in place following the murder of Professor Dickinson. So all is not lost…yet.

But I have to get this information to the Americans. Now. They must know how close the Russians are."

Igor went down the hall to review the report with his direct boss, Colonel Iuri Andropov, the 39 year old wunderkind, who had given the report to the board. Many thought he could someday run the entire MGB. He and Igor were commanding General Kruglov's favorite young officers; they worked together on numerous high profile cases.

Igor nodded at Andropov and said, "Sir, what do you make of Traveler's progress and plan?"

"You have to be impressed that Sonya got him in so close. And the guy is technically smart. We had him working in the General Electric jet engine plant in Evendale, Ohio before this. This guy is good. Do you know his history – the role he played in the Nazi's deadly V-2 rocket program that was blasting London in 1945?"

"No sir, I don't."

"Traveler quietly sabotaged a storage depot in Pnemonde where the V-2's were kept on the north coast, setting off a huge explosion at night. A returning British bomber, forewarned to look for such a blast, sighted the secret base, and the next day the U.S. Eighth Air Force flattened Pnemonde for good. It was a big gift from us to the Brits and the Americans. The guy has accomplished a lot."

"Yeah, but what about his personal habits," Igor countered. "We know he is a sexually active homosexual. Corning New York is a small place. His sexual proclivities will be easy to spot. If the FBI finds out he's queer, he'll be out on his ass real fast. He came over with Werner Von Braun and his bunch of German's, who vouched for him. The U.S. snoops didn't look too hard. But I'm sure they would reexamine him closer if they know he's queer. Then they might come upon his pre Nazi personal history in Germany. Then they would make the connection to us."

"I know. His perversions worry me Igor," Andropov responded. "But he's the best we got. And…agent Sonia already has her orders as to what to do if he comes under suspicion. She never leaves a trail. Or a loose end."

Two Weeks Later – Corning

"It's Traveler. We have a weird new problem here in Corning," Mannesmann said on the phone.

Sonya was annoyed. Whatever it is it better be important; Mannesmann had clear instructions never to call me even though it's a secure phone.

"Did you meet some guy named Herman Mook when you were here?"

"Yeah, I've seen him twice, once on each of my last two visits. I tried to teach this pathetic little worm how to have good sex. He's a Corning Glass accountant – and has unknowingly let slip some very important hints on the shipping schedule of the ceramic material we're interested in. Important stuff already passed on to our friends. Why the hell are you asking?"

"Well he's trying desperately to find you. Did you tell him you worked in personnel? He's been quizzing everyone in that department. A friend there told me about it. The jerk is off the deep end, lovesick. Giving a description of you that fits your look last time I saw you."

"Thank you. Helpful information." She hung up fast with not even a goodbye.

She borrowed one of the untraceable cars and headed out to Corning. She went to Mook's home in a cheap part of town. He wasn't in so she jimmied the lock. Took her 14 seconds. She did a quick tour and settled on the front hallway for the C4 plastic explosive with a much larger charge set to blow downstairs, where natural gas entered the home. She partially disconnected that gas line with a pipe wrench, allowing the highly explosive gas to begin seeping out into the cellar. She left the wrench by the open pipe.

She knew he would be home around six. The guy had no life and always came home right after work.

While waiting for him she heard a baby cry on the second floor of the two story rental home. Made no difference – collateral damage happens.

At 6:08 p.m., he opened his front door. She saw him through her binoculars from a block away. The radio transmitter was already in her hand. On his third step she pressed the first button, exploding three pounds of the material right between his legs. One second later she pressed the second button, resulting in a muffled blast that immediately merged into a booming explosion in the gas-laden cellar. The house imploded, collapsing into itself.

The police and utility report were later in full agreement. The explosion had occurred as a result of a gas leak in the cellar caused by Mook apparently having loosened the fitting. A wrench was found with his initials scratched into it. He probably was trying to redirect the gas flow to his furnace. The next time the igniter went on, as called to by the thermostat, the explosion was instant and massive, bringing the whole house down immediately. These things happened occasionally when a homeowner tried some stupid do-it-yourself project.

Most unfortunate that it also killed the young mother and infant on the second floor.

On the drive back she was quite pleased with herself. She never liked to leave loose ends.

CHAPTER 13

STALIN'S MURDER

Two Months Later
March 1, 1953 – 10:00 p.m.
Stalin's Country Dacha Outside Moscow

"The old bastard should go any hour now," Khrushchev whispered to Kruglov as he arrived in Stalin's ante room just outside the madman's private bedroom. "After our dinner and drinking last night he had a bad day, and the doctors have added a strong medication to his ten other drugs. Seems this one didn't mix well with the others. Provoked semi consciousness and then a cerebral hemorrhage. Now he is just muttering nonsense, and he just pissed his pants. Also, the new drug is untraceable if someone screams for an autopsy."

"Good Nikita," Kruglov responded quietly. "I have brought my aide, Lieutenant Igor Tolstoy, the one I have told you about, in case we need some muscle. He is like a son to me, fully committed and sworn to secrecy. And physically a piece of steel."

"Excellent, but we shouldn't need him. Stalin should never regain full consciousness. He will meet the devil soon in hell or wherever mass killers like this paranoid madman go."

Suddenly their conversation was interrupted by a roar from the dying man's bedroom. Stalin had regained consciousness, was sitting up in bed and screamed for his doctors, who rushed in. "They are killing me, they want me dead." Seeing Khrushchev and Kruglov, he added, "You traitors and these doctors are poisoning me, right in my own bed!" he roared.

Khrushchev, visibly concerned, glanced quickly at the head physician and nodded. The doctor gave Stalin another injection immediately, while Khrushchev said, "Koba, no one is poisoning you. We are all here at your side, and the doctor is just giving you something to soothe you."

"You bastards, you are all in this doctors' plot to kill me. After all I did for you, now you murder the father of the Soviet Union." He tried to say more but started to sink back into a dull haze. In ten minutes he was fully unconscious with vital signs slipping.

Then Khrushchev whispered in the dying man's ear, "You go to hell, you mass murderer. Twenty million of your own people. You too stupid to heed the warnings about Hitler. And the terrible things you made all of us do to calm your paranoia. Fuck your mother, Joseph Vissarionovich Dzhugashvili, you crazy Georgian peasant piece of shit! Man of steel – go to hell!"

Stalin hung on in a comatose state four more days, finally succumbing on March 5. Khrushchev called Kruglov and told him, "The nightmare is finally over. In time we will expose all the madman's cult of personality."

The entire country stopped for 10 minutes that day in tribute to their departed father figure. People openly wept in the streets, as the funereal dirges monopolized all media including the one million loudspeakers scattered throughout the country. Khrushchev and Kruglov had the "honor" of being pall bearers at the state funeral. Three years later Premier Khrushchev would publicly denounce Stalin before the Twentieth Congress in 1956.

Igor Tolstoy was one of the key MGB officers in charge of security for the funeral. Afterward and exhausted from an 18 hour day, he returned to his apartment and sought out the refuge of the hot bathtub.

The final passing of the "killer in chief" is a good thing he thought, but it will change little. A new line of monsters will come forth to succeed him. The system has no checks or balances. Absolute power corrupts absolutely. This viperous system has to be immolated at the stake. It's to that goal I remain passionately committed. Nothing changes for me. I'll help bury the lot of them.

On the other side of the world, Dominic arose to the headlines of Stalin's death and turned on to the *Today* show for details. When he got to the office he read the top secret morning reviews from State and the CIA.

He called a brief meeting of all his agents. "This is good news but it will change nothing. His henchmen will now spar for leadership, but the goal will remain – the triumph of communism. All of our cases continue – particularly the Oryol/Sonia attempt to steal our vital rocketry secrets. Let's get back to work."

CHAPTER 14

DOMINIC AND FAMILY

Dominic's wife, Laurie, and three kids waited in their new 1953 two tone brown/cream Plymouth for his arrival for their first visit to the summer cabin. Cranberry Lake didn't have a real train station, but the Cliff-Inn, just across the tracks from the parking lot, served as one. It was part of the bucolic charm. This deli/newsstand/general store was where Dominic would disembark the *Sussex County Express*, having come directly from his lower Manhattan office by ferry to board the train at Hoboken, its origination point.

Laurie had picked the kids up at school in Chatham at 3:15 p.m. sharp and had headed directly to the cabin forty-five minutes away. It was the time of year when the family would reopen their simple cottage and prepare for the season. This season they had just gotten the first TV for the cabin, a Philco model.

Even though the house had passed to them from her husband's side and though Dominic had some of his earliest memories from there, it was his wife who was crazy about the lake and their little log cabin on South Shore Road. It was a modest affair – two bedrooms, a sleeping porch, small kitchen, eating nook and a cozy little living room with an old stone fireplace, which together with the anthracite coal stove in one bedroom could heat the house in the April-May and October-November shoulder seasons. Maybe 1200 square feet on a postage stamp lot, but it was right on the lake.

Laurie had graduated from Vassar, cum laude, and was set to go to law school before she met Dominic in 1942. They got married five months after Pearl Harbor on June 8, 1942, following his graduation from West Point. After a two-week honeymoon new Lieutenant Dominic Benvenuto reported for duty. Their oldest son Damon was conceived at Camp Kilmer, New Jersey and born in April 1943.

In March, 1944 Dominic sailed to England as a first Lieutenant in the army rangers and parachuted behind enemy lines in the early hours of D-day, June 6, 1944. He later was attached to G-2 intelligence with General Patton's third army and helped turn the Battle of the Bulge, receiving a purple heart for a shrapnel wound. On V-E Day on the Elbe River he celebrated with some of Marshall Konev's Russian officer corps. Then he actually went with Eisenhower's delegation to Moscow that August and met a bunch of Russians.

Funny, he never talks about that trip, Laurie thought. Wonder why? Whom did he meet?

Benvenuto Cabin at Cranberry Lake

Dominic bounded off the train and jumped into the arms of his family, kissed his wife, hugged his children and joined them in the Plymouth. He was dressed in his stylish Hickey Freeman dark pin strip suit, newly bought at the upscale Marty Walker clothing store in Manhattan. With his promotion he had upgraded from a cut-rate retail outlet with little panache known as Barneys on 17th Street and 7th Avenue.

When they got back to the house, they put a coal fire in the bedroom's pot belly stove and a wood fire in the fireplace, had a home cooked dinner, made love and retired early.

On Sunday night the whole family had dinner at the Cranberry Lake Lodge. Dominic was surprised to see Harold O'Brien, their neighbor at the 111 John Street office, eating with his family. O'Brien waved at him.

"Mr. O'Brien, good to see you. Let me introduce my family."

Then O'Brien introduced his wife, Ruth, two boys, John and Vinny, about the same ages as Damon and Joey. His sister, May, was also with them. While the adults chatted, Damon noticed John had a Giant's tee shirt on.

"Hey, are you a Giants fan too?" he asked.

"You bet." John responded.

"You know Maglie is pitching tonight?"

Soon the boys were carrying on about their favorite team and who was the Giants best pitcher – Maglie, Jensen or Hearn. The new buddies had to be dragged apart.

After a great roast turkey dinner with all the trimmings and New York champagne for the adults, the Benvenutos returned home in time to catch Sid Caesar's *Show of Shows* with Carl Reiner and Imogene Coco on their new Philco television set. After the children were in bed, they sat in the living room, each with a rusty nail after dinner cocktail, and listened as a developing storm whistled its early breezy warning in the trees.

"I'll be going down to D.C. this week to review a couple of big cases with the heavies." Dominic offered in a quiet, concerned tone. "Serious stuff. A lot of pressure. Maybe down there several days." He never discussed any details of his work with Laurie, and she knew better than to ask. But his tone was foreboding.

"Don't know where this will take me. By the way, at least for the next few months try to drive the kids to school and back. Observe all the Bureau's precautions – you know the routine." Laurie just nodded yes and stared ahead, not wanting to go down that road. She knew the risks of her husband's job were a fact of life, one she never got used to.

"Honey, you're doing great. I'm just so proud of you." Then she ambled off to bed, sensing her husband had things on his mind.

Dominic poured himself a second rusty nail and listened to the approach of the thunder storm, watching the brilliant lightening flashes coming ever closer. The wind whistled through the trees.

I've come a long way. My father never finished high school before coming to America and spent 18 years in a coal mine only 100 miles west of here. I went to West Point, was an officer in the war and am now taking on real responsibility in my beloved FBI.

Dom thought about his enemies. They're sophisticated, covert, highly dangerous - potentially deadly. My family could be targets. They've got my name, picture. They know me. They know I'm the point man investigating the Dickinson murder. The man in charge of stopping what the Soviets really want. And apparently desperately need. They killed once and would unquestionably do it again, including disposing of me. This female operative is a cunning, ruthless adversary. It's me versus her, game on!

He gulped down his second drink, finally passing out on the enclosed porch just as the hard rain began. A sinister wind blew off the lake, pelting the windows with a cacophony of leaden drops.

———————————————————

The next day they biked and watched the Giants game at the Polo Grounds on the new TV. After a light dinner they locked the cabin, got on Route 206 South and headed toward their suburban home in Chatham. As Dominic pulled into the driveway, he thought how perfect the weekend had been.

The familiar joys and routine at the cabin also always seem to lessen his low intensity but ever-present fear. My life could end in a millisecond at the wrong end of a hot lead projectile. I'm their chief adversary standing between them and success in stealing our biggest secret. They'd do me in a New York minute.

CHAPTER 15

THE CIA DISCLOSURE

Tuesday, April 14, 1953

Dominic boarded the Pennsylvania Railroad's premier New York-Washington train, the beautiful, aluminum-clad, streamliner *Afternoon Congressional* in Newark. Pulled by a maroon colored GGI electric locomotive styled by the famous art deco industrial designer, Raymond Lowery, the entire train was brand new and state of the art, including an on board radio-telephone. It only stopped in Philadelphia, Wilmington and Baltimore.

About an hour out he went into the diner, laid out in crisp white linen, silver plated cutlery, embossed china and fresh flowers. He was seated with a lively middle aged married couple and a dour businessman type. The latter never spoke but the couple couldn't stop – stories, jokes, and endless tales of his caterpillar tractor dealership. Then the marvelous entrees arrived including Dominic's end cut of prime rib, baked potato and fresh vegetables.

As he began to dig into this movable feast, there came the usual question, "Well, Mr. Benvenuto, what line of work are you in?"

He thought a second. "I run a septic tank service business – installation, repair and a lot of cleanouts." He smiled and added, "It's been kind of erratic of late, but then this has always been a lumpy business."

That stopped the conversation cold. Dominic made a mental note – this is even better than the used car dealer routine. No one wants to talk about shit or lemons.

He got up early the next day in his hotel and was at Bureau headquarters by 7 a.m. The meeting was chaired by Director Hoover himself and his ever-present aide-de-camp, Clyde Tolson. Dominic wondered why Hoover had never married.

All the five other counter intelligence bureau chiefs were in attendance. There were also two guests from the CIA, a Dick Helms and a William Casey.

Hoover began, "We have summoned you bureau chiefs here today to review our progress in the Dickinson case and then to be appraised by Dick of some external details that I was only advised of last Thursday." As he said this, he looked at Dick, the senior CIA man, with disdain.

"What you are about to hear is for your ears only and not to be repeated to anyone, including your closest associates. Please do not take notes. We will begin by summarizing the bureau's efforts and then hear from our two colleagues here on external matters."

There followed Hoover's summary of the domestic investigation to date. "At this point the timeline, methodology and motives are clear. It was almost certainly a single male and a single female who committed the crime. The anonymous coach tickets were probably purchased by a third party at a New York area general railroad ticket agency, of which there are a dozen, where each agent probably sells to 50 customers on average a day. Most likely it was sold to someone bearing no resemblance to the perpetrator and the ticket was later handed off. The motive was to steal Dickinson's scientific papers but almost certainly not to kill him in the process. There was a dent in the heavy water thermos in the bedroom F, so we suspect Dickinson surprised him with a blow using this as a weapon, probably infuriating the murderer. The killer took his material, and they slipped off the train at Stroudsburg into a previously positioned car, which fits the physical description of a car stolen in New Jersey and not seen since. We do not know if the perpetrators were some of the Soviet hoods at the New York consulate or two of their domestic sleeper agents, or a mix of one each. We have no idea on the woman – this is the first time she has crossed our screen. We do know now with certainty that this material has reached Moscow."

He paused for effect and glanced around. Nobody asked how they knew.

This led to 20 minutes of additional questions, doubts and theories, none of which really moved the ball. All the regional guys felt they had to say something in front of the boss. Dom thought, it was typical of the kind of dreck that always came out in a cover-your-ass meeting.

Hoover stopped this rambling with the observation, "Gentlemen, let's get back on point. Dick, let me ask you to report on your developments."

The career CIA man, Richard Helms, rose and began, "What you are about to hear is obviously top secret and of the highest security classification. We speak with great trepidation, but realize that the nation's interest requires that we do so. We have an impeccable source in the Soviet Union, our most important one. We are convinced of this agent's authenticity and motivation. That is all I will say on this matter. His work is called Project Karenina. It is painfully clear that none of this can be mentioned to ANYONE on or around the Rocketry Task Force for obvious reasons – we now know there is a traitor somewhere on the inside.

Dick paused to let this sink in as he took his last puff on an ever present unfiltered Camel cigarette. He checked his handkerchief in his suit breast pocket and straightened out his chronic tennis elbow.

"Our agent has reported the following on the Dickinson case. Like us, the Russians are fully aware of the potential for nuclear armed, intercontinental ballistic missiles. They actually have a reasonably defined war plan that calls for a potential preemptive, full blown missile attack against the U.S. They are at least three to five years ahead of us on the rocketry aspects – size, thrust and guidance.

But they have one glaring engineering problem remaining – how to protect the payload during the fiery reentry into the atmosphere. They are nowhere on this. We have it. They want it. It is their last obstacle to becoming operational around 1957. They have become desperate enough to kill Dickinson to get it.

I cannot over emphasize the importance of this ICBM weapon. It can reach anywhere in the U.S. in less than an hour and there is no defense for it. Dickinson had worked extensively on our solution with a key U.S. government sub-contractor, who will go unnamed, and the Russians felt his knowledge justified the hit.

Through our source we now know what they got. Dickinson was carrying with him all his physics calculations of weight versus optimum trajectory, apogee, maximum speed and terminal speed on impact. None of this was particularly helpful to the Russians. They are extremely good at applied physics and had already figured all this out. They also got his notes on our nose cone solution as expounded at the meeting the day before Dickinson's death. These notes were of some help, but they don't understand anything about our apparently very creative approach, about which I will not elaborate. They are still baffled but will conduct research in an attempt to match our results.

Now I get to the reason and the only reason we are sharing this information with you today and regrettably increasing by twice the number of people in the world who know about our best asset in the Soviet Union. Simply stated, there is in our midst a Soviet operative, code named "Oryol" or Eagle, who is very much on the inside of the American rocketry program at a high level. I know Mr. Hoover and New York Bureau Chief Benvenuto have suspected this from the beginning. I believe you had concluded it was highly likely that someone had to be on the inside to know what Dickinson was working on. Also, what information he would likely be carrying that night, Dickinson's last minute change of plans, where he was going and how he would get there. None of that just randomly happened.

Oryol is apparently run by an agent Sonya, whose identity is a complete mystery to us. Our agent now confirms that this was the woman involved in the Dickinson murder. You gentlemen must find the traitor and this agent Sonya before even more vital secrets leave the country. The FBI has been in charge of the internal security of the Rocketry Task Force since inception. It was your responsibility to check everyone out and to clear them with the highest security rating."

He hesitated and looked around, making silent eye contact with every FBI man in the room. He added in his customary bluntness, "and…you…failed!"

There was silence and people started to fidget in their chairs. Finally, Hoover felt compelled to speak. "When did you obtain this confirmation and why is it only reaching us now, five months after the murder?"

"Because, we only got it last week ourselves. It's extremely difficult and dangerous to make direct contact with this extraordinary asset. There were two aborted attempts in December and March. Our agent is in the center of things, is very closely watched and has no privacy. But last week he felt compelled to reach out to us because of a new development. The highest level of the Soviet government has approved another attempt to forcibly gain these nose cone material secrets at any reasonable cost. They are getting desperate. They are going to hit us again."

"Does our man know who Sonya is?" Tolson asked.

"Doesn't have a clue. Apparently only the top five guys in the Soviet Union know who she is. And we don't expect to hear from them."

Dominic rolled his head back in tense pain. *Our man in Moscow can't help us. We're on our own finding Oryol and this woman who is running him. It's me against this bitch who seduces, kills and anything else to get the biggest secret in American military technology. A secret that can change the world.*

Wednesday, April 15, 1953

Dominic got home from Washington at 8 p.m., ate the quick dinner Laurie had kept warm for him, told his kids a goodnight story and then crashed. He did not notice the nondescript 1951 Mercury with a good view of his home parked two blocks away. Nor did Laurie notice the same car across from Central Avenue School in Chatham, when she picked up the boys at 3:30 p.m. the next day. Also, she could not have possibly seen the same car at 2:30 pm outside the Ladybug Nursery School her daughter, Nancy, attended because, as was usually the case, her friend Martha was picking up Nancy with her own son Peter.

The driver of the Mercury took copious notes on all these patterns. It had been a most productive twenty-four hours. She now knew everything she needed to know about the daily routine of the wife and family of this FBI Bureau Chief Dominic Benvenuto. As usual, Sonya came to a quick decision in cold, analytical terms, once all the facts were in.

Taking the little girl would be a piece of cake and devastating to her father, crippling his ability to effectively function in an emergency.

CHAPTER 16

THE BOYS AT DZERZHINSKY SQUARE

Monday, June 1, 1953
MVD Headquarters, Dzerzhinsky Square Moscow

Shortly after Stalin's death the MGB (international) was merged with the MVD (domestic), reuniting both the internal Soviet secret police with the external intelligence force. Sergei Kruglov, in effect the head of both already, was formally named the director of the new combined entity. He sat in his office wrestling with his options in America.

This Monday, like every other first Monday in the month, its governing committee was about to convene its command meeting, when all active sectors around the world were reviewed by the top brass. Today Colonel Iuri Andropov, Kruglov's 39 year old rising star, was leading the review. He began with an update on the work of MGB agents in French Indochina, which was nothing short of extraordinary.

"The arms and intelligence assistance given to Ho Chi Minh and his now quite well organized paramilitary, the Vietminh, has the French reeling. It also has the support of most of the people. Our soviet military and intelligence advisers predict total victory in the northern half of the country by 1955 at the latest."

Kruglov thought – to think that only a few years ago Beria had wanted to eliminate Ho, regarding him as a closet friend of the French and the Americans. Beria's an idiot. With Stalin gone we'll soon take care of him.

Andropov concluded his review of Vietnam and turned to the other French colonies. "All of the remaining parts of the French Empire, particularly Algeria and the African nations are now ripe pickings for us, and we are active in all these areas. The French as we knew them are finished."

Kruglov added, "We knew that when with the biggest standing army in Europe, the French, collapsed in 40 days of real fighting with the Nazis in 1940. What a bunch of spoiled dandies. Couldn't fight their way out of a paper bag."

Andropov resumed, "Totally unrelated but very promising are the stirrings in Cuba led by two very young and apparently iconic radicals named Fidel Castro and Che Guevara, just 90 miles off the coast of Florida. This is ripe with extraordinary potential for us. Soviet bombers and later rockets could loom within minutes of American soil."

Then we would see the world change, Kruglov thought. We could really intimidate the Americans or even launch Operation Preemptive Strike from there. They would have 10 minutes warning at best.

"The MGB is also far along in becoming operational with a facility deep in central Russia that will be a "Little America," where Russians and other friendlies who had spent time in America, would recreate an American town, where all the fine nuances of American life, language and customs could be learned by MGB agents to be assigned there. Some of the new "stars" of this little show will be the growing numbers of American soldiers now being captured in Korea but reported as missing in action. They will be joined by others that Soviet espionage could kidnap around the world and force them to be actors in this Potemkin Village. Maybe we should call it the Charm School." That led to broad smiles around the table.

The most time had been spent on Agent Traveler's photos of American missile warhead design, which had been quite helpful to the Russian aeronautical engineers who had replaced the executed Krivobok and his idiots.

"Traveler's photos make clear the physical design of the warhead that the Americans have now settled on." Andropov continued. "Their stress mathematics are very close to ours. Apparently an object returning from space at a speed of about 7.8 kilometers per second would experience a maximum temperature of 7800 kelvins with a peak heat flux at around an altitude of 60 kilometers. Both sides roughly agree on that.

It has now been decided that our effort will go forward on a dual track, the new one being the American design. However, the design improvement will only lower the bar for the still extremely difficult task of finding the right material to endure the enormous heat and stress of reentry. Given the new lockdown security at Corning Glass, it might not be possible for Agent Traveler to produce this, even though he is an insider, particularly since he does not even have access to that part of the building."

Kruglov's main fear then surfaced in his mind – that the politburo might at some point order him to get Oryol out. That was his nightmare. It would also mean the loss of this powerful and totally unsuspected agent in the United States, a man who could have an on-going enormous impact in helping the motherland. But the new bosses might conclude there was no other way to stay ahead of the Americans in this new area of rocketry weaponry and reach preemptive strike capability by 1957. Even though Stalin was gone, the priority of "Operation Preemptive Strike" remained the same. And the stakes were insane. Failure to get Oryol out could mean a firing squad for the MGB director.

One hour after the meeting ended Kruglov picked the phone up and asked his assistant to call in his two key aides, Andropov and Igor Tolstoy. Kruglov smiled as he thought how these two were the best examples he knew of the "new Soviet man." Andropov was 39 and Tolstoy was 36. Unlike Kruglov's generation, they had only really known life under communism. They had gone to and excelled in the new schools of the state, and had helped win the Great Patriotic War on the front lines. They also did not share the common character flaws of many of the old Bolsheviks, many of whom had survived and reached their positions of power through cunning, luck and, most important, correctly determining whom to align with and shower with sycophantic praise. Those who had guessed wrong were now worm food.

Kruglov had recently described his young star, Igor Tolstoy to Khrushchev. "He's the guy you would want to populate most of the male population of the U.S.S.R. if you could pick off a menu. Perfect combination of genetic material and practical history. A graduate of Moscow State University, number 2 in his class of 7,000. Won the school's Lenin Prize for ideological brilliance and loyalty to the party. His writings have even impressed the extremely conservative Suslov, our evolving leader of Marxist-Leninist thought, the so-called moral compass of Communism. Physically Tolstoy's a specimen, 6'1" and 195 pounds of chiseled steel with almost no body fat. Won the heavyweight wrestling championship at university competing with behemoths 50 pounds heavier. He actually considered competing in the 1952 Olympics in that sport at age 35, but I said no. In the war he had fought alongside Marshall Rokossovsky, beginning at Kursk in 1943, where his artillery unit took out over 40 Panzer tanks, and then fought with the brilliant Marshall all the way into Northern Germany.

"Sergei, I want to meet this Igor Tolstoy," Khrushchev had responded. "We will ask much of him in the coming years. I have big plans that we will bury these miserable Americans.

As Iuri and Igor entered Kruglov's office, he greeted both with the suggestion they remove their coats get informal and join him for a drink.

"I was very pleased with your presentations today, both in style and content. You both exhibited extraordinary professionalism and well though out conclusions. There was also a lot of good news today. Even this nose cone crap is showing some progress."

Andropov responded, "Thank you comrade general. We are proud to be an insignificant part in the agency's great initiatives."

"What do you think, Iuri, about this missile problem?" Kruglov asked Andropov. "How does this saga end?"

"That is a very difficult question to answer, sir. Our internal agent, Oryol, is our ultimate trump card, but can we afford to play it?" (Reportedly the

101

young genius played the Western bourgeoisie game called bridge). "That could be our eventual dilemma in my opinion. And the only way to really play that trump card might be to extricate him out of the United States. Our drops we are using now are always dangerous. To learn all he knows we may have to get him out. As you know, we desperately need the wealth of knowledge in his head, particularly details on the ceramic material conceived in Corning."

Son of a bitch, thought Kruglov, can he read my mind? This is what this guy could do – get to the core of the most complex dilemma immediately. How can he be so good?

"Igor, what do you think?"

"Sir, I am ready to help oversee and implement any effort my superiors deem appropriate" responded Tolstoy. Igor was so by the book.

Kruglov asked again, "Come on, what do you really think?"

Igor hesitated and then offered, "It seems clear to me we cannot tolerate anything but Soviet superiority in offensive missile weaponry. We really would have no options if we sensed that our great Soviet engineers could not solve this nose cone problem. I would probably favor a forcible seizure of the American material data, even if it meant further action on American soil.

I don't know about trying to get him out and losing the services of our most important agent operating in the United States. He has the potential to be the greatest spymaster of our time, making the Meredith and Chambers productions look like child's play."

And what neither man knows, Kruglov thought, is the actual identity of Oryol nor any of his particulars. So in a sense these are unfair questions I am asking. Besides me only Khrushchev, Malenkov and Bulganin in the Kremlin and Strelnikov and agent Sonya in New York know anything about Oryol.

Kruglov then said, "I appreciate your input and as usual find them well considered and thoughtful, particularly given your limited knowledge of all the facts. This is a dilemma I hope we never have to face, and we find that our brilliant scientists can solve these problems without our having to take action. But allow me to ask another frank and related question, all in the spirit of good and devoted communists.

We seem to excel in many areas of science at the most complex and large scale end of the spectrum. The Americans are clearly not as strong as we are in these areas. We are on the way to having a big lead in rocket size and range. But they seem to be very effective at what our physicists describe as 'small science', the fussy little details that transform a grand idea into a workable package. Like this nose cone material of theirs. How do they accomplish this?"

Andropov measured his response very carefully. The wrong answer could wind up in his personnel file. A really wrong answer could lead him to the basement.

Tolstoy didn't move and just stared down at his feet. His mind even drifted to his secret life as America's greatest spy, placed right here in the MGB. His mind roamed to the climactic "grand inquisitor" scene in Dostoyevsky's classic Brothers Karamazov, where one brother intellectually spars with the devil with his soul on the line.

Finally Andropov spoke. "Comrade General, this is a very fair question you have posed and let me make some comments in the spirit that you have asked it. I think a good analogy can be drawn from the Great Patriotic War. No force was larger or more effective then the mighty Red Army. No one had better tanks than our T-34's, including the German panzers or the American Shermans. We turned them out in massive volumes, and by war's end the best Panzers were fleeing in fear from the most advanced T-34's. Our tactical rocket barrages, where we unleashed thousands of these small missiles within minutes, were devastating to the Wehrmact. Our biggest problems, beginning around the fall of 1943, were always a collection of a thousand small blowups – supply inadequacies of ammunition, petrol, truck shortages. General Patton moved his whole U.S. Third Army 90 miles in just three days, under enemy fire, to relieve Bastogne. To my knowledge we never moved that fast anywhere. And how did the Americans do this?"

Kruglov thought, the young genius is on a roll, let's see where he goes with this. He just smiled back to encourage him.

"I have studied western economies to some degree in the Soviet War College. The Americans had what I would call the small minutiae of war and the supply system to efficiently deliver it – trucks of all types, jeeps, petrol tankers, hand held radios. They had the glue that holds a massive army together efficiently but in a more distributed management sense. And where does all this little stuff come from? Unlike us, they do not have a command economy with total direction from the center. The terrible aspects of this we all know – Karl Marx explained it very clearly 75 years ago. The capitalist pigs who control all of this brutally exploit the proletariat and eventually, of course, it will all blow up, and we will bury them. But at this moment in history, before we reach perfect communism, where it will be from each according to his ability, to each according to his need, we don't have the proliferation of products that are available to Americans, if they have money.

The rich justify all this with their almost religious belief in the notion of the invisible hand of free enterprise, espoused by an 18th century philosopher called Adam Smith. (Kruglov thought, what is this guy – an encyclopedia?). So while millions are homeless, destitute, starving and lacking medical care, American businesses do have a critical mass to sell goods to the exploiters, who have money for such things as cars, trucks for fun, trucks and tractors for their privately owned farms, etc, and then they produce the supply chain elements to support this- fueling tankers, tire plants, spare parts, etc. So when a war starts, the militarists just step in, turn a switch and order a transition to military and away from civilian production. So the Chrysler jeep and Ford truck plants, that already were making these things, one day just stop painting them for civilian use and the next day paint them olive green, put that damn white star on the side and magic – they suddenly have all this support stuff to service a huge army at war. Of course, we would have destroyed the fascists anyway, but for anyone who was in the field, including both of you officers, you know that those American jeeps and trucks under the lend-lease program came in very handy."

Interesting, Kruglov thought, almost no one has the balls to even mention lend-lease now. It has disappeared into the vortex of communist non-history. I admire Andropov for his courage and find myself agreeing to some degree with his insights.

Kruglov responded, "You're right, Iuri. I remember a number of times in the war where the Germans lay shattered and vulnerable before our army group. But then the attempted entrapment failed for the want of the basic materials of war that could not be expeditiously and rapidly moved forward. It was infuriating."

Andropov continued, "The most dramatic example was the massive battle at Kursk in the Ukraine in the summer of 1943. German Army Group Centre had attempted a summer counterattack there. July 12th was the climactic day. Thousands of tanks were firing point blank at each other, and over one million men on each side were blasting away with artillery, rockets, and small arms, while over one thousand planes dueled in the air. It was a battle like none the world had ever seen or probably will ever see again. By nightfall, the German offensive had stalled and a massive Russian counter offensive immediately commenced and soon overwhelmed them. Zhukov switched from defense to offense in a matter of a few hours. It had never been done with an army of this scale.

German losses ultimately reached over 500,000 men, more than 3,000 planes and almost 1,500 tanks. Our losses were greater. This was the same German Army Groupe Center under General Erich von Manstein that had smashed through Russia in 1941 and reached the outskirts of Moscow in the six month blitzkrieg. After the battle at Kursk, the Germans were never able to go on the offensive again. They were kaput but didn't know it yet.

So now travel back in your mind to late July, 1943 and the brilliant Marshall Rokossovsky is attempting this encirclement of what was left of Army Groupe centre. If successful, the war probably would have been shortened by a year. Rokossovsky missed by perhaps three days. He had plenty of men, tanks and artillery, had the German's reeling, but basically was running out of petrol, shells, ammo and the other basics of war. He was screaming for them, but our logistics had broken down. For want of maybe one thousand trucks and the fuel to run them, the Germans escaped. This never happened with the Americans."

Kruglov interjected, "Colonel, you will hear no disagreement from me. These are painful memories. As you know I was attached to Rokossovsky's army as his political commissar at that time. On July 13th German Army Group Centre lay before us at Kursk ready for the kill, severely damaged and beating a halting retreat, but we had temporarily run out of much of the supplies of war to advance. We could not close the pincers. It would have eclipsed in importance the surrender at Stalingrad of Von Paulus' Sixth Army. I wanted to shoot our general in charge of supply. Rokossovsky said, no. Marshall Zhukov or Konev would have said yes. I was enraged."

"But now let's fast forward to our current dilemma," Andropov continued. "How do my comments have relevance to our nose cone problem? As you know the Corning works primarily manufacture consumer products and apparently are far along in creating a glass ceramic material that can be used in kitchen pots and pans for the rich, a material that can withstand both freezing cold and intense heat without cracking. Agent Traveler reports that the consumer version will be called Corning Ware. But this same basic technology, with some key variations and sophisticated modifications, can support a far more robust application apparently – an effective shield for missile reentry. It seems shocking but from a kitchen pot you can come up with a vital "small science" technology produced from a highly fragmented distribution system that makes possible the creation of an intercontinental missile force that could dominate the world."

Mind boggling, thought Kruglov. He looked at Tolstoy. "Where are you on this, Igor?"

"Comrade General, I do not share my colleague's understanding of these western exploitive systems and, therefore, it is hard to comment. I do passionately share our deeply held truth that it will eventually explode under the power and moral legitimacy of communism." Just the kind of conventional ideological response Kruglov would have expected from this man whom he regarded as a devoted Marxist-Leninist, a good and faithful, but not overly imaginative, servant to the state. And, by the way, the last man anyone in the building would ever suspect as the American's leading spy in the Soviet Union, particularly his boss, General Kruglov.

"Well, whatever lucky process brought our enemies to this discovery, let us hope that our people can soon match it. Otherwise we are moving toward a very difficult decision," Kruglov concluded, looking down, lost in thought. No one spoke for about 10 seconds. Then Andropov and Tolstoy sensed that this social hour was over, donned their tunics, came to attention, saluted smartly, did an about face and departed.

Kruglov meditated. I think there is much truth to what the young Andropov said. It kind of explains how the Americans get things done. These aggravatingly small and seemingly unrelated connections that this non-command economy of theirs seems to make. Once we set ourselves to the task of building the world's best tank or largest dam, no one is our equal. Once we tell our scientists to build the biggest and fastest rocket, they do it. We kick ass. Of course, they will be shot if they fail. But for the key nose cone material that makes this fantastic new weaponry possible to come from a kitchen pot? Unbelievable! It's us against a kitchen pot."

He poured himself another glass of vodka. He passed out at his desk thirty minutes later.

CHAPTER 17

BASEBALL

Sunday, July 5, 1953 3:00 p.m.
The Polo Grounds, 155th street, New York City

Dominic and three of this top agents were driving to their annual baseball outing. They went over the Dickinson-Corning case in the quietude of the car.

"What do you think boss, are the Russians or their surrogates gonna make a try to get into the Corning plant?" Keenan asked.

"I don't know, but I would bet they'll take a shot at it,' Dom responded. "That's what the CIA guys expect."

"But security there is as tight as we can make it. How could they get in there?"

"I don't worry about their getting in. I worry that they're already in. Look at this agent Sonya. She pulls off the Dickinson theft and murder, clean as a whistle. We have no leads on who she is. All we know is she can pick up guys in a bar and she's probably an expert in disguise, a damn chameleon. The big prize, Oryol, is a complete mystery. Both have to be working under deep and convincing cover, sleeper agents that are fully integrated into American life, perhaps even native born Americans. Maybe there is another one just like that sitting in the Corning plant or offices right now. That's my nightmare. Sleeper agents are always my nightmare."

After a moment of reflection Dom asked, "What do you guys think about going over everyone in that complex again? Checking them all out beginning with their birth certificate? Assholes to elbows."

After a pause agent Morgan responded, "A lot of work but probably worthwhile. The stakes are huge. We'll get some help and start the background rechecks tomorrow."

Dom responded, "I'm afraid we've gotta do it. If later it's found out that we missed someone, you can kiss all our careers goodbye. Not to mention the disaster for the country."

Dominic and his top three agents sat in a lower field box just in front of section 17. They were two rows off the field and just behind the owner's family box in the Polo Grounds, the ancient but venerable home of the New York baseball Giants. There was no better location in this horse-track shaped oval, unique in all of baseball. It was distinguished by its 485 foot center field fence, over which no one to this date had ever hit a home run.

The Giants were having a somewhat disappointing year, entering today's game with 35 wins and 36 losses. The Dodgers were the favorite to win the National League pennant, as they had the previous year. Their starting pitchers, Erskine , Black, Row and Newcombe each had a shot at winning over 20 games , and Clem Labine was strong in his new role as a late reliever. Add to that the position players – Duke Snider, Jackie Robinson, Gil Hodges, Roy Campanella and Captain Pee Wee Reece, and they seemed an unbeatable constellation of stars – the Brooklyn boys of summer.

But the Giants were taking them to the woodshed today, behind a barrage of hitting and the efforts of Sal (the barber) Maglie on the mound, who had already decked two batters with high and tight offerings right under the chin. At the moment Bobby Thompson, the pennant winning hero of 1951, was at the plate with the bases loaded.

Thompson went to a 3 and 2 count, got the fast ball he wanted and absolutely blasted a shot to left field. His belt left the park for his second home run of the day and scored three Giants ahead of him, a grand slam. The capacity crowd went crazy, including the four FBI guys in section 17.

At the end of the inning, Dom went out to get hot dogs and beer for the gang. As he approached the refreshment stand, he saw Catherine Bowers of the *Today* show in line, seemingly chatting with a tall, dark haired and attractive man.

"Hey Catherine, how you doin'?" Dom greeted her. "How'd you like that Bobby Thompson – two home runs already and we're only in the fifth inning. Hope you're a Giants fan. And who's your friend here?"

She turned. "Oh I don't know him; we're just in line together. I was asking about the best dogs to buy. I don't come to very many games."

"Well I can tell you – get the Italian Sausage with the onions. Just like my grandma use to make – not!" He smiled broadly.

She laughed but something about her struck Dom as odd, like she was caught with her hand in the cookie jar. Then she started to mumble nonstop until the guy she had been talking to in front of her got his food and took off. Strange – maybe the guy actually is her friend, Dom thought. A boyfriend? Maybe a married guy she's embarrassed about? Or maybe she's hot for me and doesn't want to turn me off?

After a few more quips they parted. Dom pretended to head back to his seats, but then he stopped behind a column and regained sight of Catherine. His eyes followed her to her seat. There was no one in the seat to her right and on her left were two kids she obviously wasn't with. Odd, he thought, for such an attractive women to go alone to a ball game.

He returned to their box. "Here's the health food guys."

Occasionally for the next inning he looked back, seeing Catherine alone. Then he checked at the top of the seventh inning, and she was gone. At this point the Giants had a big lead, so maybe she just got bored. Or maybe she didn't want to run into him again.

The final score was Giants 20, Dodgers 6, the biggest thrashing of their cross town rivals in years. Pitcher Maglie's all time record against the Brooklyn Bums went to 16 wins versus only 6 losses; he clearly had their number. Home runs were hit by Thompson (2), Captain Al Dark, and Daryl Spencer against Dodger pitchers Labine, Black and Branca.

The four G-men left the park in good spirits but knew they had committed to a hellish week of detective drudgery beginning tomorrow.

CHAPTER 18

DEATH IN CORNING

Five days later, Friday, July 10, 2:00 p.m.
New York City

"They's been checking everything and everyone around here all week. Even been harassing me, a janitor. But my army record and time at the munitions depot doin' this kind of work kept me in good shape. No problem with me. But I don't know about Mr. Traveler. He don't look so good, boss."

The janitor, a great grandson of a former slave, was one of those rarities. An American who understood to his core how unfair America was and how Communism would change all that.

"Ok," she replied into the phone. "Keep me up but be careful. And I'm coming out to see him." Sonya put the phone down, filled a bag and left for the train to Corning.

She had called and set up the meeting in a park at midnight in Elmira heights, outside of town. As always, she got there before whoever she was meeting and observed for an hour, making sure no one was there who shouldn't be. At that hour of the night in a deserted park you could pick up noise 1000 yards away. And of course, she was in disguise – this time as a man.

She heard him approaching and watched him sit at the appointed bench. When she was convinced no one had followed him, she emerged out of some brush.

"So I understand the FBI has picked up the pace in the Corning complex, checking everyone out? You OK, Traveler?" From his eyes she already knew he wasn't.

"I don't know. They are going deep into my file, asking questions about how I got information out of wartime Germany. They know it didn't come to them or the Brits. They also know I had nothing to do with the French resistance. I'm afraid this is driving their thinking one way – east. They also asked about my sexual persuasion. I said I was too busy at work to have a woman in my life. Miserable nosey cops.

Then just this afternoon I was told that some Bureau chief from New York is coming out to see me tomorrow. I'm meeting him at the main gate tomorrow at 9 a.m."

"What's his name?"

"Some Italian name, I think it's Dominic Benvenuto."

Sonya's eyebrows rose slightly into an almost imperceptible arch. After some silence, she said, "Be very careful. Don't tell him a thing." And then she just got up, said no more and glided back into the brush.

She considered her options for the next two hours. Then she reached a decision and started to get ready.

The next morning no one noticed the young male golfer carrying his bag of clubs at 6 a.m. After all it was a Saturday, and it was expected to hit over 90 degrees later in the day, so it was entirely logical that someone was off to the public course early. What was unusual was the quick turn the golfer took, disappearing behind a string of two story apartments, all with fire escapes that went to the roof.

And, of course, it being a Saturday, things were very quiet at the Corning plant just 300 meters away.

Accompanied by three other FBI agents, Dominic exited the government sedan at the front entrance of the Corning Glass complex. Mannesman was already there, smoking a cigarette. Dominic went up to him, introduced himself and shook hands.

"Mr. Mannesman, we appreciate your making yourself available to us on a Saturday. We would like to talk with you a bit about your work and some of your history. Could you take us in to where you work and give us a little physical tour of where you spend your day, followed by a little discussion about security in the plant?

"Yes sir, I could do that." There was a slight tremor in his voice that Dominic picked up on immediately. "But you may have trouble getting by security on a Saturday. They're pretty tough on weekends."

"That won't be a problem sir," Dominic responded, gently prodding Mannesmann toward the door. They entered the facility at 9:02 a.m.

On the roof agent Sonya had shed the golfing attire and the male persona. She was now an overweight spinster type with a cane by her side. The empty golf bag and the male clothing were abandoned on the floor of the roof she crouched on. There was also a circle of highly flammable liquid around the perimeter of the roof with a five minute delay fuse ready to be lighted.

She thought about the weapon. This is my favorite for a hit like this – a bolt action, five-round modified Mosin Nagrant 91/30, high-powered 7.62 x 54 caliber weapon. The early models I trained on in 1943 were the basic soviet sniper rifle used in World War II, particularly popular in the Stalingrad siege. But this little gem's been upgraded. Most important is this new sight – the PU 3.5 scope. At this range today I'll see his nose hairs. Supported with mounts at both the barrel and the stock, it'll be rock solid when I shoot. And the rounds are all "dum-dum" ammo. They'll enter the body with a small hole. Rip up everything and blast the mangled pieces out of a huge hole as they exit.

There's probably no one in the world more proficient with the Mosul Nagrant sniper modified rifle than me. Particularly executing a head shot at a mere 300 meters – piece of cake.

She smiled internally, sitting down with her eyes glued on the plant entrance.

———————————

The group exited the plant sooner than expected. Things had not gone well. Mannesman was handcuffed and visibly upset. Dominic had his hand on Mannesmann's elbow, guiding him quickly along the 100 feet to the waiting car. He was euphoric that he had his first huge break in the case.

———————————

On the rooftop 300 meters away the eyes instantly moved to the sight, the finger to the trigger, the rifle anchored solidly in its supports.

———————————

Dominic tried to relax the suspect. "You're going to feel better after you get it all out. And your complete cooperation will result in an easy deal for you. You didn't kill anyone. We just need information about those who did."

It hit suddenly out of nowhere. The explosion of Mannesmann's head was surgically precise – atomized in less than a second. Chunks of flesh, bone and blood cascaded onto Dominic's face and clothing. Like a smashed pumpkin. The force of the blow threw Mannesmann's now headless body backward.

Dominic reacted instinctively, his infantry training returning. If it was a bolt action rifle he had a chance – might have 2 seconds to race before the next shot. "Cover" he screamed, as he sprinted toward a protruding wall of the plant. It was later determined that the second shot, clearly intended for him, had missed by six inches, only because of his speed. The other three agents found cover. There were no more shots, but the agents were slow to move. Armed with only handguns versus a skilled sniper with a high powered rifle in an unknown location was hopeless.

Agent Morgan was the first to stir on Dominic's yelled order. "Jesse, get to the car and call in. I think the shooter wants me, not you guys." Morgan ran to the car and got on the radio phone. In six minutes backup arrived. In 17 minutes a ten block square area was cordoned off. Nobody could say exactly where the shots had come from, so they had to search the whole area.

In the chaos no one noticed the elderly old woman limping in the opposite direction away from the shooting. She was outside the cordoned area by the time the checkpoints were set up. Also, the authorities were now being distracted by a fire that had strangely broken out atop a two story apartment building three football fields away from the scene of the crime.

The FBI's exhaustive investigation report on this disaster would ultimately conclude the following:

"Nothing of use was found in the fire ravaged building, the source of the shots. There was a badly charred gun barrel recovered of undeterminable origin. The arson had been very expertly planned. This is perhaps the most professional assassination of a heavily guarded suspect and successful assailant escape in the history of the Bureau."

For years later it would be studied by new agents in the FBI training academy. Perfect execution of a precision kill.

The next day Dominic was debriefed in his New York office by agent Bugliari and others.

"We found the second slug meant for you, Dom. Clearly from a Russian Mosin rifle. What the hell are they doing, going right after one of us on U.S. soil? This has never happened here. And putting a key sleeper agent, Mannesman, right in the middle of a facility crawling with security, where he would be at such high risk. The need for this intelligence must be of unimaginable importance to them."

He showed Dominic the slug. Dom just stared at the small lead mass intently. He thought, this could have left my kids fatherless, Laurie a widow. This shot might as well have been aimed at my beautiful four year old daughter. His anger grew to a crescendo of white-heat hatred.

"It had to be her. This Sonya. Besides wanting the nose cone secrets, she also personally wants me out of the picture…so now this is personal. I will hunt her down ruthlessly – every waking moment I will devote to getting THIS BITCH," yelling the last words.

No one in the room said a thing. They recognized a man possessed, a man now on a vitriolic crusade. Kill or be killed.

113

He went into his office, closed the door and locked it. Then they heard it – the vicious kicking at his walls, smashing big chunks of plaster with each violent blow. Finally they knocked his door down. It took four men to restrain him. His face was grotesquely distorted with rabid hatred, spittle flowing from his mouth, convulsions raking his body. A doctor had to give him a strong injected tranquilizer to sedate him to the point where he could be moved to a clinic.

In the subsequent weeks the anger subsided – replaced by a deep melancholy.

As the Bureau's shrink told him, "Dominic, this is a bout with depression. Anger turned inward is really what most depressions are about. We see this with agents and their families who have had grievous losses of some sort or came close to it, but feel helpless to avenge the transgression or find the perpetrators. This will pass, but you will be in pain for a while. Don't do something foolish."

Some pain indeed, Dom thought over the coming month. I feel impotent in the face of the most important mission of my life. Some nights I drink myself to sleep, a sleep racked by a recurring nightmare. The dream involves my family. They're injured, hit by gunshots. Surrounded by shooters. And me, impotent. I fire my gun and it doesn't work. New rounds are hitting my family. They're screaming for help through their pain. Then I awaken in a river of sweat.

Each day is a little worse than the last. And that haunting dream comes almost every night.

CHAPTER 19

A DIVERSION IN NEW YORK

Friday August 7
New York City

For the first time in his life Dominic sensed his future was not under his control. Out of nowhere something could destroy him. And maybe his family. There were profoundly evil forces orbiting around him and his beloved country. And I can't do anything about it.

I've lost two key players; one of theirs, Mannesman, and one of ours, Dickinson. I came within six inches of getting shredded myself. It's that woman, that master of a thousand looks. And she's an American – under deep cover, fully submerged in mainstream American society. She certainly has a real job somewhere, maybe even a family. A lifetime of perfect cover. The hardest kind of agent to find.

This one's a real pro. Assassinates a shaky cohort about to talk. From 300 yards out, just as he's about to spill his guts. A decapitating, high explosive bullet right between his eyes, spattering the brain over a ten foot circle. Then ignites the fires she set up on the roof with a delayed fuse. When it lights five minutes after the hit, it follows a trail of flammable liquid. In ten minutes the roof collapses on the apartment below. All evidence destroyed. And she's long gone – vanished.

She hits you first, coming out of nowhere. And now I know she wants me. And I'm failing on the most important case in the Bureau's history of counter intelligence.

He'd had a few drinks, as he did most nights now. He had one more glass straight up from the bottle and finally collapsed. And like most recent nights, he woke up after only three to five hours sleep compared to the usual eight he had enjoyed all his life.

He was about to head out the door the next morning a little after seven o'clock, when he noticed the TV story on the *Today* show his wife was watching. It was about the Port of New York, very upbeat and favorable about the effectiveness of its management and in particular, the union. This sounds like a paid commercial, and it's running coast to coast. Here are hard hats with

American flag decals on their helmets. One guy had sewn on his work jacket, *Better Dead than Red.*

Then he froze in amazement – here was a scene with Don Bonsignore, the union boss who ran the port – a man he had never met but had that unspoken arrangement with – keep the reds out of the port, inform us on anything strange you see, and we'll stay out of your playground – within reason.

Bonsignore was smiling and talking with the men. The reporter was mouthing some gibberish about strong union leadership and no strikes.

Jesus, the mob as media stars. At the end the camera focused on the host, Dave Garroway, who thanked Catherine Bowers for leading the story team.

Damn, she pulled it off. That woman is good. I wish she was working for me. Maybe I should talk to her about a connection.

Dom left the office at six, the usual funk setting in, that suffocating grayness that would descend at the end of each day after the diversions of the office routine wound down. It was with him now every day. It came earlier and lasted longer. Everyone noticed it was getting worse. His secretary Prudence tried everything to cheer him up, but nothing worked.

Tonight, he thought as he exited, I have to be up, seem effective, in charge of things. Director Hoover is giving a public speech at the Commodore Hotel. It's about the "Red Menace" and all the Bureau is doing to fight it here at home. And right now on the loose is some master spy who is going after the big prize - a secret that could bury America. And he's or she's controlled so effectively by some female super spy who shows up out of nowhere, always with a different look.

And I can't find either of them. I'm in charge of the investigation with 300 guys and getting nowhere. On center stage – presenting Bureau Chief Dominic Benvenuto – king of failure.

With that he drove a football forearm shiver into an ad poster in the subway station, breaking off a piece of it. His fellow waiting passengers moved away from him. Another nutcase in the big city.

He mingled in the pre speech cocktail party for Hoover with the VIPs from the press. Hoover's running on like a strutting peacock, he thought. Everything's under control. A damn windbag, chief lawman protecting the republic, its God-fearing citizens and the American way of life. In fact things are going to hell. Dom got his second drink in only twelve minutes.

Then he saw her across the room, chatting up Hoover like she was an old friend. Catherine Bowers – the *Today* show hotshot. Hoover, smiling at her, obviously pleased with their discussion and others around them taking copious notes. This chick is something else. And look at that black cocktail dress – like it's painted on her trim, tight body and glorious ass. If she had tits it would have made the package perfect, but damn she looks good.

When Hoover moved on to others, Dom went over to her. "How are you Miss Bowers? I didn't know you and the director were such good friends."

"Hello, mister formal bureau chief," she said with a coy smile. "Yeah, we dated in college." Dom actually laughed.

"So I see you got your story about the docks didn't you, miss star producer. How'd you pull that off?"

"Please," she leaned closer, "call me Catherine, Dominic." She smiled broadly at him. She had an absolute charm and graciousness about her, he thought. After ten minutes with her, laughing, hearing her stories including how she had dumped her last boyfriend, Dominic felt himself lightening up. I actually feel good, he thought. The cloud's there, but it's lifted some. A little sun peeking through. Best I've felt since Corning.

She suggested, "Let's head in a little early, so we can get close to J. Edgar. We look real intent, hanging on his every word. Clear adulation." Then she leaned over and whispered, "The old fart." With that, Dominic broke out into his first big laugh in months.

The rubbery chicken dinner was followed by exactly what one would expect - a series of empty platitudes about the brilliant agency and its dedicated G-men. Bunch of crap, Dom thought. Then he realized that he never would have thought like this before Corning. Hoover's nonsense was returning him to his new reality – failure, fear and…depression.

Hoover got a standing ovation during which Catherine leaned over and whispered in Dom's ear, "Let's get out of here. What a windbag. I need a drink."

They settled in the hotel bar. Both ordered martinis. Dom asked, "So how did you get Don Bonsignore to open the port to you and even got him to appear in a background cameo?"

"Oh, I thought you didn't know him." She smiled right into his eyes. Caught, Dom's face just stayed locked. No reaction. That's what the training called for after a verbal screw-up.

Then she added, "Simple, I just asked those boys. I told them how much I respected them and how different they were from the radicals on the West Coast, the creeps holding up stuff for our boys fighting in Korea. Let us tell your story, I said. They bought it.

By the way mister FBI big shot, you know Bonsignore, right? How can you be in charge of security here and not be all over the port? Plus, all you paisans, guys whose names end in vowels, always do favors for each other, right?"

Again he just stared back, not changing his smile one tick.

"Ok, don't comment." Then, after a moment, "Hey, do you ever loosen up? Have a little fun?"

"Not much of late."

She looked at him intensely. He is hot, she thought. First time I saw him he turned me on and now I'm really attracted to him.

Dom noticed the flicker in her eyes and a gentle rotation of her tongue around her upper lip. Involuntary?

"Could I have another martini, please," she asked the waiter.

"I'll have another also," Dom added.

"So, tell me about your love life," she asked.

"I'm married."

"I know – I see the ring." She smiled at him again, hesitated and then just blurted out with it. "You know…I'm very attracted to you. I have been since I visited you in your office that day."

She reached out with her hand and he took it. The new round of drinks arrived. Dominic was quickly feeling better with every exchange. The best he had felt in over a month. The cloud was suddenly nowhere to be seen – or felt.

Then he got up, a little woozy and said, "Wait here a minute. I'll be right back." As he stood up she noticed the hint of a developing fullness below.

He grabbed a pay phone and called home. Kids were screaming in the background. "The director wants to have a meeting with a couple of us. Gonna stay in town over night." This was not unusual. His work involved strange hours.

Catherine watched him as he returned. She knew from his face what would happen next. He didn't say a word – just held out his hand to help her get up. Then she hooked her arm in his, and he guided her to the elevator. They entered the room he had just checked into after the phone call.

Clothes started to fly everywhere. He picked her up and threw her down on the bed, removing the last of her lacey undergarments. He ran his hands all

118

over her thin, hard body, feeling the heat and hearing her breathing turn to moans. His tongue navigated all over her. Then he lost himself inside her, the first of five penetrations that night. A long and salubrious seven hours of torrid heat that left both of them wet and finally satiated.

They left separately early in the morning - Catherine first so she could reach the studio by 5:30 a.m.

She literally glided into work, riding on the cloud of euphoria from the most intense lovemaking she had ever experienced. He overslept for the first time in months. And he woke up feeling remarkably better. He knew it wouldn't last, but at least it was an uptick. His first good morning since Corning. And he knew he had to see her again.

Two days later, Sunday, August 9, 6:00 p.m.
West Side Manhattan

Agent Sonya, as always, arrived early at Books and Biscuits, a thriving bookstore catering to intellectuals that also served good comfort food –meat loaf, chicken pot pie and so on. She wanted the time to make sure there were no uninvited guests, nobody idly reading a newspaper or sitting in a parked car outside. She hated surprises. Particularly important at moments such as now, when she felt comfortable enough to be in her real appearance, waiting for Francois Duborg.

Not that she had much to fear. No one knew DuBorg for much of anything other than the aspiring actor and part time translator that he was. Very few knew that he also had a girlfriend Prudence, who just happened to work for FBI Bureau Chief Dominic Benvenuto.

And no one except Sonya and station chief Strelnikov knew that DuBorg worked for them.

DuBorg didn't know much about Sonya, including her code name. She was just his contact in their important work. That's all he needed to know. And if he ever shared that with anyone, he knew he was a dead man.

When discovered at the Sorbonne in Paris, he was a typical harmless French communist. He came to Marxism intellectually and idealistically, as did most of the members of France's third largest postwar political party. He was recruited gently by his economics professor and then introduced to a charming young woman who talked to him about working for the party in America – a chance to make a real contribution. He was fluent in English and could really help there. Frankly he was tired of his fellow university communists, endlessly debating the merits of Marx versus Engels, Lenin versus Stalin. Never advancing the cause one iota. So he jumped at the chance to go to New York.

As he entered the store tonight, he was greeted enthusiastically by Susan Haskins, the warm and gracious owner. "Right over here in the corner Francois. Your usual table. Your girlfriend is waiting for you." They greeted each other warmly, very convincingly a couple for anyone watching. Immediately, they held hands as lovers do and smiled broadly. They ordered an inexpensive white wine and hot turkey platters.

But the conversation was anything but that of lovers. Behind the hand holding and rapturous looks a very calculating discussion took place.

"You've got to move in with her, Francois. You've been helpful as her lover, but we need to know everything her boss is up to from now on. You're my connection to him, thru this imbecile Prudence. I need the skillful pillow talk. You know, honey, how come you're working so hard, why is your boss so demanding of you, why'd you work late, what's going on? That kind of banter. You've got to be around her all the time."

"But I've given you a lot of information already without moving in. Like the funk her boss seems to be in, moody, easily angered. Somehow related to this big case he is working on."

"I know, and that's helpful. But I want more. Hell, what are you complaining about. You'll get laid more."

Francois chuckled. She rarely made such a joke or said anything that wasn't clearly fashioned to advance her interests. In fact often she scared the hell out of him.

"Look," she added, "Let me be blunt. We're working on something that really can advance the cause. And her boss is the one trying to stop us. He's in charge of our little matter. We need to know what he's doing, how he's thinking, his movements, his key investigators on the case, everything about him, every moment."

Francois realized the discussion was over. He better move in. Hell it wouldn't be that bad. He'd kind of grown to like Prudy anyhow. Anything for the cause. And a nice piece of ass, even though her big tits did droop badly.

Whatever I need to do to keep this terrifying warrior off my case. I don't want to ever see her dark side.

CHAPTER 20

BREAKFAST WITH KHRUSHCHEV

September 11th, 1953 8:00 a.m.
Politburo Board Room, The Kremlin, Moscow

The new Premier Khrushchev had called the meeting and invited only Director Kruglov to attend. It was held in the politburo inner sanctum, the center of all world communism. From this ornate room a small group of men ruled an empire that spanned from East Berlin to Vladivostok, from the warm Georgia republic to well above the Arctic Circle. Arguably you could include newly communist China in this galaxy. The men in this room could imprison thousands at will, destabilize governments, even decide to go to war with the West. They also could rise up against any of their own, including their own Premier.

As Kruglov cautiously entered the room, Khrushchev gave him his usual bear hug. "Relax, Sergei, you're not going to Siberia, at least not yet," he laughed. "Come and sit with me and let me serve you those shirred eggs you love with spicy kielbasa and rich coffee from our friends in Egypt and fresh oranges from the Crimea." As they seated he said, "give me a ten minute update on all the turmoil your wonderful boys are stirring up around the world to the benefit of the Rodina (motherland)."

Kruglov thought how his old ally was exuding more confidence every time he saw him. With Stalin and Beria gone and Malenkov gently fading as co-leader, Khrushchev had consolidated power and was now clearly running the country. Kruglov remained the head of the entire MGB – MVD security apparatus. He was very pleased that he had sided with Khrushchev on all these matters and was now here in this place that reeked of power. Indeed, if he had not sided with Khrushchev, he probably wouldn't be anywhere, other than providing a thousand maggots with their breakfast.

Instead he sat down to a breakfast that 99.9% of the citizens of the Soviet Union would never even see, no less eat. It was a formidable repast matching the quality of the best in the West. Kruglov began his ten minute oral tour of the MGB's current intrigues around the world.

"Nikita, let me start with the good news, the Vietnamese. French Indochina, or at least the northern half, will soon fall. Ho Chi Minh has made tremendous strides. We have key operatives at his side now and also have army commandos on the ground that are helping him tactically. We are shipping in all the weapons and munitions he needs. At this very moment, there are three of Ho's generals here in Moscow at army command headquarters drawing up a plan to attack one of the major French fortifications, Dien Ben Phu, in force, which could lead to a French capitulation. Their days are numbered."

He continued his whirlwind tour. "Wonderful, Sergei. There is a lot of French real estate around the world that we want. Those cowards will retreat to their homeland and bury themselves in their fancy food and wine, the weaklings." Kruglov was always taken aback by the crudeness of his new boss, the son of real peasants.

"In the Middle East Nasser in Egypt is really in our camp now. This means we will soon raise some hell with the British and French at the Suez Canal. Of course, this means we have Syria also, and because of the American ties to Israel we are making new Arab friends in Jordan, particularly among the Palestinians in the camps. We are also working with the Algerian rebels and quietly slipping into Morocco, Tunisia and Libya. The other remaining parts of French Africa are also teetering. Also the Belgian Congo."

At this point Khrushchev smiled broadly, patted Kruglov on the back and then yelled for the waiter to bring the boss a second helping of sausage. The man could eat – and drink, Kruglov thought.

"Regarding other areas of Asia" Kruglov resumed, "good things are happening in Malaysia and Indonesia. Korea, of course, you know all about, following the truce in July.

Now China is a more complicated case. Chairman Mao, having held off the Americans in Korea, now seems to be forgetting his old friends, as you know. I think you may have to visit the chairman in China soon, making him look good in public but behind close doors remind him he is a distant number two in our communist universe."

"That ungrateful bastard – he's the biggest pain in my ass now," Khrushchev responded. "Since he got in power he doesn't want to hear from us. You know he wants to go right after Taiwan, even though the Americans have a defense pact with them. He's crazy.

I do have to admit the man has balls. I told him about our problems with the Catholics in Eastern Europe. He looked me right in the eye and asked how many guns the Pope had! Can you imagine that," he roared. "The guy has the moral compass of one of our gulag camp commandants. He looks at the whole world through the barrel of a gun." He stopped smiling. "We have to watch him closely."

"Turning to the Americas," Kruglov resumed, "Cuba is the new wildcard. As you know the young Marxist, Fidel Castro, was captured after his incredibly stupid attack on July 26 on an army base. But we have men on the inside of his prison and some well paid political allies, who are making sure he is protected. He will one day win release, and then we will make sure he has what he needs. At 26 years of age he has a remarkable hold on the people, even among many of the middle class, who hate the corrupt president, Fulgencio Battista. Castro holds great promise, but who knows, he may fade like a lot of these zealots," he conceded.

"He sounds too flamboyant and soft to be a successful Marxist to me," Khrushchev opined. "These crazy Hispanics make a lot of noise and then, like that piss-face Franco in Spain, turn neutral and do business with everyone. Forget Castro, he will never amount to anything. Tell me about the United States."

"Eisenhower has now been in power for nine months, and I can't say our people have figured him out yet. Obviously, he was a tough and smart supreme commander and, as you know, Zhukov and he got quite close after the war.

"We have previously briefed you on that demagogue and idiot, Senator Joseph McCarthy. We are manipulating input to him that will hurt many non-Communists. Eventually he will be unmasked, but maybe anti-Communism will have been given a bad name. Then our real agents can go to work.

Most serious is the Oryol matter. We continue to be frustrated with our attempts to obtain the nose cone material secrets. The Corning plant is now closed down tight as a nun. Contact with Oryol has become extremely complex. Our last message used agent Sonya but with two dead drop agents on both sides of her handoff."

"Thanks Sergei. I must say you are the consummate professional I always thought you to be. I put my utmost trust and faith in you in that little walk we had in the Kremlin gardens last year, and as a result Beria, shot six months after Stalin's death, the psychopath and the womanizer, now sleep with the dead."

"Thank you boss," he said sincerely, with a slight but warm smile. "Now let me get to the main event, what to do about the Oryol matter. The glass ceramic nose cone material remains secret and unreachable, secured in the Corning Works. Our agent Traveler broke under questioning, and agent Sonya very skillfully assassinated him herself, an absolutely brilliant hit.

She also got a shot off at this FBI counter intelligence chief, Dominic Benvenuto, one of their young hotshots who is in charge of both security for the rocketry commission and the investigation of our murder of the Princeton professor. The shot missed, unfortunately.

Our only presence in Corning now is a long dormant sleeper agent we got into the plant as a janitor, but he can't get near the classified area. His report is that there is no hope for his getting anything of value. So we are back to square one. Has there been any progress with our own people in their efforts to produce an effective nose cone shield?"

Khrushchev swallowed the last of his second portion of eggs and quietly looked down at his hands. After a 10 second pause he said in a low, measured tone, "They are getting nowhere. A bunch of ineffective academic assholes. This American high-tech glass solution is nothing we know anything about. Our scientists and metallurgists are confident they will eventually prove up some kind of metal, probably an aluminum-titanium solution, but it is years off.

The good news is we believe we are well ahead of them in everything else – size of rockets, payload capacity, guidance. Sergei, we will have the delivery system for a nuclear payload well before they will, a window where we could utterly intimidate or destroy them, but we won't have the material to protect the payload. Operation Preemptive Strike is missing the one last piece of the puzzle," he concluded staring down at his food in uncharacteristic despair and quietude.

Kruglov responded, "One thing slowing the Americans is the idiotic separation of their rocketry efforts with the army building one kind of rocket called the Jupiter, and the navy building something to be called the Vanguard, each competing with each other and dividing their effort." Recalling Andropov's little lecture on western economics, Kruglov added, "This is consistent with one of the great follies of the capitalist system with its widely distributed control – the notion of competition producing better results than our centrally planned, command economy. What nonsense and so wasteful."

Khrushchev nodded, but was quietly impressed with this comment, wondering when his friend had become such a student of Western economics.

"Our intelligence also indicates, Nikita, that their army Jupiter rocket will only be an intermediate range missile, maybe 1500 miles at most. That means it would have to be based somewhere like Turkey and would not be intercontinental. The Navy effort, the Vanguard, reportedly only will have an initial capacity payload under 50 pounds, not enough to deliver a nuclear weapon. So we have some time before the Americans will be operational – around 1961 or 1962 as a best guess."

"Sergei, we are losing a golden opportunity here to have perhaps a five year window of strategic arms superiority, to have our way, to implement or threaten Operation Preemptive Strike and reshape the world to our vision. This is one thing Stalin got right. And the answer to our problem is sitting right there in that upstate New York lab with some capitalist pigs that make pots and pans. We need to get it…now."

After a short silence he looked Kruglov in the eye and said, "Sergei, agent Sonya, your people and Strelnikov's thugs in New York need to develop a plan to get Oryol out with all the data he can carry, on everything about their program. Most important is as full a description as possible of this magic nosecone. I know he hasn't worked on the shield itself, but he will know enough to get our guys pointed toward the goal cage. He will be put in charge of our exotic materials work and get our rockets flying years before the Americans. Then we will squeeze their balls...or crush them.

I want a plan presented to me in detail in one month. Use your lead agent, Sonya. She has never failed us. Didn't she sneak George Koval, our star nuclear spy, out in 1949?"

"Yes she did, Nikita. He was in Moscow before the Americans even knew he was gone or who he really was. Sonya masterfully slipped him out dressed as a woman, through Mexico. And thanks to him, we caught up to the Americans with the H-bomb. The FBI still has not gone public about him and the incalculable damage he did. And probably never will–too embarrassing to them. Imagine, one of our guys who understood nuclear physics working in American weapons plants, watching how they made the bombs and then coming out to tell us all about it. Let's do it again with Oryol."

Khrushchev spoke quietly, almost reverentially. "Sonya can do anything, including getting Oryol out." He leaned over putting his face right in Kruglovs. "Get him out soon, Sergei. With him we get the whole picture that will make Preemptive Strike possible. I want the plan to extricate him on my desk in 30 days. Tee paneemyish? *(Do you understand?)*"

Khrushchev got up and left. Kruglov was white. While he agreed with the boss's logic, Kruglov's most feared nightmare would now begin – getting Oryol out. And he was a dead man if he failed and lost this incalculably valuable asset, a man hopefully destined to become the most effective spy in the history of soviet espionage.

General Kruglov returned to his Dzerzhinsky square offices and requested an immediate meeting with Colonel Iuri Andropov and Lieutenant Colonel Igor Tolstoy.

"Khrushchev wants a plan to remove Oryol presented to him in 30 days," he reported. Andropov and Tolstoy froze, expressionless. "I will not trust anyone else to be involved in this other than the two of you. You will design the specifics of the operation, subject to the following constraints ordered by me.

First, agent Sonya will lead the operation, as she did in getting our lead nuclear thief George Koval out. Second, there must be very creative secondary and tertiary back up plans. Third, you still will not gain access to or learn the identity of agent Sonya or her charge, Oryol. Station Chief Strelnikov in New York will be your intermediary.

Finally, as part of your plan I want specifics to deal with or impair the effectiveness of this FBI bureau chief Dominic Benvenuto, the agent in charge of all matters pertaining to the rocketry group and its members. He is the man we will be matched against in the coming extraction. Us against this tough American war hero and star athlete. And he's already upset with us – reports are

125

that he did not take kindly to Sonya's little ad lib attempt to put a high explosive round in his head."

Andropov smiled. "No sense of sportsmanship."

At the mention of his old friend from 1945 in Berlin and later Moscow, Igor froze. The man who had set up my recruitment by the CIA! Impossible – I pictured him working for some bank, drinking martinis at lunch, playing with his kids. This is an impossible development – me working for him now, and he doesn't have a clue.

"Sir, could you repeat the name of the American in charge again?

"Benvenuto, Dominic Benvenuto. New York Counter Intelligence chief for the FBI. Ever hear of him Igor?"

Summoning all his remaining strength to desperately hold the poker face, he responded, "No sir, never have."

"Well you have now. The bastard is good. He figured out the details of the Dickinson murder real fast. He's looking for an insider on the U.S. Rocketry commission and also a female agent, our little bird Sonya, who is a master of disguise. He also found Traveler within days once he got personally involved. Part of your plan should be to neutralize him in some way. And his guard is up after the assassination attempt. Probably not a direct take out – something more sophisticated and easier to accomplish that will distract him. I leave that to you guys."

Igor went back to his office and closed the door. He took deep breaths to avoid passing out, as he had done when wrestling in university and found himself painfully pressed to the mat and in danger of being pinned. He fought the vertigo.

This news was incomprehensible. Dominic Benvenuto – the contact who had changed his life, who had set in motion his new mission, and had recruited him is now calling the signals for the American game plan. He's now joined with me hunting these anti-Christ, these killers that I work against secretly every day. I have to reach him, them – some way, some how.

And soon.

CHAPTER 21

THE BOYS OF HUNTSVILLE

September 18, 1953
Redstone Army Arsenal, Huntsville, Alabama

Reviewing the historical accomplishment of the day, Professor Werner Van Braun recalled how far he had come since his move from Fort Bliss, Texas to the new rocket center that was finished in Huntsville in 1950.

At first he was violently opposed to the location. Why a state of the art rocket and space center should be built in rural Alabama totally escaped Werner. Unlike the German military leadership, which could order a transfer of a civilian under pain of death, American scientists had to be coddled – incentivized was their word – to pick up and move their families. How the hell could you get world class aeronautical engineers, metallurgists, propulsion experts and applied physicists to leave urban centers to come down to the rural and land locked deep South? What's wrong with these crazy Americans?

Then someone explained to him the power of the very senior Alabama congressional delegation and Senator John J. Sparkman in particular, whom he met in 1948 just before the new consolidated center for American missilery and rocketry was to receive final approval.

The senator had been extremely cordial and complimentary in the first half hour of their discussions on the front porch of the senator's lovely home. Then the Southern charm slipped and his game face took over.

"Now Werner," he said, "being such an intelligent scientist and gentleman, I know you can appreciate how hard I have worked to make this complex a reality for my constituents and how wonderfully supportive all Alabamians are of this landmark project. And I know, suh, how grateful you are to your adopted country for all that we have done for you and your associates from Germany. In fact, I personally have discouraged any attempts, shall we say, to over analyze the history of your group. I have successfully sold the notion that in fact your brilliant coterie of scientists were first and foremost apolitical rocketeers, who just happened to find themselves in the middle of Adolf Hitler's abomination. Now I must say that anything short of enthusiastic support from you in the upcoming hearings and review of the proposed Huntsville Rocketry Center would be very poorly received by me and my close colleagues. Do you understand my meaning, suh?"

In his excellent English, Braun replied, "Well, senator, nothing personal, but I must admit I am troubled by how I convince a Cal Tech jet propulsion expert to pick up and move his family from sunny Pasadena to rural Alabama. I'm looking for the logic here."

Sparkman leaned over and looked him squarely in the eyes. For a moment he just stared, saying nothing.

Then he responded, "Von Braun, let me be very clear here. I was a leader in the House of Representatives, and given my position in this state, everyone knows I will be a senator for a long time, eventually a committee chairman. One word from me and you and your boys could find yourself explaining to a senate sub committee exactly what you did from 1933 to 1945. I don't think you want to do that. There are some misguided souls who already think you should be tried for war crimes. Am I making myself clear, suh?" At this point he was six inches from Von Braun's face.

Von Braun saw his whole life pass in front of him. Everything – the early general euphoria with the new order, personal meetings with the Fuhrer, the celebratory dinner after the first successful trial test launch of the V-1. Who knew what this ambitious politician in his face could do to him. America was still a grand mystery to Van Braun in many respects. He looked down and froze for 20 seconds, before he could rally his words.

He said softly, apologetically, "Senator, I now see your wisdom very clearly. Huntsville it is. You will have no problems with me, sir."

Sparkman broke into a smile and the Southern charmer returned. "Excellent Werner. Then I believe our pleasant little discussion is over, and we should join Mrs. Sparkman in the dining room. I greatly look forward to our working together for many years."

There followed a lavish dinner of Southern specialty foods and the finest Kentucky bourbon, served by a liveried black man with great dignity and poise. The senator and Mrs. Sparkman could not have been more gracious. They parted company with hugs and fond farewells. As he left, Von Braun felt as though he had just dodged a very large caliber bullet. He realized he still didn't have a clue as to how America really worked. What a strange country, but…it clearly beat working for the Soviet Union.

Now five years later Huntsville was thriving and Von Braun had proven to be both a scientific visionary and a very charismatic leader. In fact, the best and the brightest did come to Alabama to join or spend extended visits with the "Boys of Huntsville." That's where the action and the money was, and you had to be there if you were a "rocket man." The people of Alabama and Huntsville couldn't have been more supportive or proud that they were, at this moment in time, ground zero, the epicenter of this extremely important new technology.

Von Braun had bought a house in Huntsville on McClung Street, and his wife Maria had given birth to two wonderful daughters. The family grew to actually like the town. And the Sparkman and Von Braun families got along famously for many years, even sharing some holidays together. Werner later became somewhat of a media hero.

He had learned the nuances of American politics and decision making very well by September, 1953. He got it – no more political naïveté and Prussian absolutism. He even now shared that peculiar American optimism - onward and upward!

Success in Huntsville

The events of this day, September 14, 1953, had been a strong reinforcement of that positive American spirit. Begun promptly at 8AM in a reinforced test bunker, the first simulated reentry test of the Corning nose cone material had passed with flying colors. A shield shaped in the configuration suggested by the work of the American engineers Allen and Eggers and covered by the composite ceramic had remained comfortably below the maximum heat specification to protect either a nuclear warhead or a human passenger. Everyone was elated. The news quickly was distributed through secure channels to all members of the rocketry task force and their FBI protectors, led by Dominic Benvenuto, who was in Huntsville to oversee security for this gathering.

At a celebratory dinner that night in a private room in the officer's club, Von Braun was joined by Harsanyi, the MIT scientist and vice chair of the committee, Dr. Stookey of Corning Glass, creator of the nose cone material, six other standing members of the rocketry task force and one non member - Dominic, who now insisted on being at any gathering of even a small segment of this group. He monitored every scientist's every word and looked deep into their eyes as they spoke; somewhere there was a devastating traitor among their midst or inside his staff.

"Let today's extraordinary result stand as a hallmark of American ingenuity and scientific progress," Von Braun offered in the first toast. "This marks the successful culmination of a cooperative process that involved distinguished members of the civilian, military and academic communities to solve a vexing problem that could have served as a definitive roadblock to our joint efforts to put man in space and develop the ultimate weapon, the intercontinental ballistic missile. It could not have been achieved without the contributions of every man here." He then went on to specifically recognize everyone at the table.

Harsanyi, the vice chair, spoke next in subdued but emotional tones. "Eight years ago I crawled out of hiding in Budapest as the Red Army approached the city. My wife had just been shipped off to Auschwitz, where she was executed in the last days of the nightmare. I walked to Vienna and stayed there in hiding until the joint forces reached the city. I sought out the Americans, who after I explained my technical background, took me under their wings. They then put me in touch with Werner, who was aware of my pre war work with Edward Teller, the famous Hungarian physicist, and together we all wound up in

Texas.

My beloved and newly adopted country has made all my personal and academic dreams come true and those of my two sons, now in distinguished universities. Accomplishments like today allow me to feel that at least I am giving back in some small way."

With that he sat down with tears beginning to form in his eyes. The group spontaneously applauded him. He was clearly a new but very enthusiastic American, what this country was all about.

Dominic was taking all this in. He noted that Professor Sharon Hallman, the disgruntled Stanford metallurgist, still was not ready to accept fully that the ceramic nose cone was the answer. Kept talking about brushed aluminum and titanium. Professional abstinence…or something else? Something about her bothered him.

The next member to offer a toast, Don Stookey of Corning, returned the focus of praise back to Harsanyi, whose role he described as, "Essentially that of a general contractor, who took the genius of the technological subcontractors and assembled it all in a model that would work or...fly so to speak." (The pun drew smiles). "True, you did not invent the glass composite or the physical shield to deflect heat. But you put it all together. You stepped into the role of our fallen colleague, Dr. Dickinson. Let us all consider our success today as a tribute to that great man."

There followed a reverential moment of silence, after which the group began their celebration with much camaraderie and good cheer, aided by quality food and liberal rounds of libations. The party broke up very late by Officers Club standards at 11 p.m.

It had been a truly significant day. While no one had said it, it was inconceivable that the Russians had found this same ingenious solution to the payload shield. But Dominic knew that Moscow was at least aware of its existence, and was trying. And somebody in this group or someone working for them was passing stuff on. He could think of little else, as he sought sleep.

It now falls on my shoulders, he thought, to keep this, perhaps the most important secret in the free world, out of the wrong hands. And to find the twin evils, Oryol and Sonya, before those bastards can even make an attempt at it.

Two days later Oryol contemplated his options given the reported results at Huntsville. He quickly came to some conclusions. His first step would be to activate the secret Macy's New York communication system that only he and agent Sonya knew even existed. Then he needed to start moving – fast.

CHAPTER 22

AUTUMN IN NEW YORK

September, 21, 1953
New York City

Sonya's system of learning that Oryol wanted to contact her was ingenious. A sleeper agent who worked in Macy's 34th street store on the fifth floor, toy department, was the key conduit, yet she knew nothing other than some simple rules. She also knew if she made a mistake or approached the authorities, her family would be destroyed.

Her name was Maria DeVincenzo, and her family's recent history was a sad one. In October, 1941 she had arrived in New Jersey from Italy to spend a year with her brother and found herself stranded in America when the U.S. entered the conflict in December, 1941. She was separated from her husband and two sons, both of whom were then conscripted into Mussolini's army. The older son was to die at Palermo in 1944. The younger son, Lucca, was in the Italian Eighth Army, which found itself in the fall of 1942 fighting its way across southern Russia with the German Sixth Army and its Hungarian and Romanian allies, until they finally reached a city called Stalingrad on the Volga River.

The Italians were assigned the job of protecting the German's northwest flank, which was overwhelmed by the Russian counterattack and encirclement in January, 1943. Over 90% of the Italians were killed or captured. The family assumed Lucca was gone, when no word of him surfaced.

Then in January, 1946 Maria and her husband, who had joined her in New Jersey, got a phone call from a man that informed them that their son was alive and well but living in the Ukraine on a farm, which in fact was the truth. They were overjoyed and marveled that their son was one of the handful of Italians that had fought in Russia and survived. In the second call they would find out why.

The Russians had a policy of getting a brief history on all the new POW's soon after capture. Of particular interest were those who had relatives living in America and England. The old NKVD security apparatus took a very long term view of things, and director Beria himself was convinced that eventually there would be a showdown between Russia and their current American and British allies. Prisoners with families in the U.S. and U.K. had potential hostage value. Lucca was one of these.

The second caller, a woman, asked for a meeting and gave a private washroom in Grand Central Station as the locus. Such facilities were available to travelers who had just completed overnight or longer trips and wanted the opportunity to shower and change in private. Maria met her at the appointed hour and found herself talking to an apparently older, very tall and quite overweight woman, who spoke perfect American English with a southern accent that could have been affected. She did not give a name.

"Mrs. DeVincenzo, I bring ya'll greetings from your son, who is alive and well as you already know. I have here a letter to ya from him written only two weeks ago and a photo showing him and his new Russian wife, who is expectin' as ya can see."

Maria looked at the photo. It was him! She dropped to her knees and thanked God, crossing herself amidst the flow of tears. She read the letter and continued to cry uncontrollably. Clearly these were words that only her son could write, and it also was clearly his handwriting. He spoke of family histories and asked which of the relatives had survived, and then offered favorite family stories, nicknames and jokes. Then to prove the date, he asked how Truman was doing and how Japan was recovering from the August atomic blasts. It was the work of the almighty, answering her prayers.

The contact let her enjoy her emotions in peace. Finally she spoke up. "So Mrs. DeVincenzo I share ya'll's joy. But I must tell ya that we do have some small favors to ask of ya. Very simple.

Every Thursday ya will receive a call at Macy's at precisely 10:35 a.m. from a person in an untraceable public phone booth who will enquire whether or not ya have in stock a Lionel electric train model, the Hudson steam engine, in S-gauge. As ya'll know, they only make trains in O-gauge. If ya have had a call that week from a 'Victor' asking the same question, ya will respond to this second caller that, yup in fact, that model has just come in. Otherwise the answer is no. Very simple, right?

That is all ya need to know. In return yah son will live very comfortably in Russia, and one day ya will be reunited with him and his family. Also ya will receive letters from him regularly at yah home address in a plain envelope, return address Brooklyn, that will have no fingerprints on it or any other troublin' evidence. We don't make mistakes, ya see?

Now I must tell ya that if ya inform anyone other than your husband of our arrangement, we will know about it and your son and his family will perish immediately. Ya and yah husband will eventually share the same fate. Am I bein' clear?"

Maria was distraught at the prospects of cooperation with what must be some very evil people. But she thought, whatever this simple signal meant, it couldn't be that harmful. Also, if I don't do it, someone else in the same predicament probably would, and they will kill my only surviving child, who seems quite happy now and with a beautiful new wife and family!

132

So she agreed, and the disguised Sonya quickly departed (moving very quickly for an old lady). A long term mutual dependency was born. Mr. and Mrs. DeVincenzo got letters forwarded from Lucca every two months with proof of authenticity and the quoting of recent world events, all clearly in his handwriting. Also, he now had two fine looking young boys.

Oryol or a middleman would call Macy's on the rare occasions when he urgently needed to contact Sonya, giving his name as Victor and asking the bogus question. She would respond affirmatively to the follow up caller (an agent calling on behalf of Sonya). No face contact was ever made, and no trail could be followed. Even if the Americans found Mrs. DeVincenzo somehow, the trail would stop there. If she was ever turned by the FBI and gave a false response, it would be harmless and would be immediately discovered. Then Lucca and his family would be executed and photos of the mutilated bodies would be unmercifully sent to the New Jersey home.

The system had worked fine now for four years. There had only been three such calls from Victor, and she had done her job. Today there had been a fourth call, and on Thursday September 25 the woman caller got the affirmative response. "Yes, we have just received the Lionel Hudson model in S gauge."

Sonya now knew that Oryol wanted contact.

This contact occurred in the middle of the planning of Sonya, Strelnikov and others on the final details of a plan to extricate Oryol. This had followed an encoded message from Moscow in the diplomatic pouch that "the highest authority" had authorized, indeed ordered, that Oryol be removed from the U.S. and brought to Moscow Center. A plan needed to be in place by early November.

Through a double "dead drop" sequence Sonya received Oryol's urgent news that the Americans had achieved a breakthrough and proven the effectiveness of the ceramic composite nose cone. Strelnikov immediately passed this on to Moscow, who responded that this only affirmed the decision to get Oryol out. Strelnikov called a meeting set for October 6. Planning began in earnest.

October 5, 6, 1953
Soviet Consulate 136 East 67th Street New York City

The consulate was chosen as the site for the final planning session largely by default. There was really no way to get General Strelnikov out to an external location without his being recognized. The FBI, CIA and NYPD all had his photo, physical description, etc. in great detail. Also Bodkin and some of the other muscle men who would be involved were based at the consulate. This meant that Sonya and two other key agents would have to separately enter the consulate through a surreptitious entrance from the basement of the adjacent building. In heavy disguise. They did so at different times on the day of October 5th.

The planning meeting started at 8 a.m. sharp on the next day. Strelnikov spoke first befitting his rank as a major general (two-star) in the MGB and the station chief for the MGB in New York.

After a short welcome to the group, he began, "Moscow Center has concluded at the highest level that the extraction of Agent Oryol is necessary as soon as possible. It is his working, hands-on kind of knowledge that requires his physical presence. It is not something that can be written up in a memorandum or stolen and then smuggled out in the diplomatic pouch. He knows how to make it happen. I will not go into any greater detail. In the U.S. only Sonya and I know his true identity.

Needless to say this is a bitch of a job we just got landed in our laps. Oryol is a big shot here, well protected and we believe, under surveillance at least some of the time. What we have going in our favor is that Oryol is not under any suspicion. We are also convinced of the commitment to us. This is no double agent who will turn and get our ass in deep borsht. Now let me turn this over to your new boss, agent Sonya here, who is in charge of the entire operation."

"Thank you, comrade general," she began. Today she was a middle aged gray lady, with an advancing stomach, some badly decaying teeth and wearing reflective sunglasses. No need to allow the others to know her true identity.

"It is my privilege to have been chosen to both plan and run this whole operation. Agent Oryol is apparently a man who can accelerate history and advance the achievement of our goals by decades. This is my most important assignment in my ten years as an agent. I have never failed…and I won't now.

Let me begin this briefing by saying you are never to mention any of this to anyone not now in this room. No exceptions. I will personally see to your execution if you do."

She paused and made eye contact with everyone in the room, including Strelnikov. The general had seen all kinds of killers since 1912, but this one was the most cunning, efficient and ruthless he had ever worked with…or against. No one like her. And there's no doubt in my mind this killer would do me in a minute if I screwed up. A brilliant assassin and serpent always ready to strike – and a native born American. Tougher and more brutal than any Russian he had ever met.

Her point made, Sonya resumed. She spent over three hours describing in exquisite detail every minute aspect of the operation. It bordered on specious exactitude, but such was the surgical detail that permeated all of Sonya's planning.

She seemed to have considered every possible threat to the plan and had the antidote for it. It was chilling, Strelnikov thought. This woman will go to any length–terror, murder, guile and kidnapping without the slightest concern. All that mattered was mission accomplished.

When everyone had signed off, Strelnikov spoke. "Now this proposal will be submitted to the Center for approval. It follows the broad guidelines that have been demanded by our superiors. Then we will await their conclusions."

Sonya did her pestiferous stare again, looking deep into the eyes of each, seeking out that fleeting sign of hesitance, doubt or cowardice. And silently transmitting to each the promise of swift vengeance if they failed in their part.

She concluded, "In the meantime you all should be scouting, practicing the details and rehearsing your different roles. Rehearse until it's second nature; you could do it sleepwalking. If you later make a mistake, it will be your last. Either the Americans will kill you, or I will."

Sonya and the outsiders departed the next day through the same covert access. The always super cautious Sonya had changed her appearance to a bearded man almost six feet tall.

Same Day
F.B.I. Headquarters, Downtown, New York

Dom was making progress with his depression. He attributed it to two things – throwing himself again into his work and counting the moments before his weekly shack up with Catherine Bowers.

I feel the guilt, he thought, but the sex with her just seems to get better and better. I'm doing things with her body that I'd thought about, but have never done. And she's doing that kinky stuff with me, too.

Frankly, it's helping me get back to normal and rejoin the living. The shroud is lifting. I'm gonna win. I'll find Oryol and Sonya, dead or alive. They're not getting out on my watch.

His new found optimism was interrupted by agent Bugliari entering his office. "Dom, we got a hit on the new camera. We caught three people at different times using the basement passageway to the consulate today. Something's up."

One of Dominic's FBI surveillance agents assigned to consulate surveillance had made an interesting observation two weeks ago. A suspected communist sympathizer had been followed to the building adjacent to the consulate. He entered it and immediately ducked into a service door. The agent followed him, as he descended to the basement, walked to another door, tapped on it and disappeared as the door shut behind him. He emerged that night, somewhat intoxicated, out the front entrance of the consulate and was caught by the FBI cameras across the street verifying the basement access to the consulate. Clearly the mistake of an amateur.

Dominic immediately ordered a tiny concealed camera installed in the basement corridor, the work done at night by a stealth team that gained access through a heating duct. The camera was attached to a concealed wire, which ran back to the duct, across the street and wound up in the FBI surveillance apartment facing the front of the consulate, where everything was recorded on film.

For 12 days no one used the corridor. Dominic had forgotten about it and the other agents were beginning to write the thing off. But late today he had been informed that the corridor had been accessed by three people within a four hour period – an old woman, a man in a plumber's outfit and a long haired, scruffy male. They had not exited as of 5 p.m. The film was being developed and would be brought downtown shortly.

At 8:15 p.m. agent Buffum entered the office with the film and immediately wove it into the 16 millimeter projector. Dominic and half his office entered the audio visual room. Buffum gave the presentation.

"What you are about to see are three individuals who entered the corridor today – the woman at 12:18 p.m., the plumber at 1:56 p.m. and the long hair at 4:07 p.m. Here you see the woman, who we think is much younger than she appears. Note how fast she walks and the two canes under her arms – an obvious masquerade that she has now dropped thinking she is safely in the secret entrance. Then the plumber enters and removes his sunglasses, thinking he also is safe, then the long hair who removes his obviously unnecessary thick glasses. The hair is clearly a wig. This creep looks familiar to us – we're running through the photo books now."

"Hold the film," Dominic shouted. "Run the long hair guy again. Ok, freeze it." He turned to agent Gogolak, the chronicler of all known Russian operatives and assembler of the photos. "Charlie, isn't that the heavy attached to the embassy in D.C., the guy we think was involved in the murder of the Hungarian dissident in Washington last May?"

"Looks like him to me, Chief," Gogolak replied.

Dominic said, "Something's up. Strelnikov may have called a meeting, and a lot of talent is converging – we need to know why. When they leave I want a discreet, rotating, three man tail on each of these creeps with backup, wherever they may go. Meanwhile, let's all hit the photo books and see if we can figure out the other two."

Nothing happened that night, but on the afternoon of the next day, three people exited at different times through the corridor and were caught by the TV camera. These images were recorded on the better quality Bell and Howell professional color cameras in the FBI apartment. The tails began their work, as the three exited.

Same day midtown, Manhattan

Sonya, now in the male configuration, did what she had done the two other times she had exited the consulate in the last seven years. She knew this was dangerous and only took the risk when she absolutely had to meet with Strelnikov personally. Since he was tailed by an army wherever he went, she had to go to him. It actually put her at much less risk, as long as she was heavily disguised. And she never repeated an outfit.

She walked to the nearby IRT Lexington Avenue subway stop and boarded a downtown local. She got off at 42nd Street and switched to an uptown express, waiting until the last second, as the doors were closing, to board the train. She watched carefully, but no one seemed to follow her. She got off in Harlem at 125th Street and went into a fried chicken place she knew and had a late lunch. She got a seat by the window and watched the street closely. She was very good at this and noted nothing suspicious. When she left she looked carefully both ways and remembered everyone on both sides of the street.

She then turned back toward the subway entrance and walked briskly along 125th Street. Ten seconds later she suddenly stopped, turned around immediately and caught him. A Puerto Rican male, who turned into an appliance store, but I got a good profile of him. He had definitely been on my uptown express in the next car. I also saw him on the stairs as I turned to mentally photograph everyone who was exiting onto 125th street with me. He's a pro, but I caught the bastard cold.

Sonya was calm and collected as always. She went to predetermined plan B, which involved boarding a southbound New Haven Railroad local train, as opposed to the subway. This would take her to Grand Central Station at 42nd Street. These trains stopped at the 125th Street railroad station to let commuters off, but no one got on at this hour to go from Harlem to midtown. She would easily spot any tail dumb enough to even try it.

Thirty minutes later the train arrived and only she got on. She went into the coach's filthy bathroom, removed the beard, donned a brunette wig from her tote bag, put on some make-up and glasses and exited fifteen minutes later as a tired woman commuter at Grand Central Station. When she submerged into the commuter rush, any possible tail who might have been called there would not recognize her. After two cab switches she was convinced that she was OK and returned to her apartment via the subway.

Although she could not figure out how they had latched onto her in the first place, she slept like a baby, fully confident that she had slipped her tails. Of course she immediately disposed of these disguises. Clothes and facial presentations to her were like one time code pads – throw them out after use.

137

The meeting in Dominic's office started at 7 a.m. "All right, all three details give me your report," he ordered. "You first, Miller."

Agent Bugliari spoke first. "We followed the operative who came in as an old lady but by process of elimination, dressed as the tall man as she exited. She/he entered the subway and first went downtown. Then she switched trains to an uptown express, probably trying to spot any tail. Agent Gonzales skillfully got on the train one car behind hers and got off as she did on 125th street. She went into a fried chicken joint, still dressed as a male. In an hour the subject came out and very cleverly reversed direction on the street, almost certainly spotting our man. He had to drop surveillance at that point. She then went to the very quiet New Haven Railroad 125th street station to await a southbound train and got on a largely empty New Haven Railroad train. We raced to Grand Central where it would terminate, but the train had beaten us. The backup we had called there saw no male of that description exit the train. She either jumped off somewhere or, more likely, changed her disguise again. Contact lost."

Dominic moaned. "That was Sonya, right under our noses. No doubt about it. I'll bet she just walked right off the train in a wholly different look. A real pro. Jesse, what about the long haired male?"

"We followed his car onto Lexington Ave, into the Lincoln Tunnel and then proceeded south to Washington, D.C. He took his wig off right in front of us. The vehicle made no pretense about belonging at the Soviet Embassy. They just drove right in, like giving us the finger. The suspect, an accredited "diplomat," got out, and, sure enough, he's the guy we suspect killed that Hungarian dissident.

"All right, forget that bastard. We can't touch him. And he's not a street soldier. Now what about the plumber?"

Agent Morgan was in charge of that detail. "This story has a happier ending, boss. Exiting in the same garb as he had entered, he took some evasive action but was successfully followed to an apartment on Flatbush Avenue in Brooklyn, not far from the Dodger's Ebbet's Field. We immediately set up shop right across the street."

Dominic concluded, "Good – this guy is the amateur. Probably reserve muscle they keep for big jobs like this. We'll follow him discreetly 24-7. He will lead us to the show, whenever and wherever it starts. Keep all over this sloppy creep."

That Night
East 9th Street, Manhattan, New York

"How did the move in go with Prudence yesterday?" Sonya asked Francois.

"Well in fact. You know she isn't a bad sort. In some ways I really am fond of her. She worships me, she cooks whatever I like, she is totally sexually submissive and, to the extent she can, she shows up at all my rehearsals and tells me how great I was. After the director has just reamed me out. I actually feel good with her."

"Fine. Has she brought up marriage? How did you respond?"

"I was excited although noncommittal. As you suggested, I told her that the demands of her job working for Benvenuto could affect our relationship. Over a bottle of Margaux I really pushed, and she now understands that the demands of her employment and our relationship are linked - the more intrusive her work, the more troubling it could be for our relationship. So I told her she needed to explain to me more of what she did, and what had kept her at work so much recently late at night and on weekends. I'm a jealous boyfriend. This got her talking for the first time about some rocketry case and the murder of some Princeton professor named Dickinson. Can you tell me anything about this?"

"No. Don't ever ask again and forget you ever heard those words. You understand? You just tell me what she said."

He nodded, but she kept staring at his eyes, as though his reply was insufficient. Finally, feeling the bile of fear rising, he said, "Absolutely not. I never heard of Dickinson and Princeton."

"Good," Sonya replied quietly.

Francois continued, though shaken up by the flash of fear. "Prudy also said that the tempo's picking up. Said there may be a new development. She's sorry about the late hours. She said she'd rather be here with me. That my body has it all over her typewriter."

Sonya smiled. She thought about her own experience with Francois' equipment. The guy does have some talents.

"Prudy added that this is why she's so well paid. She's expected to put in these hours when Benvenuto is on a big case. And this one is his biggest. Not wanting to push her too far, I smiled sweetly, said I understood, picked her up, carried her to the bedroom and made love exactly as she likes it. At the end Prudy told me how madly she was in love with me."

"You're getting good at this, you socialist gigolo," Sonya said with a grin. "Keep that approach – ask a little more each time, particularly when she feels guilty about her work. Then reward her. Perfect – you're building trust and a consistent reward pattern. Then if her information ever becomes critical, you can really be aggressive. For an intellectual communist from the French upper crust, you're doing well. It's being noticed."

Then without missing a beat, Sonia took her top off, looked at his groin and said, "Enough of hearing about this middle aged fatso. You got me going. Get your pants off – now. I need it, it's been too long."

He did know how to play her body. She approached it the same way one would satisfy the need to eat, sleep or any other bodily function. And her partner better never climax before she did. After that maybe he could have some gratification, but he better be fast.

She helped him remove his pants, pushed him down on the bed and then, mounted him. She came multiple times before she let him come once.

When they were done, Francois left to return to his new home with Prudence. Sonya watched him move down the street, graceful and sexy in a gray windbreaker, cutting through a light rain. The Sorbonne snob was coming along, she had to admit. Under her guidance learning the nuances of the work and combining it with his admittedly superb skills at playing a woman's body. And whenever she wanted selfish relief, he knew he had to comply on demand.

CHAPTER 23

WASHINGTON PREPARES

Next Day
November 7, 1953
Washington, DC

Dominic called Hoover's office and reported to the Director on the events of yesterday. He praised Dominic, alerted his other top counterintelligence people and then called the new director of the CIA, Allen Dulles, on a secure line between the two agencies. Dulles put it in the daily briefing for the president the next day, adding his comments that it was highly unusual and risky for covert agents to be gathered at the closely watched consulate. He added his own speculation that something significant was afoot and at a very high level.

Eisenhower called Hoover early the next morning. "J. Edgar, your people monitored some strange activity around the Soviet consulate in New York yesterday. What are your thoughts? "

"Mr. President, we're concerned. Agent Levin in Moscow has alerted us they are developing a plan to get Oryol out. We have put all the Northeast Coast offices of both the FBI and CIA on full code red."

"All right, I want to see both you and Allen tomorrow. My staff will arrange the time. And come prepared."

The Next Day
The White House, Washington, D.C.

The White House staff called Directors Dulles and Hoover mid-morning, informing them that the President would like to see them that afternoon at 2 p.m. Everyone knew Ike's emphasis on punctuality, which created a need to actually be 15 minutes early for any scheduled meeting with the former five-star General of the Army. The meeting commenced at 1:56 p.m.

Ike opened. "Before we get into the espionage issue, Allen give me a quick update on Iran."

There had been an American – British sponsored coup in Iran in the previous month of August. The CIA had replaced a popular, duly elected prime minister, Dr. Mohammed Mossadegh, with the restored Shah.

Dulles offered, "We did the right thing. We just can't tolerate these Islamic liberals that we can't control in such a strategically important area of the world, bordering the Soviet Union. With our help the Shah will bring Iran into the 20th century as a fully secularized state and relatively quickly, given their oil wealth. I would expect to see Iran as the clear leader of the Arab world and staunchly pro-American as well. We have done a great thing to stabilize the region and gain a real partner in containing communism there. This will be recognized by future generations as having changed the course of history in the Middle East."

Change which way? Ike had his doubts. I hope Dulles is right. But what the hell do we really know about the Middle East and Islam? We never had any real contact with them until FDR met Faisal in Saudi Arabia ten years ago. And since when do we throw out elected officials in favor of royalty?

Troubled by these ruminations he nevertheless turned to the key matter at hand. They reviewed the events of the last two days, with both Dulles and Hoover agreeing that something was in the planning stages. It was concluded that both domestic FBI agents and foreign assets would be used aggressively to attempt to develop the details.

Then Ike asked, "Can we contact our key man in Moscow, this agent Levin?"

"Sir, unfortunately he has to contact us," Dulles replied. "His last information, as you will recall, was that a plan was in the works to get Oryol out. This thing in New York is likely related to that - their guys here who will try to pull this off getting together. The curtain is about to rise on this operation. I expect they will use their best people and pull out all stops."

"J. Edgar, your man Benvenuto made the original connection at the end of the war with our agent Levin, didn't he? Does he know of Levin's current role?"

"No, Mr. President, it's an amazing coincidence of history," Dulles replied. "He knows a source exists, but his actual identity is only known by the three of us, my director of Ops, three others in the agency and Ambassador Kennan in Moscow. We have to keep it that way. It is very ironic that this Tolstoy, whom Benvenuto originally recruited in 1945, is now providing him with crucial help in the Oryol matter. Neither Tolstoy nor Benvenuto have a clue. It is one of the most remarkable twists in the long saga of state espionage."

Dulles left unspoken his regret that even Hoover had been told. I hope the pompous ass can still keep a secret, he thought.

"So what do you recommend we do going forward," Ike asked.

"Mr. President," Dulles added, "We have to be ready, fully mobilized. We know Oryol has transmitted valuable information already, and we must assume he will continue to do so. The meeting in the consulate is an ominous development. I think we should greatly increase our resources on this. I also suggest the FBI discreetly tail all members of the rocketry commission and the key staff people 24-7. We still have no idea who Oryol is. Nor this ruthless master spy, this Sonya, who is running Oryol and will probably be leading the attempt to get him out."

"What do you think, J. Edgar?" Ike asked.

"Given the risks I think those steps are highly appropriate," Hoover responded. He didn't like Dulles, and he knew the feeling was mutual. The FBI director particularly disliked anyone telling him how to run his bureau. But Dulles was right on this.

Unsolicited, Dulles then added, "We can't afford another George Koval, the master nuclear spy the Russians got out in 1948, whose treachery and escape we have never publicly disclosed. And there's reason to believe this same Sonya masterminded his escape out of the country."

Hoover steamed at this direct shot to his face, but kept quiet. The less said about the still undisclosed escape of Koval, the better. That had been an unmitigated disaster. Clearly it had accelerated the development of the Soviet bomb by years.

"All right, then implement this surveillance program J. Edgar, but do so discreetly. Call me with any developments." Then he looked both of them directly in the eyes and added, "And let me add something here. I want you to both cooperate with each other fully on this. No more of this turf infighting crap. In the nine months I've been president, it's become very clear to me that you two don't like each other and that both agencies don't like to work with each other. This nonsense has to stop...now."

Ike rose in disgust and left without any goodbyes.

CHAPTER 24

THE EAGLE'S FLIGHT PLAN

October 23, 1953
MGB Headquarters, Moscow

Lieutenant Colonel Igor Tolstoy and Colonel Iuri Andropov entered General Kruglov's office. They stood at rigid attention and reported smartly in the formal military manner, before being invited to take seats around Kruglov's desk. Today the boss was all business.

"Comrades," Kruglov began, "It's time for our decision on the Oryol escape plan. You've read New York station's recommendations. General Strelnikov and agent Sonya are waiting for our approval. And Khrushchev wants this done yesterday. I appreciate the hard work and long hours you've committed to this. I apologize that you have had to do this without knowing the identities of either Oryol or Sonya, but that could not be helped. I eagerly await your conclusions.

You know the impact this man can have. He has the secrets that can complete the puzzle, making operational an effective ICBM, our project Deathstar. We need that kitchen pot material from Corning Glass. YESTERDAY! Oryol has at least enough knowledge of it so he can direct our chemists how to recreate it here through experimentation and chemically integrate it into the structure of the nose cone. Then we'll have a clear nuclear superiority over the West by 1958 at the latest. The tide of power will have swung to us, and the West will tremble in fear and respect."

"Check, game, match, comrade general," Andropov concurred.

He and his god damn chess analogies, Kruglov thought.

"On the other hand, failure to get him out would be a disaster. We would have lost an absolutely committed and loyal agent of enormous value, an operative on the inside, fully trusted and totally unknown to the Americans. He is probably the second most important agent after Koval we have ever run in the United States. Comrades, what are your conclusions?"

There followed a long discussion led by Andropov on both the genius of Sonya's scheme and its potential pitfalls. Analytical, measured and balanced comments devoid of any political or obsequious pandering. Unlike many Soviet committee deliberations on major action plans, this group of professionals did not attempt to cover their ass. They spoke freely and thoughtfully in a healthy give and take. This was Kruglov's style. He had a reputation as a leader who would stand by his people in adversity. It also reflected a new tone at the top of the Soviet power structure following the death of the paranoid psychopath, Joseph Stalin.

Kruglov asked, "Has Sonya lined up enough guys on the docks to help her? Aren't most of those thugs just tools of their mob union bosses and the capitalist pigs who pay the Italians off?"

Andropov replied, "Yes, but Sonya has some new friends there, men in deep cover. Also she is bringing in six of our sleeper agents for extra muscle."

After two hours there was broad acceptance of the New York proposal, including its most nasty measures. But at the insistence of the skilled Andropov, a series of sequential back up plans that he had conceived were included in precise detail, in case the primary escape route failed.

Andropov would write the final response to the New York station, and the wheels would begin to turn. The date for the operation was set. For better or worse we're committed now, Kruglov thought. And Khrushchev has put my ass squarely on the line.

After the two subordinates had left, he got out the vodka bottle. He was doing that a lot lately.

Igor Tolstoy returned to his office. He shut the door and his mind raced. What action should he take? His options on getting precise information to Washington were very limited and all very high risk. Particularly if he were to attempt to outline the entire plan in writing with all its twists and back up alternatives.

However, he did have one much lower risk option. It had been set up by his CIA handler in the U.S. embassy. If the decision was a go to extract Oryol, Igor would visit a book store in the crowded GUM department store on Red Square precisely at 5 p.m. He would browse through a new printing of Lenin's 1902 call to action, *What Is to Be Done,* and then replace it incorrectly on the shelf below. It would be immediately noticed. The message would be radioed in code to Washington within hours, and the American mobilization could begin.

Igor couldn't know it, but a continent away his wartime friend and recruiter, Dominic Benvenuto, already had the intricate response finely planned, ready to implement. When the signal was received from Moscow, over 400 FBI field men would go into action. Every member of the Rocketry commission, the staff, the assistants and secretaries would be followed 24/7 and their phones tapped. Maybe even some of the FBI people, to cover the possibility of an inside traitor.

And most important – the amateur they had followed to Brooklyn and were now watching every minute of every day and night – would hopefully take them right into the guts of any attempt to get the Eagle out. And the capture or death of Sonya.

Several Days Later
East Ninth Street, Manhattan, New York

While she missed the extra sex, Sonya was otherwise happy that Francois had moved out, and in with Prudence, giving her peace and quiet to implement the plan. She also was deep in the process of notifying Oryol, as well as the "soldiers" who would provide the muscle and firepower if things went awry, and the other professional participants necessary if the more complex alternative plans had to be activated.

All this communication was seamlessly initiated risk free through Maria DeVincenzo at her post on the fifth floor of Macys. Maria did not know what to make of the sudden increase in activity but knew to keep her mouth shut.

It had started with a contact from a woman, seemingly different from the original woman and lacking a southern accent, who had asked to meet her in a ladies room in a crowded 42nd street movie theater. This one looked trashy, poor, like a street urchin. But she spoke in unaccented English with a steely hardness to her words that belied her appearance. Scared Maria to her core.

"Mrs. DeVincenzo, let me start by showing new pictures of your son and his beautiful family in the Ukraine. Also, a recent letter from him."

She read it and, as always, was moved to tears.

"Now I have some really good news for you. Your work for us is approaching its end, and you will soon see your son after you complete a few simple assignments. There will be a meaningful increase in queries about the Lionel Trains in S-gauge. You are to respond exactly the way you always have. Then you will be finished working for us, and no one will ever know about it.

Shortly thereafter, your son will be released to Italian authorities as a former POW and allowed to return to his native country. I assume he will then be free to visit the U.S., maybe join you here as a citizen. Who knows?" Then the bag lady just suddenly turned and left.

That night Maria and her husband celebrated joyously at their favorite restaurant, Teddy's, downtown on West Broadway, already planning where her son's family would live in America, even how they would decorate the children's room. They were ecstatic at the prospect of being reunited after 10 years of first assuming he was dead and then being separated by 6,000 miles. And Maria could sleep at night knowing she no longer was helping these frightening people, whoever they were.

Sonya sat at her kitchen table reviewing the entire operation in all its complexity. She liked working in the kitchen, a habit she had learned in her training in Russia. In small soviet style apartments the kitchen was always the center of energy.

The primary plan, known in complete detail only to Sonya, Strelnikov and the few in Moscow, was to sneak Oryol on a W.R. Grace and Company chartered freighter docked in midtown Manhattan, returning empty after making a sugar run from Cuba. She would accompany the super agent at all times and be in command at every step. In Havana he would be met by Russian MGB agents and some trusted locals tied to Castro's partner, Che Guevara. Then he would get on a diplomatic plane being flown in especially to rescue Oryol. After refueling in Lisbon, he would proceed directly to Moscow. The boarding of the ship in New York was really the only vulnerability and clearly the highest risk.

She thought – I'm ready, I'm set. All the pieces are in place. The plan is intricate and rehearsed. I will lead its every step. Within weeks Oryol will begin leading our rocket scientists to the completion of their glorious goal – a weapon that will bring to their knees this capitalist sewage all around me. Then America is finished. And by all rights I will be invited into the core of the ruling elite in Moscow.

November 5, 1953
Moscow

On November fifth the final approval to go forward with the Oryol extraction had been granted General Kruglov. The date set for commencement of the operation was unclear. It was left in the hands of Sonya. She had insisted on this, trusting no one to have that vital information, even the boys at MGB headquarters.

As instructed, Tolstoy visited the GUM department store complex that afternoon precisely at 5 p.m. He went to the bookstore, gazed at Lenin's "bible" and replaced it incorrectly in the wrong shelf. One hour and 14 minutes later the CIA chief in the Moscow embassy raced up to Ambassador Kennan's secure office.

"We just got the signal from Agent Levin, mister ambassador. The extraction of Oryol is a go, but we have no idea where, when or who."

"Send the message in Univac code to Washington immediately, using a one time pad," Kennan ordered without hesitation. "Demand notice of receipt."

The CIA man exited. George Kennan, widely recognized as the brilliant author of the cold war containment policy, closed his eyes. He thought, this is it, now it starts. It's all up to Hoover and his boys from here on out. If he fails, my grandchildren may well be speaking Russian as a second language. Or…may never even see the light of day.

For the first time in his life Kennan felt real terror shoot through to his very core.

CHAPTER 25

ORYOL DISAPPEARS

November 17, 1953, 6:00 p.m.
Northeastern United States

Oryol slowly locked his office door behind him. He did so knowing that no matter what happened, he would never see that office or lock that door again. He was crossing his own Rubicon, returning to his beloved Soviet Union to help in the crusade for the eventual total victory and implementation of Lenin's vision.

Communism was the true north of his moral compass. Far more so than the lessons of his youth as an altar boy in the Catholic Church. Of course, there were some excesses being taken, and Stalin had been an incredible brut. But how else could you prevail in a hostile world and win the fight to establish the fairest and most moral state man had yet conceived. What he would deliver would greatly advance the just cause of the Soviet Union and accelerate by decades the final victory of "true communism." He was defecting from his adopted country, carrying with him the data, miniaturized blueprints and general working knowledge that would permit the Soviet Union to begin testing and producing ICBM's with a nose cone envelope that worked. It would provide Russia with a clear nuclear superiority that would immediately change the world balance of power. In time he would be a revered hero, thought of by all enlightened people as a key figure contributing to the final victory of Communism.

He took one last look at the door of his MIT office with his name in bold letters – DR. PETER HARSANYI!

I have fooled everybody with my grateful refugee cover, super patriotic, new American spiel. Soon I will be liberated and get to work advancing the final victory of world communism.

It's not that I hate America. Far from it – as the vice chairman of the top secret American Rocketry Commission and a senior MIT professor, I admire much about this country, particularly the ingenuity and work ethic of its people. It was easy for me to put on that act at the recent celebratory dinner at the Redstone Arsenal Officers Club. America has its strong points, and I respect both the country and the people.

They are just misguided, glossing over the glaring inequalities in income, voting rights and the hideous racial discrimination that is so pervasive. Any thoughtful intellectual would conclude, as I have, that America will eventually implode in an internal revolution of the oppressed and disadvantaged. In the meantime it is most important that the new world order of "final communism" not arrive stillborn at the end of an American bayonet. America has to be compromised, disarmed and then occupied.

As instructed, he drove to the Ritz Carlton Hotel on Boston Commons. As a real amateur, he could hardly be expected to notice the FBI man in his unmarked sedan discretely following him. After the coded message from Moscow, every one of the 86 Rocketry Commission members and aides who could conceivably be Oryol, had such a tail, even if, as in Harsanyi's case, they were thought of as above reproach. Over 180 tails were now in 24/7 operation.

He entered the second floor dining room and ate dinner alone. At 7:11 p.m. he didn't hear the car scrape the FBI surveillance vehicle outside.

At precisely 7:12 p.m. he finished his entrée and, as instructed, got up and entered the men's room. There Sonya herself emerged from a stall, in elevator shoes and dressed in the full trappings of an overweight, pot bellied businessman, completely unrecognizable until she spoke.

"I will help you into this maintenance man's outfit, blond male wig and thick glasses. Then a 'co-worker' from the kitchen will get us out through the back hallways into a service truck and drive us to my car. Then it's on to New York. Now move."

With Sonya guarding the door, the disguise was affected in 48 seconds. They both exited quickly through a service door into the small truck. At first they headed north and then turned to the west, after which they stopped sharply to see if any of the cars in her rear view mirror failed to pass them. None did. Three miles later she repeated the process, entering a park, where she would notice any lights. There were none; they were clean. The silent driver brought them to her garaged car. They got in, exited and turned to the south. Five hours later they would be in Manhattan.

Up to now for security reasons their contacts had been brief and measured interfaces, some with not even a word exchanged, just a furtive exchange of a message or some microfilm. Indeed, given her constant changes in appearance, he actually didn't know what she really looked like. Tonight he was seeing her in her actual appearance for the first time. The woman was amazingly talented, organized and tough. Where did the Soviets find these people?

Sonya described to him all the details on the planned extraction from New York. He was very impressed with the intricate planning of the operation. She didn't tell him about the backup plans – why have him even doubt that the first attempt won't work.

150

At the end of the review he said, "You're a real pro, very sharp. I'm honored to have you overseeing my little journey. In future years historians will write of all this and how our upcoming trip made the world a far better place."

"Yes, doctor. You will change history once you reach the motherland." Silently she added, you better, you little academic, or I'll personally dissect you at some later date.

CHAPTER 26

ORYOL RECALLS HIS CONVERSION

Northeastern U.S.

At this point, feeling comfortable and with a long drive ahead with Sonya, a conversational minimalist, Harsanyi found himself reflecting on his long intellectual and emotional evolution to enthusiastic communism. Rather remarkably for someone of his low key and professorial temperament, he had evolved into the Russians' major intelligence asset in America.

It was a very different path than Sonya had traveled to come to her position. Hers had been a trail of hatred and then action; his the gentle progression of logic toward a perceived clear moral truth, finally forged in the tragic death of his wife and his saving from the same fate by his Russian friends.

His conversion actually had sprung from a deep moral sense developed early in his childhood in Budapest, Hungary. At one point in adolescence he thought he might become a priest. Then he realized his extraordinary skills in mathematics and science and had attended the country's leading university, the Budapest Gymnasium, where he became a graduate student working with Teller Ede, later known in the U.S. as Edward Teller, the "father of the hydrogen bomb," Leo Szilard, now a world class physicist; and finally Eugene Wigner, a future Nobelist. It was actually Szilard and Wigner who had convinced Einstein to write his famous letter to Franklin Roosevelt, advocating the Manhattan Project to build the first atomic bomb. All three of these world class physicists left for America in the thirties, as Hungary drifted toward the Nazi sphere of influence under Miklós Horthy. Harsanyi, however, had decided to stay with his new wife, who was three quarters Jewish, and their respective large extended families, hoping the anti-Semitism would blow over. Also, Horthy was not nearly as extreme as the Germans in his attitudes toward the Jews and, in fact, had successfully restrained the radical fascist Arrow Cross movement led by Ferenc Szalasi, a Jew hater of the first order.

These frightening political cross currents had served to increase the appeal of Marxism to both Harsanyi and his brilliant young wife, who had always been interested in Marxism on a very intellectual level, as had many Jews in the thirties. They had long but private conversations on dialectical materialism and the benevolent dictatorship of the proletariat well into many a late night. The turn toward fascism in Hungary in the 1930s had, however, redirected these academic meanderings into practical involvement. Both had found themselves first in small harmless meetings, then in direct discussion with some unusual countrymen and finally into the outright covert service of the Soviet Union.

The NKVD (the predecessor secret police and intelligence agency) treated him with kid gloves, as they did with many of the converted intelligentsia. He was an important person. Harsanyi knew not only all the scientific talent in his rather small country but was widely respected worldwide. It was generally known by the small international community of elite physicists that he had advanced very far in the deliberations for the Nobel Prize in physics in 1938, eventually awarded to Enrico Fermi for his groundbreaking work on nuclear reactions.

Hungary did join the war as an ally of Nazi Germany and, of course, Harsanyi kept his connections to Moscow a deeply hidden secret. He kept on with his scientific work, seemed apolitical and was left alone by the Horthy regime as a harmless, worldly respected intellectual.

In 1942 Hitler called in his chits and asked his Hungarian ally to support his deep foray into Southern Russia, the ultimate goal of which was to capture the oil-rich Caucasus region. Hungary actually contributed some 200,000 troops to this force, along with allied Romanian and Italian forces. That campaign had ended with the massive defeat at Stalingrad and the death or capture of 90% of the Hungarian soldiers.

Unfortunately for those Hungarians captured, Russian hatred of the Hungarians went back centuries. In the First World War in particular, many of the Russian dead in the opening years had fallen to the forces of the Hapsburg Austria-Hungary Empire, the major ally of Germany. The Russians despised their Hungarian prisoners, who had willingly sold out to the Nazis, even more than the German prisoners, who at least had no choice in their conscription.

Unknown to Harsanyi, who had two members of his extended family missing in action in Stalingrad, Hungarian P.O.W.'s became fair game for the worst Russian atrocities and experiments. Sonya, of course, would never mention it to Harsanyi, but she had actually garroted a Hungarian prisoner, a weakling supply sergeant, as part of her hand to hand combat training in 1943 in the espionage school in the Urals. She had really found it empowering to watch the little wimp squirm and flagellate spasmodically in his pathetic death dance. She had asked for additional subjects beyond the qualification standard to further hone her hand-to-hand skills, requesting specifically more Hungarians as her subjects. Sonya had prolonged the death of the last one so that she could practice the three types of extermination by hand while he was still moving, albeit in fearsome pain and bleeding profusely.

It had reminded her of the pleasure she had enjoyed fishing as a teenager, prolonging the death of the fish by keeping it hooked but returned to the water each time it was close to death. She even thought those trout tasted rather better.

For the Hungarian civilians left behind, the war was not particularly stressful until late 1944, when the massive Russian counter offensive reached the country's eastern border. No longer content with the country's lukewarm support, Hitler occupied Hungary and brought to power the fearsome Arrow Cross under Szalasi. The new leader immediately set out, with Hitler's blessing and encouragement, to attempt to cleanse the country of all traces of everything Jewish. By now the death camps were operating with extraordinary efficiency, having had years to perfect their heinous "production" techniques, and the massive new influx of Hungarian Jews were seamlessly fed into the Auschwitz monster. The last camp commander, SS Major Richard Baer, set "production" records in the last months of its existence, with up to 20,000 Hungarian Jews being dispatched in a day. In a short period of time over 400,000 Hungarian Jews were hideously murdered at a time when everyone knew the war would soon be over, yet the Nazi death factory actually worked overtime using the Hungarian Jews as the last source of fresh inventory.

Harsanyi returned home one day in December 1944 to find that his wife had been taken, just disappearing into the void of the Arrow Cross vacuum. While only one quarter catholic, she had fully converted to Catholicism in 1941 and had attempted to bury her 75% Jewish heritage. In addition, her Jewish relatives were all secular Jews, who had long ago given up practicing their religion, so she had some reason to hope she could go unnoticed. Harsanyi insisted on staying with her in Budapest, but they had dispatched their two children to a farm near the Romanian border, staying with very close Catholic friends.

Then suddenly she was gone, probably turned in by some of the scum who were responding to the Arrow Cross offer of the equivalent of $10 for turning over a hidden Jew. Harsanyi was beside himself with grief, but he knew he had to get out of Budapest. He was a very well known scientist, and the Arrow Cross fiends hated all intellectuals, irrespective of their ethnicity. Also, in effect, he had knowingly harbored a Jew, his wife, and for that he could be arrested at any time. He fled the next day to be with his children in rural Eastern Hungary outside the rail junction, Dubecen.

He was there three days when a local constable, a well known enthusiastic fascist, appeared at the door of their protectors asking about a Harsanyi family from Budapest and what they might know about that family's whereabouts. When the farmer denied all knowledge, the constable showed him a message from the capital expressing the belief that the Harsanyis had fled there. The squad he had brought with him then searched the farm and quickly found the whole lot of them. Everyone was arrested, but the Harsanyis were sent to a holding pen near the rail yard to await the daily arrival of what the Arrow Cross locals called the Jewish Express, a train that left town in the northward direction heading toward Poland.

It always returned empty. There was no round trip ticket.

The Harsanyis were forced to board the train that night, locked in a car with unspeakable conditions – no food, water or sanitary facilities. Around four in the morning the train had inexplicably stopped. All was quiet. They remained locked in that hell hole for two more days. Then they heard an ever increasing rumble of engines drawing near, eventually stopping alongside the train. They awaited the end at the hands of some fascist death squad.

Then they heard a strange language. Harsanyi knew some Russian from his visits there in the thirties.

He immediately shouted, "It's the Russians, we're saved!" Then he yelled out in Russian, "We are Jews and communists being sent to the death camps. Don't shoot."

The door to the car was opened. They faced a burly Russian lieutenant, backed by his platoon with automatic weapons drawn, trucks behind them. The prisoners cheered and tumbled out in joy. After warm embraces of the embarrassed infantrymen, they all tried to tell their stories through Harsanyi, who had also highlighted his own communist history. The hardened infantrymen, most with three years at the front, didn't know what to do with this crowd of pathetic prisoners.

Finally a captain arrived, the company commander. He heard out Harsanyi. "Listen, if your story is true, I don't know what to do with you. My business is simple – killing German scum, as many and as fast as possible. I can't deal with you. I'm sending you and your children back to regimental headquarters and our regiment intelligence officer."

Then he put his face right in Harsanyi's. "And if you're an Arrow Cross liar, he'll figure it out real fast, and you'll have a bullet in your head." He gave one last hard look into Harsanyi's eyes; then he turned to lead his men forward to more Nazi killing. Harsanyi shivered involuntarily.

A sergeant got them in a small jeep (ironically an American Willys) and took him to the operational headquarters just behind the front line. They were given field rations to eat and fresh water. Then the intel officer, a major, grilled them for four hours, after which he was gone for an hour, on the phone with division HQ. Then he returned.

"Dr. Harsanyi, we have checked with Moscow and have reason to believe you are being truthful. However, they have instructed me to ask you something." He was silent for a few seconds, leaned closer to Harsanyi and asked him, "Who recruited you initially and was your contact person in pre war Budapest?"

The colonel was ready to execute Harsanyi on the spot if he answered wrong. He didn't.

The officer relaxed, embraced him and smiling said, "Welcome back comrade. We have been looking for you since we entered Hungary. I am honored to be with such a patriot and great friend of the Soviet Union." Harsanyi wiped tears from his eyes. He was reunited with his people.

His children then joined him, and they were all transported even further behind the front lines to a large base in the rear, teeming with tanks, trucks, artillery and thousands of soldiers.

There he was introduced to a colonel in the GRU, (army intelligence) who spoke fluent Hungarian. "Comrade Harsanyi, it is an honor to meet you, and I welcome you to the liberated part of free Hungary. We have researched your background, and allow me to say that I am honored to meet such a leading and enlightened citizen of your country. Let me extend to you the greetings of Marshall Rodion Malinovsky, the commander of our glorious Second Ukrainian Front Army. "

"Thank you colonel. It is an honor to be a guest of the front line forces that are smashing these monsters."

"It is a pleasure to have you with us. I am sure the Arrow Cross criminals in Budapest were not giving the people accurate updates on the progress of the war in this theater, so allow me to briefly do so. Then we will discuss your immediate future.

In early September our Second Ukrainian Front, combined with the smaller Third Ukrainian Front under General Tolbukin, completed the liberation of Rumania, having destroyed a force of over 500,000 German and 400,000 Romanian soldiers with what can only be described as a Russian blitzkrieg, a hot Russian knife right through the fascists' decaying heart. We are very proud of what our army has just done. In recognition of this our glorious commander was promoted to the rank of Field Marshall of the Soviet Union by none other than Comrade Stalin himself in ceremonies at the Kremlin on September 10.

We then crossed the Transylvanian Mountains and laid siege to eastern Hungary, where we fortunately came upon you locked in your train heading toward Auschwitz and certain death. Our forward positions are now laying siege to Budapest itself, and we intend to advance from there right on to Vienna.

Now regarding the death camps I must tell you, as a Jew myself, that we are coming upon scenes of horror that are indescribable. We know that your wife was taken to Auschwitz, and, I am sad to say, you must assume she is gone. Your children are, of course, safe with us and will be treated very well, as will you. We would like to talk to you today on a number of subjects, including conditions and sentiment in Budapest, your scientific work, an evaluation of your physicist colleagues and then some discussion of your future."

With that a long conversation ensued. A nutritional dinner was served and they were later joined by a political officer and then an officer of the NKVD. The debriefing went on for two days. After that Harsanyi was driven to an airfield where he boarded a special plane for Moscow, leaving his children safely in the hands of a female Russian officer in the nursing corps.

In two days he found himself in the NKVD offices on Dzerzhinsky Square, facing a General Kruglov in his private office. Both men spoke near fluent English.

"Welcome to Moscow, Dr. Harsanyi, and let me be the first to congratulate you for all your help done in the pre war period and your stoicism in your homeland during its fascist occupation.

I reviewed your file and want to tell you directly that we found your insights extremely helpful following your trip to Germany for the 1939 conference lead by the Nazi Nobelist Heisenberg on the possible production, though at a prohibitive cost, for plutonium manufacture. Our physicists are still exploring those conclusions, and I will tell you under extreme confidentiality that we believe the Americans, lead by Albert Einstein and Robert Oppenhimer may be pursuing that possibility aggressively, though we do not have confirmation of that yet. Your next meeting will be with a group of our own atomic scientists, some of whom you know from pre war days. But for now let's discuss your future.

We would like you to return with your children to Eastern Hungary to a safe farm in the freed area and await the liberation of Budapest. As you know, the southern front German armies and the Arrow Cross fanatics are making a last stand there, but Marshall Malinovsky is about to crush them, after which all Hungary will be liberated and his force will drive toward Vienna. Then he may connect up with the American tank commander, George Patton, in Bavaria and close the southern pincer into the heartland of Germany. We think the war will be over by April or May 1945.

In the post-war environment our technical scientists expect that the world center of physics will move to two locales – the Soviet Union, of course, and the United States. There will not be the resources to support such work in war torn Europe any more. Preparing for that day, we intend to recruit all the leading physicists and rocketry experts we can get from central and eastern Europe and bring them here. We expect the United States will do the same. And that brings me to the delicate part of our discussion – our future relationship with the United States and your possible very important role in that future.

There are many opinions in our government as to how we will relate to our wartime ally after hostilities cease. Of course, I am not privy to the discussions of the ruling Politburo, but I can tell you that we have been told to be fully prepared for a possibly regrettable deterioration of that relationship. Some expect it to take the form of a tense coexistence, some feel it will be more overtly hostile and there are some who predict the inevitability of armed conflict between the two world superpowers. Germany will be in ruin, England is broke and France disgraced by its wartime performance. Those empires are finished. It will be the Soviet Union and America sharing the starring roles, center stage for the rest of this century. We hope for the best, but we must be prepared for the worst.

In the context of this expected post-war environment, we want you to join the Americans, whom we expect will be rounding up all the leading European scientists they can get their hands on, particularly applied physicists and rocketeers, and sending them to America. Your distinguished background and your proficiency in English makes you a very attractive catch. We are convinced they know nothing of your or your wife's sympathy for our cause.

Your mission will be to immerse yourself in one of the finest American technological universities; we recommend M.I.T. or Cal Tech. You should vigorously pursue your research in the physics of rocket dynamics, propulsion and the resulting potential for weaponry delivery, becoming as involved as possible in secret government work. We will be able to contact you but in the most discreet manner. Of course, you may take your children with you, but they must continue to know nothing of your allegiance.

That is the overview, Dr. Harsanyi. The details will be provided by my staff, after you conclude your briefings with your Russian peer group here. Allow me to stop at this point and ask if you have any questions of me."

"Colonel, let me begin by thanking you and the valiant Second Ukrainian Front troops for saving my life and that of my children. We were incredibly fortunate. If we had been arrested a few days earlier, we probably would have been executed in Auschwitz. By the way, I assume you have no further word of my wife's fate?"

"No we do not. You have to assume sadly that she did perish in Auschwitz, her ashes carried away in the smoke of thousands of others that day."

Harsanyi looked down and tears came to his eyes. Then he resumed slowly but with intensity, "You may rest assured that I am now more committed than ever. Before the last year I was an intellectual and moral convert to communism. Given what happened in my country and the particulars of my rescue, I am now committed to the very core of my soul. You will have no more faithful servant abroad."

The two men embraced warmly and then continued a tactical discussion of how to maximize the effectiveness of this potential new soviet super agent. Both concluded his potential to serve the Soviet Union was extraordinary. One hour later they had finished their comprehensive review, and Harsanyi was passed on to three days of exhaustive discussions with eight highly distinguished and trustworthy Russian scientists and a handful of high ranking members of the NKVD's American department.

Kruglov wrote the following in Harsanyi's file:

With the possible exception of George Koval and our nascent contacts in the so-called Manhattan Project, no American agent has more potential than Harsanyi. Indeed, the Manhattan project crowd lacks anyone with this clear commitment to the cause. They are mostly Nazi-haters and flowery intellectuals, some of whom merely feel the need to share their work, so that others will develop nuclear capabilities, creating a nuclear stalemate. Harsanyi's acceptance into the heart of American science should be seamless and immediate – after all, some of these American practitioners have already voted for him to win the Nobel Prize.

Then Kruglov gathered the eight scientists who would milk him of knowledge for the next three days. "Make sure you are thorough, precise and detailed. If things go well and he becomes a fixture in American rocketry efforts, we may never see him in Moscow again. And by the way, no one without an absolute need to know should ever have any contact with him. When he leaves you will erase his name from your memory bank. He's a non person. Vwee panamyetye (Do you understand)?"

Afterwards he met with a key aide, who asked, "There is one more matter to review, sir – what do we do with his wife? Harsanyi has been told she is gone, but he still harbors hope. As you know we picked her up walking aimlessly near a deserted train which had been partially destroyed by our fighter planes just eight miles from Auschwitz. She remains in a stupor in one of our field hospitals. We had alerted our people and the GRU Army intelligence personnel in the area to be on the lookout for her. While she was a pre-war communist also, I must tell you that she was a sentimentalist, a babbling theoretician who had trouble keeping her mouth shut, even after the fascists gained control of Hungary."

Kruglov looked down and then right back up into his aide's eyes. Without hesitation, "Shoot her – in the face and remove her teeth, so she can never be identified. Take off her clothes and bury her nude in an unmarked grave in the woods. And have it done by our people, not the Army idiots. Harsanyi is far too valuable to be compromised by some sniveling, chatty wife running around American academic circles having tea. We close that door today.

And by the way, from now on he will be known as Oryol – our top secret American 'eagle!'"

CHAPTER 27

FIREFIGHT AT THE DOCKS

Early Thursday Morning, November 18, 1953
New York City

Dominic and his 400 man task force had been on full alert now for almost two weeks. All they knew was that reliable intelligence had indicated the Russian extraction operation was a go. No other details as to who, when or where. With 140 tails around the country to man, no one was getting much sleep. And needless to say, he hadn't seen Catherine Bowers for weeks. No time for that.

Strangely, Dominic was now completely freed of the depression. In the pressure of the incipient battle and living on the edge, there was no time to look inward. It was D-day nine years later, but now he was the commander. He was Eisenhower.

He had remained in New York. He stayed right on top of the amateur, the "Plumber," Mr. Romanowski, who had been under continuous surveillance since caught on film in the basement of the Soviet Consulate. Further research on him had drawn a total blank. He was a non person. His whole story given to the landlord was bogus – all dead ends. He had hardly gone outside his apartment since, and then only to get food. He had contact with no one. Not even a call in or out on his tapped phone. He was taking absolutely no risks – just like you would expect of an imported soldier preparing for action. Dom was convinced the call would come to him, and then he would be followed.

At precisely midnight the plumber received a call, the first in weeks. It was in a foreign language, probably Eastern European, and very brief. It took the FBI 18 minutes to conclude it was in Bulgarian, get it to the right translator and decode the very laconic message.

"The Boys are gathering for the farewell party tonight. Leave now – don't be late. Everything should be done as rehearsed."

The plumber had merely grunted, gotten in his car carrying a large crate and headed toward Manhattan. As he had accessed the on ramp to the Brooklyn Bridge heading toward Manhattan, Dominic got the call. This was the plumber's first trip into Manhattan since the FBI had begun their surveillance.

The plumber drove across Manhattan on Canal Street, where he picked up a very large man and turned north on Tenth Avenue to 23rd Street, where he parked and both men entered a warehouse one block from the Chelsea Piers, carrying the large crate.

Dominic frantically called for back up and exited the FBI building downtown with three agents in an unmarked Bureau car. All carried automatic weapons. He arrived at 1:20 a.m. at the building across from the piers. By 1:30 p.m. there were four cars and sixteen agents in total, discreetly surrounding the building on all sides and armed with high power rifles, automatic weapons and in radio contact. Romanowski and his accomplice had not exited.

Harlem
Same time

Seventy-five blocks north there was movement at a Soviet safe house located in a dilapidated tenement on East 115th Street. Agent Sonya and Dr. Peter Harsanyi had arrived at 12:30 a.m. from Cambridge, Massachusetts. They got a breather and Sonya gave him a quick description of the plan. At 1:15 a.m. they descended the tenement steps, joined by two heavily armed men and got in a gray 1952 Buick sedan. They headed toward the West Side Drive and approached the Chelsea Piers at 1:31 a.m.

The Chelsea Piers had once been where all the great transatlantic cruise ships had arrived and departed earlier in the century. The *Lusitania*, sunk in 1916 by a German U-boat, had departed from there, and the *Titanic* had been scheduled to dock there on its maiden voyage and before its unfortunate date with an iceberg. But by now the great cruise ships such as, the *Queen Elizabeth*, the *United States*, and the *SS France*, all docked up in the west forties piers, leaving Chelsea to service a secondary lot of freighters, including the rusted Cuban sugar freighter chartered by Grace and Co. that was preparing to leave at 2 a.m. for its return trip to Havana.

Five minutes before the Harsanyi vehicle reached the pier, the plumber and now three colleagues, who must have already been inside, had exited the warehouse, all dressed in heavy winter coats and fedora hats brought well down on their heads. The four FBI cars communicated by radio with Dominic, who told them to move only on his command and then giving them assigned vectors to cover. As Harsanyi's gray Buick drove up, the plumber and his three accomplices moved across the avenue to meet them.

Dominic saw four people get out of the car, one of them not as spry. His mind raced. It was highly likely that this was Oryol. They had been led there by a subject caught on film entering a tunnel to the soviet consulate, and a large party of men were now escorting a somewhat older man onto an empty Cuban freighter due to embark in one hour to its home port, Havana, a center for soviet activity in Latin America. Jesus, this it!

161

He yelled into the car radio, "Everyone but the drivers out of the cars – NOW! Surround them and block their way onto the boat." Immediately 12 agents with automatic weapons and rifles drawn raced toward the group.

———————————

Sonya, dressed in male attire, saw what this was immediately. She started barking orders. Harsanyi was thrown back in the car, and then the Russians opened up at the men approaching, firing particularly heavily at the FBI cars approaching from the south. Almost immediately a heavy weapon, a 50-caliber-type machine gun firing from a second story office window on the south side of the piers, also started to rake the agents in that sector, the large rounds quickly dissecting the two vehicles they were seeking cover behind. Two agents fell immediately and the others retreated to better cover as the cars were torn apart. Then an automatic weapon in the warehouse also opened up on the FBI. Dominic had not seen the likes of this since Bastogne, France in December, 1944.

He screamed, "Watch the south end." He immediately recognized this as a typical L-pattern infantry ambush with fire that would favor an escape to the south. He ran over to the southern-most group. Sure enough, as soon as the cars there had been chewed up by the 50-caliber, Harsanyi's car with Sonya and a driver accelerated hard to the south. The FBI agents opened fire, but as soon as they revealed their new positions, an automatic in the south part of the warehouse joined the 50-caliber and opened up on them full bore. Lead was flying everywhere, and they had to stay behind cover, as the Buick made its escape.

The noise was deafening. Another agent fell, and a burst traced both sides of the garbage dumpster Dominic and agent Bugliari were behind. He thought, these bastards have practiced this contingency cover plan and done this before; these are special-forces, military type assault skills.

Harsanyi and Sonya stayed on the floor as the car broke through the south part of the attempted entrapment and raced south on Eleventh Avenue, turned east on 21st Street, and went two blocks where they entered a garage. It was the same garage that Bodkin and Sonya had gone the night of the Dickinson murder. The door was open and the lights were out. They entered, changed immediately into a non-descript 1951 Ford, engine running and car facing the open double door just as the backup plan called for. They exited turning eastbound and then a left northbound on Eighth Avenue, now moving in the opposite of their exit direction from the firefight. They moved with alacrity but not at a speed that would draw notice. Sonya was now driving and in a woman's hat and gray wig. Harsanyi had laid down on the back floor and Bodkin rode shotgun. Literally.

At 34th Street Bodkin quickly got out of the car and disappeared into Penn Station. Then Sonya and Harsanyi got on the West Side Highway, drove north to 125th Street and then east to the unattended Willis Avenue Bridge into the Bronx. Harsanyi got up off the floor. At that late hour, they had escaped the island in fourteen minutes. Perfect–just like Sonya and Bodkin had rehearsed for this backup plan.

Dominic got on the only secure car phone still operating and reached the FBI communications center. They alerted all FBI units and NYPD headquarters. Within seven minutes every law enforcement officer on duty in New York City knew of the APB for a gray 1952 Buick sedan with armed and extremely dangerous occupants, last seen heading south on 11th Avenue.

Meanwhile the firefight at 24th Street had continued. Over a dozen NYPD officers with rifles had joined the firefight. It was becoming obvious the unfriendlies were now skillfully trying to extricate themselves. Romanowski and his two comrades, who had approached the station wagon with him, were now dead. The 50-calibre had ceased firing as soon as it had disabled the FBI cars and the sedan had escaped. Then the agents had surrounded that second floor office and had the shooter, who was returning fire with a smaller automatic weapon now, trapped. Finally he broke for the street, firing on the agents and was cut down.

"Get that prick in the warehouse." Dominic roared, the only unfriendly who was unaccounted for. "He has to get out the way the plumber got in. Get in that building. I want him alive."

Meanwhile ambulances were arriving, sirens wailing. Two of the four downed G-men were dead, one was severely wounded in the chest and critical, and one was shot in the leg but, with a tourniquet already applied, would clearly survive. At 11:55 p.m., thirty-two minutes after all hell had broken out, the holdout was found in the warehouse, hiding in an air vent and was sped off to an FBI interrogation center.

It was over. Dominic got on the car phone to call into the FBI emergency hot line.

Two Hours Later
4:30 a.m., Thursday, November 19, 1953

The Officer in Charge (OIC) at FBI headquarters in Washington that night set up a call that connected the top FBI brass including Hoover, CIA director, Allen Dulles and, of course, Dominic Benvenuto, still on site at Chelsea Piers.

After Hoover called roll, Dominic spoke. "At approximately 2:23 a.m. this morning, roughly two hours ago, 16 FBI agents all under my direct command were in a tight surveillance stakeout of a warehouse building entered by a subject of considerable interest to us, who went under a fictitious name, Lech Romanowski. He had been filmed on a secret camera placed by us in an underground access tunnel to the Soviet Consular building on 67th Street. We had followed him, staked out his residence in Brooklyn and tapped his phone. Last night he entered his truck and headed for Manhattan for the first time since surveillance had begun. He picked up an accomplice, and they entered a warehouse that faced the Chelsea Piers through a side entrance on the north side of the building carrying a heavy box. He later exited west with two other men as a car approached the pier at 23rd Street, where a sugar ship of Cuban registry was preparing to return to Havana. The car stopped and four men got out, one clearly less agile than the rest.

As you are all aware, we have been on high alert for the possible Soviet attempt to extract Oryol from this country. We don't know who he is or how to identify him, but the older man there was most likely him, given all the circumstantial evidence just described.

I ordered our agents forward and our four cars into blocking positions on all sides. Immediately we were met by heavy gunfire, including a 50-calibre weapon that was raking us from a protected position in a pier office to the south of us. Also automatic fire from the warehouse across the street, as well as four shooters around the car which then sped off to the south with only three occupants. After our cars were all incapacitated by the 50-calibre, the suspect car sped off to the south. We could not pursue.

From my army experience this was clearly a classic L-shaped ambush using concentrated fire power usually to aid an escape by a unit, to remove valuable material or a senior officer in a predetermined direction. They were protecting something or someone very important. We think it's Oryol. Also, these gunmen were extremely professional - special forces quality. That was a military operation.

We have two dead agents with an accumulated 24 years of service, one agent now fighting for his life at Lenox Hill Hospital and one in surgery with a badly wounded lower leg, who will survive. We recovered the weapons, and they were all U.S. Army issue, reported missing on our master list from different bases here in the U.S. over a surprisingly long period of time, apparently being saved for an operation like this. There is no doubt these were Russians and/or their Eastern European cohorts, although we have only identified two for sure. The only survivor may be an illegal but he is claiming diplomatic immunity. We have no idea who he is, but he is getting our full interrogation attention now.

As soon as the firefight ended, we went on the radio to FBI headquarters and the NYPD. Every law enforcement officer working tonight in the New York metropolitan area has the APB for the Buick sedan and a description of the male driver, somewhat short, very fit and trim. All the bridges and tunnels are being watched closely. If that Buick is moving, we will find it. We also are inspecting the Cuban ship from bow to stern, but have found nothing yet other than a captain who is nervous and a crew that speaks very little English.

We also are now checking the whereabouts of all members and staff of the Rocketry Commission, who, unknown to them, have been under physical and phone surveillance since we got the news that the decision had been made to extract Oryol. At this point we have confirmed the whereabouts of all but three, the most unusual being the vice chair of the Commission, Dr. Harsanyi.

Last night he was followed to the Boston Ritz Carlton hotel, and was seen entering the dining room, where he apparently eats alone on occasions. Like all the Rocketry Commission participants, he was followed by one of our agents, who remained outside in his car where he could surreptitiously see both formal exits from the hotel. At 7:11 a car sideswiped our man's parked car, badly scraping the driver's side, and continued driving on. This distracted the agent, who called in the license and make of the car.

About 15 minutes later the agent was informed through his car radio that the scraping vehicle had a fictitious license plate and fit a description of a car recently reported stolen. He raced out of the car into the dining room only to discover that Harsanyi had disappeared without paying his check. There has been no sign of him since. The fender bender was done to distract the agent and have him on his car phone as the suspect escaped, probably out a service entrance.

Harsanyi was about our most unlikely suspect. A mild and brilliant academic, he is widely regarded by his peers as a very enthusiastic converted American, who has been extremely important to the Commission's work. And Van Braun swears by him."

At this point CIA director Dulles, on the call from his home, groaned and thought – we used a former Nazi, Van Braun, to vouch for his vice chair, who knows everything about our program – a vice chair we can't seem to find right now. And we have been warned that the Soviets want to get their leading spy out. Wonderful, just wonderful.

Hoover then spoke up. "First, Agent Benvenuto, you are to be congratulated on your successful disruption of the escape attempt. Going forward it's my view that we should go public to the press with the description of the Buick escape car and a cover story that the shootout was drug related and connected to contraband activity on the pier. We need the public's help to find that car quickly. We plan to release this in the early morning. Anyone disagree?"

CIA Director Dulles responded, "If this is Oryol, we have to do everything conceivable to catch him. We have, at great risk, told the Bureau information from our most important sources and have put at risk our most valuable asset in the Soviet Union. It would be disastrous if we let this Oryol slip out of the country."

After an awkward pause, Dulles continued, "Go ahead with the release to the press. If we determine it is Harsanyi, and we damn well better and soon, we will have to release this fact as well and change the story, perhaps to a kidnapping of the physicist. I will awaken the President now and brief him. I expect he will agree with me, as he does on most matters of this nature. And find that god damn Buick." No one on the call had ever heard the aristocratic Dulles publicly swear before.

One hour later the automobile that had scraped the agent's car in Boston was found engulfed in flames behind a deserted Boston wharf. This closed the loop in Dominic's mind. All of the night's events were now tied together, another highly complex symphony concocted by that fiendish genius of a conductor – agent Sonya. We knew it was coming, yet we couldn't stop it. But at least they're not out yet–we stopped them and have a chance.

We foiled this attempt through excellent and well coordinated surveillance work that led us to the scene. But they must have a quick backup plan to attempt to get Oryol out. My only lead is the Buick. And that vehicle has just disappeared into thin air, despite the fact that every cop on duty within 100 miles is looking for it.

Of course unknown to Dominic and all the pursuers, the Buick was now resting comfortably under a tarp in a locked, dark garage in lower Manhattan and was going nowhere. Tomorrow night it would get a paint job in red and again be covered up.

They did have the quick glimpse of the Buick's occupants as they briefly exited the car before the fusillade of bullets had exploded. But Dominic knew, given Sonya's involvement, that these were merely one set of disguises that by now had morphed into some other total makeover.

In fact, Sonya was now a graying woman with a round girth, having driven a 1951 Ford to a safe apartment in Metuchen, New Jersey, where she and the most important Soviet spy in the free world were having some tea after a most eventful early morning. They felt thwarted but hardly beaten, and were reviewing plan B as conceived and designed by the best minds in the Moscow MGB headquarters. Sonya assured Dr. Harsanyi that they would be out of the country in a matter of days.

Friday, November 20, 6:00 a.m.

Hoover got up early and placed a call to Mr. Pat Weaver, the president of NBC and formerly the creator of the *Today* show. He owed Weaver a favor on a previous matter. He also knew that the morning papers were already out and the *Today* show was now the way that "Mr. and Mrs. America" got their first update of the overnight news. He hoped Weaver would run with the story on short notice. They desperately needed public help to find the car, the assailants and, of course, Oryol and Sonya.

"Mr. Weaver, I apologize for awakening you, but I have sad news of some import. As the broadcaster of the only national morning news show, you could assist us in vital law enforcement efforts in this matter.

I am prepared to give you the following information, just ahead of our general release to the press in a conference at 8 a.m. here in Washington. I am aware that your news show *Today* goes on the air in only 55 minutes at 7 a.m., and this will be difficult for you to implement in such short time.

Early this morning there was a very violent shootout at the Chelsea Piers in Manhattan, as FBI personnel apparently interdicted an attempted large narcotics delivery. Two FBI agents perished, one remains in critical condition and two are being treated in the hospital with lesser wounds. Five of the assailants were killed and one was captured. Unfortunately one car with two lead suspects got away in a 1952 gray Buick sedan headed southbound. We will be asking all citizens to be on the lookout and are extremely interested in recovering this car and its occupants. We would like you to use this material as you see fit as you open the *Today* show, but there is to be no mention of your source for this, and, if asked, I will deny we ever spoke. Also your people will not be able to get any confirmation from anyone before our 8 a.m. release. They have to run this story on your authority. Is that all clear?"

Weaver was stunned. "Sir, how can we report such a story with no collaboration or time to investigate? Isn't there someone I can call?"

"Mr. Weaver, how would it serve my interests to embarrass you. However, you or your people are certainly free to call the NYPD and confirm the general event. You might also ask them if the action terminated around 3 a.m. and initially involved the FBI with NYPD personnel joining later. We will disclose both of these true and correct facts at the 8 a.m. press conference, whose schedule you can also confirm through our press office.

I am certainly not in the business to tell you how to run your business, but it would seem to me that it would be very helpful for your new show to scoop, as you press people say, all the conventional media on a most important and tragic story. If you do not take this opportunity, I am afraid you will be very upset at yourself at 8:30."

"My assistant, agent Tollson will provide you with the details now. What is most important is public awareness of the missing assailants and help in locating the vehicle they escaped in."

Weaver was silent for a few seconds. Then he responded, "Mr. Director, I thank you. We will make those two calls, but I expect to run the story. Please put your assistant on."

Eight minutes later Weaver reached Garroway, who whistled, asked a few questions and hung up. At a moment like this Dave was delighted that they had in house such a talent as Catherine Bowers, exactly the person to pull this off in the remaining 41 minutes before air time. He smiled with confidence as he dialed her. She was great at this stuff, particularly under pressure. What a godsend at a moment like this.

CHAPTER 28

ORYOL UNMASKED

Same Day – Thursday, November 19, 1953
10:00 a.m. – New York City

Dominic's New York Counterintelligence office now was the coordinating nerve center for the massive effort the government of the United States was directing at understanding the climactic events of the previous night. Following the 4:30 a.m. conference call, over 100 FBI agents had been added to the New York cadre, and frantic efforts were underway to find the car and identify its occupants. Unfortunately, upon further investigation, the gunman caught alive at the site did have diplomatic immunity, a minor "trade" official, and would soon have to be released under the strongest of secret protests to the Soviets. The Soviets would also be forced to expatriate two of their KGB "consulars" in Washington."

At 10:15 a.m. the last person unaccounted for serving on or for the rocketry commission other than Dr. Harsanyi had been located, an army general in California, who it seems, had spent the night with his female enlisted aide. He had shown up on his base at 0700 hours Pacific Time to find a squad of agents looking for him. His career was over – for more than one reason.

"So, as suspected, Harsanyi is our man. Incredible," Dominic reflectively announced with a big sigh to a gathering of his key aides and senior agents. "He has not been seen since he entered the Ritz Carlton hotel in Boston for dinner. He never paid the check and got out of there unnoticed, our man in the tail car outside having been distracted by that stolen vehicle scraping his side.

This means Harsanyi must have immediately left for New York, no doubt accompanied by some muscle. They knew he was being tailed, and so they arranged the car diversion. By the way this means some bastard on the inside is still feeding them info. We've got to find the traitor.

Once in New York they regrouped somewhere before heading to the Chelsea Piers at 2 a.m. We were damn lucky last night to be on the scene of their attempt to sneak out of the country. The only reason we were there was our secret surveillance camera in the bowels of the consulate and the sloppiness of the Brooklyn agent. Without him "Oryol," aka Dr. Peter Harsanyi, would be on that freighter in international waters right now headed for a quiet but warm welcome in Cuba. And toasting Sonya on her masterful extraction.

Just before this meeting I called Hoover and gave him these conclusions. I said we should get an army of analysts right now to review everything we know about Harsanyi, including his full history in Hungary and the people we interviewed who swore by him, including his fellow scientists Von Braun, Teller and Szillard. We also want the CIA to use all their Hungarian resources to get data.

It's no secret that the Hungarians hate their Russian occupiers. It is a secret that there is hope that they may ultimately revolt as the East Germans just attempted. There is plenty of anti soviet sentiment in that country, and we expect our people there to get us the real story on Harsanyi. While we probably didn't distinguish ourselves on all our background checks, our CIA buddies, who have been dumping all over us, in fact committed the biggest screw up in this case – missing Harsanyi. This was their territory. They checked out the foreign guys and they blew it with Harsanyi.

I'm calling a meeting for tomorrow morning at 8 a.m. of everyone on the commission. We have spoken to all of them, and they have been ordered to get on planes immediately.

Finally, we have been authorized to release Harsanyi's photograph and a broad public appeal for input on his whereabouts. It will be characterized as possible foul play or even kidnapping of a leading scientist. No further details to be given and no tie to the pier shootout."

Dominic concluded the meeting. The entire overcrowded office sprang into action, activity everywhere. It resembled the intensity of a battlefield command bunker.

10:40 a.m. - Washington, D.C.

After Hoover had gotten off the phone with Dominic, he briefed his staff on the conclusions released and the plan of action. Then he asked for an immediate joint call with the president and CIA Director Allen Dulles. Hoover was upset and deeply disturbed by the Harsanyi developments, but he did relish the chance to rake Dulles over the coals.

Ike had to excuse himself from a conference in the oval office with a congressional leadership group led by Senator Everett Dirksen. Dulles was on a secure phone with the CIA station chief in Iran, orchestrating the new "independent" regime in that country. Within three minutes all were on the line.

Hoover began, "Gentlemen, I must bring you up to date on the Oryol matter. We have now determined that Doctor Peter Harsanyi, the vice chair of the top secret rocketry commission, is missing, last seen on November 17 in Boston at approximately 7:10 p.m. We now believe it highly likely, although not proven, that the shootout at the Chelsea Piers was an attempt to get him out of the country and was foiled by some very strong surveillance work by our New York office and led personally by our chief of counter intelligence there, Dominic Benvenuto.

We have never seen such a violent effort by the soviets on our soil and believe it only could have been justified by a matter of the greatest importance. Our Moscow agent had indicated that an escape would be forthcoming. This all points to this attempt to extricate Oryol, who is, it seems, none other than Dr. Peter Harsanyi, a man who knows all the details of our rocketry program in its entirety. An unmitigated disaster if he makes it out.

I have just authorized a national release of his photograph and a speculation that he has met with foul play, perhaps kidnapping, but no further details. We have not connected it with the so called drug related shootout in New York last night."

Dulles interjected, "Mr. Hoover, I would have appreciated it if you had consulted with us first."

"Given the urgency of thwarting his escape, I did not feel it necessary or appropriate," Hoover responded. "Now we need to talk about the joint effort to gather immediately as much data as possible on Harsanyi. As you know Director Dulles, the CIA did the full background checks on all of the commission people not born in the U.S. We did the research only on their domestic history. There is little doubt that Harsanyi was completely clean since coming here. Now, Director Dulles, I have to ask you to review your work on his history in Hungary and quickly. If he is in fact Oryol, my strong suspicion is that he has been a communist sympathizer for a long time and his coming to the U.S. was no accident."

Ike groaned and asked Dulles, "Allen, was there anything in his history in Hungary that gave you doubts?"

"Mr. President, I did the final review of his file and that of all of the foreign born commission members personally, but I saw nothing to question. To our knowledge he never demonstrated any pro soviet feelings, but admittedly that would have been very dangerous in fascist Hungary before or during the war. We also looked very closely at how all the recruited European scientists found their way to us as the war wound down in April and June of 1945, fearing a possible plant. Harsanyi was hiding out in a rural area as the regime folded and found us in Vienna shortly after it fell. We didn't see much time lapse that would have permitted him contact time with the Russians, although it's possible."

Hoover responded, "Well Mr. Director, someone got to him somewhere before he came to our shores. Then he proceeded to run a very good act as a committed new and loyal American, a low key genius that everyone liked and respected."

Sensing that this bent was non productive, Ike interjected, "Look, what matters now is finding this guy before he gets out of the country. Allen, stop everything else you are doing, including this Iran stuff, and personally oversee an exhaustive review of Harsanyi's background. Use all our clandestine resources in Hungary and Eastern Europe to find out not only his history, but also how it might be predictive of how he will personally perform now under pressure, following a foiled escape attempt. J. Edgar, you know what you have to do; don't hesitate to use any resources or employ extreme action. If he gets out, the balance of power will take a dangerous shift toward the Soviets within a few years. Gentlemen, get to work."

The call ended abruptly. Ike was physically upset. Also, for the first time since D-Day, June 6, 1944, the former general was actually scared.

11:00 a.m. - Metuchen, New Jersey

Sonya had driven to a busy set of payphones on Route 1. She dialed an untraceable local number.

"We will need your flight services after all Mr. Breen. Our car broke down last night and we will need to fly to Canada. Are you still available to leave on Sunday morning, two days from now?" In Moscow they had concluded that a Sunday, the busiest day of the week for pleasure general aviation, would be the best for the back up extraction, and Sonya had agreed.

"Yes Madame, I am fully prepared." He had only a trace of an accent. "How many travelers will be in your party?"

"We still expect only two, but as we discussed, a third, a young person, could join us at the last minute."

"Very well then, I look forward to seeing you Sunday at 9 a.m. Allow me to assure you all is ready."

2:00 a.m. (6:00 p.m. New York)
MGB Headquarters, Moscow

General Kruglov had called a meeting with Andropov and Tolstoy to review the last 24 hours in America. He was very agitated and visibly upset.

"From the moment Khrushchev ordered this, I anticipated that all might not go smoothly, and we could well find ourselves exactly where we are now – in real trouble." Kruglov stared at his hands. "Somehow, the FBI was lead right to the scene. If it weren't for the alternate escape planning and the brilliant execution of those plans by Sonya, they would all be dead or, even worse, captured. Even so, now we find ourselves with Oryol clearly identified, even though Hoover is playing some game about a suspected kidnapping. Sonya and Harsanyi are hiding out, trying to sneak out Sunday in a small plane to Canada, probably with a hostage as insurance. And the whole world hangs in balance," he screamed and pounded the table.

"And we have succeeded in totally pissing off the Americans with a cowboy shootout in their biggest city, dead FBI agents in the streets and maybe more violence to come as we turn to our high risk contingency plans. Even Stalin never attempted something like this, and if we did and fucked it up this way, he would have shot us all by now.

When I called Khrushchev on today's developments, he went crazy. It was he who ordered this, but I was the only witness to it at our breakfast. I don't know if he has shared this with other members of the Politburo or not. He can blame this whole miserable disaster on me and offer me up as a sacrifice. And you guys. We damn well better get them out."

The group sat silently and stared down for awhile. Then they reviewed the course for the next day and the contingency plans in place and adjourned to get some sleep in their offices.

Tolstoy contemplated his options. It was highly likely that his message had gotten to the Americans and that they were on high alert, expecting an extraction attempt. He had hoped that would be enough. But it hadn't been. Sonya had managed the escape from the American trap like a skilled ranger. She was in a class by herself, a native born American who thought like a caged Russian. She's unbelievable.

It was helpful that the Americans now knew the identity of Oryol and were being aggressive in hunting him down. At least Igor would not be the one who would have to expose himself to get that information to the Americans. But they better find him, and soon. The plane attempt may well work and if that failed, the second backup plan probably would succeed. And only Sonya knows when she would try it and exactly where.

11:00 p.m. - East Ninth Street, New York

Prudence was sound asleep now. She had come home at 8 p.m. exhausted, having been called into work at 4 a.m. that morning, following the shootout at the piers. Once Francois was sure that she was in deep slumber, he went out into the living room and dialed the number Sonya had given him to use in case some really urgent news had been divulged by his lover.

A male voice answered. Francois responded, "I was told to call you in the absence of our mutual woman friend if something really urgent came up."

He answered, "OK, so what is your news?"

"She mentioned that they now know who the suspect is, the identity of the bird. Apparently it is some professor from Boston."

The voice on the phone was briefly silent. Then, "Do you not watch television, listen to the radio or read the late newspapers, you idiot. That man and his photo are all over the place as a faked kidnap victim. And you broke silence for this?" He quickly hung up.

But not quickly enough.

Friday, November 20, 1953
8:00 a.m. – F.B.I. Offices, New York City

The meeting of the newly arrived members of the commission, the senior agents and staffers was called to order by Dominic right at the appointed time of 8 a.m. As he stood to speak, all eyes turned to him, the room marked with total silence.

"Before beginning our update, I would like to play for you a telephone call recorded last night in Manhattan at approximately 11 p.m."

The room was soon filled with the voice of Francois DuBorg and his brief call to the garage. Everyone but one attendee looked around in bewilderment. As it ended, Prudence dropped her steno pad and began a low level sob. Dominic looked at her but did not speak for 20 seconds, as her sobs grew stronger, echoing throughout the silenced meeting room.

Finally, Dominic spoke to the very confused assemblage. "I must inform you all now that we sought and were granted by a federal judge permission to wiretap all of your homes, including commission members, staff and FBI personnel, following a long litany of security issues that had concerned us. This call originated in the apartment of Miss Owens, my previously trusted assistant of many years, by a man who had moved in with her several months ago, which by agency rules should have been disclosed to us but was not. We have only had this tape for five hours but have already identified the man as Francois DuBorg, a semi employed actor of French citizenry, who has been in this country two years.

Our counterparts in Paris have responded with very cooperative alacrity following our urgent request for information. Mr. DuBorg could be described as a French intellectual and a graduate of the Sorbonne, who is estranged from his conservative family, apparently of noble ancestry. He has an arrest record from a Parisian demonstration that got out of control. During interrogation he described himself as an intellectual communist, hardly a crime of any sort in France, but nonetheless of great significance to us. We are pursuing all leads available to us aggressively. Miss Owens, do you have anything to say now to us?"

She just continued sobbing and finally broke down. "I had no idea, no idea…I am…a good American," and then lost it. She was escorted from the conference room by agent Keenan and was placed under arrest and quickly removed from the building to a nearby interrogation room, where she would spend the next eight hours being grilled non-stop by the best.

Dominic then began the briefing of the stunned and shaken participants. "So it is now clear that, right under my nose, my very assistant was, probably unwittingly, divulging generic information to a soviet agent, which they were able to amplify and use much to their advantage. They were two amateurs, but they hurt us – badly. This relationship, undoubtedly assisted by other clever drop arrangements by professionals, is how the group communicated both among themselves and with Oryol.

Now it also is my deep regret to have to inform you that Dr. Harsanyi is missing and is almost certainly agent Oryol." He paused, the group gasped and groaned. It resembled a joint clinical state of shock.

Van Braun spoke first. "Surely there is some mistake. Peter will show up somewhere; this is impossible to believe. Every chance he gets he lauds the United States and all that this great democracy has done for him and his adult children, now in university…"

Agitated, Dominic broke in, "Let me give you the facts, Werner. First, it is absolutely clear that there has been a flow of information from someone on the inside of this commission, beginning with Professor Dickinson's last minute change of plans the night of his murder right up to and including the importance of the Corning connection. Second, we have clear direction from an unimpeachable source that an inside agent exists. Third, we know the Russians have decided to extricate him. Fourth, a participant in the shootout had previously been seen exiting the soviet consulate with other known agents, probably from a planning session on this very escape attempt. He was the one that finally led us to the scene. Fifth, you just heard a phone tap from the apartment of my clueless assistant recording a call to the very garage where one hour ago we found the suspect car from the scene, a gray Buick, which had been recently painted and was partially dismantled. And finally, everyone else on this commission or still working for it is within 100 feet of where I am speaking except for one man…Dr. Peter Harsanyi. Now, what part of this is unclear to you sir?" he ended derisively, screaming in his face.

The group sat in shocked silence, staring at their hands. Dominic looked about at each, taking time to regain his composure. He was furious at his assistant and his own stupidity in this disaster. But now ready to go forward at a breakneck pace.

They had a ton of new leads to pursue now. He gave very clear and detailed instructions to all the commission members and the staff. Each was then interviewed by one or two of the over 60 agents that had now been assembled to exhaustively question everyone.

The Bureau had picked up DuBorg at 8:45 a.m., asleep in his and Prudy's New York apartment. Ten remaining agents tore the apartment apart looking for evidence. By 5:00 p.m. they would know everything there was to know about Prudence, Francois and their relationship, right down to sexual preferences and oddities.

The proprietor of the garage, an East German illegal entrant into the U.S., had been traced by the phone tap on Prudence's number and was now being grilled in a holding cell but had so far not opened up. There were at least three other vehicles in the building that were reported stolen and were being researched.

At 1 p.m. the crew that had meticulously gone through the lovebird's apartment had largely reconstructed Francois's life through bank statements, cancelled checks, phone bills and payroll stubs. Among other things, they knew the address of his two previous apartments, where he ate, shopped, got quick cash and his doctors. Agents had already been dispatched to canvass all of these locations, interview his neighbors and the people he would have dealt with frequently. The pursuit was now a furious race operating at warp speed.

2:30 p.m. - Chatham, New Jersey

A block away from the school, Bodkin and a large muscled man watched Dominic's four year old daughter Nancy enter the car of the family friend that picked her up every day after preschool. As they pulled away, he followed at a distance in the recently stolen car. At the chosen intersection he and his associate donned the ski masks, cut the car off and jumped out quickly. Bodkin grabbed the little girl, while his associate put a gun in the driver's face and pistol whipped her once. That was enough to get her hysterical, as blood flowed from her face. Later the driver couldn't even say for sure if her assailants were men or women, no less offer a description of them or the car.

It had gone very smoothly, just as most of Sonya's meticulously planned operations usually did. This had been so easy, he thought, as he glanced at the bound and taped little girl and managed a slight smile. Let's see how effectively her famous father functions now, once he knows we have her.

They would deliver her to the Metuchen apartment and Sonya as soon as darkness fell, around 5:30.

3:30 p.m. "Books and Biscuits" store, Upper East Side, Manhattan

Miss Susan Haskins, the proprietor of the store, had greeted agents Keenan and Bugliari cordially, after they had shown their badges and explained the purpose of their visit.

"Let me first say that I am the daughter of the chief of police in my home town in Kentucky. I love my dad, and I have always loved and respected law enforcement folks and their work. Let me know any way I can help."

"Thank you Miss Haskins. We are very appreciative of your cooperation. The focus of our interest is a man named Francois DuBorg. I believe you are familiar with him." They showed her a photo.

"Yes. He would come in often, until he moved somewhere. Kind of an odd duck – a French intellectual artistic-type, who was trying to break into live theater. He had some success, but I know he also did something in a bank to really pay the bills. I would cash his checks to pay for food and books. They never bounced. He was a voracious reader – mostly political stuff. Nice enough guy. Occasionally he would come in with his girlfriend, who struck me as attractive but somewhat cold and hard, kind of a strange couple."

The agents looked at each other. "Did he come in with any other men or women ever, anyone with an accent perhaps?"

"Not that I can remember."

"Do you know or recall seeing this man?" showing her the circulating picture of Harsanyi.

"No, but wasn't his picture in the paper this morning," as she reached for the New York Daily News.

"Don't worry about that now, ma'am. Did you ever get a flavor for Francois DuBorg's politics?"

"Not really, other than the general malaise I see in a lot of frustrated artistic types that believe that somehow the system is conspiring to deny them their rightful place as a star," she said with a smile. She was also feverishly trying to recall the story that accompanied the picture in the paper.

"Ok, then let's turn to this girlfriend. Did he seem genuinely interested in her? Did she give you the impression that she would do anything for him, anything he asked?"

"Well, I'm not sure I know where this is going, but I would have to say no. It just had the feel that she was the dominant one in the relationship. She was kind of tough – I can't remember ever seeing her laugh, barely a smile. He was somewhat meek around her. I saw her mad a couple of times and never saw that in him. He really seemed a sweet, harmless guy."

The agents looked at each other. Could Prudence Owens have been the consummate actress all these years, feigning devotion to the Bureau as a basically shy and retiring middle age woman?

Then Keenan asked, "Did it strike you that they were a bit of an odd couple – he a dashing man in his early thirties, who probably had his choice of lovers, and she over 40, somewhat overweight and not distinguished by her looks?"

Susan looked at them for a few seconds and cocked her head at an angle. "What are you talking about? She was about his age, very trim and athletic looking, hardly overweight. She moved quickly and with grace. And, very attractive with her short blond hair and chiseled features."

Keenan and Bugliari stared at each other. The latter, as the senior agent, spoke first. "Miss Haskins, we may have a misunderstanding here. Allow me to show you a photo of his girlfriend." They produced a recent photo of Owens.

"I don't think I've ever seen this woman in my life, and certainly not with Francois. Who is she?"

At this point after exchanging another glance with Keenan, Bugliari said, "You are saying that you never saw this woman with DuBorg? And you're implying that he had another girlfriend?"

"Well," she laughed, "this would hardly be a first for a young, good looking single guy in the big city, now would it?"

"Miss Haskins, this is a very serious matter. It is somewhat connected to the man's picture we showed you earlier, a man of great interest to us, whom we are aggressively trying to locate and may be in great danger. Now let us start over in detail from the first time DuBorg first walked in here and please describe with care and as much detail as you can everything you recall about him and especially this girlfriend."

One and one half hours later the agents concluded the interview, thanking Haskins profusely and left their card in case she recalled additional facts or impressions. They left her with a police portraiture artist to get a drawing done of this blond.

As they left she asked them, "Should I call you if Francois comes in again?" Keenan looked her square in the eye. "That is not a risk, ma'am. And I would doubt you will ever see this girlfriend again either."

Her jaw dropped. No words came out as the agents left.

They got in the car and immediately got on the secure car phone and called in on Dominic's private number. Strangely he wasn't there- his aide answered. "Dominic has had a terrible emergency develop – some sons of bitches took his four year old daughter from the car she was riding in coming home from nursery school over two hours ago. No sign or contact since. He is, of course, devastated."

Bugliari and Keenan were astounded. "What the hell…" Keenan moaned in a very subdued voice. "It's them, the Russians – where will they stop? They're breaking all the rules. This guy Harsanyi must mean everything to them. They never tried any of this stuff even with the nuclear thefts."

"Well I'm sure you didn't call in on this line to curse these creeps. What have you got?"

"It seems lover boy had more than one girlfriend, and the second one is a lot more interesting than mousy Prudence. We are now looking for a 31-35 year old short haired blond, about five feet eight inches, very trim and athletic, fine facial features, tough, cool and not very friendly. She seemed to tell DuBorg when to jump and how high. Not seen in the last two months, probably about the time DuBorg moved in or, perhaps more accurately, was told to move in with Owens. We're guessing, but this woman probably ran DuBorg and his activities. She is either in charge of this whole operation or would lead us to whoever is. We have our best bureau artist there now working with Haskins on a portrait of her. As soon as he's done, get it out to all law enforcement. ASAP."

57th Street

While this conversation was occurring, a massive force of FBI investigators were all over the wealth of new leads that had been developed following the trail of Francois, Prudence and the garage. In uptown Manhattan, agents Morgan and Cissel were sitting down with a Dr. Caryn Ronan, a psychoanalyst whose name had shown up on a number of DuBorg's checks.

After a formal and mutually polite introduction, the agents gave Mrs. Ronan a limited description of a potential kidnapping case of a leading scientist, including the possible roll of her patient, Mr. Francois DuBorg. "We should tell you that your patient has been arrested and will unquestionably be charged with some meaningful degree of involvement in a most serious federal case that we are aggressively pursuing. We are, of course, sensitive to confidentiality concerns that I'm sure you have for all your patients, but you will have to put this in the context of a developing case of the utmost gravity.

Mr. DuBorg had moved in several months ago with a Miss Prudence Owens, an employee of the federal government with access to matters of national security of the highest order. Did he talk to you ever about that move in?"

Mrs. Ronan looked down, cleared her throat and answered, "Yes, he did."

"And what did he say about it?"

"There are limits that I can go with you on this without abusing patient trust. Let me just say that the relationship troubled Francois. He is a sensitive and caring man, an intellectual radical like many of his countrymen's intelligentsia."

"Was he using Miss Owens?"

She cleared her throat again. "I can't say. But there was an outside influence that had pushed him to aggressively move in. He never did tell me,

178

however, what it was that they wanted to know. But it did trouble him to the point that he had sought out my counseling and analysis. He never did get specific."

"Was he emotionally attached to Miss Owens?"

"Unclear, but I think he was growing more fond of her, particularly after he had moved in with her."

"Did he ever talk about the people who wanted him to stay close to Miss Owens or what they wanted to know?"

"Only in a limited fashion. He did mention a woman, with whom he at one time had been romantically involved. Their relationship was mostly physical. Later he had come to fear her in some ways. My guess is that she used romance to first involve him and then used fear to sustain it."

"Did he ever give you a physical description of this woman?"

"No he did not, although he did once say she was quite striking."

"What can you tell me that he said about her - any proclivities, traits, interests, beliefs, biases, sexual habits?"

"I am not going to describe their personal lives in any detail. That would be a betrayal of client confidentiality."

"Did you ever meet her, see her picture, learn her address or occupation?"

"No to all of that except the occupation. He had told me that she was in the media – worked in some way for the *Today* show. One time he did talk about the two of them running into an FBI guy she knew, while they were at a baseball game, and he had to pretend he didn't know her." Both agents wrote that comment down in detail.

"Did he give you the name of this *Today* show person?"

"No."

And so it went for another hour, although it got testier as the agents repeatedly asked the same personal questions that Mrs. Ronan had earlier refused to answer. Finally they left her office.

She struggled for the next few days about her refusal to discuss more of the sexual – psychological specifics of Francois's relationship with the TV woman, her downright abusive treatment of him and her damaging sexual dominance. In the end the FBI finally moved on, and Caryn Ronan was able to return to her work in good conscience that she had not revealed the truly personal

179

details. But she had given them a lead far more valuable – the link to the *Today* show. They got right on that.

CHAPTER 29

THE RACE IS ON

Sunday, November 22, 8:45 a.m.
Hadley General Aviation Airport Raritan Township, New Jersey

They would be flying on a chartered Beechcraft Bonanza, the most respected general aviation aircraft in the high end, single engine market. Introduced in 1947 at the hefty price of $7,975, the Beech Aircraft Company had sold thousands of this Model 35 produced by highly skilled workers in Wichita, Kansas. It had a range of approximately 1000 miles, more than enough to reach the Carp general aviation airport in Ottawa, Canada, its pre approved flight destination. The Bonanza enjoyed an exemplary record of performance and safety in its first six years. However, like all aircraft it could not take off with its wing flaps and tail rudders frozen in place and with heavy ice on its wings. And that was exactly the current condition of this Bonanza.

The weather forecast the day before had been for light rain and a temperature around 40 degrees Fahrenheit for the scheduled take off at 9:00 a.m. – nothing that could impede or probably even delay the flight. Within an hour they would be out of the warmish system and clear air for the remainder of the flight. Surprisingly, the low pressure system coming up from a southwesterly direction and bringing the rain had been joined by a strengthening cold front down from Lake Erie and upstate New York, producing freezing sleet/snow in 29 degree weather.

Sonia had made the choice of little Hadley Airport because it was low key, no tower, all general aviation and certainly not a likely place for an escape from the country of the major soviet spy in the United States. No one could ever put all that together. On a typical clear Sunday in November there was usually more action at the golf driving range and miniature golf course across the street. The bad news was that no sophisticated services were available, particularly de-icing capability on a Sunday.

"There is no way we can get out of here until this sleet/snow stops and/or the temperature rises for 3-4 hours above this freezing," the pilot said in his barely distinguishable, perhaps Czech accent and clear military tone. "At that point our approved flight plan to leave the country, filed with New York Center and accepted by the Canadians, will not be valid. Also, we would not make Ottawa Carp Airfield until darkness, which would preclude our landing this aircraft under their rules. This afternoon we might be able to take off to another domestic destination, re-file a new flight plan and make the Canadian leg when approved by the authorities, but this would take several days."

Sonya stared at him. If looks could kill, he would be a dead man. He had assured her that weather looked good for Sunday. It now was clear there was no alternative backup plan, at least not for several days. Sonya never asked where these sleeper agents came from, their background or their commitment to the cause. Generally they were very good. This guy was not. He seemed in it for the money. The MGB was letting her down as never before and at the critical point in the most important assignment in her life.

Her contained but fearsome rage was partly a function of the failure she herself had felt after the bungled escape attempt in New York Wednesday night. One of the goons had screwed up somewhere and had to have been tailed to the site. Clearly the FBI did not know of the Harlem location, or they would have stormed it directly. It was also clear that they didn't know what was about to occur at the Chelsea Piers, or they would have had more firepower there. No, they had gotten lucky, following one of the foot soldiers to the site and were led right to the scene.

And now our brilliantly conceived and executed contingency escape had worked, even in the face of a massive law enforcement dragnet followed by regional publicity in all the media. We also have the girl and have emotionally disabled my nemesis, Benvenuto. Was it now all to be for naught because of some flyboy idiot? Rage – barely contained rage.

Then her mind cleared somewhat, and she suggested an option. "What do we risk by attempting to get airborne? If we see that the flaps will fail, we have a 2200 foot runway to accommodate a safe deceleration, correct?"

"We can attempt it but it will be very problematic. We have ice on our rudder, flaps and wings, which serve to reduce flexibility and adds weight."

Sonya commanded, "Let's give it our best shot." The pilot shrugged, argued for a while but eventually prepared the plane. Bodkin brought the sedated daughter of Dominic, Nancy, out of the car and carried her to the Beechcraft.

In 15 minutes they were taxiing to the furthest end of the longer runway. He opened the throttles on both engines to maximum takeoff RPM's, and the plane started to roll.

With 700 feet of runway left, the pilot realized the speed could not be increased, and he had to try now. Sweating even in the cold weather, he pulled back on the wheel, and slowly the plane rose to about 10 feet, at which point the stall indicator sounded its loud and clear warning. The Bonanza could not gain takeoff speed and, rather than risk a nose-plant, he brought it back down. They had failed.

They returned the Bonanza to its mooring. Sonya weighed her options. After some thought she said, "I like your idea of attempting to fly closer to Canada later today when things clear up and then re-file a new flight plan to leave for Ottawa. Come back to the car and let's return to the apartment, where we can review all this unnoticed and unseen."

The pilot hesitated and felt some discomfort in this change of plans. Finally he did understand that they would look very strange hanging around Hadley Airport in the sleet with a sedated four year old. But secretly he was afraid of this steely eyed woman.

They joined Harsanyi, Bodkin and the blindfolded, gagged and traumatized Nancy Benvenuto. Sonya drove them all back to the Rose Street apartment in Metuchen, which they entered through the back door with Nancy. They took her out, reinforced her sedation with another pill mixed in apple juice and left her sleeping in a bedroom.

Harsanyi went to his room and left Sonya and Bodkin to plan with the pilot, who promptly announced that he deserved more money for this more complex job. Sonya looked furtively at Bodkin. Then she got up to make some tea, which she served to both men.

Bodkin, given his limited English, was conducting a minimalist but distracting conversation with the pilot, which he tried to accelerate as he saw Sonya get in place. In a split second she put her right hand on his chin, her left on the back of his head and did a violent twist of his head up and to the right, snapping the top of the spinal column at the C-6 and C-7 vertebrae. His head fell lifeless on his chest, and she then kicked him violently off the chair onto the floor. Then threw his hot tea on his dead face.

"I don't want to even look at this scum while I enjoy my tea."

Bodkin managed a smile and said in Russian, "We could have used you at Stalingrad. You're one tough broad."

"Thank you. Coming from you I take this as a compliment. I do like the opportunity to use my hands, comrade. I just don't get enough opportunity to do much of it these days."

Bodkin rolled his eyes, astounded as always by the stealthy and calculated precision of his boss. He lifted the body and in the darkness quickly put it in the trunk of their Ford. He then garaged the car in the enclosed heated space that came with the apartment and returned to the unit, grabbing a beer and turning on the television set. Sonya joined him as the CBS Sunday Evening News with John Cameron Swayze came on.

After a lead off story updating Secretary of State John Foster Dulles's activities, a photo of Harsanyi was flashed on the air, describing the disappearance of a "leading American scientist" late last week. The photo had been in the papers Saturday and the two had seen it, but now the story was evidently escalating.

Then to their mutual shock a police drawing of a woman strongly resembling Sonya's real appearance was flashed on the screen, as Murrow mentioned that "the authorities were looking for her in connection with the case, and were seeking any help in determining her identity."

Bodkin groaned in Russian, "Jesus, how did they get that? Who could have described you so well but yet not know your American name."

"I don't know," Sonya replied quietly, seemingly lost in thought. After a 30 second hiatus she spoke, "They will soon know all about my true identity and possibly the name Sonya. It is time for both to disappear...now." She glided into the bathroom with her suitcase of cosmetics and disguises, not to reappear for over an hour. As she exited, totally unrecognizable now with her hair dyed black, she looked Bodkin squarely in the face and said, "Sonya, rest in peace. Her days are done."

Same Time
Dominic's Home, Chatham, New Jersey

Dominic answered the doorbell of his suburban home. It was agent Bugliari with the police sketch of the female subject. Dominic was trying to run the search for his daughter from his home and had asked only to be contacted on other developments in the case if they were extremely important.

"Chief, we're releasing this sketch of DuBorg's other girlfriend, not Prudence, but this other female who the witness Haskins described as a frequent companion. Our French lover boy liked to spread his good cheer around. Witnesses describe her as very tough and strong willed, perhaps the dominant figure in the relationship. Our guys have studied our old tapes, when the operatives were caught on film going to the big confab in the Soviet consulate. They now think the woman disguised as an old lady with the canes going in and a man going out is in fact a young spry female who fits the general description of this subject...highly likely this is Sonya."

He slowly removed the sketch from its envelope and placed it in front of Dominic.

His world fell out from beneath him. It was his lover – Catherine Bowers! Of *Today* show fame. Impossible!

The air left his body, replaced by a fear and rage that surged inward. He let out a scream of rage.

There she was – the *Today* show's rising young producer, the hot lady who had literally screwed him out of his depression, the woman who had been in his very FBI office. Apparently the bitch who had assassinated Mannesmann and tried to kill Dominic himself in Corning. Undoubtedly the woman on the night train who had helped pull off the Dickinson murder and theft.

Agent Sonya – the bane of his existence. The most cunning and thoroughly American agent in the history of soviet espionage here. Trying right now to get out our most vital secrets and their best spy. While I've been looking for her everywhere, part of the time she's been in bed with me.

Then he made the last connection – the fiend who also had to be the mastermind behind the kidnapping of my daughter. Doing God knows what to her right now. All to destroy my effectiveness in pursuing her by running this emotional train wreck through my mind.

With that he screamed, then roared, "I know this bitch. She works at the *Today* Show. Catherine Bowers. I met her on a publicity deal. She's been right under my nose."

He spared the details of how much under.

"Call the office and get that name out now. I need to do some work here."

As the agents left, thoughts raced through Dominic's mind, as he considered his options. Then he dialed the number he had called only once before. The phone was in fact being answered at a mob safe house in the Bronx. He gave his code name, "Edgar" to be used to signal that he wanted to talk to Don Bonsignore, the boss of the Port and the head of the council of New York's five crime families.

The Don was quickly located "in flagrante" at his 19 year old mistress' apartment in Manhattan. The aide had him on the phone, albeit naked and still panting, in 28 seconds.

"Bonsignore, it's Dominic Benvenuto. I need your help. Now! I will be concise and to the point.

You know all about the shootout at the Chelsea Piers. You also certainly know it was not about a drug bust. What you don't know is that it was an espionage matter of the gravest concern and threat to America. Also, that Catherine Bowers, the *Today* show writer who did that puff TV piece for you and the union, we suspect is involved with this, working for a foreign government. She did the story to have a cover for her research into how the docks work and probably make some new friends there. So she could use them to get high value operatives in and out.

I'm coming to see you now, and I want everything you have on her. Her contacts on the waterfront, the union guys she worked with, any other friends she might have made in the port, anybody she may have screwed. Capisce? She had some inside help in that attempt to escape and I need to find them now. All this took place in your territory."

Bonsignore paused, took in a big breath and began to speak slowly in response. "Dominic, I can't believe all this. From that TV broad? We knew that firefight had nothing to do with us, with drugs or any port problems. When we saw the army of Feds and cops there the next day, we just stayed out. None of our business, ya know. And that hot little bitch Bowers was behind all that?

That comment made Dominic spontaneously ask the next question. "Did you do her?"

The don was silent for five seconds. Then Dom prodded him, "Did you do her, Dante?"

"Yes," was all he quietly said.

This truth blew him away. Jesus, he realized, I share the same girlfriend with a mob boss. Wonderful. Dipping my unit in a mafia ink well. Christ, what more will we learn about this women. So that's how she worked her way into the port for that story. And that's how she made at least some friends or got some of her guys already on the inside to help pull this off.

Dom continued. "Now I have to add one more terrible fact. Her people kidnapped my four year old daughter yesterday. Trying to throw me off. Distract me from the job of finding her and her valuable cargo. The bastards know I'm the agent in charge of this."

The Don whispered something in Sicilian Dom could not make out.

"So Dante, I need to talk to you right now about how you will help us. You understand – will help us, not if. Where can we meet?"

Bonsignore gave an address in the solidly Italian section of north Newark, halfway between them. Dominic got in his car, put the portable red light on the top and never dropped below the speed limit.

Thirty Minutes Later
North Newark, New Jersey

Bonsignore, his consigliere and a driver-bodyguard got there first. When Dominic drove himself up, he parked, got out, introduced himself curtly and went inside. They sat at a table in a back room. The place was a station for number runners bringing in their tickets and cash but was quiet now.

Dominic opened right up, dispensing with any pleasantries. "Bonsignore, do you have any daughters?"

186

"Yea, I do. They are 8, 14 and 16 and they are my little flowers, the loves of my life."

"So I will start this little discussion of ours with this. Nancy is my only daughter, age four. You know my background is southern Italian. You know how I feel now imagining that little girl is with some killers, probably gagged and sedated? Maybe in some trunk of a car, probably wetting herself because of fear or lack of a bathroom. Sobbing for her mom and dad. Not understanding how they did not protect her from this nightmare. And in the hands of a woman agent who has among other things taken a sniper shot at me?"

The Don answered, "I would probably be going nuts–screaming at people, out looking for her, ready to shoot anyone who looked at me the wrong way. I would be insane with rage now. I understand. How can I help?"

"I am giving you three boxes of pictures – one batch of my daughter, one set of Bowers, one of a college professor. You don't need to know anything about him except that we want him big time. Prefer alive but not essential. No questions. Two days ago pictures of the professor went out to all the press, described as a possible kidnapping as the cover story. Possible foul play. My daughter's photo was rereleased yesterday and Bower's picture will go out tomorrow. None connected with each other. In fact they are probably all holed up in the same place as we speak. Trying to get out of the country.

Bowers is wanted in connection with the shootout. Separately my daughter is described as the missing child of a government employee, assumed kidnap victim. I want you to have every trucker, numbers runner and foot soldier of yours looking for them. An order from you, the top, a command. Nothing in writing and no questions asked. Just find any or all of them. Fast."

The Don added in a respectful low tone, "Especially your little girl."

After a pause, Dominic whispered, "Yes...especially my little Nancy."

There followed a discussion on details, contacts, and next steps. All surprisingly calm and businesslike. Bonsignore was somewhat surprised. He had expected that this Calabrian FBI big shot would go off the handle and rip into him. After all, it was Bonsignore's docks, his territory where all this mess had gone down. He had let his very silent absentee partner down in their mutual understanding.

Dominic got up to leave. Without any shouting or drama, he just methodically said, "Bonsignore let me make something clear. All this took place on your watch on your turf. This bitch infiltrated your operation. Then she made friends in the port who helped her. Two shooters with heavy caliber weapons got into the piers and more in the warehouses. Somebody gave them keys, opened doors, and made it possible. Up to now my department and the FBI has stayed out of your territory. You had a pass. An unspoken deal – you keep subversives and strangers out of this center of national security, keep the port humming, and we don't bother you when you dip your beak a little.

If you don't produce results and soon on this, I promise you that will change. A mob of federal agents will descend on your offices, on the docks – getting records from shippers, studying commission payments and examining tax returns. We'll rip it all apart and follow the stink to wherever it takes us, which is probably right up your Sicilian ass." With that he turned and left.

The Don stood frozen. He saw his whole gold mine potentially about to disappear, not to mention the feds trying to send him away – or deport him on some technicality. What he had worked for, battled for, killed for all those years of rising through La Famiglia. The respect he had assembled. Now threatened by a senior fed whose daughter had been taken as a result of a failure to catch some big time spooks right in the Family's feeding ground.

He had to get right to work. He turned to his consigliere and said in Italian, "Get the four other family heads to meet me for breakfast in our suite in the Waldorf Towers, tomorrow at 8 a.m. No exceptions."

Monday, November 23, 1953; 9:03 a.m.
NBC Studios

Garroway signed off at 9 a.m. Eastern Time. At 9:03, he was talking to Jack Lescoulie, the on screen sports commentator, when an aide whispered in his ear, "Mr. Weaver wants to see you upstairs. Immediately."

Weaver, who Hoover had called the night of the shootout, had conceived the *Today* show and as a result had been promoted to the Presidency of NBC. As Garroway entered, Weaver put down his notes on his latest idea–the creation of a new late night show called simply the *Tonight* show. That day he had a lunch scheduled with General David Sarnoff, Chairman and founder of NBC, to review the idea and get permission to talk to possible hosts he had in mind. He had knocked the ball out of the park with the *Today* show and his choice of Garroway.

"Take a seat Dave." Coffee service was brought in on an elegant silver platter. "Did the feds make your weekend as miserable as mine?"

"Pat, they went through everything of mine here and at home. Turned it upside down. Then they hauled off half of the stuff in my office. They grilled me on every conversation I ever had with her, everyone who I knew about who had worked with her or had anything to do with her getting the job. They knew about two lunches we had at the Plaza for year end reviews and wanted the full details. Wanted to know if I had ever slept with her.

"Had you?"

"Absolutely not. Although…I did think about it. She is stunning."

188

"How did we first hear about her, Dave?"

"A harmless connection through the NBC affiliate in Chicago. She helped write local news. Before that she had done similar work at their radio station. The Chicago guy raved about her. Didn't want to lose her but she had already said she was planning to leave, to come here to New York, wanted the big time. Our personnel people liked her. University of Wisconsin grad. I met her and hired her on the spot. And she never disappointed."

"What about her work leading to the story on the Port?"

"She brought it up with me and I told her it was nuts, too risky. People who are curious about that union and its mob bosses tend to disappear. Next thing I know she's got all the top union guys on film, answering her questions. Granted it was a bit of a puff piece, praising their patriotic role in the war and the Korean conflict. But still, no one had ever gotten inside that union. It was an absolutely unique story."

"Well, sadly we didn't know how unique this woman was. An American born in Iowa, working for God knows whom. For all our sakes I hope they get her soon, and take the heat off our ass."

Same time, Same Day
Waldorf Towers Hotel

Don Bonsignore sat at the head of the table. The four other Dons had now taken their places with selections from the breakfast buffet that had been set up in the room. They included Carmine ("Stones") Spoletti, Massimino ("the Cleaver") Tarantino, Giovanni ("Olio") Monte and Salvatore ("the Banker") Andretti. Their five consiglieres sat behind them along the walls of the dining room.

No one knew what this was about, except that they had been told to be there in no uncertain terms. There was a grave undertone and uncharacteristic silence permeating the room. You could hear a pin drop. Finally, Dante Bonsignore put down his coffee, cleared his throat and began to speak calmly in hushed tones in his native Sicilian-accented Italian.

"Gentlemen, it is with the utmost appreciation that I thank you for gathering here today so early and on such short notice. I will remember the respect you have all shown me by your quick response and this accommodation. What I am about to tell you will shock you as much as it has me and my organization.

My office got a call last year from this Catherine Bowers, a writer-producer for the new *Today* show on TV. We paid no attention to it. Then she called again and gave us a pitch about doing a story on our union members, what good guys they were, patriotic, a good line of bullshit, capisce? Also, how we were different from those pinko fairies on the West Coast.

189

As you know even with all the guys working for the newspapers that are on our payroll, we still get a lot of bad ink and it's been hurting us. Then Hollywood gets in the act with a new movie starring this young prick, Marlin Brando. That really hurt.

So we let Bowers a little into the tent. Thought she could help. A curious little lady who went all over the docks, meeting people, getting connected, looking up a lot of people. But at the end of the day she played ball with us. Let us see the rough cut and made some changes we wanted. The final product was real good. I even agreed to show up on the film, arms around some of the boys with American flags on their tee shirts loading tanks headed for Korea. Real friendly, right?

Then it runs on TV and she sends me a film copy. I show it the next Sunday dinner after mass with my whole family. Everything ends – splendido.

So yesterday I get a call from a certain important federal employee, whom, I'll just say, we have a very quiet relationship with. That's all – mutual respect. Don't ask any questions. All legit, just a business understanding. We will help them on certain national security stuff that matters big time to them. In return they just happen to lose interest in us. A very nice accommodation. Mutual respect."

He stopped to look at the four sets of eyes, each in its turn, to make sure they all were on the same page. And if one of them asked a tough question or gave him any heat for letting the press in, his operations would get a little visit from Bonsignore soldiers, who might just get a little sloppy. You know, a bar trashed here, a whore house broken up – the kind of untraceable stuff that just sort of happens in our businesses when people forget who their friends are.

"So yesterday my Fed buddy calls and asks through our buffer system for an emergency meeting. He told me this Bowers lady is most likely involved in some kind of spy activity, has shot and killed two FBI guys and wounded three others at a shootout at Chelsea Piers last week. She is now trying to sneak some turncoat commie scientist out of the country. And, most unbelievable, she has had the cajones to kidnap my contact's daughter for hostage value."

The four other heads of the families sat spellbound, frozen in their place. They couldn't believe what they were hearing, like some tragic Italian opera happening real time. They all had some problems with the feds, but none of them would ever take these kinds of ghoulish actions with an FBI guy's family. Not only would it be incredibly stupid, but it also squarely violated their own weird code of ethics. You rarely touched a woman and certainly not a four year old girl. That was an unthinkable sin, a violation of the natural order.

They all were quietly reaching the same conclusion. We either set this right and fast or we are all in real trouble. First it would be Bonsignore's head. Then the rest of us. Just the way the feds had gotten Capone through tax stuff and other paperwork. It didn't matter that Capone had 10,000 civilians on his payroll – the feds still got him on technicalities. Don Bonsignore, The Boss of all bosses, knew exactly what they were all thinking.

His eyes showed a subtle glimmer of his developing success; he had co-opted them all to join ranks behind him. He thought, there are reasons why I am "The Boss of all the bosses."

"So gentlemen, I ask you all now for an urgent accommodation that will serve all our interests. We get the word out NOW to be looking for this woman, the scientist creep and the little girl. Their pictures are all over. But, and this is important, don't connect them. Just three separate things we are helping on. For the good of the country…and our businesses." With that he ran the top of one hand beneath his jaw and upward – the Sicilian gesture signifying the request for agreement, a nod yes.

"Every teamster, hotel worker, numbers runner, loan shark, hooker and doper on our payroll. All our Capos, soldiers, bookies. Everyone, capisce? We better find at least the little girl or we may all be in a world of hurt like never before."

Then he stopped and looked around. Now it would be OK for them to open their mouths. I'm done.

"What questions do you have?"

Carmine Spoletti, boss of most of Brooklyn and Staten Island, spoke first. "Don Bonsignore, do you have anything on this TV girl? Have you checked out the people she spent time with on the docks? What the hell was she all about?"

"We have checked out everyone she had contact with. Mostly our key people. And none of them would ever get involved with some spook. They're good Americans, and they never would do anything to hurt the business." Then he paused. "Except for a few exceptions we are looking into now."

The room went stone cold silent. Nobody moved. What the hell did he mean by *a few exceptions*?

Bonsignore put his head down and spoke quietly.

"Three union members and a former member were killed in that firefight. Shot by the Feds. All Eastern Europeans – no degos. Turns out they were all three illegals – phony papers, social security, the works. Fooled my people. All forgeries by a real pro, not done in this country according to the feds."

Everyone in the room stayed quiet. They knew what a full court press by the feds could do to all of them. The smell of fear in the room was palpable –

very unusual for this group of vicious survivors, who had reached the top by never showing fear.

But this game was clearly out of their league. These were the guys who fought the big wars with tanks, planes and now the new nuclear bombs.

The leaders and their consiglieres got down to the practical business of organizing the manhunt. By noon, everyone whom the mob controlled or who owed them a favor was looking for Bowers, Harsanyi and little Nancy. Nothing on paper except photos but on the lips of thousands in bars, restaurants, construction sites, trucking warehouses and night clubs in the New York metropolitan area. With big rewards offered. The whole shadow economy that marched to a different drummer.

And sometimes very effectively in matters like this.

4:45 p.m. - Chatham Pre School

The administrator, Mrs. Miller, was the first to see the little girl, lethargic and dressed in very dirty clothes, get out of a large Eastern Freightways truck. A big man was holding her hand, as they walked to the office. Who could this be so late in the day, she thought. Then she looked more closely. She flew out of her office, running to grab little Nancy Benvenuto.

"My God, it's her," she screamed to no one in particular. She ran up and hugged little Nancy, still somewhat groggy from the anesthetized state she had been kept in for days.

The driver said "Yeah I seen this poor little kid wandering about four miles away near route 24 with this here school name and address pinned on her jacket, crying. She also fit the description that we all got from our union shop foreman, when we started our noon shift, for some missing girl. So I brought her here straight away."

"Oh my god you are a hero. This little girl was stolen from her family just three blocks from here. She's in our preschool." With that Mrs. Miller picked her up, raced into the office and called the FBI number she had been given.

"She seems OK but kind of doped up. Get over here and call the family."

"Thank you, Mrs. Miller. Don't move, we will be right there."

In six minutes five FBI agents arrived in two cars with Dominic forty five seconds behind them and the ambulance and local police 90 seconds later. With great emotion the little girl was reunited with her father and mother - and then the brave little warrior finally broke down, crying uncontrollably. Dominic went up to the trucker, gave him a big hug and kissed him on the cheek,

192

whispering something in his ear. He got his name and then they drove off in the ambulance to Overlook Hospital in Summit, New Jersey for a battery of tests for little Nancy.

The first agents had fanned out in the Chatham area rapidly in three cars on a long shot attempt to sight any of the 112 stolen cars listed in the greater New York list of unsolved car thefts in the last two years, a list they had practically memorized. The New York garage had housed three cars that had been on that list. Although repainted and relicensed, they had been identified by the VIN numbers. It was reasonable to conclude when the escape car from the pier had gone into that garage, the passengers quickly switched into another repainted stolen car and had made their escape in that new vehicle. In fact the 1951 Ford was on that list, but neither that nor any other suspect vehicle was sighted. Three hours later they gave up.

Twenty miles away from where little Nancy was found, Sonya, Bodkin and Harsanyi were driving northwest away from Chatham on Route 10 in the car of the lately deceased pilot, whose decomposing body remained in the trunk of the 1951 Ford still in the apartment complex garage. The Ford everyone was now looking for.

"See Dr. Harsanyi, we are nice people after all. We returned the little girl, hardly any worse for wear, right? Just a few drugs for the little fusspot, what the heck." Harsanyi swallowed hard.

Later that evening "Edgar" called Bonsignore on the back line. "Please extend my warmest thanks to your people. Particularly to the Teamsters at Eastern Freightways. And as one father of girls to another, I personally thank you. And keep your people on the outlook for the woman and the professor.

Let me just add that I hope and expect your business in the port will continue to prosper. Within reasonable limits of course."

The Don responded, "God bless your little girl!" They both hung up, never to talk directly to each other again. Ever.

Tuesday, Nov 24, 1953
8:00 a.m. - F.B.I. Headquarters, New York

Dominic had just returned to the office to the cheers, hugs and embraces of all. "I want to thank you for all of your thoughts and prayers for my beautiful daughter, now safely resting with her mom. She will be fine. I applaud you for all your great investigatory work in my absence. We now have the name, Catherine Bowers, the probable leader of this operation, and we are piling up information on her. It's only a matter of time before we get her and Harsanyi. I pledge to you that these bastards will never get out." A roar followed. "Let's go."

Hell hath no fury like that of a Calabrese American, whose beautiful four year old daughter had been held captive and doped by creeps with pants left to soil for three days. Dominic was a man functioning at a high pitch, but doing so in a barely controlled state of rage. The truth was he wanted to find them and rip them apart with his hands. But he had to bury these thoughts and professionally lead an effort now involving over 500 Bureau agents spread throughout the Northeast, right up to the Canadian border.

"Tell me about DuBorg, Jesse. What have we learned?"

"You know, as a French citizen and given the language difficulties, we thought it appropriate to invite some of our French consulate Securitèe associates of Corsican descent to question the subject at their consulate on French soil. A lot of guys with knife wounds on their face and body – you know how the Corsicans are. We suddenly felt an urgent need for coffee, so we left them alone for awhile."

"I have to tell you we returned to find Francois highly upset with that wet electric prod up his ass with continual shocks running through it, his feet in water and a hot wire running up his nose, all of which had caused him to wretch and defecate all over himself.

The puissant has now spilled the beans completely. He was recruited in Paris, where he was a member of the Party, and told of a great service he could render the international proletariat through work in New York. His cover was as an actor, in fact a real passion of his, and he had a real, part time job at Credit Lyonnaise Bank, translating loan contracts.

Catherine Bowers, AKA agent Sonya, made contact with him, at first wooed him with hot romance and then started to bust his balls at every turn, humiliating him and sexually abusing him. Then he was instructed to pick up Prudence Owens and learn all that he could from her, given her position with the Bureau. This all began to bother him mentally, and he sought professional psychological help. His doctor has been somewhat helpful, although these types tend to protect their patients. But she did give us the lead to the *Today* show."

Dom asked, "OK, now give me the full data dump on Bowers. What do we know at this point?"

Agent Morgan continued, "She grew up in Iowa in a fatherless household. Her mother was a total radical at an early age and actually visited the Soviet Union in 1918 with that John Reed crowd of left wing Americans. She got pregnant there; father listed as unknown. She raised the daughter as a closet communist, reading to her from the "Manifesto." Catherine adored her mom and bought it all. Total radical by the time she went off to the University of Wisconsin. Majored in communications, minored in Slavic Studies, fluent in Russian. Some of her college acquaintances said she had at least two abortions and used males for physical pleasure as she pleased. Also had clear psychological issues. When the war broke out she openly worked for a radical socialist paper in New York until late 1942.

At that point the trail goes completely cold. We have had 120 agents and analysts in four different offices working around the clock now for 24 hours just on her, and yet we don't know where she was or what she did for eighteen months. No U.S. passport, no record of travel outside the country. Boss, my bet is she went somewhere to get the best training the soviets could give her and returned as a key agent, deeply submerged as a mainstream and talented American.

In 1944 she resurfaces with a gopher job at a newspaper, which led to writing for a Chicago radio station affiliated with NBC. That led to the *Today* show. We can't find any smoking gun in that chain of jobs. She wanted media, worked hard, was very smart. She earned it all, and moved higher and higher in the communications industry."

"Damn, a native American poised to strike on Moscow's order. Who knows what other work she has done without our knowing it."

Then he suddenly realized, hell, that super spy George Koval was from Iowa also. The bastard who stole all those nuclear weapon construction secrets. The guy we've never disclosed. Maybe he recruited her. He made a mental note to report that thought to Hoover's office immediately.

Then Dominic asked, "What about the garage manager – is he talking yet?" Dominic asked.

"No," replied Morgan. "Of course as an illegal entrant he has no rights, so we haven't been overly concerned about his comfort. He seems to have lost some teeth, and his balls are apparently bothering him. Also, he's not smelling very good – he doesn't seem to believe that the bathroom in that wing is unusable. And he keeps dropping his cigarettes on his skin, very clumsy." Even Dominic broke a small smile.

"Regarding our Prudence Owens, chief, we are almost certain she was just a hapless dupe, hopelessly in love with DuBorg and willing to do anything for him. There was clearly a sexual hold he had over her, and after making love, there would be pillow talk. She thought it harmless, but that info would be passed on to a voice in a phone booth the next day. And I must add that she is now a psychological mess, and the department shrink with her does not expect her to ever recover. And she's suicidal."

Dominic looked down silently for 10 seconds. Then he asked, "What about Bower's mother?"

"She is still in Iowa in the house that Catherine grew up in, but is not at home. Our Chicago office got a search warrant and are now going through the house inch by inch. Interestingly no pictures of her daughter taken in the last 10 years. Some radical magazines but other than that nothing unusual. Apparently she works odd jobs, cooking and cleaning but seems to be out of town now. Some friends, but none close. The agents are making inquiries and have the house under subtle surveillance with the phone tapped."

"All right, a lot of good work has been done. Keep pursuing all of this. We have to find them before they leave the country. I want a real presence in the airports, the shipping ports and the Canadian border. This is personal for me now. I want Bowers, Harsanyi and their associates to burn in the chair, and I want to witness it."

The group looked quietly at each other and realized their boss was now a man on fire – as a patriot, a professional and a father. They gave him wide berth as he stormed out of the room.

CHAPTER 30

TO THE BORDER

Wednesday, November 25, 1953
Dzerzhinsky Square, Moscow

General Kruglov had assembled Andropov and Tolstoy in his office.

"Comrades, our lead agent in Canada has been called by Sonya on a secure phone. He has reported the following to our embassy in Ottawa, whose message has just arrived. Sonya has eluded the Americans after the failed port connection and the first contingency plan to fly out in a small plane failed. She is now activating our second contingency plan, the ground escape over the border into Canada. She will do this by car tomorrow on the American holiday of Thanksgiving – apparently a very busy day, as many families visit their relatives just across the border. Reportedly the heavy traffic presses the border guards to be more accommodating and just wave more through. She has many crossover options and will not reveal her choice of place or time, as she worries about how secure our channels are. She's convinced by the way, that we have a problem here. And high up."

He paused to let that sink in.

"She will avoid bridges, instead choosing to cross land to land – a smart decision. Harsanyi will be masquerading as an old man and she will be in one of her bizarre disguises – to be determined. Once across, she will call our agent, who will have been waiting for her near one of the most remote border options. When they reach Canada, they will be safe, in my opinion, and as good as here in Dzerzhinsky Square. And this nightmare may end like a crescendo in a Shostakovich Symphony. Questions?"

"Is there any muscle still with her? Is Bodkin there?" asked Tolstoy.

"Yes he is, and they have several automatic weapons with them, disguised in the structural parts of Harsanyi's supposed wheelchair."

"Ingenious," Andropov mouthed in a low, almost reverential tone. "This woman is good. What will she do afterward, by the way?"

"That cannot be discussed, even in this group. I don't know who is more important – Harsanyi or agent Sonya. Many important people here in Moscow want her very badly for their work."

"Comrade General," Andropov asked, "a small detail: what is to be the fate of the Italian, the former POW, and his family in the Ukraine whose mother has been our blind drop agent in the department store in New York City? You will recall that she was our conduit for many years? What do we do with her son?"

"He will have an accident on the job, be buried as a good communist and his two sons will be admitted to Kosmonol – the Communist Youth League. We just can't afford to have a loose end like that running around America. Regarding the woman in New York, no contact with her ever again. She and her husband will keep their mouths shut, fearing American action against them."

Tolstoy looked down, as loathing and disgust filled him–the woman's family just a loose end to be added to the pile of 20 million other civilian loose ends that had died in Russia under communism.

Kruglov adjourned the meeting and Tolstoy returned to his office. What to do? Apparently the Americans have no idea where Sonya and the escaping party were now or any aspect of the new plan. If he did nothing they would all get out. He would have to contact his liaison, but how, and on such short notice?

Later that Day–Same Building

"What the hell! Someone is calling the American embassy from this very building and speaking to them in English. We just closed the trace from the bugged lines we have in their embassy building. Get the security officer of the day here now!" shouted the technical sergeant running the eavesdropping desk.

All calls were monitored in or out of Dzerzhinsky Square except Kruglov's lines, and everyone who worked there knew it. The sergeant could not believe what he had just heard.

By the time the security officer arrived, the call had been terminated, but, of course, it had been taped. They played it back. The two technicians and the officer knew enough English to know this was really bad. Also the speaker was disguising his voice. He said something about the escape being on a holiday and that the bird's wings could be clipped crossing by land into Canada. They ran upstairs to General Kruglov's office.

Lieutenant Colonel Igor Tolstoy, the new "model soviet man," had left the empty office three floors below him after completing his phone call to the U.S. embassy. He flew up the back stairs to his floor, making a point of immediately dropping into a colleague's office to establish his whereabouts.

He knew, however, now it would only be a matter of time, but at least the Americans were warned and roughly knew the plan. His fate was sealed – the only question was when and how.

8:00 a.m. EST – Same day
Jefferson Parks Apartments Metuchen, New Jersey

Vinny Kelly lifted the door to his heated garage and noticed that the smell had gotten worse. Now Vinny was a fussy guy, a clean freak, who also had a very sharp sense of smell. It was said by his wife that he could smell a fart 100 feet away.

Some new tenant had recently rented the garage next to him and parked his 1951 Ford there. The units were only separated by chicken wire on the inside, so that one heater could heat all four of the parking stalls in each cluster. But this meant Vinny could see and smell his garage neighbors, and the odor, though still slight, was starting to bother him.

He called the superintendent, who was sick of Kelly's complaints. Two weeks earlier he had bitched about the stink of a neighbor's garbage outside his apartment two doors down. However, the super agreed to call the tenant who had the stall the Ford was in but got no answer, so he joined Vinny at the garage, knowing Kelly would otherwise just keep bothering him.

As soon as he opened the door, he let out a low whistle. The super had retired two years ago from the Runyon Funeral Home in town, having served there as a mortician for thirty years. Besides the upscale work, he also did jobs for the county on decomposing bodies, frequently seniors without family found days after death, usually when a neighbor noticed the smell.

He looked in the car and saw no one. The smell seemed stronger in the rear. "Something is decomposing in that trunk. I'm calling the cops just in case."

The Metuchen PD came quickly, crow-barred the trunk open and found the pilot's body. The four men gasped from the odor. The patrolmen called in the emergency to detective Lieutenant Eddie Leese, who said he would get there immediately. He also asked for a description of the car and its vehicle identification number. The 1951 Ford rang a bell and he checked the APB list for stolen cars possibly involved in this ongoing FBI matter of the highest urgency. The circuit closed.

Thirty seconds later he was on the emergency phone line that had been set up with Dominic Benvenuto, bureau chief of FBI counter intelligence in New York, who ordered nothing be touched until his men got there.

One hour later over 15 agents were going over every square inch of the car, garage and apartment. Agent Cissell called in to Dominic. "Chief, I would guess no one has been here in about 3 days. The milk and other food stuffs have gone sour in the 'fridge. Before they left they tidied up and threw out all the garbage, which unfortunately got picked up two days ago. But I've got prints and hair samples galore. And Chief...one of them looks like it could have been from your daughter."

Dominic was taken aback by that. He was reminded how personal this was – some scum had held his doped up four year old beloved daughter there. He worked hard to contain his rage. When he had recovered he asked, "Do you have the victim's ID?"

"Yes we do. His wallet was left on him. A Gustave Breen. Of particular significance, he has a general aviation pilot's license."

Dominic's eyes rolled. He started to connect the dots. "OK, Ed, you keep on it there until every inch has been covered, but get the prints, hair and other evidence to the lab now." He hung up and barked to his new assistant, a male, "Get me that security chief here in New York for the FAA on the phone."

Twenty eight minutes later, an FAA manager described a flight plan filed last Friday by Breen to "take two or three passengers from the Hadley airport in Raritan Township, New Jersey to the general aviation Carp Airport in Ottawa, Canada that Sunday. He had cancelled the flight due to weather and no alternative has been filed."

"Don't hold your breath," Dom muttered to himself, thinking of the decomposing body just found. He thanked him and hung up. Sonya aka Catherine Bowers and the pilot had probably quarreled over something and, no surprise, the pilot had gotten the worst of it. The usual Sonya pattern.

Eight agents in his office were set to work learning all they could about Gustave Breen, his history, previous flights and, most important, his automobile registration. The Ford had gone in and something else had come out, most likely Breen's car, and it was highly likely that Sonya, Harsanyi and accomplice were in it.

Dom was fast developing a character profile of Sonya – ruthless, cunning, violent, but also capable of rapid readjustment of complex plans, conceived well in advance and skillfully executed. So she whacks Breen after the flight failed because of weather. Who knows why she found it necessary to kill him? Then she sees the police artist's sketch of her and a connection with the Harsanyi matter. She had to assume the Manhattan garage had been hit and Francois was in custody. This meant their Ford was now dirty.

They still wanted to go to Ottawa. So now you dump his body in the Ford's trunk, which won't be found for a while, take off in Breen's car for an escape into Canada. Then hide out in the Ottawa embassy until the Soviets can get him back to Moscow, where he turns the world upside down. Sorry, but the Royal Canadian Mounted Police are not the same as FBI counterintelligence. If they get over the border, they're as good as home.

Dominic's thoughts were interrupted by his new assistant on the intercom. "Chief, there's an urgent call…" at which point Dominic cut him off.

"Hold all calls Frank – period."

"Sir, it's director Hoover."

He thought to himself, oh, just what I don't need now, some request for a long update.

"Yes, Director Hoover, Bureau Chief Benvenuto here."

"I'll get right to the point. The CIA just reported a call to their top man in the Moscow embassy from our source in the MGB. At great personal risk he revealed the plan is to get Harsanyi out on Thanksgiving Day by car into Canada, exact location unclear, but through a secondary land-to-land border crossing. I have our people on the phone now with the army, and we plan to bring in hundreds of our agents plus the military to help the border control people. We have less than 24 hours. Your next call will be from our operations director, and you and he have to get all the bodies we can up there. Call me every two hours throughout the night to let me know of your progress." Then he just hung up.

They had just obtained the description of Breen's Oldsmobile, so an APB went out to all law enforcement on the eastern Canadian border. Sixty New York agents were given 90 minutes to report to a military hangar at Floyd Bennett Air Field, just outside Queens. Dominic would go with them. Two other transports at Newark were being packed with army personnel. They had to control that border and fast.

Later that same day
Upstate, New York

Dominic grabbed a map and studied the land-to-land border crossings in the Northeast. He tried to think as Sonya might. There essentially were 200 miles along the Canadian land border with New York, Vermont and New Hampshire. Beyond that there was a long border with Maine, but that was a much longer trek from New Jersey over marginal roads and far to the east of the desired Ottawa destination, revealed by their former FAA flight plan. Sonya would want to minimize exposure time. Unaware that the Americans knew what she was going to do, the odds were strong that she would take the easiest way, crossing into Ontario along the 150 mile border along New York and Vermont.

To cover that 150 miles he would need at least 500 armed men in the woods. These snipers would cover the wooded areas between major roads with high powered, site - enabled weapons. As the closest and most accessible, the New York border would be emphasized.

The occupants of the late Gustave Breen's Oldsmobile were, of course, oblivious to all of this and actually were quite upbeat, as they were now within thirty miles of the border and looking for another non-descript, low key motel to spend the night with their fake ID. They had taken all secondary roads for the long trip beginning two days ago in New Jersey. They wanted to be well rested for whatever tomorrow would bring.

As they had been doing throughout their journey, they would tune into the local news station just before the top of the hour. Now they had a station from Plattsburg, New York on, as the five o'clock signal sounded. After some national news from the network the local man came on.

"Area-wide police have just put out an APB for a tan 1953 Oldsmobile, New Jersey license plates. Anyone seeing such a vehicle should call local police immediately. In other news…"

Harsanyi cut him off, "Oh my god, they know we're in this car. How could that have happened so soon?"

Sonya thought for a few seconds. "They must have somehow found the Ford, which they knew was a stolen car. God damn lucky. Then they find our flyboy in the trunk and quickly deduce that we are likely now using his car. Dammit!"

Sonya thought for several minutes. Bodkin knew not to disturb her. Harsanyi asked several questions but got no response.

"I need to take a few years off this face and get changed." She did that while the men got out of the car and walked a bit. Bodkin tried to calm Harsanyi down in his contorted English.

When they returned she looked younger than her 35 years, wearing a blond wig, and Jane Russell bra with sizeable "falsies" under a very tight sweater. Indeed, she had always increased her bust size in every disguise, so different from her naturally very modest breasts and athletic build. Briefly she thought back to the huge tits she had in place for the seduction of the shmata guy on the train. Also on her trip to Corning when she picked up the Goldman Sachs jackass. Men like tits and that's all they would remember about her. But Catherine Bowers of the *Today* show was a natural 32A.

Bodkin whistled slowly as she emerged from the car and smiled. He immediately knew the plan without even having to ask. The woman is just unbelievable, he thought.

They drove a bit until they came upon a large restaurant in Plattsburg with a big bar scene attached, the locals getting well greased at the beginning of the four day holiday weekend. As Sonya got out, she said to Bodkin, "Just follow us discretely in the car when I come out with the guy. Then wait outside the house until I come get you." Bodkin nodded and smiled. He'd done this drill before.

She went in and saw plenty of candidates. The guy definitely should not be married with kids, expected at Grandma's tomorrow. She also needed a guy with enough money to have his own place where he lived alone, preferably a house out of town and a car. It would help if he already was half shit-faced and very horny.

She took a bar stool near the men's room, so every guy would have to see her at some point. She was friendly, very friendly. The first to come up to her was a 25 year old kid, who wasn't even close to the right profile. Then three guys got her in conversation, whom she was sure were all married and would soon leave their buddies and head home to the little woman and their 2.2 kids. Sure enough, they all were gone in 45 minutes.

Then a somewhat older guy, maybe 45 came in, well dressed and somewhat overweight. Apparently he had eaten alone in the dining room and now was going to have a few drinks and a look around the bar at the talent pool. He spent about 10 minutes with two ladies at the bar, then decided he needed to visit the men's room. Sonya smiled at him, as he went by. He smiled back, was obviously struck by her but continued into the men's room.

Sonya called the bartender over. "I may start ordering bourbon sours. If I do, don't put any booze in them." She smiled at him, winked and put two dollars in his hand. He responded, "You got it, honey."

As he exited the men's room, Sonya had pulled her shoulders back and her skirt up. He went right up to her.

"Well, I don't think I've ever seen you in here. Are you new in town?"

"Actually, I'm moving to Plattsburg as soon as I can find an office job in town. I've always liked the area, particularly out a little bit, in the country, a little land, you know."

"I certainly do. That's exactly what I've got. I've been here for six years since my divorce, managing the used cars lot for the local Chevy dealer. By the way, my name is Billy Atchison."

"And I'm Elizabeth Mackey."

"Well, how do you do, Miss Mackey? Am I correct in assuming you're unattached?"

"Oh, please call me Liz, and yes, I just broke up with my boyfriend last month after spending three bad years with him. Found out he was cheating on me. We gals are just too trusting," she said, ever so sweetly.

"My goodness, that guy needs to have his head examined for cheating on such a beautiful woman as you. What can I buy you to drink, Liz?"

Ninety minutes later, after dancing twice to the juke box and having had three bourbon-less sours, while Billy had four real scotches, they left together and got in his car, a brand new 1954 Chevrolet Bel Aire. Bodkin followed, driving at a discreet distance as instructed. The house was perfect. Nothing fancy, but on ten acres, seven miles out of town. Bodkin had followed and stopped out on the country road, well out of sight.

They weren't in the house seven minutes when horny Billy grabbed her and kissed her on the lips with his tongue already moving. She quickly pivoted, put her right hand under his right armpit and grabbed his right wrist with her left hand, pulling him around her extended hip and flipped him down hard, his head smacking the wooden floor. She then kicked him hard in the balls, and while he shrieked in pain, she looked for the right object, settled on the fireplace andiron and bashed in his skull with it. Three times, just to be sure. He stopped all movement and noise, as the blood filled his fatally damaged brain. She dragged him into a closet so as to not upset Harsanyi.

Sonya went outside and in the porch light waved Bodkin and Harsanyi in. They gathered in the kitchen over some tea and turned in early – very businesslike as though it was just another night at the Howard Johnson's motel. Tomorrow would be liberation day.

Same day
Camp Kilmer, New Jersey

Staff Sergeant (E6) Lavanna was quietly packing for the Thanksgiving holiday in his Camp Kilmer, New Jersey barracks for unmarried, senior non - commissioned officers. Like most army barracks built in the time of the two world wars, the wooden building had two floors, each with a latrine at one end. Unlike typical enlisted men's barracks however, this one had improved private rooms for the sergeants, all of whom were regular army lifers.

Lavanna had distinguished himself in combat and also was a fully qualified sniper. Included in his kills were a Chinese army equivalent of a Colonel, whom he had stalked in the cold and dark until he got a clean shot, which at 400 yards he put right through the man's chest, with a second in his head as he lay on the ground. While he was a perfectly well balanced and committed soldier, Lavanna could throw a switch and become a stealth killing machine, capable of coolly delivering clandestine death at great distances with uncanny precision.

His holiday ruminations were now suddenly interrupted by the battalion commander, who had stormed into the barracks, accompanied by a special forces major, giving the command to "fall in" on the first floor. The light colonel then gave them the command to stand at ease.

"Men, a most unusual emergency is developing. Division headquarters wants expert riflemen, preferably with sniper experience, for a most important mission over the holiday weekend. It could be dangerous. Something about a kidnapper trying to get over the border. Volunteers will receive a hazardous duty pay bonus and a personal letter in their 201 personnel file from commanding general Cassidy, expressing the army's deep gratitude. I am sorry, but those are the only details I am authorized to disclose, and I cannot answer questions." After a pause he added, "Who would like to volunteer?"

Sergeant Lavanna and three others stepped forward. What the heck, he thought, I could use the money. Since Korea I've been bored, and it sure beats going to grandma's house in Seaside Heights, New Jersey for the always overcooked turkey. (Grandpa had gotten campylobacter once from undercooked turkey, and grandma never had forgotten it. So it was always way overdone.) Man, I'd rather have army chow, he thought.

Soon without any further explanation he found himself on an army transport plane with 67 other army marksmen heading north. They landed in several small airports in areas where there was direct contact between the land mass of Quebec and the states of New York and Vermont. Lavanna got off in Plattsburg, New York, only 30 miles south of the border and just 60 miles south of Montreal. While unknown to Lavanna, a fugitive could turn due west at Montreal to reach the capital, Ottawa, about 150 miles away on excellent roads.

Before disbursing in many directions by car, they got a briefing from FBI agent Bugliari, Dominic's right hand man. "We appreciate all of you giving up your Thanksgiving holiday for this critical assignment. I can only give you a general background on this case before I give very specific instructions on your role. All of this is highly classified."

He flashed Harsanyi's photo. "You may have seen this man's photo on television or in the newspapers. He is a leading American rocket scientist, whom we have publicly said may be a victim of foul play. We now believe he is voluntarily attempting to flee the country with classified material." The rangers groaned and Lavanna let out a low whistle. "This woman is probably the leader of the agents trying to sneak him out. We know they tried to escape by private plane last Sunday, but the weather didn't cooperate. Probably suspecting we were closing in, they killed the pilot and almost certainly are now fleeing in his 1953 Oldsmobile. Their air destination was Ottawa, location of the Soviet embassy, so we have to assume that is their planned way out. Other sources support this conclusion.

We have rushed to get more people on the border crossings, but with the holiday, short notice and a long border, the Bureau's very stretched. We are going to position you men on the border in the woods between the border stations that separate New York state and Quebec. Other units are doing the same thing in Vermont and New Hampshire, although in lesser numbers.

Unfortunately, each of your coverage areas will be about 500 yards long. However, there are very dense and almost impassable woods in many places that will encourage an attempt in the open farmed areas, particularly with a heavy set, middle aged man in the group. We plan to have over 700 FBI, state and local law enforcement people helping. They will also take you to your line of responsibility and show you how the border runs.

You are herby given the order to stop and detain anyone you see moving across the border in your area of coverage. Then reach us on these field phones, not unlike the ones most of you used in Korea. We'll get there fast. If they refuse to stop, you are authorized to shoot to kill, before they cross the border, aiming first at the older, slower man. If somehow they get out, inform us immediately and we will ask for help from the Canadians on the other side, but we really don't want that option. Gentlemen, do I make myself clear?"

Lavanna couldn't believe what he was hearing. Shoot some people on the chance they were the bad guys? What if they were just hikers or people drinking and partying in the woods on a holiday weekend? And a woman – how could you tell it wasn't some drunks planning to get laid. At least in Korea you knew that anyone moving toward you from the north was a bogey. Damn, Grandma's burnt turkey was starting to look pretty good.

Then there were several questions, to which Bugliari largely gave hedged responses. Somehow they had to figure out whether any group coming into their sector were these terrible bad guys or just harmless civilians.

"Besides the field radios you also will receive a M1D sniper rifle with the most advanced sniper sight, which, I believe, you all have used. As you know, you can bring a man down from 600 yards with this weapon, and if necessary, we expect you to execute a head shot on the older man if you're at a range of 300 yards or less. Now we will all move to a local police firing range, where you will quickly zero-in your weapons, and then you will be taken to your areas of responsibility."

At 4:30 a.m. Lavanna found himself at a location about 35 miles northwest of Plattsburgh on the Quebec border. The last town he had seen in the U.S. was Mooers, New York, a tiny rural community. He climbed the tallest tree he could find and settled in with the border just 300 yards behind him. Just like being back in miserable Korea, he thought, but at least here any hostiles won't have the whole damned Chinese army right behind them. Still, he was missing grandma more with every new twist in this bizarre operation.

8:00 a.m. - November 26, Thanksgiving

Bodkin and Sonya had been up at dawn, planning, talking and getting in their chosen outfits. She would be his mother, Harsanyi the father and Bodkin would wear the Chevrolet jacket he found in Billy's closet. They cooked a hearty breakfast of Billy's eggs, bacon, coffee and orange juice.

Harsanyi had not slept well and had little appetite. He didn't look for Billy and didn't ask what happened to him. He just wanted to be out of the hands of these killers and back in Moscow with the Communist intelligentsia, changing the world. That vision alone had sustained him in the last eight days of hell with this psychopath and her killer accomplice

The Oldsmobile had been put in Billy's garage last night and out of sight. At 8:15 a.m. they all got in the new Bel Aire, ready and in costume with their forged U.S. passports in hand, in case anyone asked. They had already assembled the two automatic weapons that had been concealed as part of the wheelchair structure. They headed due north on route 15, hoping to enter Canada legally and without incident, but as they got near the border crossing, they saw the traffic back up.

Sonya parked the car and got out on foot to see what the issue was. In her 1940's floral print dress covered by an old blazer and wearing a ridiculous old lady's hat pinned to her hair, she looked like the typical grandma off for a Thanksgiving visit with the Canadian relatives. No one gave her a second thought, as she walked closer to the checkpoint.

She immediately recognized what was going on. The border guards were joined by local police, and there were far more of them than she would have expected. They were overseen by some guys in civilian dress. They were getting all passengers out of their cars, examining the trunk, the engine compartments and everything in between. There were also dogs sniffing the vehicles and mirrors were being rolled under the cars to examine the undercarriages. She took a short look, turned around and walked back. She mumbled to herself, "A fucking traitor somewhere, probably right in Moscow!"

On her way back a driver poked his head out and asked her what was going on. "Sonny, I don't know. They're checking each car so close, maybe they think John Dillinger is back in town." She waved and laughed along with the driver, as he closed his window.

She got in the car and turned to Bodkin. "They're looking for us, that has to be it. Someone, somehow, tipped them off - Dominic Benvenuto isn't that good. We have to assume that the border is like this for a hundred miles. They can't know exactly where we planned to cross because, fearing exactly this, I didn't tell anyone. And I mean no one.

It has to be a leak in Moscow, and that traitor could have told them the day, the rough area and the method. But not the exact place.

"Get that map out, Bodkin. The beauty of picking this area to cross is that there is no St. Lawrence River here to separate the countries, just woods and farm land. If the road crossing points are a problem, we just have to enter the woods. That's why I chose this spot."

She studied the road map and quickly made her decision. There was no time to waste – Billy's body would be discovered at the latest tomorrow after the holiday, when he didn't show up for work. Also the more time the border patrol and FBI had, the more resources that would be poured in here.

They turned the car and left the line, giving the impression that they were going to find a better crossing point. Then she found a phone booth and made a quick call – into Canada.

She drove back south to Route 11, where she turned west and went through Mooers to Rural Route 203, onto which she turned north again toward the border. About one mile from the border, Bodkin got out, found some higher ground and got a clear view through his binoculars. While far fewer people were manning this point, there were uniformed guards with weapons examining the cars. There were no border personnel on the Canadian side.

Sonya made the decision. They drove onto the frozen field and got almost a mile east of the check point on 203 before the Chevy finally got stuck. Then they got out on foot and headed due north toward the border, intending to cross well out of sight of the guards on 203.

One Mile North

While it was only 10:15 a.m., Lavanna was just finishing an early lunch consisting of his C-ration can of spam and a container of applesauce, all washed down with canteen water. "Happy Thanksgiving" he muttered to himself.

Snipers had to have certain key talents to even be considered for this elite military occupational specialty. Most important were perfect hearing and better than 20/20 vision. He had both. He also had scored a 76 out of a possible 84 on the rifle range test at the end of basic training, just one below the base record of Fort Ord, California. After advanced sniper training his skills were finely honed by 18 months in Korea, sitting on high points and desperately needing to hear and see the other guy before the other guy saw him first.

So it struck him as odd when he faintly heard what sounded like a car to the south where there was no road. Very strange. Then it ceased, and all was quiet for a few minutes until he began to hear the sounds of feet on frozen, crackling dirt. He reached for the glasses and instantly saw them, now about 700 yards off and heading north right at him – a man moving adroitly, a somewhat

208

older man proceeding with more trouble and, amazingly, an old woman moving with the grace of an athlete. Both the woman and younger man were carrying automatic, sten gun type weapons. He silently laid the glasses down and put the radio to his head.

"Delta one this is Delta six, over." When the base radio operator came on he said in a low tone, "Delta one, I have three people coming right at me on the edge of the woods seven hundred yards out, two with automatic weapons, one a woman disguised to look much older and an unarmed man moving with some difficulty. I need backup ASAP but will now implement my instructions. Out." He signed off and turned off the radio, so it would not be heard. No time for a discussion.

Then he went into automatic army ranger/sniper mode, a learned response where each muscle and reflex performed instinctually, not unlike a lion seeing prey walking right toward him. Fear was not an emotion that was included in this ritualistic, coordinated movement.

He raised the M1D very slowly, now supported by the shooter's cradle in the boughs he had fashioned, and observed his bogeys approaching through the world class sight. He made sure the broken sunlight did not reflect off the barrel, sending a brief reflection that could be seen, the mistake that had often led to the death of a sniper. The weapon had an effective range of 600 yards, in his hands probably more. But there was no sense in rushing things, as the intruder's automatics were effective only at close range. He was concerned that the group was walking along the line where the woods joined the field, potentially allowing some of the party quick cover or even escape when the firing would begin.

Against his every instinct he had to give them the option of surrender, those were his orders. At 200 yards, with his weapon aimed at Harsanyi's head and finger on the trigger of his killing machine, he yelled "Halt, drop the weapons."

Sonya leapt like a cat for Harsanyi, grabbed his arm and was starting to pull him toward the woods, when his head opened up like a smashed watermelon - soft tissue, bone and blood flying everywhere from the impact of the 7.62 millimeter round. It entered Harsanyi's skull right between his eyes and exited through a much larger hole in the back of his skull. He was dead instantly.

Bodkin had aimed at the yell and began firing wildly to help Sonya do what he knew she would attempt, but it was over too fast. As he then broke for the cover of the woods, he took a shot in the leg from the sniper, who, after taking out the primary target, had turned, as trained, to the source of return fire. In great pain Bodkin leapt into the woods, took cover and looked for the shooter.

A few seconds of silence followed. Then Sonya could be heard moving fast into the woods, and her sound drew Lavanna, who had now alighted from the tree. Bodkin hoped for a shot. He saw the American race into the woods and

Bodkin opened up at his last seen position with a fuselage of automatic weapon fire, shredding the foliage but not getting a hit. His weapon was designed to spray out fire at close range but not particularly accurately. At 200 yards it was almost worthless. But it did stop the sniper from pursuing Sonya.

Lavanna had gotten the primary target and had correctly assumed that the woman in disguise was the leader, as the briefing had emphasized, so she was the next highest priority. He wanted her but was not free to move because of the covering fire from the male. Bodkin picked up what looked like a muzzle reflection 60 yards out and fired five rounds quickly. Bodkin's position revealed, Lavanna dropped the four foot stick that held the reflective foil and immediately put three rounds into Bodkins body, the third piercing his chest and exploding his heart.

The sewer rat of Stalingrad, the peasant from the small village in the Urals, lay dying on a far off and strange frozen field in America. As life left his body, his last vision had been of his home in the Caucasus Mountains that he had not seen in such a long time, with his mother, expressionless, waving goodbye to her only surviving son.

Same Day, Nightfall
Plattsburgh, New York

The first wave of help, an army national guard squad, had reached the wooded site 18 minutes after the radio call from Lavanna. The FBI followed shortly thereafter. They all fanned out to search for the third player, the female disguised as an old woman. Lavanna had predicted it – that they would never find her and they did not. After felling Bodkin, Lavanna had listened intently but had heard nothing and found no one. She had probably been sprinting over the border while he and Bodkin had stalked each other for those five minutes. She was long gone.

Dominic was on and off the field phone to Washington. Five hours after the shootout he reported to Hoover directly.

"Mr. Hoover, we have pretty much tracked her escape out of the woods with the help of dogs. She crossed the border about a quarter mile east of the shootings. The Canadians allowed us to follow the trail into Canada, where it ends on Route 203 one mile south of the tiny rural town of Havelock. A local farmer recalls seeing a dark sedan parked on 203 around 8:30 a.m., but paid no attention to it. It was gone when he returned around noon. No one else in town recalls seeing such a car. The Canadians have this slim information, but my bet is that car is already in Montreal or Ottawa, and the female agent is long out of it. Unless the Canadians pull a miracle, we've lost her."

CHAPTER 31

THE FINALE – IOWA, MOSCOW, WASHINGTON

November 30, 1953
Home Of Helga Bowers, Des Moines, Iowa

Agent Keenan was wrapping up the dissection of Helga Bower's home, where Catherine Bowers, a.k.a. agent Sonya, had grown up. He would soon leave the Chicago FBI men to continue surveillance and report to Dominic in New York as to what they had found, which was confusing to say the least.

There was nothing from or about the daughter anywhere in the house later than 1942. Several photos as a child with her mom, high school senior photo from 1937, college graduation shot from 1941. Then nothing. Maybe they had had a falling out, Keenan guessed.

He was reviewing the situation with the agents who would now resume hidden surveillance of the house after he left. "In my opinion I think it's pretty clear. The mother was, and probably still is, a committed idealistic Marxist. Her daughter Catherine takes a deep dive in 1942 into the labyrinth of soviet espionage, materially helped by the fact that we were wartime allies with the Russians then. She gets some formal training somewhere. To protect her daughter, maybe mom just claims she moved to Chicago and doesn't return home. The neighbors buy it, and the Soviets have just acquired a valuable sleeper agent, with 100% American credentials raised in Iowa no less. How much more perfect could it get. So she had a little flirtation with socialism in college in the thirties, but so did a lot of people.

Catherine sets up her new existence in New York waiting for her friends to call her. And call her they did, and she answered big time.

So you guys have to wait here until mom shows up, which may be never, given that they know that we have Catherine's full history now and are looking for her everywhere from Canada to Mexico. My bet is we never find mom."

They continued to restore the house to its prior condition.

Then, thirty minutes later a key turned in the front door. The agents dove for cover in the closets, the sole bathroom and the garage. Helga Bowers entered and froze. She immediately sensed intruders had been in her home. There were some of her private papers on the floor, and the furniture was not the way she had left it. It also smelled of men. Then she opened the bathroom door and saw agent Keenan.

"Who are you and what the hell are you doing in my home?" she said in a rising voice that she hoped would belie her fear and shock.

"Miss Bowers, I am agent Keenan of the Federal Bureau of Investigation." He showed his badge. The other agents also moved out of their hidden positions and flashed their ID's. "May I ask you where you have been for the last week?"

"I was visiting some old friends in Portland Oregon. I took the train and have been gone for two weeks. Now what are you fascist cops doing in my home? Where is your warrant?"

Keenan showed it to her. "Miss Bowers, could you tell us the whereabouts of your daughter, Catherine?"

"My daughter, Catherine? You miserable pricks, what are you talking about?" she screamed. "And I thought you gave up tailing me years ago. What's the matter, you have nothing to do these days? That demagogue McCarthy isn't keeping you creeps busy?"

Keenan looked her right in the eyes. "Ma'am, where is your daughter, Catherine?"

"You bastards." Her eyes started to mist up. "She is lying in the local cemetery one mile from here, where she has rested in peace since dying a hero's death on a battlefield in the Ukraine in 1943."

The agents looked at each other.

"She had volunteered to serve on the true frontier of the war against fascism, while the Americans and Brits were living it up in London, taking their sweet time to invade France until the Russians had softened up the Nazis. Then the Americans walked through France and Germany to do their land grab."

Keenan turned to look at the other agents, who seemed in as deep a shock as he was. "You are claiming that your daughter has been dead for 10 years? Who then is the Catherine Bowers who until very recently worked as a writer-producer on the *Today* show and claims this as her place of birth and you as her mother, pray tell," he asked.

Helga sat down, her voice starting to get louder. "I don't have the faintest idea what you sons of bitches are talking about. My daughter left her journalist job in 1942 to volunteer for service in the Soviet Union, who, if you happen to remember, was then our ally. The next time I saw her was in the coffin the Russians shipped her back in as a decorated war hero, as they did for a number of

American volunteers of that period. She was passionate about the war and defeating the fascists, and yes, she was an ardent socialist. And don't tell me or my friends who came to the open casket wake that that beautifully preserved body was not my daughter. They did as good a job on her as they did on Lenin."

Keenan and the agents were in shock, speechless.

They later visited the grave and interviewed the friends, including two army vets of World War I, who had seen the body in 1943, all of whom said there was no doubt that the woman interred in the local cemetery was, in fact, Catherine Bowers, whom they had known from infancy. The agents actually got a court order to exhume the body, and, indeed the remains were identified as that of a young female dead around ten years and the correct height. Finally even the two vets were calling the FBI guys pigs and told them they would not cooperate any more.

The New York office soon confirmed that a coffin had been shipped to the United States from the port of Murmansk, Russia in November 1943 in a returning lend lease convoy and was delivered to Des Moines, Iowa for burial.

"So who the hell is agent Sonya?" Dominic demanded of his men. "Get back in the field and check every trace we got of this chameleon!"

When Keenan returned to New York, he sat down with Dominic. "Chief, all the experts and certainly the eyewitnesses of the wake, most of whom are very patriotic Americans who have served their country, say that the body in 1943 was indisputably that of Catherine Bowers. I think we have to accept that. These locals can't be that good a coordinated gang of liars – they are not complicated folks."

Dominic looked laser like into Keenan's eyes. "Then who the hell is the woman who was masquerading as Bowers, worked for the *Today* show, shot up our agents here, almost killed me, almost got Harsanyi out and may now be somewhere on the loose in North America? And what will this shrewd bitch do next, when we no longer have our man in Moscow to warn us of her every step?"

November 30
Moscow, Dzerzhinsky Square

"Tolstoy still hasn't broken, the bastard," Andropov reported in a tone of barely suppressed fury to Kruglov. "The balls to call the U.S. Embassy from this building. We will keep on destroying pieces of his body until he talks. Or dies. A shooting squad is too good for him. What a God damn actor – the perfect communist man, indeed!"

Kruglov nodded, "At least we now know that Sonya got out and entered the Ottawa embassy incognito. She functioned like a professional at every turn.

There is no agent we now have who is more effective in North America. A cool, tough and emotionless leader. Without this Tolstoy traitor in our midst, she would probably be standing with us right now in celebration, with Harsanyi spilling his guts to our rocketry people and our Premier Nikita bragging about what a genius he was to order the extraction.

Sonya will now enter a new phase in her life. Even the idiot Hoover will figure out that Sonya was in fact not this Catherine Bowers, a hot headed Marxist enthusiast from Iowa. That Catherine Bowers actually flunked out of our top secret training base in the Urals because of her extremely volatile nature and in 1943 volunteered for the Ukrainian front, where she died in action. We shipped the body back with a hero's trappings. If nothing else, her mother will tell them so and show them the grave."

"Then boss," Andropov asked, "Can you say anything about who this master agent is?"

"Our woman was in fact a contemporary of Sonya's in training, and she assumed Catherine's identity when Catherine was killed at the front. When she returned to the US, she used all of the dead Catherine's papers and just slipped smoothly into her identity – birth certificate, social security card, college diploma – everything she needed to convince employers she was Catherine Bowers. Stupid American employers don't call applicant's mothers.

Even I don't know any more than that. I have asked a couple of old NKVD types around here who she really is, and they just smile. They won't say anything. Which means someone, somewhere who is very powerful is protecting Sonya and condoning their silence. Or was. Her true identity may have died with Stalin and Beria. I've given up asking. All I care about is she always gets the job done. Except when foiled by a god damned traitor right in our midst like Igor Tolstoy."

"Will she get a new identity now? Is the name Sonya history?" Andropov asked.

"Of course," Kruglov replied.

"Do you have any idea where she will be assigned?" Andropov asked.

"Many want her, but I think Khrushchev leans toward Cuba. There's a lot of potential there if that hot head Castro's talents can be channeled."

"Fascinating. And by the way, Comrade General, has our esteemed Premier talked to you about these events?"

"Yesterday Khrushchev called me in, and I was ready to pack up for the gulag. He was ranting and raving for ten minutes, and I said nothing, just stared at my feet. Finally, with his face six inches from mine, he warned me that if I speak to anyone about his role in ordering Oryol out, I would not survive the day.

I said I fully understood and that I had already forgotten our breakfast conversation. Then he told me to get back to work, and I just flew out of there like a man freed from death row.

Someday, who knows, comrade Andropov, you may run this massive security apparatus. I have reason to believe you will soon be our ambassador to Hungary, a wonderful promotion for a 40 year old. But a tricky job – those Hunkys are an obstinate and rebellious lot. But be that as it may, if you ever do get to run this place, always beware of the political webs being spun behind your back. You may fondly recall these days where only your professional results mattered in your advancement, and you didn't really have to pay attention to the top political bosses."

"Thank you, comrade. By the way what do we expect in the way of an American response?"

"Our ambassador and General Strelnikov, station chief in New York, are somewhat optimistic that the public reaction will be muted to nonexistent. In private we expect to get reamed out in the strongest terms by those moralistic turds. Screw 'em – they can't go public; it would be too embarrassing.

And, most important, imagine what McCarthy would do if he knew the truth. The whole government could fall."

December 1
The Oval Office, Washington, D.C.

The president was joined by Secretary of State John Foster Dulles, CIA director Allan Dulles and FBI Director Hoover. The latter opened the meeting with a brief update and summary.

"There is no question that Harsanyi was the man shot during the escape and that he was willingly fleeing the country. The fingerprints are perfect matches. There is absolutely no sign on his body that he was forcibly kidnapped or restrained. This was an attempt to get him, code name Oryol out with all he knows and get him to Russia. Everything overseen by this master spy Sonya.

He was accompanied by the short gunman, whose prints tie in with some of those found in the sleeping car compartment of the murdered Dickinson on the Lackawanna night train last November. We are unable to identify him; he is not registered in the Soviet embassy or the New York consulate. The female agent's prints in the escape car are the same as those we obtained from several sites in Manhattan, where the woman using the alias Catherine Bowers lived and worked. She was agent Sonya, no doubt about it. Director Dulles, what would you care to add?"

Dulles began, "It appears Harsanyi had definite communist sympathies going way back that he began to cleverly conceal in the mid 1930's, when things started to get difficult for a communist sympathizer in the developing fascist mood of Hungary. His distinguished countrymen, Edward Teller and Leó Szilárd – both of whom are making great contributions to our nuclear effort – vouched for his character in the years they worked together in Hungary and the enthusiasm with which he had embraced his adopted country. His children are thriving here in university.

We have thoroughly reviewed the circumstances of his meeting with our forces in Austria at the end of the war. We are suspicious but have been unable to disprove the story he gave us on his exodus, although there was much chaos and slaughter, particularly of Jews, in the collapsing fascist Hungarian regime in the spring of 1945. By the way, the records the Russians gave us in 1945 do show that his 75% Jewish wife perished in Auschwitz days before the Russians arrived."

Ike made a mental note that, despite Dulles's explanation, there was no question that his people in Europe had missed key particulars of Harsanyi's true history. How many others have slipped in he asked himself and are working in universities, aerospace facilities and even the armed forces. This information could save the otherwise declining career of that raving demagogue McCarthy.

At least, he thought, the Russians never got the formula for the reentry material. With that he looked to his left where a model missile nose cone stood. He stared at it for a few seconds and silently smiled. Dulles and Hoover both caught it.

After a further review of the details, Ike raised the key question. "Gentlemen, what do we go public with?"

"Mr. President," Dulles began, "we should quietly review the many pestiferous facts in this saga, make personnel and policy changes where appropriate and relentlessly seek all connected to these covert operatives. But we should, in our opinion, continue the plausible cover story of a forced kidnapping for monetary gain, the death of one of the kidnappers, identity to be determined, and disappearance of the other into Canada. Our previously released explanation of the Chelsea Piers shootout seems to be holding, and no one has put the two together."

Hoover then picked it up. "We also have to consider the McCarthy issue. He and his wildly ambitious associates have made a mockery of both our and the armed force's programs to deal effectively with the real communist menace. He has submitted hundreds of innocent men and women to a witch hunt. The newsman Edward R. Murrow and CBS are really after his hide now, and, frankly, we are quietly feeding them insights and facts for their investigation. They will soon challenge him openly and his house of cards may collapse. It would be an unmitigated disaster, let me repeat, disaster, to re-arm McCarthy and Roy Cohn with this new information. He would pound the table saying how he had been right all along and then haul before his committee hundreds of people who had been involved in this Harsanyi matter in any way. In this witch hunt careers of truly dedicated and skilled public servants in the

army, CIA and FBI would be destroyed. The country could be torn apart and our precious democratic fabric could be irrevocably harmed. In any case the big winner would be the Russians, who would be ecstatic as our counter-intelligence network potentially self destructed."

CIA Dulles added, "Mr. President, I fully agree with my distinguished colleague."

Hoover noted with satisfaction Dulles's new conciliatory tone toward the FBI. Given the CIA failures to properly check out Harsanyi's foreign history, the Brahman had adopted a new patina of cooperation. Besides that, the Bureau had saved the day, thanks largely to Dominic Benvenuto's bold action to close the border and, on his own initiative, the coordination, mobilization and field placement of a large group of experienced army snipers, one of whom had scattered Harsanyi's brains all over a wooded field 200 yards from the border, averting disaster. If Harsanyi had gotten out, this highly principled president would have felt compelled to step forward, accept blame and probably been a one term president. Not to mention that he would have to ask for the resignations of both Hoover and Dulles.

Ike asked, "I agree with you on maintaining this low profile. I justify it on the basis of our continuing ongoing extensive investigation, the need to identify all the domestic participants, particularly this vicious agent Sonya and the scourge of Joe McCarthy.

Let's close the loose ends, change our procedures and privately scream at the Russians, letting them know we're aware of everything they were up to. And gentlemen – most important – can we figure out who this fiend Sonya really is and get her behind American bars or six feet under before she turns the world upside down somewhere else? Put major resources into that effort. Who knows what this efficient killer will do someday, somewhere else if we don't find her."

Same Day
A Minor Tag end...closed

It was unusual to see three men in ties, overcoats and business hats drawn down low, just above their eyes approaching the simple DeVincenzo home in Fort Lee, New Jersey. In that Italian neighborhood news spread like wildfire as soon as it happened. "Mrs. Maria DeVincenzo, we are agents of the Federal Bureau of Investigation. Here are our identification badges. May we enter your home to discuss certain matters?"

The trail from certain low-level phone operatives had lead directly to Maria. Her signaling system on the phone at the Macy's toy department became quite clear under intense questioning of these low-level men in the contact network. After only three minutes of discussion Maria and her husband broke down and admitted everything. All they could claim was that they were ignorant of what they were enabling in the bigger picture of things.

A federal judge and jury in Newark, New Jersey, would not be sympathetic to that plea in their decision nine months later. He was sentenced to 10 years in a Federal penitentiary and she was committed for life. Neither lived beyond five years – their son dead, their grandchildren communist youth deeply hidden somewhere in the vast Soviet Union, their hearts broken by the enforced separation in maximum security U.S. prisons.

After being told of her husband's death five years later, Maria was found hanging from the prison laundry pipes by a noose of sheets fashioned by her own hands.

When told of this in her then current assignment, the former agent Sonya was understood to have said, "Just another meaningless bit of collateral damage to people of no consequence."

EPILOGUE

Dominic had retired in 1975 but remained an active consultant for the FBI. He also had served on a number of congressional panels and attended many security conferences around the world. A very fit 71 years of age he was still in considerable demand. People that mattered knew not only his public history of accomplishment but also had heard the rumors of several never disclosed but apparently masterful feats. He had been awarded the Distinguished Service Medal upon retirement

With the failure of the 1991 coup attempt in Russia, President Yeltsin found himself firmly ensconced as president of the fledgling democratic new Russia. In an unprecedented gesture of openness (and given an unstated desire to purge the old KGB men who had backed the failed coup against him), the regime invited an American delegation of FBI and CIA present and former leaders to Moscow and cooperated meaningfully with them in reviewing old files to answer some of the unsolved mysteries of the 46 year cold war. Dominic was part of the blue ribbon panel, and number one on his list was figuring out who the diabolical Sonya was and what else she might have surreptitiously participated in after the events of 1952-1953.

His Russian counterpart and guide was a retired KGB Major General. Together they had, at Dominic's request, visited the unmarked grave of a Lieutenant Colonel Igor Tolstoy, officially dead of pneumonia in January 1954. In fact he had died from a cerebral hemorrhage following 45 days of violent beatings and drug interactions, during which the security apparatus had gained little from him.

Dominic placed flowers on the grave and then stood in silence before the remains of a man he had met only once in 1945, when he offered him the avenue to reach American intelligence if he ever chose to do so. Thank God he did.

He turned to the general. "My friend, it is so breathtakingly ironic that this man, whom I recruited at the end of the war in 1945, should turn up eight years later in 1953 to save our butt, and my butt in particular. The Harsanyi thing was my case. Without Tolstoy Sonya would have succeeded. Who knows what the world would have looked like today? And they only missed getting him out by 200 yards."

They left the gravesite and had a quiet lunch at a field grade officer's club on Gorkovo Ulitza (Gorky Street). After ordering, he looked at the general, breathed deeply and then asked "the" question.

"Georgi, who the hell was Sonya, and what did she do afterwards? Despite enlisting the help of every friendly intelligence ally, we never caught her scent again. And this request is somewhat personal. She actually kidnapped my then four-year-old daughter, now 43 with three of my grandchildren, for a few days to cover their escape." The general rolled his eyes.

"My friend, the agent who went by Sonya at that time was a whispered legend around the private inner sanctums of soviet intelligence. The last person who knew the full story was Andropov, who met her well before he rose to the head of the KGB and then, as you recall, was briefly the leader of the Soviet Union in 1981 – 1982. As a young and rapidly rising colonel, he used her both on your Oryol matter and later in Cuba, while Castro was leading his rebel force to their ultimate victory on New Years day, 1959.

I do know that she helped Castro with "wet operations" for the two years leading up to that final victory and eliminating enemies immediately afterward. Most spectacular was that she personally slit the throat of what I think your mafia boys call the head "button man" of Meyer Lansky's Cuban operation. Lansky and his mob buddies had really kept the Cuban dictator, Fulgencio Batista, in power with money and bribes that they hoped would insure the mob's lavish new casino hotels built in the 1950's. Sonya, then known as agent Lena, severed the head of Lansky's lead goon and had it delivered in a box of roses to Lansky's hotel."

Dominic let out a slow whistle. Old visions were being stirred.

"She had helped the naïve Castro several times before that. She was later his unrecorded head of security. Also, reputedly his lover for a while. And Che Guevara. Sexually she was apparently another Catherine the Great.

After the success of the revolution, she left Cuba. Beyond 1959 it is all rumor and innuendo. There were stories that she oversaw the Profumo scandal in England that brought down the government in 1963. I do know she was a native English speaker, but I don't even know if that meant American, British, Canadian, Australian, whatever."

Then the general paused, apparently struggling with a thought. Finally he just came out with it. He squared up and looked Dominic in the eyes.

"Most dramatic, but never more than a whisper, was that she had at least met President Kennedy's assassin, Lee Harvey Oswald and his Russian wife Marina, in Texas. But I must hasten to add that this has never been even remotely substantiated."

He paused for dramatic effect and looked squarely into Dominic's eyes, looking for a clue that the Americans might have picked up her trail in their investigation of the Kennedy assassination. Was there any truth to this old KGB whispered rumor?

Dominic didn't move a muscle or change his facial expression one millimeter. But his pulse picked up and his thoughts raced to his time with the Warren Commission that investigated that horrific day in Dallas in 1963. Nothing came to mind and he remained silent, but internally he was spinning. Could it be?

Realizing Dominic had nothing he would offer, the general broke the silence. "Like you said Dominic, kto znayet. Who knows with her? She is the greatest enigma in the history of Soviet espionage."

The two men exited the club and walked slowly back to Dzerzhinsky Square. Her eyes picked them up as soon as they came out of the building. She had been told of Benvenuto's arrival by the last person in the new KGB she still trusted. She followed them like an aging bird of prey might have, wishing she was younger and could grab Dominic with her claws and rip him apart. As she watched, she thought about how close she had come. A bullet six inches from his temple.

So we meet again, you bastard. You ruined my life, defeating me in my greatest mission. Without you I might have achieved my dreams and been among the ruling elite of a world dominated by us. Forty years ago I should have ripped your balls off in that hotel room in New York and then put a blade in your heart. We would have gotten that Hungarian toad out without your interference, even with that traitor Tolstoy in our midst. Then the world would have quivered and quaked before the new Soviet nuclear rocket dominance. Now our cause is hopeless, at least in my remaining years (she had just turned 74 and suffered from lymphatic cancer. Her time was short.).

We only missed by 200 meters, you lucky bastard. A miserable 200 meters may have stopped the victory of socialism. *Kto znayet*, or as you Americans like to say, "Who knows?"

She spat in disgust, turned away and, as she had done so many times in her life, slinked back into a shadow – unnoticed, unseen and undetected. Always the ethereal cloud that not even a direct onlooker could later describe or, indeed, even say with certainty actually had even been there.

THE END

FACT AND FICTION
Notes from the Author

The Premise

I created the premise of the book, the Russian "nose cone dilemma" following a careful review of the historical facts of major rocketry and space developments in the 1950's. I made a set of deductions drawn from certain facts known in the spring of 2006. However, the premise, while logical, was still speculative.

Serendipitously, as I was finishing the second draft, a superb historical review of the early space race was published in the fall of 2007 – *Red Moon Rising* written by Matthew Brzezinski (copyright Times Books) – to commemorate the 50th anniversary of Sputnik's launch. It ended the speculation. This distinguished former Moscow correspondent for the *Wall Street Journal* and current *New York Times* magazine writer drew heavily on input from Professor Sergei Khrushchev, the Premier's son, himself a rocket scientist.

In fact the Russians had serious nose cone reentry issues. The launch of Sputnik was to distract Premiere Khrushchev's attention from the failure to have the ICBM fleet go operational in 1957 by putting up a civilian satellite where successful reentry was not a needed result.

The Characters

This has been an attempt to be historical fiction with an emphasis on historical. Whenever possible I have used actual facts, events, and figures correctly, rather than making up names or history. Obviously the lead characters, Dominic Benvenuto and "agent Sonya" are fictional, as are Harsanyi (Oryol), Tolstoy, and Strelnikov.

The many major historical figures are presented as true to form as my research allowed – Stalin, Khrushchev, Eisenhower, the Dulles Brothers and J. Edgar Hoover. General Sergei Kruglov was in fact the head of the Russian security service, the MGB, predecessor to the KGB. He was so secretive that I have been unable to find any photograph of him, although a former American diplomat, who had met him, was helpful in filling in details for me.

George Koval is mentioned in several contexts – a true super spy, whose existence has only recently been fully appreciated. Russian President Putin publicly disclosed Koval's role in the theft of American nuclear weaponry secrets by awarding him the highest honors on the occasion of his death in 2007.

Amazingly, there had never been a full American disclosure of his deadly effectiveness and the FBI's total failure in that disaster.

Iuri Andropov, Kruglov's aide in the novel, did become the Ambassador to Hungary and oversaw the brutal repression of the revolution of 1956. In 1981 he became the last true communist premier of Russia, to be followed by Gorbachev and the collapse of "the evil empire."

Dick Helms and William Casey, present at the meeting described in chapter 15, both eventually rose to be directors for the Central Intelligence Agency.

All the battlefield accounts of World War II are accurate, as are all the Russian field marshals–Zhukov, Rokossovsky, Malinovsky, Konev, the giants who commanded the largest land army in the history of the world and the army which broke the eastern front of the Third Reich.

The railroad luxury streamliners, characters in themselves in this adventure, are historically correct right down to the train names, time schedules, first class accommodations and car names. These result from a lifetime of fascination with the later years of sumptuous train travel, and those storied trains that transported important Americans to magic places in long gone splendor – places and splendor that a five to ten-year-old, middle-class kid growing up in New Jersey could only fantasize about.

ABOUT THE AUTHOR

D. L. Wanna, a pseudonym, lives in San Francisco with his wife. He has six adult children. He is the founder and chairman of the Making Waves Educational Foundation and related foundations that have for 21 years served over 1000 inner city youth in Northern California. The Foundation also operates one charter middle school and plans to open at least three more.

He is a vice chair of the Stanford University Board of Trustees, vice chairman of Stanford Hospital and Clinics, a past trustee of Princeton University and a director of several public companies.

He also does some investing.

7343500R0

Made in the USA
Lexington, KY
12 November 2010